THE SACRED AND PROFANE LOVE MACHINE

Iris Murdoch was born in Dublin in 1919 of Anglo-Irish parents. She went to Badminton School, Bristol, and read Classics at Somerville College, Oxford. During the war she was an Assistant Principal at the Treasury, and then worked with UNRRA in London, Belgium and Austria. She held a studentship in Philosophy at Newnham College, Cambridge, and then in 1948 she returned to Oxford where she became a Fellow of St Anne's College. Until her death in February 1999, she lived with her husband, the teacher and critic John Bayley, in Oxford. Awarded the CBE in 1976, Iris Murdoch was made a DBE in the 1987 New Year's Honours List. In the 1997 PEN Awards she received the Gold Pen for Distinguished Service to Literature.

Since her writing debut in 1954 with *Under the Net*, Iris Murdoch has written twenty-six novels, including the Booker Prize-winning *The Sea, the Sea* (1978) and most recently *The Green Knight* (1993) and *Jackson's Dilemma* (1995). Other literary awards include the James Tait Black Memorial Prize for *The Black Prince* (1973) and the Whitbread Prize for *The Sacred and Profane Love Machine* (1974). Her works of philosophy include *Sartre: Romantic Rationalist, Metaphysics as a Guide to Morals* (1992) and *Existentialists and Mystics* (1997). She has written several plays including *The Italian Girl* (with James Saunders) and *The Black Prince*, adapted from her novel of the same name. Her volume of poetry, *A Year of Birds*, which appeared in 1978, has been set to music by Malcolm Williamson.

ALSO BY IRIS MURDOCH

Fiction

Under the Net
The Flight from the Enchanter
The Sandcastle
The Bell
A Severed Head
An Unofficial Rose
The Unicorn
The Italian Girl
The Red and the Green
The Time of the Angels
The Nice and the Good
Bruno's Dream
A Fairly Honourable Defeat
An Accidental Man
The Black Prince
A Word Child
Henry and Cato
The Sea, The Sea
Nuns and Soldiers
The Philosopher's Pupil
The Good Apprentice
The Book and the Brotherhood
The Message to the Planet
The Green Knight
Jackson's Dilemma
Something Special

Non-Fiction

Acastos: Two Platonic Dialogues
Metaphysics as a Guide to Morals
Existentialists and Mystics
Sartre: Romantic Rationalist

Iris Murdoch

THE SACRED
AND PROFANE
LOVE MACHINE

WITH AN INTRODUCTION BY
Elaine Feinstein

VINTAGE

Published by Vintage 2003

2 4 6 8 10 9 7 5 3 1

Copyright © Iris Murdoch 1974
Introduction © Elaine Feinstein, 2002

First published in Great Britain in 1974 by
Chatto & Windus

Vintage
Random House, 20 Vauxhall Bridge Road,
London SW1V 2SA

Random House Australia (Pty) Limited
20 Alfred Street, Milsons Point, Sydney
New South Wales 2061, Australia

Random House New Zealand Limited
18 Poland Road, Glenfield,
Auckland 10, New Zealand

Random House (Pty) Limited
Endulini, 5A Jubilee Road, Parktown 2193,
South Africa

The Random House Group Limited Reg. No. 954009
www.randomhouse.co.uk

A CIP catalogue record for this book
is available from the British Library

ISBN 0 09 943357 5

Printed and bound in Great Britain by
Cox & Wyman Limited, Reading, Berkshire

TO
NORAH SMALLWOOD

INTRODUCTION

When Iris Murdoch began to write in the 1950's, Jean Paul Sartre was the dominant sensibility of the age. Europe, and what had happened there in the recent past, was of monstrous significance to any educated reader. Murdoch's own distinguished commentary on Sartre was published before her first novel *Under the Net* (1954) and she might well have spent her life's energy in academic philosophy. Instead, an amazing flow of novels thereafter confront the great issues of morality and human freedom with a passion for truth almost unequalled in the last half of the twentieth century.

By the seventies, one of Murdoch's greatest creative decades, the possibility of living without God and without guilt was no longer seen in European terms. The world shift towards a hegemony of Anglo-Saxon values had already made itself felt. Yet Murdoch remained a writer with the morality of a European intelligence. Her novels often make use of an exotic, frequently foreign, character who is allowed to enter and disrupt a comfortable English coterie. There is no such figure in *The Sacred and Profane Love Machine* (1974). Indeed, there is an almost total absence of the glamour that Murdoch likes to throw over such characters. These are very ordinary lives. There are no enchanters, little overt philosophical speculation, no mystic resolution. *The Sacred and Profane Love Machine* has often been considered a lesser work than *The Black Prince* (1973) or *Henry and Cato* (1976) because these great issues and their relation to the responsibility of the artist are so much less in evidence.

Yet it is a novel with Murdoch's unmistakable stamp upon it. A book haunted by her understanding of human brutality, even though the preoccupations of her characters seem far removed from any apprehension of European experience. It is entirely fitting that the conclusion of this seemingly English tale should be an arbitrary act of terrorist violence in a Hamburg airport. A rereading of the novel shows both how carefully we have been prepared, if not for such an event, at least for an explosion that reveals how a cosy Buckinghamshire village is as unprotected as any other. Moreover, the story has unexpected and uneasy symmetries built into its structure.

A boy appears in a darkened garden. His presence is an early signal, though neither the reader nor the two witnesses are yet aware of it, of the breakdown of the pleasantly ordered world of Hood House, where Blaise Gavender lives with his wife Harriet. The boy is a stowaway from Blaise Gavender's London world across Putney Bridge. What has been kept conveniently separate is about to be brought into anguishing collision. It is a novel about the pain which quite insignificant people can inflict on one another and themselves, and the consequent vulnerability of all we think of as normality.

The man at the centre of the action is a commonplace, second-rate adulterous husband. Blaise Gavender practises psychotherapy without distinction and with little belief in its central tenets, flirts half-heartedly with the thought of abandoning his lucrative practise in order to study medicine, and covets an orchard owned by his neighbour, Montague Small. Unknown to his wife, he has kept a mistress for the last nine years; the sharp-witted, pretty Emily MacHugh, much younger than himself who indulges him in perverse sexual pleasures. Montague Small, a popular detective story writer, is privy to this secret and helps to facilitate Blaise's visits to Emily by inventing a particularly disturbed patient, Magnus Bowles, who can only bear to be visited in the hours of darkness.

Monty, as he is usually called, finds the lives of the Gavenders a diversion from his own unhappiness in the aftermath of his wife Sophie's recent death from cancer. Murdoch observes his grief brilliantly, particularly the way he wakes up to the pain of it a split second before remembering that Sophie is dead. It is a sick and bitter bereavement, however, since theirs had been a tormentingly miserable marriage; Monty has kept a tape recording of one of their last arguments; and remains bitterly jealous of the adulteries with which she taunts him. Since Monty has come to loathe the character of the cold and clever Milo Fane on whom his detective stories centre, and has found he is incapable of writing serious fiction, he has a constant sense of failure, and for a time wonders whether the job of school teacher might offer a decent means of escape.

Unlike Arnold Baffin in *The Black Prince* whose facility is a matter of savage envy to the blocked Bradley Pearson, there are no other aspirant writers in the novel. Monty paces himself against the artist he had hoped to become, and is largely the victim of his mother's heroic vision of him as a child. Indeed, the struggle against the power of maternal love is an important theme in almost every family group this book brings into focus.

The only character whose intelligence is likely to be considerable is the classical scholar, Edgar Demarnay, now the Master of an Oxford College. His intellect is not much in evidence for most of the novel, however, since he is often drunk and a buffoon socially, it is far from surprising that his life has been a history of unrequited love. He had once felt an adolescent admiration for Montague as an undergraduate and even now has a desperate wish for his friendship. He had also once been in love with Monty's wife, Sophie, and we first meet him making an undignified entry into Monty's house to find the stream of letters he had written to Sophie over the years. Both men suffer from self-loathing, but Monty has no fellow feeling for Edgar, and offers him even less tolerance than he usually affords his visitors.

Blaise Gavender, on the other hand, has always found it perfectly easy to like himself, and accommodates to the double life he is leading without much difficulty. When he first met Emily she was twenty-two, small, thin with a harsh London accent and a brain good enough to undertake a thesis on Merlau Ponty, though she abandons any such ambition once she has committed herself to Blaise. In the first ecstasy of their lovemaking Blaise feels that he and Emily are living 'like gods together', and sees his marriage as a pitiful and unworthy mistake.

Blaise has no intention of throwing in his lot with Emily on a permanent basis, however, still less of telling Harriet about his new feelings. He attributes his dissatisfaction with his life to his wish to study medicine, and in this Harriet encourages him. Over the nine years he and his mistress have been seeing one another regularly, Emily has gradually begun to realise how unlikely it is that Blaise will take any action to change the situation, and so they have begun to quarrel bitterly. In her disappointment, Emily has gradually ceased to care for her own appearance or that of her flat, which now smells of cats and the bedwetting of her near autistic small son, Luca. When Luca was a small child Emily had loved him with an obsessive violence: 'they had lived like animals nestling together in a hole'. But now she cannot get close enough to touch him.

Emily endures financial, emotional and physical insecurity. Her teeth hurt. She has lost her job. Blaise continues to enjoy their sexual games, but has little temptation to destroy the rest of his life for her sake. His excuse, which has some validity, is the likely response of his legitimate adolescent son, David. His evasions and indecision are the familiar concomitants of a man who wants to continue his secret pleasures without disturbing his comfortable domestic life. Truth is a condition to which Blaise may sometimes tell himself he aspires, but he has neither the courage nor the appetite to confront his own weakness. Even as he laments his 'lost goodness', he excuses his infidelity by remembering that he had never had a true erotic passion for Harriet.

Harriet commands far more respect than any other figure in the novel, though her trusting placidity is not the sign of a sharp intelligence. She is the daughter of a military family, her father a Major, her mother disappointed in some way, which is never fully examined. Her own ambitions ran for a time to painting but she abandoned any such aspiration without much regret soon after her marriage to Blaise – in this rather resembling Emily – and has been contented enough in her role of country matron, caring for her husband and son and keeping her kitchen pleasantly old-fashioned. Her strongest passion is maternal and centres on her fastidious son, David, bound for Oxford the following year. She longs to show him physical affection but he draws back from her in an adolescent awkwardness she has no choice but to accept. It is one of the many parallels between her situation and that of Emily, who also longs to clutch her son to her and is rebuffed. Emily has filled her house with cats. Harriet directs her affections towards a number of homeless dogs to whom she gives names drawn from Greek mythology and who, throughout the novel, seem likely to threaten some unpredictable classical vengeance. She also takes great interest in the problems and symptoms of her husband's patients, particularly the fictional Magnus Bowles, for whom Montague Small invents persuasive dreams and obsessions.

Blaise's disclosure of his affair to Harriet only comes when he fears that the presence of Luca in his garden will inevitably lead to his own exposure. He is terrified of Harriet's reaction to the discovery and constructs, with the help of Montague Small, a letter of confession which cleverly fudges the history, suggesting that his sexual involvement is in the far past and that only duty binds him to the mother of his illegitimate son. In a masterstroke, he throws himself on Harriet's saintly goodness for forgiveness.

Harriet rises to the bait, and behaves at first with exemplary courage and briskness as befits a soldier's daughter. It is in the spirit of military stoicism that she holds herself together, and takes some strength from her new role of forgiving wife. Her pain, however, is overwhelming. Murdoch observes with cool accuracy how it is not so much the abstract knowledge of betrayal that hurts her, so much as the trivial evidence of a domestic intimacy shared with someone other than herself. Blaise's relief at her evident command and togetherness empowers her further. The first sign that she may be overreaching her own strength is her insistence on meeting Emily, and then inviting her home to Hood House for tea.

On this magnificent set piece the whole novel turns. Blaise, who has naturally continued to lie to both women, is correctly alarmed at bringing his two lives together in one room. At first the women are perfectly polite to one another. It is the sudden drunken incursion of Edgar Demarnay, who has formed an attachment of his own to Harriet, which unbalances the proprieties. He accuses Blaise of breaking his marriage vows, and lunges at him elbowing him in the eye. As the ensuing scuffle dies down Emily rushes away and almost involuntarily Blaise follows her. The balance of the seesaw has tipped, and it suddenly seems clear to him that it is Emily who is indispensable.

Indeed, he is soon involved in altering the whole shape of his life so that Emily buys and furnishes the new home she and Blaise will occupy together. Harriet is expected to content herself with occasional visits, as Emily had. He does not immediately explain this plan to Harriet, telephoning her instead to reassure her that he is spending the night with his invented patient, Magnus Bowles.

Harriet is an unpretentious woman; her greatest weakness her need to be needed. Hence the outpouring of love she offers the neglected child, Luca, the ease with which she can relate to him, and her delight in taking him to choose a dog from the pound. Blaise's second defection affects Harriet more seriously than his first. 'For a situation where she was not needed she had no heroism.' When the role she is supposed to play becomes clear to her, she at first reacts with vigour, and moves out of Hood House altogether.

Unfortunately, she has fewer friends to turn to than she had imagined in the days when she felt herself to be a fount of benevolence. Montague Small offers her a grudging hospitality, though he has always found her intrusive, and is far more interested in her son David's beauty and intelligence. Edgar Demarnay, who has a great country house and had suggested she might like to take refuge there, withdraws his offer when it looks as if Montague Small might consider moving in to keep Edgar company. Harriet's need to love is so intense that she even considers turning to Magnus Bowles, whose own desperation she feels she could relieve. In a spirit of compassion, and to cover up Blaise's years of falsehood, Montague abruptly explains that Bowles has committed suicide.

Everything that had once given Harriet's life meaning is stripped away from her in the second part of the book. It is not clear that she deserves this, but there is a sense that her discovery pulls her down into the common condition of humanity. Her powers to help have never been as great as she had imagined. Significantly it is to Edgar, rather than Harriet, that Monty confesses the most intense source of his misery, which is the part he played in his wife's death.

That Blaise should wish to see Harriet again is extremely plausible, as is his expectation that she would receive him back with gratitude. Blaise has caricatured Harriet throughout the book, even as he calls her his 'sacred love', once observing unkindly: 'it comes to asking her to sacrifice, but she is the sacrificing type, and in the end she'll see it as her duty.' To his astonishment, he finds Hood House dark, and the dogs both unfed and loose. As Blaise blunders into them, and the teeth of the largest and fiercest dog, Ajax, come for his throat we seem to be witnessing an alarming retribution. Indeed, reading the novel for the first time, it seems likely Blaise is dead. He is not, however. It is Harriet, in flight with Luca to her brother in Germany who meets an arbitrary violent death under a hail of terrorist bullets fired randomly at a Hamburg airport.

Harriet, alone among the characters in this book, has already been forced to take a harsh look at herself, and concludes: 'I am not the good person I used to think I was'. The brutality of her end, followed by the unseemly survival and happiness of those who have betrayed her, gives the close of this novel a peculiar cruelty. Blaise no longer remembers that he had once seen Harriet as his 'sacred love'; Emily is triumphantly, self indulgently happy. All Harriet's possessions are burned and her old-fashioned kitchen modernised. She is expunged from their lives. Most heartrendingly of all, Luca who had blossomed under Harriet's attentions into an inquiring, hopeful and intelligent person is so traumatised by the events at the airport that he has to be taken away to an institution. There is a tragic horror, recalling that at the end of Dostoevsky's *Idiot* in the character's mental collapse

This is not a novel without flaws. Neither Pinn, first Emily's redoubtable char, then her lodger, nor again the nubile Kiki St Loy have much depth or resonance, though Pinn's account of the destruction of her brother's intelligence by her father's persistent blows to his head has a poignant authenticity. David worries about his sexual desire and longs for its fulfilment, but is far less vivid that Luca; perhaps it is fitting that when he finally loses his virginity he should do so to Pinn rather than Kiki about whom he fantasises. It is in these areas where we have cared least that the book offers a certain optimism. Monty is cheered up a little by Kiki's – rather unlikely – gift of her virginity, and Edgar is given the prospect of a new life, and the interest of several beautiful women.

We do not altogether believe in Edgar's privileged life as the owner of a great house, but his classical training makes him a credible voice for the only moral comfort in the book. It comes after Edgar has heard in full the tape of a conversation made by Monty three days before Sophie's death. As Edgar tells Monty, 'Sophie is dead and you are alive and your duty is the same as any man's to make yourself better'.

This is an ambiguous novel, even to its title, which is taken from a Titian painting of 'Sacred and Profane Love', where the same model is used to show both the desired women. Parallels and similarities between Emily and Harriet have already been noted, and Peter Conradi suggests that most of the differences between the two women can be attributed to the fluctuations of their situation. 'Instead of being based on a medieval moralism that would wholly separate the good from the wicked mistress, it presents them as a single principle, Eros...Emily, formerly shrill and bitter...actually improves; and Harriet comes to offend in various ways the aesthetic sense of those who cared for her'.

This is ingenious, and may partly account for the coldness with which Harriet is first despatched and then forgotten. But it is special pleading, for the end in no way suggests any poetic justice at work in judgement. Both the bleakness and the beauty of this memorable novel lie in our realisation that the world around us works neither by justice nor a sense of the aesthetic, that only children attempt to believe otherwise, and that even their innocence offers them no protection.

Elaine Feinstein
2002

THE BOY was there again this evening, and the dogs were not barking.

David stopped in the act of pulling his curtain against the dark twilight and gazed intently down into the garden. The boy was standing under the acacia tree, just on the near-side of the fence that divided the Hood House garden from the orchard. The figure was so still and so merged into the blotchy spotty half-darkness of the scene that David would have been at a loss to explain how it was that he was so sure that it was a boy and that the boy was staring at the house. In fact, he had seen the shadowy boy before, two days ago, scarcely more clearly, at about this time. A small figure, a small boy, eight or nine years old perhaps. Why did none of the dogs bark?

David jerked the curtain across and turned on the light. He felt no urge to go down and investigate. The pulling of the curtain had already made the incident seem unreal and unimportant. A sensation which he felt almost all the time now, a sort of mild aching disgust and lassitude, made him unable to concentrate his mind. He sat down heavily upon a chair and turned unfocused eyes upon the blur of his school books lying about him upon the floor. Then with an involuntary evasive movement he turned back towards the window curtain and blinked hard three times.

He had just been engaged in removing the paper covers from all his books. A large cardboard box contained the mass of glossy sturdy polychrome smashed-up jackets which in a sudden fit of irritable energy he had ripped off, revealing the glowing sides and discreet gilded lettering of the volumes beneath. There was no doubt about it, the books looked more beautiful and more real without their covers. Montague Small had once told him that he had celebrated his fortieth birthday by thus undressing all his library. 'A wrapped up book is waiting for something,' said Montague. David had decided not to let his wait for his seventeenth birthday. He picked up a sleek slim dark blue book and stroked it. Catullus, Oxford Classical Text. *Excrucior*.

I

The pain in question was not the agony of love, however, and women were not yet David's problem, apart from his mother of course. He was visited by highly localized burning erotic anguishes which he relieved (with distaste but without guilt) in the privacy of his room. He dreamed of a Miranda, but none had so far appeared, and the exclusively masculine life of his day school was devoid of love objects. His distress was obscurer, a sort of fear of never being able to be a real person at all. He felt obscenely amorphous, globular, a creature in metamorphosis trailing a half discarded form. Even his terrors were blunted and unvivid, not enlivening. Lassitude and disgust staled all.

David was a fastidious boy. The wet red mouths of the dogs offended him, and the sight of his mother smiling upon that row of slobbering noisy feeders. He noticed how things dropped from his father's fork at meal-times, even from his father's lips: his father who now turned crimson in the face after a second glass of wine. The involuntary spasms of the body, its slimy moist interior, inspired horror. Shameless kissing in the cinema made him turn away. He would have given up eating altogether if that had been possible, would at any rate have eaten only in private, picking up dry small fragments with his fingers. Any slovenly messiness in the kitchen made him squeamish. His mother licking a spoon, then using it to stir the food. Greasy stuff trodden underfoot. The dogs made the garden foul, however much his mother ran about, and sometimes inside the house itself a vile smell would destroy both appetite and peace. They were not even very nice dogs. An early reading of the *The Hound of the Baskervilles* had made David afraid of dogs. Only of course he told nobody about this.

Last night he had dreamt about a huge blue fish struggling in the breaking waves upon the very edge of the sea. As it opened its dripping mouth towards him he had seen that its tail was half a girl with long flailing legs. He woke in horror to the sound of a howling dog. He had so often told his dreams to his father when he was a small child, it was as if his father still roamed inquisitively in his dream world, a co-spectator rather than a denizen. A blessed silence upon almost every subject had fallen between them in the last year. After the dream, he had lain awake tormented by images, faces that imposed themselves upon his closed eyes. Often it was the face of Christ, hanging just before him as upon a veil, amazingly beautiful, then turning gradually into a sneering mask. Christ was a problem to David. Prayer had been an addiction once, but the perpetual presence of this ubiquitous intrusive Friend amounted now almost to hallucination. Why had such a weird belief been induced in him when he was too young to defend himself against it? And how had his mother's vague gentle faith and the mild Anglicanism of his public school spawned in him the secret superstitions of a mopping mowing slave? Compulsive stupid rituals had replaced those frenzied conversations with God. There was a smelly intimacy about it all, connected with his mother, his mother's knee, sentimental gushings of a ridiculous familiarity offered to a deity devoid of dignity, devoid of austerity, devoid even of mystery, but now just proving horribly hard to get rid of.

Moving towards the door he saw himself in the long mirror which his mother had insisted on installing. He looked at himself, at his slim figure and blue-eyed long-tressed head. His hair, flaxen at birth, was still a lightish gold. Long uncut it fell in unruly Pre-Raphaelite splendour to his shoulders. He looked at his thinness and his straightness and his cleanness. He was a solitary being, he thought, a loner, always would be. Sometime soon he would be a *man*: he pronounced the word to himself as if one were to say a gryphon, a chimera.

Then he smiled at his image, suddenly finding it ridiculous. He had always seen himself as the Beloved Disciple.

Harriet Gavender (née Derwent) had also seen the boy; only in her case it was the first sighting. And she too had noticed the silence of the dogs. Coming out quietly into the midsummer twilight of the still garden to breathe the rich polleny fragrance of the silent air, she had seen the small perfectly motionless figure standing just beside the fence of Monty's orchard, merged almost into the dark trunk of the acacia tree. Harriet stopped abruptly upon the paved terrace and great fear invaded her heart. Why? Surely there was nothing to be afraid of in an inquisitive trespassing child. Then she recalled a dream which she had had on the previous night. She had dreamt that she was in her bedroom, in her bed (only Blaise was not with her), and that she had awakened in the darkness to see a strange light shining at the window. This is no dream, she said to herself as she rose in fright and went to look out. Just outside in the branches of a tree was the source of light, a radiant child's face, the face only, suspended there and looking at her. She ran back at once and burrowed under the bedclothes, thinking in great terror: suppose that face were to come and look at me through the window?

The dream, only now remembered, seemed to dazzle her for a moment, and turning her head away towards the sombre façade of the house she suddenly saw the dim face of her son at the window of his darkened room. David too was gazing down the garden, looking at what she had seen. He did not notice his mother. After another moment he pulled his curtain across and the light came on brightly behind it. Harriet looked down the garden again. It all seemed to have become much darker. The boy was gone. A bat had noiselessly appropriated the space between, a flittering weaving almost substanceless fragment of the invading dark. Had the child, she wondered for a moment, been really an apparition, a visitor strayed over the border from another world? Or had she imagined that small silent watcher? How stupid I am, she thought. It's just a boy, it's nothing at all.

She walked out a little way onto the lawn, breathing deeply and sighing. A collared dove groaned once in the final light. A pink rose reclining upon the big box hedge glimmered with contained electric luminosity. A blackbird, trying to metamorphose itself into a nightingale, began a long passionate complicated song. The birds sing so much more carefully in the late evening. The great cloud fields had faded behind the bumpy tops of the orchard trees, whose silhouette was so familiar to Harriet that she seemed to be thinking it rather than seeing it, and the sky had dulled to a sort of dark lightless white netted over with grey, a colour which it would retain all night. It was midsummer. Midsummer night in fact, Harriet thought. The thought came to her with a bitter-sweet sense of time passing. How much she loved the slow parade of the English year, and how sad it was too, with its increasing store of memories. And her mind flew back to the summer balls of her girlhood when, in a totally vanished world, she had danced all night in the arms of agile lieutenants.

A light had come on in Monty's house, obscured by the trees but gleaming through them. Harriet walked as far as the fence and looked at the light. What was Monty doing now? Moping? Weeping? Did he really not want to be visited?

4

Harriet's woman's heart yearned towards the mystery of the sad solitary man. Montague Small occupied the adjacent house which was called Locketts, a smaller place which the then owner of Hood House had made to be built about 1900, and had subsequently occupied, at the bottom of his own very extensive garden. Most of the garden, including the orchard so much coveted by Blaise, now belonged to Locketts, and Hood House, which had later been sold separately, had only a square of lawn to bless itself with, and the long fat box hedge and the acacia tree and Harriet's herbaceous border and her few roses. As Blaise had often observed, the logical way to divide the garden would have been to cut it beyond the orchard, which was continuous with the Hood House garden, whereas the garden 'proper' of Monty's house was at a right-angle, round a corner, and in fact the house was in another road. But as Harriet said to her complaining husband, perhaps Mr Lockett (for he had called his new house after himself) had not been a very logical kind of man.

Because of the form of the garden, and also because Locketts was such a charming and somehow significant little house (quite a gem of *art nouveau*) it had always been a matter of great importance to the Hood Houseites who their neighbour was. Of course they had another next door neighbour, but that was an elderly lady, a Mrs Raines-Bloxham, who politely declined to know them. (This was not snobbery: she politely declined to know anybody.) And when the Gavenders had first come to Hood House, not so very many years ago, Locketts had been empty. The arrival of Montague Small (*the* Montague Small, as David, who was a thriller reader, had gleefully informed them) and his intense pretty little Swiss ex-actress wife had aroused an interest and a curiosity which were not long unsatisfied. The Smalls were gratifyingly friendly though the tiniest bit aloof. It seemed so right that it should be a *writer's* house, Harriet had thought. They all liked Monty. Harriet pretended to like Sophie, and tried to, but never quite did. For Harriet, Sophie was hopelessly foreign. As for Blaise, he prayed openly 'Oh Lord, let that woman never want to be a patient of mine!' Then a bit later Monty had come round one day with an utterly changed face to tell them that Sophie had cancer. There had been an interval of withdrawal, Monty cold, Sophie invisible. Then Sophie died. That was now nearly two months ago. Monty was very very bereaved. 'I have never seen a man mourn so, 'said Blaise.

Harriet turned back across the dim garden. The lightless light looked down from the white night sky. The blackbird's long song was over. A distant owl was hooting. One star was visible. Jupiter, David had told her. Venus did not rise until after two. How thick the silence was, though it was not really country here of course, not like in Wales in her childhood. Wilder Buckinghamshire was a little away, and the houses went on continuously among the trees in the direction of London, whose pink glare illuminated the night sky in winter. A light had just come on in Blaise's study. How pretty, how foursquare, how quite ridiculously *housey* Hood House looked with its shallow slate roof and its pretty flint and stone patterning and its tall early Victorian windows, quite the oldest as well as the handsomest house in its area. A sort of seaside house she thought of it as being, without quite knowing why. Perhaps the little white wrought-iron balconies on the first floor gave it that slight air of marine quaintness. It was not a very big house but it was the grandest house that Harriet had ever lived in. She and Blaise had been far from well off when they got married.

There was a soft almost soundless flurry and something wet and warm brushed Harriet's hand. It was the nose of Ajax, the black Alsatian. Then all the dogs were suddenly round about her, not ecstatic but gently pleased with her, undulating in a circular ballet of quiet orderly prancing. The dogs had been a lovely accident really. They were her pets, not David's, not Blaise's. They were outdoor dogs of course. They lived, in as much comfort as Harriet could contrive, in the old garage. She had wanted to bring little Ganimede into the house once, but it had proved impossible to house-train him. Dogs, like humans, can be disturbed forever by an unhappy childhood. Anyway it had seemed so unfair to the other dogs of whom at that time there were four. Now there were seven in all: Ajax, the Alsatian, Ganimede, a black miniature poodle, Babu, a black spaniel, Panda, a black labrador mongrel with white markings, Buffy, an airedale, Lawrence, a Welsh collie, and Seagull, a small black and white terrier. The idea that they should all be black and have classical names had been early abandoned. Harriet had originally acquired Ajax because she felt nervous at Hood House when Blaise was away from home at night, as he sometimes had to be to see patients. (Magnus Bowles, for instance.) When she was a child she had had a morbid fear of cats, and used to search her bedroom carefully every night in case a cat had secreted itself there. In later life

6

she feared burglars, tramps, gipsies, violent intruders. Of course Blaise had told her that burglars symbolized sexual intercourse, but this interesting revelation did not cure her fright or prevent her from holding her breath to listen for strange noises in the dark. Harriet had acquired Ajax as an adult dog from the Battersea Dogs Home, and then the thing had become rather an addiction. 'When you feel depressed you go and pick a dog!' said Blaise with exasperation. But it was so touching to go there and rescue some pathetic affectionate beautiful animal, it was a kind of creative act.

'No, outside, boys, outside, boys,' she murmured. 'You've had your dinners. Now be good dogs.' She shut the kitchen door upon the concourse of dark muzzles and turned on the light. Harriet had never let Blaise modernize the kitchen and, also in spite of him, they usually took their meals there, at the rectangular deal table covered by its red and white check cloth. The big chaotic rather obscure room suited Harriet. It was friendly and undemanding and smelt humbly of the past, full of dark lined old wood that needed scrubbing. She passed through it now, gazing unmoved upon a pile of greasy plates, and mounted the stairs, resisting as usual the usual temptation to go and call on her son, and went into her 'boudoir'. This was a tiny cluttered room, originally a dressing-room. Blaise's more austerely pretentious taste reigned in the rest of the house. Harriet, who could not bear to discommode a spider and who would spend ten minutes washing a lettuce rather than let any miniscule creature inadvertently elude rescue, extended her charity in a quite instinctive way to things. Now that both her parents were dead most of the serious family stuff was at Adrian's flat in London, but Harriet had carried away, together with her various childhood treasures, a lot of awkward homeless oddments, brass ornaments and such, which no one else seemed to want or love, and which now mingled with an exotic miscellany of gaudy little gifts which Adrian and her father had brought her from various parts of the world, from Benares, from Bangkok, from Aden, from Hong Kong, the casual spoils of innumerable bazaars, jars and trays and boxes, little animals, little men, little gods of whom she did not know the names, all that 'junk shop rubbish' for which Blaise scolded her so, although he secretly found her absurd animism rather touching. And now, stuffed into the middle or hanging onto the edges, were the things that Monty had given her lately, since Sophie died, handing them out at random whenever she called, plates, ornaments, cushions, bits of embroidery, as if he wanted to strip Locketts and deprive it of all memory.

The walls of the boudoir were covered with paintings and photographs. The paintings were Harriet's own (she had thought herself a painter once), pale splodgy water-colours, laboriously high-lighted oils whose paint seemed to have thinned with the years. The photographs were all of family; of her parents' wedding, of Harriet's wedding, of David as various children, of a younger slimmer hawkier Blaise, of her soldier father in uniform, of her soldier brother in uniform, of her disappointed pretty mother. *Ubique quo fas et gloria ducunt* had been a tattered pilgrimage for Harriet's mother. Harriet had been born in India when her father was Gunnery Instructor at the School of Artillery at Deolali. Harriet's mother, doing an Indian season with a diplomatic cousin, had met and married the romantic Captain Derwent. A caparisoned elephant attended their wedding. (There was a photograph of the elephant too.) Soon after came a home posting and the war. Captain (now Major) Derwent became an instructor at Catterick, then commanded an anti-aircraft battery in Wales. Later on he was at Woolwich, later still in Germany. He never rose above the rank of Major. Harriet's mother followed the camp, living in furnished lodgings (only she drew the line at Germany). There had been a Welsh mountain cottage which the children had liked. There had been too little money and no romance. The days of the elephant were far off now. As a widow Harriet's mother had lived in Ireland. Harriet rarely saw her in the later years. The thought of her came tenderly back in connection with country things: blackberrying, sloes for sloe gin, quinces for jelly, ponies and heather, the smell of honeysuckle or damp hay, the vanilla taste of russet apples. Harriet cherished these intense yet shadowy almost pointless visitations. It was so important to think quiet loving thoughts about people in idle moments, especially perhaps about the dead, who being substanceless so desperately need our thoughts.

Harriet looked into her Dutch marquetry mirror (a Christmas gift from Blaise) and patted her very long intertwined coiled up golden tinged dark brown hair. Instinctively her broad calm face became even calmer. She was wearing the long spotted voile dress which Blaise said made her look so Victorian. She was always careful not to dress too young. Some of her friends simply never noticed when they put on weight. Harriet sat down at her desk and relaxed into a melancholy idleness. She felt at these times empty, floppy, disjointed, as if she covered a huge area quietly like a large limp suspended sea animal, like an immense uninhabited continent: and this was for her really a form of being happy. Each person doubtless has a sort of form or structure or schema (only that would not have been Harriet's word) into which his consciousness lazily stretches itself out when uncoerced, and which is, however unglittering and inglorious, his happiness. Harriet was happy. The house around her felt happy too with the stored-up warmth of her anxious yet composed and unassertive temperament.

Of course she had her worries, especially David and sometimes the aching sense of a tiny lost talent, but she was loved and loving and had an untroubled conscience and that was quite enough, for one of her temper, for happiness, that deep confiding slow relationship to time. Hers was a sometimes sad but always smiling happiness. She loved her husband and her son and her brother and carried every discontent into the light of that love to be consumed. Sometimes she had a feeling of what she thought of as 'littleness' ('small fryness') when she thought: how I wish I were a great painter or a great *something*. She had been to art school and had had ambition. But early marriage, combined with the fact that Blaise never took her vocation seriously, had led her to lay aside her brush. She knew that she led a selfish life because all her otherness was so much a part of herself. There was no strain or distance really, even her charities were easy and pleasant and rich in the rewards of gratitude. I am a deeply selfish person, she told herself sometimes, and so I shall never be great, not like men are great, or touched by greatness.

Now however she was thinking about her son. Every mother has to endure it, I suppose, she thought. The marvellous intimacy could not last. He had withdrawn first from Blaise, now from her. Blaise said it was natural and proper. He had become untouchable; and Harriet, with her long habit of touching, was suddenly in a dilemma, in an anguish. She was visited by alarmingly precise ghostly yearnings. Feelings very like the torments of an unrequited love made her blush and tremble. It was indeed dreadfully like being in love. She wanted to hold him in her arms again, to cover him with kisses, to untangle with caressing fingers that untidy and now absurdly long golden hair. But nothing was less possible. He had become, as if further to confuse her, dauntingly good-looking in this last year. What Blaise called David's 'archaic smile' haunted her like a sort of erotic enigma. He was so tall now and often so stern, and yet inside this dignified angel there was surely the same awkward adorable small boy. He had odd mannerisms, new ones, secret ones. There were so many things one could not talk about. Did he still lay out his penknife and his compass and all his other little treasures before he turned out the light? How happy it had made her once to think that David prayed nightly for herself and Blaise. The thought had soothed her own growing disbelief. Did he do so still? It was inconceivable to ask. She knew of mothers who flirted with their adolescent sons. It was impossible for her to do so. David, in his new grown-upness, had already a sort of authority, an absolute ability of veto. Harriet knew very well what she could and could not dare. I must pull out, she thought: it was like the ending of an affair, giving somebody up. Would one be thus condemned to break the links one by one? Of course it was simply natural change and not an ending, and of course her love could not end, could not in the faintest detail of its being diminish ever. The trouble was that she could not see at present how her love for David could change sufficiently for her not now and henceforth forever to be in the position of concealing something which he would uneasily suspect. She leaned forward over her hands in sudden anguish. What was that quotation about love being 'woman's whole existence'? It was certainly true in her case, and how terrifying it was.

Blaise Gavender had enjoyed his supper. He enjoyed his food. There had been asparagus, which so deliciously scented the urine. Harriet was an untidy slovenly housewife but a decent cook. Earlier he had been upset because he had been rude to a man who came to read the electric meter. The man had been a little casual. Blaise had suddenly acted the country squire. Why? These little outbursts would have interested him once. Now he let the incident fade, efficiently digested like the asparagus. Perhaps he thought of all 'callers at the house' as patients, and so as properly obsequious. At this moment, while desultorily mending with glue and sellotape a broken Japanese bowl of Harriet's, he was trying with fair success to keep his mind strictly on his patients. Sometimes he hated his patients. That was bad. His sort of healer could only operate through a love relationship. Of course that could be bad too. Monty had once said to him that all curiosity divorced from love or science was necessarily malign. Monty had been talking about a writer and his characters. But the phrase had struck Blaise in relation to his own work. He enjoyed his work, but why? That he had long ago seen through his motives did not tell him what to do next. It did not even mean that he could not help people. He could and did.

The thought of Monty always caused irritation, though Blaise was fond of his interesting talented neighbour. He had talked too much to Monty. In other parts of the animal kingdom males instinctively threatened each other in a mechanical and meaningless manner. The blackbirds on the lawn were doing it every day. Of course he had been a fool ever to accept Monty as a patient, though that interlude had been mercifully brief. Had he ever understood Monty's motives? Blaise quickly terminated the relation when he realized that the healer was in danger of being taken over by the sufferer.

Fiddling with the jigsaw puzzle of the Japanese bowl (was a piece missing?) he recalled a dream which he had had last night. He was standing in the garden beside the acacia tree when he saw that part of the trunk appeared to be moving. A huge snake was gradually descending the tree towards him. He watched with horror and a kind of joy the approach of the snake. Only it was not exactly a snake, since it had a pair of large wings folded upon its back, in the way in which a beetle's wings are folded. As it came near to him it reared its head and the wings spread out and began to buffet him on either side, half suffocating him in their strong soft violence. Meanwhile the creature's large tail, tapering to a point finer than a pencil, had wound itself round one of his legs. He was a woman in the dream. He had no difficulty in interpretation. He knew the muck heap of other people's minds. He knew the muck heap of his own.

How dull and unmagical his own dreams seemed to have become, he thought, as if he were stolidly interpreting them even as he dreamed. And how rarely did a patient's dream astonish or move him now. Well, it was not his business to be astonished or moved. The patients had become, for him, a grubby grey contingent of predictable people. Whereas for

Harriet they remained objects of reverence and mystery. Since they mostly came to the house, she knew them a little bit at a saying 'Good morning' level. But Harriet, who would have been an excellent wife for a headmaster, had always yearned for a closer relation, a more positive kind of service. Not that she wished in any way to encroach upon Blaise's priestly function. She would have liked to mend their clothes. Of course there should have been six children, not just David. They had hoped for more. Blaise had been sad about that. But Harriet positively and half-consciously suffered from a sheer excess of undistributed love, like having too much milk in the breasts. She suffered from having these huge resources by which she could directly benefit only her husband and her son.

Some of the patients indeed had been with him for years and could almost have played the role of children. In a way they did people the house. They were not easy to get rid of. He had lately begun to take them in groups as a way of preparing them for the end, the parting, the severing of the umbilical cord, their cure. Also this meant that he could, and not only for financial reasons, take on new patients. There was, alas, no substitute for the unravished chastity of the new patient. The existing ones were in fact wonderfully various. Each had his *idée fixe*, something which he took to be his 'reason' for consulting Blaise, although this 'reason' often concealed a complex of other lesions. Stanley Tumbelholme had an obsessional fear of his sister. Angelica Mendelssohn suffered paralysing jealousy through being in love with members of the Royal Family. Maurice Guimarron thought he had committed the sin against the Holy Ghost. Septimus Leech was a blocked writer. Penelope Biggers was insomniac because she feared to 'die' in her sleep and be buried alive. Horace Ainsley (who had once been Blaise's doctor and was still Monty's) exhibited chronic indecision caused by irrational guilt. Miriam Lister had a daughter with homicidal tendencies whom Blaise was treating by treating the mother. Jeannie Batwood simply wanted to save her marriage. Not that Blaise necessarily discounted or even radically reinterpreted what his patients said they thought. He received an early lesson from a patient who always wore gloves because she said she had the stigmata. It was a little while before it occurred to Blaise to ask her to remove the gloves. She had the stigmata, and was later successfully treated for hysteria.

Blaise knew perfectly well that he was not really qualified to do what he professed to do. He was by now very experienced and no longer feared making radical mistakes. However, though he never said this except jokingly to Harriet (who hotly denied it) he knew that he was some sort of charlatan. He had never taken a medical degree. He had studied philosophy and psychology at Cambridge, he had done a thesis on psychoanalysis, and later taught psychology, at Reading University. (It was during his first year at Reading that he had met Harriet at a dance.) He had started to practice his own sort of therapy first of all as a temporary and risky experiment, and also because what he saw of others in the field led him to think that he could do better. He had probably not been wrong. Of course he enjoyed power, all meddlers with the mind enjoy that. And of course he was aware that this absorption in other people's misery had more to do with sex than with either altruism or science. He had passed far beyond worrying about that either. The fact was that he could indeed like a priest make to cease the biting mental pain which, in the interstices of 'real' tragedy, so needlessly erodes the lives of men. He had the gift. He had the *nerve*. He was a strong and thoroughly able person. Why now this absolute crisis of confidence? Surely he was not such a fool as to grow sick of the thing simply because it had become so easy and so lucrative.

When the idea that he ought to throw up his practice and take a medical degree had first occurred to Blaise, he had rejected it out of hand as an irrational fantasm, a project of self-punishment generated by some quite differently located sense of guilt. To surrender his steady income, to run, at his age, the gauntlet of tedious and possibly difficult exams, to accept alien judgment and hard work: no. This was just the (so familiar among his patients) disingenuous craving of a middle-aged man for a cleansing spiritual test. Also, as his father had been a successful doctor, his motives were even more miserably transparent. However the idea inconveniently persisted so that he began positively to fear it. Of course there were plenty of facts about the brain and nervous system which, wielding the power he did, he ought to know and did not. He was surrounded by mysteries. But as time passed his painful idea presented itself less as a desire for specialized professional improvement and more as a desire for absolute change. For many reasons, he had ceased reading, ceased thinking, of late. He needed radical intellectual change.

His fascination with the enchanted enchanting curiously self-determining world of psychoanalytical theory had now begun to seem, in his own case at any rate, to be a form of

13

self-indulgence. The different 'schools' were like so many magical gardens, each with its own flora and its own design, and each surrounded by its own high wall. As a practitioner Blaise was pragmatic, 'empirical' in the simplest sense of the word. He simply tried to see what would 'work', and was prepared to take a fairly *ad hoc* common-sense view of what constituted 'working'. He had long ago stopped worrying about which school he belonged to, nor did he feel this resignation as a failure of science. He had intended to write a big book about it all once, but had given that up. The discriminations no longer seemed to be worth making. He occasionally recorded an idea for an article, and let Harriet continue to believe in the existence of the book, since she seemed to care about it. His present *malaise* was more profound. As a result of experience, of his patients and of himself, he had begun to lose faith in all 'deep' theories of the mind. He could quiet his patients by telling them that it was a 'long haul', by telling them to 'accept themselves'. He could prevent *them* from being crippled by guilt. But what he had once, theoretically at least, regarded as 'surface phenomena' of morality and freedom retained, for him, their unassimilable awkwardness in a way which made him sometimes feel that he lived with his patients in a world, for all its horrors, of comfortable illusion. The torment which he tried to spare his patients he could not escape from himself: the pain of irrevocable decisions taken in the old-fashioned blindfolded responsible way. Perhaps he was just sick to death of the human mind, sick of himself and his habits and his doings, and as some men tire of the world and turn to God, he was turning to science.

He had talked to Harriet about it of course. She only partly understood, but she was all sympathy, all support. He knew that Harriet would feel sad if they had to sell Hood House and live for a time more modestly. She would feel lonely during the long hours when he would be a hospital slave. (Yes, it did seem like a punishment.) But she wanted his happiness and his fulfilment more than anything, she willed his will, she willed him. Already she saw herself as 'the doctor's wife'. God, he was lucky. He had never when young imagined that he would marry a woman so totally non-intellectual. But her intuitive attention to him was so shrewd, he could do without intellectual chat. She was never tedious, always fresh, intent, intense, but with a sort of immediate graceful animal intensity, quite unlike the cunning reflective shifts and transports of his patients. Harriet's intensity did not exclude, what Napoleon valued most in a woman, repose. Even her vague Christianity, which he had taken care not to uproot but had hoped to see quietly wither, now seemed something he could not do without, any more than he could forego the special way she stretched out her hands to him when he entered a room where she was. There was no doubt that she had influenced him, and not only by making him kinder to spiders.

As Blaise sat thinking these, and now other, thoughts the twilight had come, and he had set aside the completed Japanese bowl. He got up and went to the window, standing there in the dark and looking down at the paved terrace. He saw the pale form of his wife who was just outside the kitchen door, gazing away down the garden. Her motionless figure seemed brimful of the stillness of the evening, her quietness made the garden more quiet. She still had much of that 'story book' beauty which had once seemed to him like a vision of another moral world. He loved those silly flowing girdled robes which a more critical eye would have wished to see upon a slimmer woman. He looked away down the garden at the tall poised silhouette of the acacia tree and the denser darkness of the orchard beyond. Monty Small was talking of leaving Locketts. Would he consent to sell the orchard? Yet, really, was this a moment for buying orchards! Harriet had moved away down the garden and now there were her neurotic dogs swirling about her like little black ghosts. Blaise pulled the curtains and turned on the light.

It was nearly reading time. Would David come? Harriet stared so, he must speak to her. He must speak to David about giving up Greek. And he must talk to Monty about Magnus Bowles. Oh God, he had so many troubles. He had so much wanted a daughter.

' "Where is Nastasia Philipovna?" asked the Prince breathlessly.
"She's here," replied Rogozhin slowly, after a slight pause.
"Where?"
Rogozhin raised his eyes and gazed intently at the Prince.

"Come," he said.'

Blaise closed the book. Of course both Harriet and David knew the story, though Harriet usually claimed to have forgotten. But Blaise liked to finish at an exciting moment. He read aloud well, with spirit but without too much emphasis. The reading aloud custom dated from David's childhood. They had read most of Scott, Jane Austen, Trollope, Dickens. Blaise loved it. There was an actor *manqué* somewhere inside him.

The reading took place in summer in what Blaise called the breakfast-room (though they never breakfasted there) and in winter in the kitchen. The breakfast room was really the sitting-room. The drawing-room was rarely sat in or withdrawn to. Harriet, ensconced in an armchair opposite to her husband with a box of chocolates at her side, was sewing. She always sewed at reading time because David as a small child had once said that he loved to see her sew. Did he still, or did it merely annoy him now, she wondered. This was the pattern of so many of her dilemmas about her son. Because of him, so many of the silly little rituals of a happy marriage were put in question. Harriet was (not very skilfully) blanket-stitching the frayed cuff of one of Blaise's old jackets. The jacket smelt of Blaise, not a tobacco smell, as he was a non-smoker, but a sweaty doggy thoughtful male odour. How much that smell expressed the difference between men and women. Harriet would have liked to embrace the jacket, now at this very moment, and bury her face in it, only she had learnt long ago to modify her transports in the company of either of her two men, let alone in the company of both.

David was sitting on the floor, not near Harriet (he used to lean against her knees once) one foot tucked under him, his head drooped, quietly grimacing and blinking as if the story were producing extraordinary trains of thought. His fair, now rather greasy, tangly hair, which was beginning to turn slightly upward at the ends, flopped around his face in a random and unintelligible chaos of criss-crossing locks. Does he *never* comb it, she wondered. Oh, if only he would let me. She felt his consciousness of her ardent look, and shifted her attention to his faded jeans, one slim boney ankle, one dirty sandalled foot, the carpet. She sighed deeply and laid aside her needle.

Blaise meanwhile was quietly reading through the next section of the book, half smiling with appreciation and pleasure, then suddenly frowning with thought. Harriet was a little

16

older than her husband and she felt the age gap in these moments of contemplation. How young he still was. He was less handsome than her son, but he looked so strong and decisive and manly. He had straight faintly reddish hair, which he kept cut very short, a pink large square-jawed face, a long thin mouth, and long blue-grey winter sea eyes. David's eyes were his father's, only much bluer. Harriet's eyes were a clear plain brown. The presence of both the men in this sort of quietness filled her with a kind of happiness which was also anguish, was terror. Life had been so terrifyingly generous to her. She sighed again and helped herself to another chocolate. At that moment she suddenly remembered the apparition of the intruding boy. She was about to tell Blaise about it, but then decided not to. Blaise would think it was one of her 'night fears', and he always thought that her fears meant something when in fact they meant nothing. Perhaps she had imagined the boy anyway.

David was feeling tense and miserable. The reading sessions had embarrassed him horribly ever since the days of *The Wind in the Willows* which were now some time ago. The silent will of both parents beseeching him, compelling him, to come made now a nightly drama. Once or twice lately he had just not turned up, and had sat alone in his room grinding his teeth. He gazed at a greasy food stain upon his father's lapel and inhaled the smell of milk chocolate with which his mother's audible munching was polluting the atmosphere. If only his mother would not stare at him and sigh like a love-sick girl. Of course he loved his parents dearly, only now everything about them grated on his nerves until he could scream. Their self-conscious air of a happy home life made him want to go and starve in a garret. If only he had gone to a boarding school, then home might have been a treat. He rose and mumbled good night and went out quickly and silently. Later in his own room he listened to the murmurous sound, so rarely heard by an outsider, of spouses communing privately with each other. How much it had soothed him when, as a small child, he had fallen asleep night after night, lulled to security by that noise as by the murmur of a friendly brook.

'You did my Japanese bowl so beautifully.'
'I'm glad David came.'
'I wish he wouldn't keep blinking like that.'
'I wish he'd either cut his hair or wash it.'
'He says he's going to grow a beard as soon as he can.'
'Oh God.'
'What does the blinking mean?'
'Adolescents are full of ticks.'
'He ate no supper. Do you think he's got *anorexia nervosa*?'
'Dear girl, I do wish you wouldn't read those Sunday supplement articles!'
'Don't worry him about Italian, leave it a while.'
'I'm not going to let him give up Greek. He can do Italian in his spare time.'
'By the way, the Andersons have asked us for tomorrow night.'
'Tomorrow is Magnus Bowles night.'
'Oh dear. Can't you change Magnus for once?'
'You know I can never change Magnus.'
'I suppose he must be recovering after all these years. He doesn't need you quite so often.'
'It is hard to say,' said Blaise, 'what recovering would be in the case of a man like Magnus Bowles. He so much is his obsessions.'
'If only he could paint again.'
'He messes with paints.'
'What was that horrible thing you said about paint?'
'Paint equals shit.'
'The unconscious is so coarse. Does he still go around his room on his knees touching things?'
'He is surrounded by gods which he has to placate. Everything is holy. In another age he would have been revered as a saint.'
'Poor crazy creature.'
'Primitive man lived in a world of frightful small deities. Roman Catholics still do.'
'I know you think all religion is just obsession!'
'Dear girl, I don't think anything so silly. Religion is very important. It's just that it isn't what it seems. Few things that are very important are.'
'I'd love to meet Magnus one day. I feel sure I would help him to feel more normal.'

'Women always think that about homosexuals'.

'I don't mean—I'd just tidy his room and talk to him about painting. He sometimes sends me his greetings after all. He must think about me a bit.'

'Oh you quite exist for him. Perhaps you are the only woman who does. But your meeting him would simply destroy my ability to help him. So it's impossible.'

'A man it's impossible to meet. How interesting. I just hate to think of him being all alone, seeing practically nobody but you, sleeping in the day and waking in the night, and terribly frightened of things that aren't there.'

'You'd be surprised, dearest girl, how many people have such fears, and most of them manage to lead quite ordinary lives.'

'Well, he doesn't. One is lucky not to be pursued by imaginary devils. He has quite a funny one, hasn't he?'

'A Bishop with a wooden leg who follows him like Hook's crocodile.'

'That's rather nice. I can't quite feel I'd be frightened. But those awful hallucinations about having killed his mother and the corpse sprouting up like a young girl. And telling you he'd cut his finger off and not being convinced he hadn't even when you were showing him his own hand! He's much madder than the others. I'm sure he should be having electric shocks or something.'

'I understand Magnus's case, for God's sake, Harriet.'

'All right, all right. It's just that he must be so unhappy.'

'These acute anxiety states aren't quite unhappiness. They are not quite believed in. Magnus feels he's going to be punished for some crime which he can't remember, and not being able to remember is part of the guilt. But this is quite an exciting condition, and all the bumping and touching keeps the punishment at bay.'

'Is he as fat as ever?'

'He's a compulsive eater.'

'How I sympathize. So am I. Pass the chocolates, darling. I think you should write his case history, he's so picturesque. I wish you could persuade him to see you at a civilized time of day.'

'He's incurably nocturnal. He even looks like a potto. He only comes alive in the evening.'

'Then he takes half your night and exhausts you. Those patients are eating you.'

'No, I eat them actually. Let's get off Magnus, can we?'

'Well, I'll ring the Andersons. No, I don't want to go without you, not there. Anderson just wants to talk shop with you. And she is so intense and odd. They asked Monty too, by the way. He refused.'

'He needs to get out and see more people. Are you going over tomorrow?'

'Yes. That's unhappiness.'

'He's got to get through his mourning like a long illness. You are good for him.'

'I hope so. You don't think he's likely to kill himself?'

'Monty? No. No.'

'He looks so pathetic and wretched, like a sort of lost Harlequin. And yet he looks so sort of pale and clerical too, like a mad priest in one of his stories. He only needs a black hat. If only he could start writing again.'

'I suspect he's sick to death of Milo Fane.'

'All the same it must be wonderful to have invented a character that everybody knows about. There are even Milo Fane Detective Sets at the Supermarket.'

'Old Monty must be coining money.'

'I rather wish we had TV. There's another Milo Fane series on. The papers say Richard Nailsworth is marvellous as Milo.'

'No, girl, no. No television. Anyway you don't like Monty's books any more than I do.'

'I've never said so to him.'

'Don't. Writers may know they're bad, but there's always a precious bit of vanity left. I'm afraid Monty's books are all the same, at least the later ones are.'

'I know, Milo has gone all moral and the victim turns out to be the murderer's long lost mother or something. I wonder why Monty has never written a straight novel?'

'He probably can't. And there's the cash. Earning those sums could become a habit.'

'And then he marries a rich girl. Odd how money always finds money.'

'Sophie might have been a better actress if she hadn't been so confoundedly well off.'

'B. darling, shall I ask Monty about—you know—lending us money?'

'No, for God's sake. Nothing's decided yet.'

'You keep saying that and I feel it's because of me. You think I wouldn't want to be married to a poor medical student. How wrong you are!'

'I know, my darling,' said Blaise, 'that you'd stand by me in anything. You'd weather any crisis. I thank you and bless you. But it's a big step and we must think—'

'I've thought. I'm for it.'

'You said it was mad.'

'I just said that at first because I was surprised. And I only meant wonderful-mad. Let's go straight ahead, and let Magnus Bowles and the rest of them find another trick-cyclist.'

'You are so brave, girl darling.'

'I'm not, dearest B. I'm not making any sacrifice. I don't want to be anywhere else but right behind you, looking at the world through your eyes. I have no other being, no other vision.'

'My own girl—'

'Shall I say anything to Monty about the orchard?'

'We can't both borrow his money and buy his orchard!'

'So I should say something about the money?'

'Not yet, I've got to think—'

'I've got those securities, and of course you might get a grant.'

'Go to bed, girl dear, will you, go to bed.'

'All right, all right, moody man. Don't work too long on your book, will you. Why, it's still quite light outside. How odd the garden looks.'

Montague Small was awakened suddenly by a curious sound inside the house. Or had he dreamt it? He sat up. The memory that Sophie was dead came the usual split-second after waking. As if one were to see the flash of the sword before it bit. The intensity of the pain took all his attention for the moment. He listened again. Silence. It must have been part of his dream. Then he remembered the dream.

On a huge empty plain, a large strange monster lay decapitated. Monty approached and saw the long iron-grey neck, scantily covered with black hairs, the dried blood, the gaping mouths of the severed blood vessels. The huge hideous head lay a little way away from the body, and he saw with fear and horror that something on the surface of the head was moving.

Then he saw that a tiny monster, a baby replica of the slain beast, was clinging to the hair at the side and weeping piteously. He saw the falling tears like seed pearls. Suddenly he felt himself to be choking with wild grief, weeping and weeping.

He sat now dry-eyed. Odd that he had been crying so in his dream, but could not cry in real life, had not cried since. Oh, if only tears would come. How terrible all his dreams were now. The freshness and brightness of dream images, as he had once known them, was gone. His hand quested over the night table touching the glass of water, the bottles of sleeping-pills and tranquillizers which Dr Ainsley had given him, his watch, the base of the lamp. He switched the light on. Not yet four o'clock. He would not sleep again now. Dreams conspire with the sleeping consciousness, they feed each other and draw into forgetfulness. But now the thread was broken, the critical suffering mind hideously alert, not to be coaxed and charmed; switched on like clockwork, it raced in misery. It was no good turning the pillow over and pretending to start afresh. He put on his watch. If he wore it in bed it always somehow crept up beside his ear and woke him with a deafening beat, the sound of eternity heard in a child's delirium.

He got out of bed and put on a dressing-gown. His abandoned bed lay crumpled and terrible behind him, like snake skin, like a vile face. It smelt foul. He had dismissed the charwoman. How dreadful Sophie had been at the end, clawing at him savagely to share her terror and despair. He thought, she screamed horrors at me to help herself endure. She could not so have loaded any other being. It should have been a cue for compassion, even for pride. He ought to have accepted that suffering from her with profound gratitude as a proof of her love. Instead, when she spitefully attacked him, he shouted back. Their life together ended in a mess of stupid quarrels. They were quarrelling when she died. He would never forgive himself. After all that filth of suffering one might have felt that death was a clean agent: the vile rubble of consciousness cleared away forever, the poor victim safe beyond the hooks and pulleys of pain, beyond the malignity of the world and of God. But he had made even this austere consolation impossible for himself. He felt that joy, which is a part of all essential things, had departed from his life forever. Sickening terrors, which he had long wished to spurn away, fed by catastrophe now prowled again. There were moments when he could not see how he could go on living with his mind.

He pulled back the window curtains and switched off the lamp. The garden was already fully visible in cold white lightless dawn light, very quiet, very appalling. The long empty lawn receded, colourless, textureless, like the sheet spread for a ceremonial disembowelling. The two big Douglas firs were motionless, brimful of alienated enigmatic being. The tall privet hedge was featureless as a wall, its chubby leafy roundness flattened by the white light. In the orchard, round the corner towards Hood House, a few birds were tentatively calling, with a compelled despairing clarity. Monty then remembered the boy whom he had seen on the previous evening, standing in the Hood House garden in the twilight and gazing so fixedly towards the house. At first he had imagined for a crazy moment that it was Sophie. He so constantly expected to see her. Could one think so intensely of someone and not be visited? Can ghosts *decide* to manifest themselves, he wondered.

It so often seemed to him that Sophie was in the house, a breathless quick presence whisking maliciously out of rooms just as he entered them. She travelled with him, already even now changing a little. Was she perhaps really travelling, receding, through some sort of dark echoing *bardo*? For in that sleep of death what dreams may come. . . . If she survived as a tormented dreamer did she dream of him, and could her dreaming mind now somehow doom him? Was she wasting in resentful suffering now in death as he had seen her waste in life? Perhaps our thoughts hold the dead captive as they do the living; and perhaps their thoughts can touch us too. 'What are you thinking?' she had cried. 'Oh how it maddens me not to know!' Or was it he who had said that? Alive, their love had been a mutual torment. Death, which might have imposed a merciful silence upon this dialogue, had not done so. He had so often wanted to silence her thoughts. Were they silent now, or were they still gabbling away just on the other side of his awareness? Could not the survivor end this wicked servitude and set at liberty the frenzied ghost? How was this to be done? They had loved each other. How little this seemed now to avail. Love was itself the madness.

How little he had helped himself by meddling with his mind this test told him. For years he had tried to control his dreams, to remain conscious while dreaming, to connect sleeping and waking. He had partly succeeded, making thereby the waking world less real, not the sleeping world more so. That was right in a way. But as so often, he had got hold of the wrong form

23

of the right answer. Horrors swept freely in on him from the land of dreams, and what should have been wisdom turned into nightmare. All his spiritual efforts had been mere adventures ending in fright and muddle. After it all he was but an apprentice and his master was a sorcerer. Not even a very important sorcerer. Of course the little figure under the acacia tree could not possibly have resembled Sophie, though she was so small and had often seemed to him like a boy. Yet for a moment, in exquisite pure fear, he expected her to turn, expected to see her spectacles glinting at him like an animal's eyes in the half dark. But of course it was just a boy. The fear remained however. Supposing the strange boy were to hear him and to turn round and look at him? Monty hurried silently back to Locketts, touching the reptilion trunks of the twisted orchard trees for comfort. Inside the house Milo Fane, cool, ironical, slit-eyed, mocked his pusillanimous scurry.

As he now looked down into the relentless morning garden he recalled his mother's promised visit. Underneath an unfailing lady-like politeness his mother had detested Sophie. His mother had doubtless willed Sophie's death, who knows how ineffectually. The feeling had been mutual, of course, and Sophie had scarcely even attemped to be kind. She had a sort of foreign awkwardness with her mother-in-law which seemed designed to exasperate. Monty's mother, who thought of herself as impoverished gentry, had been delighted by her son's literary success but disappointed by his marriage. Sophie, though gratifyingly well off, came of a nebulous alien 'flashy' background of Swiss business people, which Mrs Small could not and would not attempt to understand. She regarded Sophie as vulgar, and she and Sophie's mother were instant enemies. 'The creator of Milo Fane can marry *anybody*,' Monty had been earlier informed by his mother. She had imagined for him a frail elegant delicately nurtured English girl (possibly with a title) whom she would have dominated and made into a junior ally. In fact, she would probably have found means to hate any woman Monty married.

Monty's father, a poor curate, had died when Monty was eight. A week after the death, his mother had instructed him henceforth to call her by her given name: Leonie. Something unintelligible and dark entered with this portentous name into the relationship. Leonie, who had always wanted to be an actress (doubtless another reason for Sophie's unpopularity) gallantly supported her son and only child by teaching elocution and singing at a girls' school. She was delighted when Monty went to Oxford, dashed when he did less than brilliantly, yet more dashed when he became a schoolmaster, delighted when he ceased to be a schoolmaster, and became a successful writer, dashed again when he married a shrill-voiced unreticent foreigner. Now the time for delight had come round once more. Sophie was dead and tidied away. Leonie could not, and indeed scarcely tried to, conceal her satisfaction, but at least she kept away. She had been discreetly 'ill' on the day of the funeral. Perhaps she might have been unable to restrain herself from dancing. Now she had retired quietly once more to the little house which Monty had bought for her in a Kentish village, where she played at *grande dame* country life. She had not yet, but soon would, inflict her triumphant presence: eater-up, taker-over. The first wild period of rejoicing (mourning) must shortly be deemed to be done with. Her sugary letters arrived now almost daily. She wanted the house, she wanted the things in it, of course she wanted him. She had hungered for a grandson, but there had been only the one miscarriage.

The thought of his mother caused Monty little emotion. That did not matter. He was fond of his mother. He understood her attitudes. He even sympathized. Her glee simply did not concern him. He was so scoured by death, so scalded and sterilized, he could not feel the petty irritations of which ordinary life is composed. His mother could not touch him, he had become untouchable. He felt indestructible because destroyed. An awful separateness had come upon him in the later days of Sophie's illness. He could not bring himself to take his wife in his arms, not (as she thought) because her illness had made her hideous: it was that death had already taken hold of her and he could not bear the sense of utter loss which her still-breathing body inspired. He had heard of people embracing and kissing their dead. He could not have done so. The absence of the loved person is so absolute. And as she lay dying he felt even more the tormenting impossibility of touching that body where, every day, she so dreadfully still was.

What a tumultuous history their married life had been. There had not been very many years of it. Monty had married late. Sophie had always been stupidly flirtatious, a muddler. He had been chronically jealous, a harsh judge. He lectured. She wept. She reviled him. They went to bed. It was too often like that. The great sphere, as he pictured it, of their love had often been strained and made to shudder, but had never actually broken. There had just been endless trouble, endless

25

rows, endless new starts. Locketts had been a new start. Before that they had lived in a series of flats in Kensington and Chelsea. Sophie then professed to want to live 'in the country', and Monty, although he did not particularly care for the country, had been pleased by the idea of at last 'carrying her away'. He would have liked to lock her up, to chain her. They compromised upon this umbrageous pretty almost-suburb. Sophie had liked the house, but started complaining at once of being lonely. In fact they had rarely managed to make joint friends, to compose, as most married couples do, a new world which they inhabited together. They had no people to gossip about. They never somehow quite managed to set up the ordinary married state between them at all. Sophie continued to flirt with her old friends and to make new friends who did not want to meet her husband, and Monty, increasingly isolated, watched her.

Perhaps, he thought now and had sometimes thought then, his love for Sophie had been in his life something too intense, too magical. He had fallen in love with her instantly when, after he was already a well-known writer, an old college friend had introduced him to her at a party. She did not even then look like an actress. (She was in fact a very bad one.) She looked like a poor little rich girl. He recalled still with great clarity and purity, that first vision of her, leaning eagerly a trifle forward, her elegantly shod feet neatly together, her dark eyes glowing with self-satisfaction, her shiny little hand-bag held up childishly in front of her, her powdery turned-up nose, her clever provocative elaborate make-up, her very smart very plain dress. Her laughter. Her pert little vanity, her absolute rich girl's confidence, tempered by a certain touching simplicity and waifishness. All this penetrated straight into his heart. She was not the sort of woman he liked or approved of. He loved her crazily and at once, not for 'reasons' but just because the totality of her particular charm made her suddenly entirely indispensable to him. He entered into an immediate frenzy and proposed two days later. She refused him. He kept on proposing. At last she said yes. Of course there had been other women, but they were unimportant.

Naturally he had loved her more than she had loved him. That had been written into the contract. They had spoken of it and laughed over it. She had married him, partly at least, for reasons, which she frankly acknowledged. She was old enough (her thirtieth year was in sight) to feel that she had been a waif for long enough. She *thought* (as he put it to her later) that she wanted to stop racing around. She admired Monty and she trusted him absolutely and she was impressed by the way he loved her. She proposed to rest upon him. It all added up. For him, there had been no addition sum. He had lived thoughout upon magic, upon romantic love in its fullest sense, and this magic, now that she was gone, seemed sometimes likely to kill him. He had never been able, as most husbands are, to make the transition from frenzy to deep quiet communion. Sophie had not let him. Later she had grown fatter and had put on the thick round glasses which soon seemed so much a part of her. Only as she became less dazzling she seemed to collect even more admirers. There was no rest. She never settled down.

Sophie had isolated him. So had Milo Fane. Milo had even cut him off from the world of literature. Obsessively writing, he scarcely now read at all. At times he felt that Sophie and Milo between them had done for him properly. Novel-writing is at the best of times a lonely occupation. Monty wrote fluently and fast, hoping somehow that each novel would excuse and rescue its predecessor. He had intended at first to write a few best-sellers and then to settle down to serious composition. Perhaps he had even just intended to impress his mother. But he had reckoned without Milo. Milo turned out to have tremendous vitality and staying-power. Of course the sedentary man enjoys pretending to be the man of action: that is banal. There were deeper and stranger links between Milo and his creator. Some men, perhaps most men, are the lifelong dupes (or beneficiaries) of self-ideals or self-pictures developed in adolescence. Monty adolescent, fatherless, insecure, saw himself as a sort of 'terror'. He even at Oxford, among his radical friends, affected to hold extreme right-wing views. He lived by and in a professed contempt for others, for the stupid sheep of the world, which suffered a rude blow when he obtained only a second class degree. Milo was also of course created in order, with his right-angle grip Mauser and his ruthless courage and his invariable success, to expunge that second.

As a young man Monty had rather crudely mimed the 'demonism' which it pleased him to feel within him. Later he began, when it was almost too late, perhaps altogether too late, to feel himself to be an intellectual. If only, he thought, he had become a scholar, a collector, a scrutinizer, one whose life *progressed*. He had hated school-mastering and had never attempted to fructify it by real study. He was 'rescued' by a seemingly felicitous personification of his 'demonism' combined with his intellectualism in the person of Milo Fane, the ironical disillusioned diminished man of power. Milo was, at first, almost therapy. With the help of this scornful sceptical homunculus, Monty could criticize his earlier yearnings while at the same time quietly gratifying them. An author's irony often conceals his glee. This concealment is possibly the chief function of irony.

Years went by and Monty at intervals decided to say farewell to his sardonic *alter ego*. It was, after all, such a mean stupid inglorious aspect of the masterful spirit within him which he had externalized in his detective. Monty felt the need to transform himself, to discipline himself, but Milo drained him of energy and made him sometimes feel that if he abjured this mean exercise of power he would have no power at all. The serious novels which he occasionally attempted did not engage his feelings and soon collapsed, and he would then decide that he may as well give himself a quick rest by writing another Milo. It was now so easy. Monty and Milo watched each other. Long before the critics noticed it, Monty began to see the attenuation of his hero. Milo had developed a weight problem in reverse. He was a skinny man who constantly wanted to fill himself out. Milo lived on cream and Guinness and chocolate biscuits, all in vain. Monty had at first invented this idea for fun, but later it began to seem symbolic. Milo got thinner and more shrivelled and was more sarcastic and more contemptuous of the women who fell at his feet. Milo with his chocolate and his glass of milk became almost malevolent; and as he did so the therapeutic intellectual ferocity of his creator began to lose its way. Monty made at last a wild attempt to 'save' his cute unwanted familiar, to humanize him, to 'relate' him. Milo developed a sudden passion for justice, a pity for victims, a concern for young people. But the result was an unsavoury unconvincing priggishness which the original unregenerate Milo, now become as thin as a piece of wire, seemed to be wearing as a scarcely serious mask.

Monty had wanted to rid himself of Milo. Later he felt he wanted to rid himself of himself, so huge had this growth become which had seemed at first so liberating. 'You just *are* Milo Fane', Sophie had cried in moments of anger, perhaps of resistance after his hectoring and lecturing had reduced her to such touching tears. When he contemplated the impoverished world, the cold smart ultimately passionless mind, of his now so famous and somehow so powerful hero, Monty knew that he was *not* Milo Fane. But he felt frightened all the same. Something of all this he had once wanted to explain to

Blaise Gavender, just in order to be able to *explain* it to some intelligent person. But Blaise, without listening properly, had been in such a hurry to connect everything with everything, to connect Milo with Sophie, and Sophie with Monty's mother, with great over-simplifying leaps. Monty, annoyed with himself for having even for a moment seemed to be Blaise's 'patient', soon set to work to mystify his doctor. Then he exerted his power against Blaise, trying almost frivolously to subdue him. Blaise quickly terminated the discussions.

Even when he had been happiest with Sophie (and they *had* been happy) Monty had sometimes wondered why all his life he had so wantonly deviated from an image of calmness (he was loath to give it any grander name) which he had (it now seemed to him) from his earliest years had plain before his face. Even as a silly exhibitionist undergraduate he had known about *that*. Even what he was pleased to think of as his demons themselves suggested the only form which his salvation from them could take, assuming that he wanted to be saved. Of course this had nothing to do with God, who had passed out of Monty's life very early on. He spoke to no one about this matter, least of all Sophie, with whom he never talked about deep things. He meditated on it secretly; and as he sat, frenzied with pain, watching Sophie suffer (she was not good at it) he had thought almost with longing of the time after her death when he could, as never before, take refuge with *that*. (As if Sophie's death could enlighten him in a sort of spiritual orgasm.) But how unlike his expectation of it this later time had turned out to be. He had thought to live in suffering like a salamander in the flames. He had not expected or conceived of the sheer horror of her absence, he had not expected mourning to be a sort of fruitless searching, he had not foreseen the remorse. Why had he, quite apart from anything else, not made Sophie happier? It would not have been difficult. If he could not even see that, what could he see? How could he have behaved so *stupidly* badly? And now in the stead of the blank quietness he had hoped for, he felt like a hunted informer seeking a new identity. He felt, in a way so familiar as to be almost dreary, the chosen victim of the gods, the self-admitted traitor, the one destined for judgment. His old friends kept changing their masks, but he and they had not moved an inch.

He had lost all sense of direction. His life seemed at an end, yet he felt no urge to kill himself, the hours and the days had to be got through somehow. And thought continued, cold thought, in the midst of it all. He even coldly asked himself, can I not turn all this misery into art, into real art, not the pseudo-art of Milo Fane? Can art for me ever be more than vile self-indulgence? This involved the question, can I *now* get rid of Milo? And this sent him back again to the question of the calmness, the question of getting rid of himself. Was he too old a leopard to change his spots? Could he undo himself completely at the age of forty-five? Could he get rid of *them* and achieve *that*? What anyway, in the most mundane sense, was he to do with himself? Richard Nailsworth, the actor who played Milo, had invited him to stay at his villa in southern Italy. But that would be the last place to seek consolation. I must simply stop writing, thought Monty. If he wrote now or in the foreseeable future he would write muck. If he wrote another Milo Fane novel he was done for. What could he do? Why not become a schoolmaster again? he thought to himself at some point in his reflections, and then the thought kept recurring. After all, this was the only work, besides writing detective stories, for which he was trained. He had done it once, why not again? It was decent ordinary work, and he must somehow find his way back to ordinary life or lose what was left of his soul. Much much later he might try to write again. Or perhaps never. Meanwhile, why should he not simply put himself in a position where he *had* to attend to the needs of others? This was no spiritual orgasm, but it looked a good deal more like the way. This still vague notion, passing him at intervals in the maelstrom of his distress, alone carried some hint of a possible future.

Monty moved back from the window where the pale cold light was increasing, the sky not yet declared as blue. In the dimness of the room he peered at himself in a mirror. How well he knew that disingenuous face which seemed to try to conceal itself even from its owner. Small head, dark eyes which the tired wrinkles were already hooding, dark straight hair a bit stringy at the end, now unobtrusively balding a little. Soon he would have a tonsure and would even more resemble what he sometimes felt himself to be. A suspicious Jesuitical face. A cold thinker's face. A clever face. A narcissistic face. The face of a man who had wasted his talents and ruined his marriage and who still thought himself wonderful and exceptional. A stupid posing false face.

How insanely obsessed he was even Harriet, who cared so much to find out his thoughts, had not the faintest idea of. Of course bereavement is a darkness impenetrable to the imagination of the unbereaved, and later forgotten when the bereaved one recovers. Was this misery simply bereavement or was it some more final mental ruin from which there was no recovery? I must *be a man*, he said to his image, and turned from it. The banal phrase struck him. Could it carry to him any sense of possible ordinary living? After all, the day returns and brings back a few at least of the small concerns and duties he had once prayed about at school. He had to see Harriet. He had to *pretend* to Harriet. That was a sort of duty. He had to talk to Blaise about that foul slug Magnus Bowles. He had to write to Sophie's mother in Berne. He had to write to his own mother. He could do all these things. Why should he not become a schoolmaster and live a simple decent lucid life at last? He looked at his watch. Oh God, it was only half past four.

He decided to go downstairs. Then he felt like physical invasion, like sudden profitless sexual longing, the awful temptation coming to him again. He had a tape recording of Sophie's voice, only one, which he had taken without her knowing it a very little while before she died. He knew that he would have to destroy the tape but he could not yet bring himself to do so. He padded out of the bedroom and down the stairs and through the arched hallway that traversed the house. Sick with black painful excitement he entered the dark little drawing-room, switched on a lamp, pulled the tape recorder out of a cupboard. Sophie's voice was such a summary of her history, such a rich personification of herself. Her Anglophile father had had business interests in Manchester, and Sophie had spent a year at a girls' boarding school in the north of England. She had 'come out' in England, she had done her stage training in London, she had been a starlet in Hollywood. Her voice carried it all: the not very strong French-Swiss accent, a touch of the north, a touch of 'deb', a faint touch of American, more than a faint touch of the Royal Academy of Dramatic Art. And with it all that bright peevish energy which stayed with her to the end: utterly Sophie, little rich girl, waif, actress, flirt, demon, goddess, dying. Monty sat down, switched on the machine, and covered his face. 'Take it, take it, it's so heavy on my feet. The book, take it. Ach. Could I have the drops now, I have got the shakes today. Let me have the glass, will you — no, not that, the glass, the looking glass — '

There was a loud sudden sound nearby, the sound of something crashing to the floor. Monty leapt up and switched off the tape. He stood stiff, listening. Then there was another softer sound. The noises came from Sophie's little 'study', the

31

room where she had kept all her special things, the room where she had so largely been occupied in dying. Monty had not entered it since. Mad fear crept on his neck and in his hair. Then he strode quickly out and across the hall and flung open the door.

A shaded lamp was on. On the other side of the room, just beside Sophie's desk which had been opened and obviously rifled, a man was standing. He was a big stout man, holding a letter in his hand and staring open-mouthed at Monty.

'Hello, Edgar.' said Monty, 'What are you doing burgling my house?'

After a second of shock he had recognized Edgar Demarnay. They had not met for several years. An Edgar grown fatter and grosser and older, but Edgar still, with his big pink boy's face and his fat lips and his copious short fluffy hair now pale grey instead of pale gold.

Edgar stood there in appalled silence. Then he motioned with his hand towards the hall.

'It was a tape recording,' said Monty. Then he turned and left the room and returned to the drawing-room. He switched on various lights revealing peacock blue tiling alternating with dark panels covered in mosaic saffron and grey lentil plant designs. Mr Lockett had been in Moorish mood when the drawing-room was conceived.

Edgar Demarnay had been Sophie's great admirer, possibly her lover (Monty carefully never established this) just before her meeting with Monty. Edgar was in fact the old college friend who had introduced them to each other. Edgar had remained, or so he claimed, hopelessly in love with Sophie. Monty had later succeeded in forgetting about Edgar. There were by then other far more dangerous people to worry about.

Edgar, who had followed, now sat down heavily on the purple silk and wool sofa which occupied the curtained recess. He stared fixedly across the room, not looking at Monty.

'Oh come on, Edgar, say something.'

'I'm sorry,' said Edgar, 'I'm sorry. It was hearing her voice like that—it was such an awful shock. I still can't believe she's dead. Can you?'

'Yes,' said Monty, leaning against the elongated cast-iron chimney-piece. 'I can. She is dead. She has been cremated. She is ashes. The ashes have been scattered. There is nothing left of her at all.'

'How can you,' murmured Edgar, 'how can you—'

32

'What are you doing here?' asked Monty. 'Since when have you taken up burglary?'

'When did she die?'

'Ages ago. Weeks ago.'

'Oh—I thought it was just—much more lately—a day or two ago—I've just got back from America you see—I only heard the news this evening—yesterday that is—I simply had to come here at once. What did she die of?'

'Cancer.'

'Was it a long business?'

'Yes.'

'Oh Christ. No one told me.'

'Why should they?' said Monty. 'It wasn't any special business of yours. And you still haven't told me what you were doing thieving in my wife's room. Looking for souvenirs?'

'Well, as a matter of fact,' said Edgar, 'I was looking for my letters.'

'Your letters?'

'I didn't intend, you see, to break in. I just drove here as soon as I heard the news. I was at a dinner party, I left at once. I didn't intend to do anything but stand in the road all night. There didn't seem to be anything else to do. I did stand there for ages.'

'How interesting. What time did you arrive here?'

'Oh about midnight. I didn't mean to trouble you at all, of course. I imagined you'd be prostrated.'

'As you can see, I'm not.'

'Then I started thinking about my letters. I suppose you know that ever since she—got married—I've been writing to Sophie every week.'

Monty had not known this.

'I kept in touch with her, you see. I wanted her always to know what I was doing, where I was, just in case she ever needed me.'

'How touching. In case she ever decided to leave me, I suppose.'

'She always knew my telephone number,' said Edgar. 'Even if I was away for two days at a conference I saw to it that she always knew where she could ring me. It made me happier to think that she could always find me, it made me feel in touch. And then tonight—they said she was dead—and I ran. I just intended to stand all night and mourn. I didn't even know— you see I ran straight out—if the funeral was over or anything. I thought they said she'd just died. And then as I stood out there I started thinking of all those letters, hundreds of them. I expect she showed you some of them, did she?'

'No.'

'I wouldn't have minded if she had,' said Edgar. 'Of course I didn't mean it to be a secret or anything, there was nothing for there to be a secret about. It was all very simple. I just loved her. I couldn't stop. I haven't stopped. Oh God.'

'Get on with it. I'm tired.'

'Could I have some whisky?'

Monty took a decanter out of the stained glass corner cupboard and poured out half a tumbler of neat whisky.

'Thanks. I've got a drink problem. Won't you?'

'No.' Monty could not conceive of ever touching alcohol again.

'I thought of course you'd see the letters and I didn't mind, but I didn't want anyone else to see them. They were good letters, the best I could write. Then I suddenly thought—of course I did visit this house once, just after you'd moved in.'

Monty had not known this either.

'I called when you were in New York that time, and Sophie gave me tea in—that room over there—so I knew where she kept her letters and things—and I suddenly thought I'd try to get in and if there was a packet of letters there I'd—take them away. It was a stupid idea—yet I just thought, in the night there, that it would—console me and I felt the letters were there, so near, and I could just—and then the garden door being open—'

'Did you get them?' Monty had not looked into Sophie's desk, since. He had been afraid of what he would find. Sophie had burnt a lot of papers when she first became ill.

'No.'

'I'm afraid I interrupted you. Do go and look properly now.'

'You don't mind—?'

'Of course not. Go and look for your bloody letters. Then clear out. I'm going back to bed.'

'You always were a funny chap, Monty,' said Edgar.

'Go out by the garden as you came. Good night.'

Monty made for the door. Edgar jumped up.

'Monty, please, are you mad? You can't just go away and leave me!'

'Why not, pray? I think I've been rather kind to you.'

'Of course you have, but—please don't go, please talk to me. I've got to talk about Sophie—you may be—but I'm not—'

34

'Don't you want your letters?'

'Yes, but now—you—if you find them—'

'I doubt if Sophie kept them. Not all those thousands.'

'Well, she might have kept some—the ones she liked best—I'd sort of like to know—which ones she kept—'

'Oh, you make me sick,' said Monty. But he made no further attempt to go. He sat down. It was the first time since her death that he had been in the presence of someone who had known her and loved her. Sophie's mother, who had plenty of troubles of her own, had not attended the funeral. He felt an inclination to talk to Edgar, though at the same time he knew that it was a mistake, after the awful absoluteness of that ending, to bandy words with this mucky *revenant*.

'Did she answer your letters?' said Monty.

'Didn't you know? Hardly ever. And then just a little scrawl. You didn't answer my letters either, if it came to that. Did you keep them?'

'Me? Keep your letters to me? Of course not! I can't remember getting any. I receive hundreds of letters a week. My secretary takes them away in a sack.' He had dismissed his secretary too. The letters now pilled up in tea chests in the hall. Harriet said she wanted to deal with them for him.

'You *must* remember,' said Edgar. 'I wrote you all about California—quite long letters—about the animals and so on —I knew that would interest you. About the sea otters. Don't you remember about the sea otters?'

Monty did now remember. 'Yes. But how tedious you are. You always were.'

'You're just the same too. This is like all our old conversations somehow. Could I have some more Scotch? I can't converse without it these days.'

'What was the party you rushed out of?'

'The Latin Mass Society Dinner.'

'Congratulations on your new appointment, by the way. I saw it in *The Times*.'

'Yes,' said Edgar, helping himself to the whisky. 'I never thought I'd end up as Head of a House. An Oxford college to play with. I just couldn't resist it. I expect I'll hate it though, it'll wreck my work. Oh God, I wrote Sophie such a long letter about all that.'

'I imagined you'd settled down forever in California.'

'So did I. It's a terribly wicked hedonistic place. But I felt somehow—free there—you know, like they say Englishmen get in America—uninhibited—let their hair down. I told Sophie all about that too in the letters. Of course I don't mean I had women or anything.'

'Of course not.'

'I'm such a puritan. I'm the most frustrated man in the northern hemisphere. I've got semen running out of my ears. Oh God, I'm talking quite ordinarily, aren't I, as if—and she's dead—thank God for drink. Getting through time has always been my problem. I'm always more or less sozzled now, only nobody notices—at least I hope they don't—I never get quite sober—if I did I'd be screaming—I'm always just topping up, you know—I live on a plateau of permanent quiet inebriation. A single drink and I'm back up there again, right up. I can work all right too. God, I'm such a wet, such a failure. I talked to Sophie about all that in the letters.'

'What a bore you must have been,' said Monty. 'I can't think why you regard yourself as a failure. You were always full of erroneous ideas about yourself, as I remember. You're a successful world-famous scholar, fellow of the Royal Academy, head of an Oxford college—'

'I was a pupil of Beazley once. When I think of that I want to crawl under the carpet. I'm no good. I'm not like you—'

'Like *me*? I'm just a failed novelist.'

'An artist—that's best of all,' said Edgar, dribbling a little at the mouth and gazing into his drink. 'Yes, that's best of all. I wish to Christ I was a writer. Anyway, you know what I mean.'

Oddly enough, Monty did know.

'You're just better than me,' said Edgar. 'Always were. You got Sophie. You deserved to get Sophie. Oh Christ. She's dead. Oh Christ. You've got a sort of hardness in you, a centre. I'm soft all the way through, I can't cope with life manfully, never could. Maybe I'm retarded, yes, that's it, retarded. When I see any sort of nobility or strength in somebody else I just resent it like hell. At least I don't resent it in you, but that's because I admired you so much at college. *Te Consule*, you know, as we used to say. You remember—"the prince whose oracle is at Delphi . . .". All our old private mythology—you were some-how at the centre of it all. Everyone has someone they admire at school or at college, and go on admiring forever after. You're just my admiree.'

'This is drivel,' said Monty. 'And since you admit to being retarded, I can only agree. If there is anything which you admire in me, it is probably what I least value in myself.'

'I don't mean your frightfulness—remember what we used

36

to call your frightfulness—at least not exactly that. You've got
a centre, you can think, you can invent. Are you writing
another Milo Fane?'

'No.'

'You know I've never really been loved by a woman.'

'*Tiens.*'

'Somehow I've always wanted the ones that didn't want me.
I'm the absolute queen bee of unrequited love. And then with
Sophie—it was so especially awful—Oh God—what can you
be thinking of me—'

'I'm thinking,' said Monty, 'of how we all used to call you
"Rosie" in College.'

Edgar had indeed not changed much. The drink problem,
if it was one, had not marked him yet. The plump smooth full-
lipped uniformly pink youthful face had been so mysteriously
and discreetly touched by middle age, it was not clear how one
knew it was not still the face of an undergraduate.

'Yes, "Rosie", yes. I think you invented that. I rather liked
it. You were bloody kind to me in those days. I've kept all your
letters, even from then. And all Sophie's letters of course.
There weren't many. I'll show them to you one day. Would
you like that?'

'No.'

'Do you mind if I have some more Scotch. In a weird way
this is like old times. How we used to talk about women before
we really knew any! Do you remember saying to me *laissons les
jolies femmes aux hommes sans imagination*?'

'No.'

'We used to talk all night. Women, philosophy. "Nothing
in reason supports the assertion that it is good absolutely to
relieve suffering." How we broke our heads on that one, do
you remember?'

'I think you'd better go now.'

'Hitting something soft back hard, like in badminton, that's
what our friendship has always been like. I used that image
once in a letter to you. I kept all your letters—Did you—No,
of course, you said you didn't—'

'Oh, go away,' said Monty. 'There isn't any friendship. I
know, now that you remind me of it, that you were once all set
for some sort of big emotional intellectual friendship between
us, full of challenges and responses and rows and reconcilia-
tions and exchanges of clever letters, but it never existed except
in your mind. After we left college the only real connection
between us was Sophie, and now she's dead.'

'You sound so cold,—as if you'd accepted her death.'

'Of course I've accepted her death. I accept facts.'

'That's your—frightfulness—again. You always hated vulgarity and sentiment. Oh God. Coming home to England you know—I kept thinking and thinking how I'd see her—I didn't even think of her saying anything to me. I felt I'd be like a dog, just sitting and looking at her. I was faint with joy at the idea of seeing her. Did she talk about me ever?'

'Occasionally.'

'What did she say?'

'She made jokes.'

'Well—I'm glad of that—if I was good for a laugh—that was all right. Coming home I felt—'

'Have you still got that big house? I forget it's name.' But as he spoke Monty remembered the name.

'Mockingham. Yes. It's been a bit of a problem since my mother died. And you know my sister lives in Canada now. It's only twenty miles from Oxford, so I suppose I'll partly live there. Do you remember coming to Mockingham?'

'Yes.' Monty especially remembered the first occasion. It was his first visit to a large English country house, where all was 'accustomed, ceremonious'. He had been impressed, but had carefully concealed this fact from Edgar.

'You remember the coolness with my mother about your not coming to church?'

'Are you still devout?'

'Well, I go. I tag along. I don't know what I believe. But it helps me not to go to the dogs. Not so fast, anyway. I say, Monty, that tape you were playing. Do you think you could—?'

'No.'

'Will you sometime?'

'No. Could you go now! I'm going back to bed.'

'I'm sorry—don't be angry with me, Monty.'

'I'm not angry. Just clear off, will you.'

'I'll come to see you tomorrow.'

'It is tomorrow. And you won't.' Monty rose and pulled back the curtains and opened the shutters. Bright sunshine flooded the dark elaborate little room, drawing blue flashes out of the de Morgan tiling.

'Can I come this evening?'

'No.'

'When, then?'

'Look, Edgar,' said Monty, 'I'm glad we've talked, but

38

that's that. We have nothing more to say, unless you count
drooling on about Sophie as saying something. I don't want
to see you and I can't imagine that you really want to see me.
Maybe I'll look you up one day in Oxford. Except that I'm
never there. Anyway, good-bye.'

'But, Monty Monty—' Edgar had risen.

'Go, go. Here, take this.' Monty reached out to the chimney-
piece and took up a Coleport mug brightly painted with sprays
of red roses. 'Take it, take it away. It's nothing personal. It's just
that I want to dismantle the place, like Aladdin's palace. Whenever anybody comes, I give them something to take away.'

'Oh thank you—how pretty—I'll put it in my room in
college. Monty, do you think, later on I mean, when you've
had time to sort things out, you could give me something of
Sophie's?'

'No.'

'Anything, anything at all, one of her shoes—'

'No!'

'Monty, you don't mean it about not seeing me tomorrow?
I've *got* to see you, I've *got* to talk about her, I shall go mad.
You may have had time to get used to it, but I haven't—'

'Go away,' said Monty. 'I don't want to see you. *I don't want
to see you.* Understand. Go away. Please.' He opened the
drawing-room door and went out into the hall.

Edgar followed. He stood, arms hanging, holding the
Coleport mug by the handle. Then suddenly he gave a little
whine and began to cry. His face grew red and seemed to be
instantly wet all over with tears. He said. 'I can't bear it, I
can't bear it.' He continued silently to cry, staring at the
ground and not wiping his tears.

Monty studied him for a moment or two. Then he went to
the front door and opened it wide. A spurt of bird song
entered into the house. Edgar set off along the hall and, with a
powerful whiff of whisky, went past Monty and out of the door,
still crying.

Monty went back up to his bedroom and darkened it again
by pulling the curtains. He got back into bed. He wondered if
the sight of Edgar's tears might now help him to cry. He tested
himself hopefully, but it was no good, His heart was beating
hard and his head was aching and he lay sleepless. It was
nearly six o'clock.

'Blaise is away,' said Harriet. 'He's with Magnus Bowles.'

'Oh really,' said Monty. He got up and wandered restlessly to the window. They were in the little Moorish drawing-room which the intense evening sunshine was illuminating with a rich powdery light, making the turquoise ducks upon the tiles to glitter like jewels and the saffron and grey lentil trees to glow with a pearly radiance. Harriet was sitting among the patchwork cushions upon the purple canopied sofa, looking with her pale mauve robe and her half-tumbled glinting brown hair, like some sultan's delight. The room was somnolent and the garden fragrances were lacking in freshness, heavy like incense. Monty felt a little faint, perhaps from lack of food, perhaps from lack of air. A large pink-silver-paper-covered milk chocolate fish (a salmon perhaps?) which Harriet had brought with her lay upon the low table beside Edgar's empty whisky glass. It was once again six o'clock.

The morning post had brought another letter from Monty's mother, who was mercifully still at Hawkhurst.

My darling boy,
I am thinking of you all the time and will come to you soon. I just *brood* over your grief, wishing so much that my loving thoughts could make it well. I know by intuition, telepathy, what you will, how much you are suffering. We have always been so close and known each other's minds. I would draw off that pain if I could. I can at least share it. Be quiet within yourself, dearest child, try to be quiet in your mind. I don't mean resignation, you are not a resigned person. We know what we think, don't we, of 'the will of God' and all that false comfort that weak people fly to. Just be gentle and relaxed with your sorrow. And be sure to take all those pills the doctor gave you, won't you, dear. I was so glad of your letter though it said so little. I may telephone you soon. I did ring on Tuesday actually, but I got no answer. I expect you were in the garden. *Do not make any decisions about property until I have seen you*, you are in no state to do so. We shall have to think it all out carefully together, won't we. I look forward to a long quiet conference about practical matters. Taking decisions will make you feel that

time has passed, and time *does* heal, you know. It will do you good to face these ordinary things, but you must not attempt to do so alone. Our job is to get you writing again, isn't it, to get you and Milo on the road again! You will feel so much better then. And we shall arrange your future for the best, and decide what to do about Locketts. So leave all these tiresome things until I come, dearest. Do not worry about me. Your little mother is perky, and full of her own concerns. Do you know, I have just bought a new dress? It is a lovely cornflower blue, I think that you will like it. I send you, dearest boy, like little birds, so many loving thoughts. My heart flies to you. I think about you with such an intensity of love. Know that, as you read these words, I am thinking of you.

Ever your loving and faithful Léonie.

Harriet was looking at Monty and wondering what he was thinking. He was not thinking about his mother. He was not afraid of Léonie's telephone calls, since he had silenced the telephone bell with a piece of plastic wire. He was thinking: I must destroy that bloody tape recording. He had played it again that morning.

Harriet had spent the afternoon at the National Gallery. She usually did this on Magnus Bowles days. Blaise would drive her into town in the afternoon and drop her off at the Gallery, or at some other art exhibition, while he went on to the British Museum Reading Room. Then in the evening he would drive to the southern suburb where Magnus lived, and Harriet would make her way home by train and bus. She had never learnt to drive the car.

She had felt very strange that afternoon in the National Gallery. An intense physical feeling of anxiety had taken possession of her as she was looking at Giorgione's picture of Saint Anthony and Saint George. There was a tree in the middle background which she had never properly attended to before. Of course she had seen it, since she had often looked at the picture, but she had never before felt its significance, though what that significance was she could not say. There it was in the middle of clarity, in the middle of bright darkness, in the middle of limpid sultry yellow air, in the middle of nowhere at all with distant clouds creeping by behind it, linking the two saints yet also separating them and also being itself and nothing to do with them at all, a ridiculously frail poetical vibrating motionless tree which was also a special particular tree on a special particular evening when the two saints happened (how odd) to be doing their respective things (ignoring each other) in a sort of murky yet brilliant glade (what on earth however was going on in the foreground?) beside a luscious glistening pool out of which two small and somehow domesticated demons were cautiously emerging for the benefit of Saint Anthony, while behind them Saint George, with a helmet like a pearl, was bullying an equally domesticated and inoffensive little dragon.

Hypnotized by the tree, Harriet found that she could not take herself away. She stood there for a long time staring at it, tried to move, took several paces looking back over her shoulder, then came back again, as if there were some vital message which the picture was trying and failing to give her. Perhaps it was just Giorgione's maddening genius for saying something absurdly precise and yet saying it so marvellously that the precision was all soaked away into a sort of cake of sheer beauty. This nervous mania of anxious 'looking back' Harriet recalled having suffered when young in the Louvre and the Uffizi and the Accademia. The last visit on the last day, as closing time approached, indeed the last minutes of any day, had had this quality of heart-breaking severance, combined with an anxious thrilling sense of a garbled unintelligble urgent message. This experience had been a stranger to her for some time now since Blaise was not interested in pictures and she had not visited the foreign galleries. Why suddenly this emotion, on this occasion, for this picture? Was it something prophetic? Already a number of times she had walked away, determined not to look back, and had looked back. It was absurd. After all, these were her very own London pictures which she could see again any time she wished. She had intended to tell her little story to Monty, but by the time she reached him it already seemed too trivial. She knew better than to tell it to Blaise. He would say it was something to do with sex.

How very much I depend on people, she thought, looking at Monty's profile. What a charming short straight nose he had. Everything about him was proportioned and neat, not like the knobbly looks of most men. Any girl would be pleased to have a nose like that. Harriet had no impersonal abstract world, except perhaps the world of pictures, and that seemed to come to her as pure 'experience', not anything she could possibly talk about. What I feel with the pictures is different, she thought, it's like being let out into a huge space and not being myself any more. Whereas what I feel looking at Monty is so absolutely here and now and me, as if I were more absolutely my particular self than ever, as if I were just throbbing with selfhood. It's odd because I love the pictures and I love Monty, but it is so different.

Monty had a hard and rather fixed gazing face, not like Blaise's face which was so mobile, always changing and dissolving into laughter or annoyance or thought, as if it had no surface but were actually part of what it confronted. Blaise lived his face; Monty peered through his, looking from behind it, and not necessarily, Harriet sometimes uneasily felt, through the eyes. Monty had a sort of intent *voyeur* face, yet livened at times by a sort of puzzlement or chronic surprise. Only since Sophie's illness his face had hardened further into a mask. There was a pale smile he smiled for Harriet, but it was quite unlike his old real smile. Harriet loved Monty, not of course in a 'sexy' way, but in the way that she loved almost anybody whom she got a chance to love, and perhaps a little bit especially because he always seemed to her so clever and yet so lost. That woman whom he mourns so has ruined his life, she thought to herself.

Monty did not in fact want to see Harriet at all. He let her come to him in this emotional impetuous way out of a kind of politeness, because this was something which *she* needed and wanted. She needed the sense of helping him, she wanted the flavour of his grief. A weary sense of duty upheld him in receiving her, in giving her that little wan smile which she so rightly recognized as peculiar. On the other hand she did not irritate him as his mother would certainly have done. Harriet was capable of being silent, and although she very much wanted to touch him (to hold his hand for instance) she accepted his renewed evasions with tact and grace. She had qualities of physical repose which his mother entirely lacked and which poor Sophie had lacked too.

How awfully neat he is, Harriet was reflecting, and how much I have been looking forward all day to seeing him. Even now he has put on a clean shirt and a tie and such smart cuff-links which he must have *chosen* to wear, I'm sure I've never seen them before, and he is so fantastically clean-shaven, and so *clean*, even his fingernails are clean, which Blaise's never are. Of course Monty's father was a curate, I'm sure that's significant, he looks so absurdly clerical. And he's so compact and small-scale, though he is quite tall, he seems so dainty after Blaise's untidy smelly masculineness.

'Don't grieve, my dear,' she said, just to say something. 'She had a happy life.'

'Oh Harriet, please don't talk rubbish. You don't know whether Sophie had a happy life or not. Even I don't know. And what does it matter now what sort of life she had?'

'I always felt that Sophie—'

'*Please.*'

Harriet kept trying to make him talk about Sophie, she wanted to hear him rehearse his loss, she wanted, unconsciously of course, to triumph over Sophie. Any woman is glad when a man loses another woman. Harriet wanted, in a sense, to 'move in'. It was natural and Monty did not resent it.

'Are you eating? Your kitchen looks too tidy.'

'I open tins.'

'I do wish you'd let me deal with your letters.'

'I sort out my mother's ones, the rest don't matter.'

'But aren't there any letters from friends—'

'I have no friends.'

'Oh *nonsense*!'

It was true, thought Monty. Sophie had pretty well cleaned him out of friends.

'Well, I'm your friend, Monty.'

'Thanks.'

'Oh Monty, don't—do break down or something—don't bottle it all up—it's not good to be so remote and calm about it all.'

'Women always want men to break down,' said Monty, 'so that they can raise them up again. I am quite sufficiently broken down, I assure you, without any demonstrations. In fact I'm behaving in an extremely unmanly way. If I had an ordinary job to do I'd have to get on with it. Being self-employed I can brood all day. It's undignified and bad. Bereavement is not uncommon. One must just treat it like the 'flu. Even Niobe stopped crying eventually and wanted something to eat.'

'You mustn't blame yourself—'

'I don't. I ceased some time ago to believe in goodness. My judgments are purely aesthetic. I am behaving like a milksop.'

Harriet got up and moved to stand beside him. A ragged-winged white butterfly, resisting the slight warm evening breeze, was clinging on to a tassel of mauve wistaria just outside the window. Monty and Harriet watched the butterfly together in silence. Beyond, upon the close-cut lawn, three of the dogs, who had come round with Harriet by the road, were

44

waiting to escort their mistress home. (The only dog who, at great danger to his organs, Harriet felt, could jump the orchard fence was Ajax.) Babu and Panda, who usually went about together, were playing a familiar game of taking it in turns to lie down and be sniffed over, and then to leap up when least expected. Nearer to the window Ganimede, his tail now languidly set in motion by the sight of Harriet, was stretched out in his typical slug-like pose, his muzzle on the ground, his front and back legs fully extended.

'Dogs are normally pack animals unless redeemed by attachment to an individual master. But your collection of creatures seem to display both characteristics.'

Harriet's hand gently sought out Monty's hand and took it in a firm cautious gentle grip like a retriever holding a bird. Monty smiled the wan smile, lightly pressed the intrusive hand, and moved away. He repressed a shudder at the unwelcome contact. His flesh mourned. Harriet sighed.

Oh get out, get out, get out, thought Monty. He said, 'Please go, Harriet dear.'

'All right, all right. Aren't we going to eat our chocolate fish? Just a little bit.'

'It's melted,' said Monty. He began to pull off pink silver paper coated with gluey pale brown chocolate.

'Not really.' The fish lay disclosed, staring-eyed, a little amorphous but quite whole. Harriet swooped on it, detaching its tail and conveying it to her mouth, licking her fingers. Monty pretended to eat a sticky fragment. He wiped his fingers on a (Harriet noticed) freshly laundered white handkerchief.

'Can I ask you something else quite abruptly?' said Harriet. 'You know Blaise's doctor plan. Well, if we go ahead with it, could you if necessary lend us some money?'

'Yes, of course.'

'And if you leave Locketts, though of course we hope you won't, would you consider selling us the orchard? You know how much Blaise has always wanted it.'

'Yes, of course.'

'It seems awful to ask *both* things! We may have to sell Hood House anyway.'

'Don't worry about money for Christ's sake. And of course you mustn't sell Hood House.'

'Thank you, Monty, you're perfect. Yes, yes, I'm going. And you will talk to David, won't you, about his not giving up Greek? He's so attached to you.'

'It's mutual.'

'Thank you, dear Monty. May I have just another little bit of our fish?'

'Thank *you*, dear Harriet. Here wait a moment, take this.' Monty picked up a large blue and white Chinese vase from the table in the hall and bundled it into Harriet's arms.

'Monty, you are absurd, you mustn't give away all your things, whatever will your mother say! It's so huge, and you gave me that Persian plate thing last time!'

'The apparent scene is slowly falling to pieces revealing the reality behind.'

'I don't know what you're talking about, and I don't think you do either!'

The opening door revealed Monty's front garden, a large paved area dotted with dwarf veronica bushes, lavender, rosemary, hyssop, santolina, and sage. The declining sun made a pattern of long rounded shadows upon the grey paving. Rushing round the side of the house the three dogs began to race about among the bushes, lifting their legs against them, almost without pausing, like canine athletes. The door also revealed, half-way up the path from the gate, Edgar Demarnay, now dressed in a light brown summer suiting and a very large green tie, his fluffy pale hair neatly combed, and carrying a straw hat.

Harriet, who had emerged, stepped aside. Edgar, reaching the door, also stepped aside, placing his straw hat upon his heart and bowing to Harriet. He then turned and bowed to Monty.

'Professor Demarnay, Mrs Gavender,' said Monty.

'Not Professor any more actually,' Edgar murmured, staring at Harriet.

'Thanks, Harriet. Good night.'

Harriet moved away.

As Edgar began to say something to him Monty said quietly, 'I'm sorry, but I meant it. I really don't want to see you. At all. Good-bye.' He shut the door in Edgar's face and went back into the drawing-room feeling very upset.

A moment later he realized that he had made a ridiculous mistake. He ought to have held Edgar in play long enough to let Harriet leave the scene. As it was he had practically thrust them into each other's arms. Cursing, he crept into the dining-room and peered through the curtains.

Harriet and Edgar were standing at the gate in close converse, Harriet holding the large Chinese vase as if it were a baby. Damn, damn, damn, thought Monty. Did he then feel

46

possessive about Harriet? Evidently. And how very much he did not want Edgar hanging around. Edgar typified all that messy mysterious side of Sophie's life which had so much tormented him. And all those bloody letters and giving her his telephone number! Now Harriet would feel sorry for Edgar. She must have been intrigued by Monty's treatment of him. She was a woman, that is an inquisitive interfering busybody. Edgar would be questioned. Edgar would be delighted to tell all. Edgar would acquire a contact, a foothold. Edgar would be back. Oh damn, damn, damn.

Edgar and Harriet began to walk slowly off together in the direction of Hood House.

Monty went back into the drawing-room, wrapped up the milk chocolate fish in a copy of *The Times*, and took it out to the bin in the kitchen. Then he went out into the garden. The light had its velvety dramatic evening quality, a portentous vividness conscious of the dark. In the still absurdly light green greenery of the privet hedge a wren was singing with piercing accuracy, and two blackbirds and a thrush were having a musical contest in the orchard. Less coherent birds, ostentatiously unimpressed, were contributing chaotic background noise, like an orchestra tuning up. Monty felt frenzy, anger, despair, and a stupid bitter resentment against everything. He had been very irritated at being asked to sell the orchard. That was not Harriet, that was Blaise. Typical Blaise, clumsy, greedy egoist, wanting to have everything at once, however incompatible. A large black animal emerged strolling from the orchard. Ajax. Monty did not entirely trust Ajax and never patted him. 'Clear off!' he said to the dog in passing. There was a faint growl. Monty thrust on into the orchard, his shoes and trousers soaked by the long grass which, already heavy with dew, was hanging in arches over the clipped path. He reached the fence of the Hood House garden. Was it conceivable that Harriet would invite Edgar in?

Someone was standing in the garden, on the lawn, underneath the acacia tree, a boy. It was David. Monty watched him in silence. David stood a while with head thrown back, arms limply hanging, gazing up into the tree. Then he turned slowly towards the house, trailing his feet and making long slithering tracks in the dew. His attitude and his movement expressed the self-conscious histrionic dejection of youth. Poor David, thought Monty, poor poor David. A dog barked, rather hysterically. Another answered. Hood House remained enigmatic.

Monty turned back. Sophie had wanted him to build a wooden platform in one of the orchard trees so that they could have their evening drinks sitting on the platform. Monty had told her it was a stupid idea. He threw himself face downward in the long wet grass.

Emily McHugh now very much regretted having taken Constance Pinn into her confidence. And why had she now let her into the house? Pinn must have mesmerized her. Pinn, who had once been her charwoman, and was now her lodger. In fact it had for a long time been impossible to conceal anything from Pinn. Pinn's coping with Luca had made possible Emily's job, now defunct. The job was gone and Pinn was installed. How Emily lost the job was as follows.

Emily had been employed part-time to teach French at an expensive progressive girls' boarding school in the vicinity. The academic standards were not high. The children, doubtless like their parents before them, were being groomed for life's lower pleasures. The young ladies rode, swam, danced, fenced, played bridge and read a little sociology. There were no examinations. Languages were regarded as a hard option, and Emily, who had now no taste for study and was no star at French, had survived because her pupils were lazy, untested, and easy to connive with. An unspoken pact kept the ineffectual lessons rolling along somehow. Then one day what Emily had long dreaded occurred. A French girl turned up in the class.

Kiki St Loy was in fact a mixture. Her father, a diplomat, was half French, half Cornish. Her mother came from Andalusia. Kiki spoke English, French, and Spanish, all fluently and all not quite perfectly. She was every schoolteacher's nightmare: a beautiful precocious popular bossy over-sexed rebellious *intelligent* pupil. Emily, who saw the danger signals at once, could not help liking Kiki. In fact to begin with she almost 'fell for' the girl, and imagined that she could recruit her as an ally. This proved vain. As soon as Kiki realized her power she began to use it. She went into long infectious fits of laughter over Emily's accent, which she amusingly mimicked. She gravely corrected Emily's now even more frequent mistakes, pretending that she was the teacher and Emily the pupil. The class adored it. Emily began to be not just upset but frightened. She tried to 'buy them off' by

49

yet more connivance, yet more concessions to rebellion and disorder. All pretence at serious work was given up. Her lessons became 'shows' directed by Kiki. Other teachers complained of the ceaseless uproar. At last after warning Emily several times, the headmistress, who had never understood the situation, since Emily could not bring herself to explain it, asked her to leave. Humiliated, and yet also with a sort of despairing end-of-the-world relief, Emily left.

All this too it had been impossible to conceal from Pinn who, through Emily's own good offices, now also worked part-time at the school, as a clerk. She was said to be doing well. Emily watched her friend's success story with mixed feelings. She had accepted Pinn as a lodger partly for financial reasons after the demise of the teaching job. Pinn was useful. She was better at dealing with Luca than Emily was. She was also much better at cooking and professed to enjoy it. Pinn, who knew all about Emily's curious way of life, was the only person with whom it could be discussed. And of course Emily was fond of her. Only Emily had somehow not foreseen how irritating Pinn's sheer *knowledge* would prove to be at close quarters, although Pinn, who was very shrewd, was also very tactful. Of course Pinn was fascinated; she could not conceal that. Since Pinn had become what she called a 'secretary bird' she had become much smarter. Her short auburn hair was stylishly cut. Her long narrow spectacles were of the latest fashion. Her clothes contrived to look expensive. She hummed and buzzed with vitality. Emily, since she had lost her job, wore the same old slacks and cotton sweater every day. With less to do, she felt far more tired. She had been unemployed for nearly a month.

Luca was now eight. The bed-wetting phase was over at last, thank God. He had been named (he was never christened) Luke, but the name had somehow become Italianized. Luca lived in Emily's consciousness as a ceaseless mysterious dark pain. When he was a small child she had loved him with an obsessive violence, hardly able to stop touching him, holding him, hugging him. They had lived like animals nestled together in a hole. She loved him in this way still, perhaps even more; but at some strange and awful moment, perhaps two, perhaps even three, years ago, as dawning consciousness filled his eyes with puzzlement, he had begun to withdraw from her. He pulled himself away from her embraces. His chattering ceased. He also cried more rarely. Now, and Emily simply dared not think about this, it was so appalling, he hardly spoke to her at all. Sometimes it was as if he had actually become dumb. If she asked him a question he would reply, if he replied, with a gesture. Now and then however she overheard him talking to Pinn. And although he was always at the bottom of his form at school, no one had yet suggested to her that he was handicapped or mentally deficient.

He could not read, but that was true of a lot of children at the rotten school he attended. He watched television a lot, as Emily did too. Sometimes as they sat silently together in front of the screen she would turn her head surreptitiously to look at him, and find that he was gazing quietly at her. 'What is it, Luca?' No answer. He would turn away again. How much he understood of the indiscriminately miscellaneous programmes they watched together, she did not know. He never spoke about them, and rarely laughed or smiled, even at the children's programmes. He did not seem to want to play with other children out of school hours. Emily suspected that he was afraid of them. When she asked him if he would like to invite a friend to tea he simply shook his head. He had no difficulty in occupying himself, however, and was in this respect at least an 'easy' child. What he did was not always clear to Emily, but when not watching television he seemed to be constantly up to something. He played outside by himself, and sometimes simply vanished for long periods. When at home he spent a lot of time quietly in his room with the door shut. He communed at length with the two cats, Richardson and Little Bilham. Richardson was an elegant peach and grey cat, Little Bilham was a dwarfish tabby with white patches. Both were neutered males and running somewhat to fat. He would carry one of the cats about with him for an hour on end. He was extremely interested in insects, and kept a sort of insect zoo in his room, where spiders, woodlice, beetles and other creepie-crawlies were periodically kept in boxes. He was not a violent child.

For some time now Emily had been trying to persuade Blaise to go to see Luca's form master to get some sort of proper report on him. 'They'll attend to a *man*,' she told him. 'It's no good my going. They'll pull their socks up if they see the child's got a real father who wears a tie and can speak English.' However Blaise kept putting this off. He said, 'Luca's all right, we'd be told if he wasn't.' Of course Blaise was always nervous about what he called 'security'. But Emily felt that really he was frightened of finding out that Luca was in some way abnormal. 'He may need treatment,' said Emily. 'Treatment for what?' said Blaise. In fact the school was so chaotic that it was doubtless very difficult to identify a retarded child. Of course Luca *looked* all right. He was even quite a presentable boy, with Blaise's square face, and Emily's almost black hair and blue eyes. He enjoyed perfect physical health, and when he was intently watching a wood-louse or a house-fly he appeared to be quite intelligent.

Emily had just had her bath. Not a bath-addict, she always bathed on the days when Blaise came. He used once to like to come and discover her in her bath. That was one of the many discarded rituals. Now she was feeling warm and clean and faintly fragrant with bath essence. Her breath smelt nasty though, or so she, trying now to sniff it, suspected. Yesterday her dentist had told her that she ought to have three back teeth out and have all the front ones crowned. Extensive 'bridge work' would be necessary. The crowning and bridge work would cost more than a hundred pounds. She would have to tell that to Blaise. She would also have to tell him, which they had so far concealed, that Pinn had moved in. And that the rent of the flat was going up again in September. And she had not yet dared to break it to him that she had lost her job. She had decided to tell him that she had resigned it of her own accord. This sounded more dignified and could be made part of the campaign which Emily intermittently waged against her lover.

Emily, in a rather dirty quilted dressing-gown, was reposing in the sitting-room, nursing Little Bilham and sipping sweet sherry and absently watching the images upon the television screen. Pinn had turned the sound off. Pinn, in her petticoat, was intently engaged in painting her nails. Blaise, who liked Emily artificial, used to try to persuade her to paint hers, but she could scarcely ever bother, and now he did not bother either. Pinn, who worked afternoons, was usually home by five, and would then spend a long time flossying herself up. She often went out in the evenings. Emily was the one who stayed at home these days. Watching her friend doing her nails beside the flickering television set Emily thought, we are like a couple of prostitutes waiting for clients. Poor prostitutes, of course, not *poules de luxe*. Emily had once imagined herself as a *poule de luxe*. That seemed a laugh now. The sitting-room proclaimed something which was almost poverty which had crept over Emily like an illness, a symptom of the disorder of her life. Some people were doubtless just destined for poverty and muddle. Emily had probably inherited it. Earlier Pinn had been going on boringly about her rotten childhood. Emily had had a rotten childhood too, only she didn't talk about it

all the time. Bloody rotten. No wonder the place looked like a
slum. The cats didn't help. Richardson was sharpening his
claws on the side of the greasy armchair. Tear, tear, said Emily
to herself, that's right, tear, tear, tear. Odd to think that she
had once paid Pinn to clean the flat. Nobody cleaned it
now.

Watching Richardson destroying the chair, Emily suddenly
remembered a dream she had had last night. She had dreamt
that she was skinning a cat. She was in a fishmonger's shop and
the fishmonger was her step-father. 'Put it here,' he said.
Holding the skinned carcase by the tail, Emily carefully laid
it down on the fishmonger's slab. There was no blood. Then
suddenly she saw the carcase moving a little. 'It's still alive,'
said the fishmonger. It can't be, thought Emily. Oh, what it
must be suffering! It can't be still alive! The carcase continued to twitch and move. Emily woke up. She now drove
away from her the memory of the horrible dream. There were
so many thoughts which simply had to be sent away. She
spoke to Pinn.

'Who are you off with?'

'What?'

'Who are you off with tonight?'

Pinn had mysterious men friends.

'Kiki.'

'Kiki again?' Pinn seemed to be developing a nasty little
friendship with Kiki St Loy. 'Since when have you started to
adore Kiki?'

'I don't adore Kiki. I adore her car.' Kiki had a very long
yellow sports car.

'Well, don't bring Kiki here. I've had Kiki.' Also Blaise
might see her. Emily had lately begun to develop an agonizing
fear that Blaise might abandon her for a younger woman. But
of course that was a ridiculous idea. Ideas like that were an
illness too.

'Of course I won't bring her here, don't be a clot. We're
meeting at the pub.'

Thank God Kiki's leaving at the end of the term, thought
Emily. Kiki was seventeen, though she pretended to be
eighteen.

'Aren't you going to cook for him?'

'No.' Emily used to cook elaborately for Blaise. Now they
just drank for hours, opened a tin, and went to bed.

'You should have let me do you that casserole.'

'It doesn't matter.' She used to dress up for him too, once.

Now she just put on a casual evening top over her old dirty trousers. 'Won't you have a drink, Pinn?'

'No, thanks.'

Pinn used to be a drinking companion, in fact it was in this role that Emily had first got to know her so well. Pinn, arriving to char, had been offered a drink. Confidences followed. Alas. Now, however, while Emily was drinking more and more, Pinn was drinking less and less. Alas, alas. 'I hate drinking alone,' said Emily. But these days she often did it.

Enter Luca. His presence in the room altered everything down to the atoms and electrons. There was cosmic change. Luca had an awful condensed thereness, as if he had an exceptionally high specific gravity. As he spoke less, he seemed to have become more concentrated and opaque and dense. He was light-footed. The effect was mental. Pinn looked at him with detached curiosity, stopping her nail game. Pinn, like many childless women, rather disliked children and had never once, Emily noticed, referred to the boy with affection. However there seemed increasingly to be almost an understanding between them. Perhaps it was just the lack in Pinn of those awful black balls of emotion which so crammed Emily, which made Luca feel easier with her. 'We rub along,' Pinn had once said of her relations with the child.

Emily also stared at her son. He walked straight up to the television set and turned the sound up very loud. 'DANGER OF SERIOUS LONG-TERM DAMAGE TO THE ECONOMY . . .'

'Luca! Don't do that!'

It had been a dancing programme. Now it was evidently the news, yes, there was that man's silly face. Slopping her drink, Emily leaned over and switched the set off altogether. The room was tiny. Even Little Bilham could not have been swung.

Luca, paying no attention to his mother, had retired to a corner and was carefully examining something he had in his hand.

'What have you got there, Luca? What is it? Show mummy.'

Luca went without haste to the door and departed again. The door of his room closed softly.

'Oh *God*,' said Emily.

'He wants a snake,' said Pinn.

'A snake?'

'Yes. He wants a pet snake.'

'Well, he can want.'

'Do you mind if I pull back the curtains?'

'Yes, I do mind. Put the light on.'

Emily kept the curtains pulled a lot of the time now. The flat had had to be on the ground floor because of the cats, because of Richardson anyway, since Little Bilham had not been born or thought of when Blaise first found the flat and moved Emily into it seven years ago. The windows looked out onto a square of shadowed weedy grass which it seemed to be nobody's responsibility to turn into a garden. People sometimes stood there, as if transfixed with horror, but never strolled, and even the children preferred to play elsewhere. The block of flats which surrounded this gloomy patch was situated in a now rather shabby backwater off the Upper Richmond Road where the undulating nervous sound of traffic (in no way resembling a river) did not cease by day or by night. Though still fairly new, the place already had a battered filthy knocked-to-pieces air about it. The concrete walls outside were covered with long multi-coloured stains, and the dark corridors inside were full of perambulators and bicycles and large broken toys and piles of old newspapers and mysterious horrible smells.

Pinn had turned on the light and was now tacking a newly laundered white lace collar on to her little black dress.

'Isn't it nearly time you went?'

'Yes, yes, yes, yes, yes!' Pinn jumped up and left the room, carrying the dress.

Emily sighed and gave herself some more sherry. She ran her tongue along her painful gums. No need to look for the aspirins, the drink was making her feel better. Time to put on her trousers and her brushed nylon evening top. What fun it had been dressing up for Blaise in the old days, when he watched her at it, boots first of course. He had put her into some pretty uncomfortable rigs in his time. And he usually brought some new gadget, sometimes she could not even guess what it was. How they had laughed, and then suddenly become silent. They had had fun. Did she feel excited now at the prospect of his visit? Yes, a bit. But the little element of fear was no longer delicious. Their conflicts were no longer held firm inside the fabric of their love. They smashed through it, revealing awful vistas of solitary suffering. There was always something to be confessed, an extravagance or some awful worry about Luca, and now the rent, her job, her lodger, her teeth, the increasing unmanageableness of her existence. Blaise's eyes would go blank. There was always a row. His visits upset her so much, upset Luca so much. There were moments when

55

she almost wished he would not come. Misery grew in her heart like a plant. Sometimes she was so unhappy she just wanted to be unconscious, not to die exactly but to sleep for months. Any unpleasant happening tapped a deep base of nightmare. She was so full of vain regrets. If only only only, she reflected for the thousandth time, she had forced him to leave his fat cow wife then, nine years ago, when he was utterly mad about her, when he was her slave. I could have made him bust things up then, thought Emily. He was crazy. If I had threatened to break with him, he would have done anything. I should have forced him. Instead, I was sorry for him. I was sympathetic and understanding and kind. He asked for time and I gave him time. And look what time has done for me.

Blaise Gavender was driving his Volkswagen over Putney Bridge. Crossing the river was always a bad moment. People sometimes wonder how spies can live an ordinary life. Blaise knew. One simply divided one's mind in two and built impenetrable barriers between the parts.

It was low tide. As he looked at the sluggish light-brown meander of water he remembered a dream he had had last night. Some fishes in a muddy pool were ceremonially drowning a cat. The fishes had pale semi-human faces surrounded by flapping layers of repulsive finny matter. They had pushed the cat's head under water and were holding it down with their fins. Surely it must be dead by now, Blaise thought with fascinated pity. But the cat's tail, still visible above the water, continued to jerk about.

This doctor business, Blaise was thinking. It's all an illusion. I can't put that part of my life straight without putting it all straight. But I can't do that either. I can't stop earning money, I daren't stop. Even with Emily's job, even if I get a grant to become a medical student, I can't stop her allowance, I can't ask *her* to suffer more. And I'd hardly ever be able to see her then. Thank God I never told her about the doctor idea. I can't drive her mad. Besides it would be dangerous. No wonder I've never been able to save any money. I've given so much time and so much life to something which has turned out so badly. This bloody lie has ruined everything. And now just when I see some really good possibility in my life at last, I can't have it because of this, because of her. However I shift the pieces about I'm trapped. I can't afford to be poor. If all this came out it would ruin my practice. Anyway, it can't come out, it would kill Harriet. I don't want it to come out. But I don't want it to go on either. God, there must be some way of sorting it out, there must be some best course. But there isn't. Anything good is immediately cancelled. Because I feel vile I can't spur myself to do good. What is good here anyway? It is entirely hidden.

Sometimes, reviewing his dilemma, Blaise felt that the thing he resented most of all was the loss of his virtue. Another man might have called the lost thing his honour. A girl might have called it her innocence. Blaise mourned for his lost goodness. He was condemned to live in a sinful state, although his mind did not consent to sin and rejected it. Reflection about his psychology did not help him at all. Much of the machinery was painfully clear, but irrelevant. The agonizing fact was that he could not now be good because he had to go on and on and on acting a bad role, it was as simple as that; even though he so often and so frenziedly felt the role as entirely alien. What an ordinary thuggish *homme moyen sensuel* he appeared to have turned out to be, and yet of course he was not. His virtue had mattered to him. He had treasured it when he was young. His fellow students thought him 'wise', his patients still did. A sense of himself as wise and good had led him into his chosen vocation, had given him the 'nerve' required to practice. The same guiding star now, with wonderful clarity, pointed him onward. But he could not go. It was as if his virtue did not know that he had lost it, could follow it no further. It kept on pointing. This was the anguish. And Harriet: she had so perfectly fostered in him that happy sense of being a good man, which sometimes almost forgetting, he seemed still to retain. When had the wickedness started, where was it located? How ever had he managed to put himself into this position of torment?

In fact he had not slipped into it either accidentally or unwillingly. He had rushed into it with cries of joy. This memory was sometimes an agony, sometimes a consolation. Blaise had known ever since boyhood that he had certain peculiarities. They had never troubled him. This exercise of common sense was indeed part of his wisdom, and reflection on his own oddness had also led him to study psychology. He was not all that odd, he early concluded. Most people were pretty odd. It was interesting. He had early discovered, partly by introspection, partly by intuition, partly by questioning others, and partly by a study of literature, that human minds, including the minds of geniuses and saints, are given to the creation of weird and often repulsive fantasies. These fantasies, he concluded, are in almost every case quite harmless. They live in the mind, like the flora and fauna which live in the bloodstream, and like these may be in some ways beneficial. They are of course symptoms of mental structure, but are not themselves usually causes, except perhaps in art. Fantasy concerning murder may make a man write a book about murder, but is very unlikely to make him commit murder. So, theoretically and by instinct, Blaise lived cheerfully with the oddities of his mind (which did not, in his case, concern murders). He knew his ridiculous undignified inner self very well; and it never occurred to him that he might ever want to act his fantasies or that it would be of any interest to meet a cognate fellow-dreamer. Obsessive rituals and the search for *alter-egos* was a sign of mental ailment, and Blaise was thoroughly mentally healthy. He was not going to develop any of those precise needs which lead ultimately into the little cupboard. He later studied such cravings in his patients with the cool eye of science. He *knew* all about it. Was he not a wise man?

Blaise believed it to be a sign of mental well-being to like all sorts of people, and he liked all sorts of people. He had certainly no pre-conceived theory about the sort of woman he might marry, except that he thought she would probably be an intellectual. Then one day suddenly there was Harriet, not an intellectual but—what?—a sort of saint? Well, not a saint so much as a noble lady. Harriet's sweetness was very ordinary really, her selflessness was selfish in a very ordinary woman's way. But she had a beautiful, as it were, aristocratic, dignity and tact. Harriet was neither socially grand nor rich, but Blaise's rather snobbish mother approved of her at once. Blaise was much in love. Something that he loved in Harriet was her absolute openness, her non-peculiarness, her (dreadful word) normality. Harriet was right out in the open, in the light. Had there been after all some tiny fear in him which Harriet's sunniness had extinguished? Harriet would never let him shut himself into any dark cupboard. When he married Harriet he felt that all *that*, though still there of course (such

58

things are ineradicable) had become utterly unimportant and harmless and small. Of course he never imparted any of these reflections to Harriet. He did not want to trouble his lovely calm wife with tales which might alarm or sicken her. Anyway she would not have understood. What went on in her mind he soon found out without her even noticing. It was nothing at all unusual.

Blaise had been happily married for nearly ten years when he met Emily McHugh. He met her at a lecture on Merleau-Ponty at the French Institute. Of course Harriet was not with him. Emily was a student at a teachers' training college, writing a thesis about Merleau-Ponty. Emily was twenty-two. Her appearance struck him at once. She wore her nearly black hair long in those days, tied roughly back with an elastic band. She was small and very slim, with a small ardent face, a little sharp nose, and brilliant rather hard and stony blue eyes. She spoke in a deliberately harsh and unobliging voice with a slight London accent. She immediately, though somewhat mechanically, flirted with Blaise when they met (no one introduced them) at the cocktail party after the lecture. Blaise flirted too. He found himself, however, almost at once finding some pretext for referring to 'my wife'. Emily gave him a strange look. It was clear to Blaise after about twenty minutes that he could not let this fascinating chance acquaintance disappear for ever. How had he so early known? They often discussed this later. Even at the first meeting he had felt (yet on what evidence?) like an animal who had thought that just *his* sort of animal did not exist anywhere in the forest—and then had suddenly met one. They talked of Emily's work. Merleau-Ponty readily provided an excuse for another meeting. Blaise promised an offprint of his early paper on *Phenomenology and Psychoanalysis*. He delivered it to her two days later in a pub near the British Museum. Emily never finished her thesis.

'Did you meet anybody interesting at the French do?' 'There was a student working on Merleau-Ponty. We had an argument.' This was the only thing Blaise had ever said to Harriet about Emily. Harriet had noticed nothing, had never for a second suspected. Her trust in him was perfect. In the early days it had seemed inconceivable that Harriet should not have read the truth off his blazing face, off his trembling hands. The day after the British Museum pub, he and Emily were in bed together. It was ecstatic, sudden, total. As total as Harriet's trust, its cataclysmic necessary counterpart. Sin was an awful private happiness blotting out all else; only it was not sin, it was glory, it was his good, his very own, manifested at last. This was the dark cupboard all right, only it was not dark, it was blazing with light and as large as the universe. Everything he had done before seemed feeble, shadowy, and insincere. A combination of pure free creation and pure causality now felicitously ruled his life. The dark forces had never been stronger or more clearly seen, but he was not their puppet. They rose into the bright air like a fountain and carried him skyward with them. He had never fretted after, never even dreamt of, a woman who could so complement his own strangeness. This was not just intense sexual bliss, it was absolute metaphysical justification. The world in its detail was revealed at last to an indubitable insight. His whole being was engaged, he was identified with his real self, he fully inhabited his own nature for the first time in his life.

Though she had had, in a casual and unimpressed way, a good deal of varied sexual experience, Emily McHugh had never really been in love before. She had been true to her deep thing, she informed Blaise. *She* had remained free, *she* had known how to wait, *she* had made no compromises with society, *she* had not given up hope and accepted a second best! Blaise hung his head. It had indeed been a failure of faith and courage, not to wander on through the forest, not to search faithfully for his true mate, not to believe and endure. He did not ever exactly curse his marriage or curse Harriet, but he saw it all as a pitiful and unworthy mistake. He wished with the most biting remorse that it could all be undone and made never to have been, and in this rather abstract sense he sometimes wished that Harriet could die or be somehow just spirited away for ever. In fact, when he was with Emily, Harriet seemed like a dream and tended to slip out of his consciousness altogether. As for Emily's reproaches, he wore them like rubies. What they were even pleased to call their vices penetrated the texture of their whole life down to the minutest details of repartee and verbal wit.

Of course Emily was not really an intellectual, but she had the style of one, she was literate and sharp and witty. Illegitimate, poor, fatherless, she had struggled into her education against great odds. How brave she is, he often thought, she does not even know how brave she is. What will and courage had carried such a girl to the length of even hearing of Merleau-Ponty! She did not however 'live herself' as a thinker. She had an integrated animal quality which was unlike, but complementary to, her partner's psychological texture. She was not unconscious of her being, but wore it without the quick anxieties and awarenesses which formed part of Blaise's pleasure. She found nothing odd or ridiculous in rituals which she had never except mentally performed before; and it was this deep calm priestless-like *confidence* which led her lover on into the land which crystallized gorgeously about them like a solidifying dream, the thunderclap blending of the fantastic and the real. The ritual aspect of their relationship proceeded with intuitive spontaneous ease and occupied them quite a lot at the start. There were objects the sight of which, or even the thought of which, could give Blaise an erection. But as they soon even more rapturously discovered, it did not really matter much what they 'did'. All this, everything, like the earth upon the last trump, was caught up and included in the miraculous quality of their spiritual-physical grasp of each other. The particular thrilling violences resided more purely in looks and in tones and in the intimate sway of one consciousness in its fierce blissful wrestling with another. However, that they had also 'done everything', gave them a virtuous sense of completeness. They lived like gods together.

Except of course that they could not live together. At first, incredible as it later seemed, the sheer force of love made them seem scarcely aware that Blaise was married and that he had to spend much of the week with his wife. The cruelty of absence stirred them to hotter transports of love. Blaise crossed Putney Bridge faint and molten with desire, and when they met they wept and danced. It seemed at first frivolous to worry about, even to be conscious of, their more worldly difficulties. A change came (erotic love is never still) when Emily started posing questions. The questions could not disturb them of course, since there had to be suitable answers. Their love had to triumph, to work, so it just would. Still, there were questions. Blaise put off telling Harriet. He *would* of course tell Harriet and dispose of Harriet. But he did not want to be too unkind and he needed time in which to arrange it all for the best. Emily was not anxious, she did not drive or press him. It was enough for the present that he so indubitably loved her, it was enough too that she *knew* and Harriet did not. She even pitied Harriet, who was elderly and deceived and fat and no longer loved by Blaise. 'Mrs Placid' was Emily's name for Harriet. Poor Mrs Placid.

Luca had been an alien growth. Their love, so dense, so seamless, so complete, had not seemed framed with any space left for a child. They had not wished for, dreamt of or anticipated children. *That* problem belonged to quite another world, to quite another set of arrangements. They did not even, though they might have done so, conceive of it as belonging to the time after Blaise should have 'disposed of' Harriet. At least this was what Blaise felt, and he was fairly sure that it was what Emily felt until she actually found herself pregnant. Blaise later accused Emily of concealing her pregnancy until it was too late to terminate it. Emily retorted that she had no need for deceitful stratagems to entrap one who was so utterly bound to her in love and trust. However that might be, Luca arrived, and across his cradle Blaise and Emily looked at each other with eyes which sparkled with a new anguish.

Blaise, who had up to now visited his dark goddess in a discreet one-room flat in Highgate, moved his second *ménage* to Putney. It is hard to say at what moment it began to dawn on both of them that some longer and more complex trial period lay ahead than they had envisaged in the days of their first rapture. 'You aren't going to do it,' said Emily one day. 'You're going to funk it.' Blaise said nothing. They sometimes quarrelled, and the quarrels began to be really painful, not like the joyous pain of the twin fighters which they had once been. Then on an evening when Emily had screamed at him with what for an instant looked like near hate, he had said, 'Wait. Please. When David is older I will come to you. I can't do it now. I can't.' Her reproaches then brought him no pleasure. David's life had lengthened. Public school, and now later university, had been set up as the stage when all would be changed and reversed. With shame and with resentment Blaise read in Emily's eyes her slow loss of hope, her desperate contempt. However, with a spirit which he often, with a rekindling of his old dark joy, admired and adored, she gritted her teeth and carried on. At other times he felt: well, what else can she do, poor girl?

There was one other thing she could do, as he of course knew, and that was kick everything to pieces. She could go and confront Harriet. In fact all she needed to do to ruin him was to write a letter. Emily did not know and had deliberately never wished to know where he lived with his wife. 'I don't want to know anything about your bourgeois existence,' she told him. 'I don't want to think about it at all.' In this she had never wavered, and Blaise knew that she regarded with an almost superstitious horror and disgust the existence of that elsewhere into which he vanished. Not only did she feel no curiosity about it, she symbolically annihilated it in her mind.

However that did not imply that she might not suddenly in some moment of hatred and despair take it into her head to smash through the barrier. She could easily discover his other lair and invade it.

Fear of this did not in fact trouble Blaise very much. He had once told Emily that if she decided to ruin him in this way he would never see her again. The threat was unnecessary. Emily, intelligently brooding upon the situation, quite sufficiently saw that this sort of wrecking action would not serve her turn. He saw the intelligence working and working in her suspicious alienated eyes. Did she still believe that when David went to college Blaise would quietly break it all to Harriet and come and live with Emily? Did he believe it? As the years went by he came to see her slightly less often. Neither of them commented. 'You know I'll never leave you, never give you up,' he said to her in moments of tenderness, and there were still many. 'I know,' she said. And she did know: but this did not help much either.

'Magnus Bowles' was of course a fiction, invented by Montague Small. Soon after Monty's arrival at Locketts, and in fact during the brief and inauspicious time when Monty was allegedly Blaise's patient, Blaise had blurted the whole business out. This was when Blaise was beginning to feel very anxious, but was still very much in love. He told Monty, in the confessional quietness of his own parlour, partly out of a ridiculous bravado and *joie de vivre*, partly in order to get Monty's help and advice, and partly because he had to tell another man. Monty of course was fascinated. When Blaise saw that glow of delighted curiosity in his friend's eye he already began to suspect that he had made a mistake. However it *was* a relief, and Monty *did* help. How the whole thing failed to come to light (to be obvious to Harriet) in the early stages was a mystery in retrospect. Blaise was constantly recklessly absent, sometimes for days on end, at important 'conferences', seeing urgent 'patients', studying in remote 'libraries'. Only Harriet's monumental calm trust (what Emily called her stupidity) kept the structure up. It never occurred to Harriet to doubt or in any way to check statements whose falsity would have been clear under the lightest scrutiny. Her poor husband was very very busy, that was all. She and David, much absorbed with each other, endured his absences and ecstatically welcomed his returns. He always came back so tired, poor thing.

It was Monty, with his sophistical detective story mind, who pointed out to Blaise how poor his 'cover' was and how easily he might be 'blown'. 'You need a consistent story,' said Monty, 'and one with a built-in safeguard against investigation.' Thus 'Magnus Bowles' came into being, invented and kept going as a changing person by Monty. Blaise could not have invented such an elaborate lie: at the start because this degree of deliberation seemed a sacrilege against his love ('I must just take my chance,' he had said to Monty), later because he was so drained of energy and spirit by the whole business, he could invent nothing. He found that he could not even, given Magnus as an accepted fiction, keep him going without Monty's continual help, which was increasingly necessary after Harriet began to take such an unfortunately passionate interest in the poor fellow. Indeed by now Monty had crazed Magnus up to a point where Harriet was thoroughly distressed about him. The deception involved weekly conferences with Monty, during which the latter continued Magnus's history and produced fresh 'Bowlesisms' for the consumption of Harriet.

This dependence on Monty irked Blaise, though of course he trusted Monty's discretion absolutely. He never introduced Monty to Emily, though Monty occasionally dropped hints on the subject. Magnus Bowles was indeed a great convenience, ensuring regular unquestioned unalterable absences. The earlier panics, when Harriet had innocently contested her husband's determination to be absent on a certain day, had reduced Blaise to nervous frenzy. And Magnus could also be relied upon as a device to cover any sudden emergency. Harriet, who regarded Blaise's relationship with his patients as something sacred, would not, of course have dreamt of 'investigating' Magnus on her own account. She was now entirely used to Blaise's regular absences with his nocturnal patient. Only, as it seemed to Blaise, Harriet's curious and more frequent night fears attested some unconscious feeling in his wife that all was not well. Hence the increasing regiment of dogs, hated symbol to Blaise of his own secret depravity.

And now the whole situation had existed for nine years. Luca's sturdy growth was evidence of its longevity and of its solidity. Blaise's relation with his second son had never been a happy one. He had been in every ordinary and natural way connected with David's upbringing and he felt, even when David became 'difficult', that he and David belonged to each other. He had no such connection with Luca, though when Luca was a very small child Blaise had been there often enough to play the father, and indeed had felt a frenzy of tender confused love for the hapless creature. He had often put his arms round Emily and Luca and felt how unfortunate they were all three, and how desperately he wanted to protect his little second family and ensure their happiness. Their somewhat derelict and deprived condition, compared with the arrangements at Hood House, even gave him a sort of pleasure, and spurred his possessive love. Inevitably however he had, and especially as he began to turn up at Putney less often, to leave Luca's nurture and the decisions concerning his daily life to Emily. Luca naturally became Emily's child, although there was a time when Luca was about five, when his mother seemed positively to hate him. She used to hit the child, though she denied this to Blaise. Blaise felt guilty and helpless. Luca was backward, a bed-wetter, beginning to look like a problem. Blaise was relieved that Emily took it for granted that the child should go to the local state school, although she knew that David went to a public school. Later she used to raise the matter, but only to taunt Blaise. 'Mrs Placid's boy's at a posh school, but that hell-hole is good enough for my son!' Also later she used to say, 'You'd have left me long ago if it wasn't for Luca.' Was this true, Blaise wondered. Possibly. And 'I hate that child. If it wasn't for him I'd be able to ditch you and have a proper life! I love Little Bilham more than I love Luca.' Emily did deeply love her son, however, only she could not help constantly using him as a weapon against her lover.

There were frequent quarrels about the boy of course, including some rather unexpected ones about religion. Blaise had no religious beliefs, although he had been a devout Anglican as a youth. He had plenty of religious 'feelings', but he knew perfectly well what they were all about. His religion had been based on he knew what and had gone to he knew where. He had had however no impulse to resist Harriet's wish that David should be brought up as a Christian. Harriet introduced David to Jesus Christ at the earliest possible moment, in fact very soon after David had revealed a dawning consciousness of herself and Blaise. Harriet taught David to pray as soon as he could speak. Blaise not only did not object, but actually approved, since he felt that it was very much better for a child's mental health to be a vague Christian and to drift out than to be a deliberately protected atheist constantly wondering what the mystery is from which one has been excluded. (By 'vague Christianity' Blaise meant of course the Church of England. More enthusiastic creeds were another

65

matter.) Besides, a little mild devotion was a painless introduction to the history of Europe.

However when Blaise propounded this reasonable doctrine in relation to Luca, he met with ferocious opposition from Emily, who regarded religion as not only false but (and this was perhaps even worse) 'bourgeois'. 'I will not have my child bowing and bobbing and mumbling prayers. Thank God he's not at a posh school where that farce still goes on.' Blaise was annoyed, but he was in no position to resist. Luca's school did profess to teach 'scripture', but Luca seemed to gain no contaminating insights from these sessions. Once, quite recently, in Blaise's presence, he had pointed questioningly to a picture of a crucifix. Emily had replied. 'A religious idol.' Luca seemed to know as little about religion as about anything else. And yet: what did Luca know? When he was five he had asked why his Daddy was going away again so soon. 'To his work,' Emily said, and laughed nastily. Later the child stopped asking questions. Of course neither of them had 'said anything' to Luca, but Blaise saw sometimes in those very dark round eyes suspicion, hostility, perhaps some kind of knowledge. Blaise suffered very much, and with a sort of hopelessness, as he saw that consciousness, with its inevitable condemnation, beginning to take form.

A philosopher said that the spiritualization of sensuality is called love. Blaise had certainly felt his early love for Emily to be all sense, all spirit. The absolute interpenetration of the two gave him, together with experiences of pleasure which he never previously knew existed, a sort of certainty about the whole thing which seemed to create its own truth and its own morality. In the light of this truth his relations with Harriet seemed hopelessly insincere, not only in this situation now, but fundamentally and always. Emily told him that he had married Harriet for snobbish social reasons, and he did not deny this, because although it was not true, something rather like it, it then seemed to him, was. He had loved Harriet. But he had married her in a muddled compromising impure deliberately blinded state, thinking this to be the best possible. He had committed the sin against the Holy Ghost (which so much troubled Maurice Guimarron) by wilfully excluding the possibility of perfection.

All this he saw in the illumination of the dark rays of his glinting girl. Could one doubt the absolutely *incarnate* truth when confronted by it, as by God? He felt like a disciple in the presence of Christ. So in leading Emily to think that Harriet was unattractive and ageing (he even exaggerated her age for Emily's benefit) and that his relations with Harriet had become empty, in letting Emily picture Harriet as a stupid fat cow and a snob, he had again not exactly been lying, for these images in Emily represented something which was true in him, though not exactly true of Harriet. In any case were these in any sense lies? There is a level (not necessarily the deepest one) in any marriage where love fails. Emily was a chemical which showed up what had been previously concealed, not making the rest false, but completing the picture.

How Blaise came gradually to change views which he had held to with such certainty was never entirely clear to him. Were the causes of change simple, even vulgar ones, he sometimes wondered? An irregular liaison is always likely to be under strain. He had mad periods of suspecting her fidelity, and used to turn up unannounced. There was never any trace of another man, though Emily often threatened him with a rival just to torment him. There were so many strains upon his relation with Emily, strains which began as soon as she started to suspect that he was not going to leave Harriet immediately or even soon. At that time, when Emily's suspicions were beginning, Blaise was going through a phase of alternating exasperation and euphoria. He realized obscurely that he and Emily had somehow missed the boat, at any rate they had missed the first boat. He could not so easily set himself 'free' (a word with which Emily was constantly beating him). But why after all should he be expected to go through the disagreeable and murderous business of becoming 'free', if that was what the state was rightly called?

Men in other ages and societies had been able to have two, or many more, women whom they kept incarcerated in separate places and visited when they felt in the mood. An elderly less-loved wife could be retained as an amiable companion, or simply out of pity, and should feel no resentment at that. A man, any man, surely needed various women, there were so many possibilities and styles of love and affection and habit. Why should some of them automatically exclude the others? He led a double life. Did that make him a liar? He did not feel a liar. He was a man of two truths, since both these lives were valuable and true. Thus went his exasperation. His slightly crazy euphoria consisted of a feeling of 'Well, I'm getting away with it anyway!' There seemed to be something noble in this, an heroic exercise of power as if he were a sort of interiorized Atlas, holding the two ends of the earth apart by sheer strength. Unfortunately this image in turn suggested that of Samson. And his dilemma now sometimes expressed itself in the feeling that he could only end it all by ending himself.

The 'vulgar' causes of change included of course the question of money. Emily omitted no chance of telling him how second-rate, how second-best her own establishment was. She endlessly complained about her lack of independence, while refusing to take a full-time job and tormenting him with her needs. 'Luca is the iron ball tied to my foot, Luca is my iron foot,' she sometimes used to say. 'Surely you wouldn't leave me if there was no Luca?' was what he was supposed to reply. (Their conversations were becoming increasingly mechanical.) 'You wouldn't see me for dust!' Emily would then answer. Emily was remarkably, given her character, resigned really to her iron foot, but there were many ways in which she could still make war on Blaise, putting on him a pressure, sometimes intelligently designed to persuade him at last to make what they referred to as *the move*, and sometimes (it seemed to him) designed in a purely vengeful spirit to reduce them both to misery and spoil their time together.

She ceased to attend to the appearance of either herself or the flat. Both were untidy, slovenly, even dirty. The flat smelt abominably of cats and, during Luca's prolonged bed-wetting, of urine. The colourful love-nest had become a slum, and Emily seemed to preside with a certain satisfaction over its decline. Money which Blaise gave her to buy a new gas stove was spent on drink. Emily drank more and so did Blaise when he was with her. They quarrelled noisily, careless whether Luca heard them. And lately Emily had taken to waking Blaise up at night when, weary with drink and strife he had fallen into a deep slumber, to continue reproaching him or to announce that she and Luca proposed to emigrate to Australia. Their spiritualized sensuality could scarcely now even serve them as an anaesthetic. The old ambiguities of physical pain had merged into the truly maiming horror of mental pain. The cruelties of their situation could no longer be transformed into its glories. Their quarrels, which had been sham fights, the image of the bed where they ended, became real fights involving real hurts. The raucous hard-edged voice which he had loved so much, now telling him that he was weak and cowardly and contemptible, filled him with a self-lacerating rage which could gain no sexual release.

Shame, which had once been entirely absent, became the

atmosphere of his life. He felt ashamed and venomously angry before Emily, ashamed and obscurely frightened before Luca. When he thought of David he felt a sort of absolutely pure shame which was more piercing than any other. Whereas Blaise experienced his fatherhood of Luca as an obscure form of punishment, he experienced his fatherhood of David, still in spite of everything, in a deep ordinary almost happy way; and it was this defeated happiness which produced the pure and particularly poignant suffering. It was as if David's father had never been told and could not but be happy. He loved David so much and was so proud of him, and could not help completing this picture by filling in David's love for him and David's pride in him. Any boy wants and needs to admire his father. In earlier and more rational discussions with Emily, Blaise had argued that the shock to David should be postponed to an age when it would do less damage. Emily asked why she was supposed to be concerned about the welfare of Mrs Placid's boy. But she seemed sometimes to accept the consideration as an argument; perhaps because she needed to feel that there were reasons for the delay in making 'the move' which were not simply Blaise's uncertainty about the absolute value of their love.

Meanwhile David passed in protected ignorance the various milestones of his life, while the tormented lovers continued to argue. How, Blaise constantly wondered, could he bring this desolation and this misery into the serene innocent lives of his wife and son? Of course the desolation was already there, right in the middle of the scene, making Harriet fear burglars and collect dogs, making David's eyes contract and turn away. For David too, in the black depths of his adolescent distress, unconsciously 'knew'. Yet this knowledge was infinitely more merciful and less harmful than that unimaginably awful real knowledge which 'the move' would involve. How could Blaise, after that, look into David's face again? He would earn his son's lifelong contempt, perhaps hatred. Harriet and David had done nothing to deserve those horrors. However much one suffered from the pain of conscience had one not a duty to keep quiet and digest one's own scandals? Was it not perhaps right that he and Emily, the guilty ones, should continue to hug the poison to themselves, perhaps forever? Oh, if only he could set it all to himself simply as a task, however wearying, however difficult, however long! How he envied ordinary men their innocent problems, their jobs, their mortgages, their overdrafts! How he envied the bereaved Monty his clean pain!

Blaise felt shame before Emily, before David, before Luca. Where Harriet was concerned something much stronger had been happening which was now his chief and most awful preoccupation. As one mystery wound its way on into deeper defiles of horror, the other mystery, though without thereby bringing him any hope or release, had emerged into a new brightness. At one time Blaise had scarcely recalled Harriet when he was with Emily. Now he scarcely recalled Emily when he was with Harriet. Once Emily had seemed real and Harriet a dream. Now Harriet seemed real and Emily a dream. He had told Emily that he had no sexual relations with Harriet. This had been true. It was true no longer. Harriet had of course silently, perfectly, waited. How much, if only it were not for the devils, he would have enjoyed, and somehow in spite of them did enjoy, being once more with his chaste modest virginal dear wife. How much more satisfying this was than 'doing things' with Emily. Harriet had once seemed to lack what Emily possessed in such abundance, 'seductive vitality'. But now his wife drew him with quiet power, rousing in him mixed intensities of reverence and desire. He had never felt any such emotion in his life before, and he regarded himself with awe. His 'spy' life became, in a terrible deprived way, simpler, as a function of these changes which made his whole existence more precarious by supplying him with a new but equally baffling set of motives.

Of course memory falsifies to conceal disagreeable causal connections. But the shift was becoming increasingly clear. It had been anguish to experience the continued maiming of his great love for Emily. It was an even greater anguish to discover that his love for Harriet, which had been obscured and gone underground like a river, was not only intact but was emerging into the light stronger and deeper and purer than it had ever been before. After all, his innocent love for Harriet, as if unaware of his badness, had simply gone on growing in the natural way in which married love grows. And he instinctively longed for Harriet's sympathy in his sufferings. If he hurt his finger she sympathized, so why not now? To see the vision of healing love, but no longer to be able to profit by it: is this perhaps the worst suffering of the damned in hell? The fruits of virtue and evil are automatic; he saw that now. But surely, surely, he repeated to himself, there must be a best moral choice, some decent and not too painful, not annihilating, way out, some salvation which could expunge his fault? Could not gentleness and patient imagination somehow unviolently unravel this, or was he condemned to die like a rat in a storm drain? If someone suffers terribly, surely at last it can be said: let there be forgiveness, he has suffered enough. But who could utter these releasing words?

He felt now so absolutely 'in the truth' with Harriet, as if he had already told her and been forgiven. Because of her there seemed, oddly, to be nothing fake in their relationship. He drank from her calmness, her tenderness, a sort of spurious strength which ought to have been, but could not be an instrument of his salvation. Oh how could he have been such a witless fool as so to ruin and lose what, in his continued false possession of it, he saw now to be supremely valuable? If only he were living now in ordinary honest wedlock with such a wife and with such a son he would be the happiest man in the whole world. Emily had cheated him not only of his goodness but of his destined happy life. Sometimes he hated her for this so much that he wanted to kill her.

It was all becoming increasingly urgent for him as a question of truth, a choice for him between truth and death. Where truth was death too. Yet could he still be saved by an angel and could that angel be Harriet? At night he often dreamed that he had told Harriet and that all was somehow perfectly well. And in waking moments too he thought, could there not be some way of getting safely past that awful barrier that stood before him as an implacable iceberg, as an image of absolute smash: some way of telling the truth, and yet keeping everything just as it was before, like a juggler with a pile of balanced plates who jerks one out and keeps the others steady?

How spoilt and wretched his life was through his own fault. And how miserably unjust it all was to Emily. 'Our love has just never had a chance. It's had to live all its life under the carpet. No wonder it's as flat as a pancake!' Still, however unjustly, it was simply the case that the balance had shifted, the picture had changed. Had Harriet, just by innocently loving him, just by smiling and arranging the flowers and being his legitimate wife, finally *won*? And if so what followed from that?

Blaise remembered that he had not fed the dogs. He had had these two dogs since he was quite a little boy, both of them smooth-haired fox terriers, named Tango and Rumba by Blaise's father, who was fond of dancing. Blaise felt terrible guilt and fear because he remembered that the dogs were shut into the old stables and no one knew they were there and no one would hear them barking. They had been there for days and days, for weeks. How could he possibly have forgotten them, and what would his father say? He began to run, but his feet had become large and heavy and were cleaving to the earth. At last he reached the stables and unbarred the top half of the door of the last loose box and peered into the obscure interior. There was no movement within. He looked and looked. Then with horror he saw the two dogs. They had become dark and dried up and elongated and were hanging from hooks upon the wall. He thought, when I did not come they must have hanged themselves. Then he thought, no, they have died and become something else, and the gardener thought they were some sort of tools or implements and hung them up. But what sort of tools or implements have they become?

'Wake up, damn you, wake up!'

Emily was shaking him by the shoulder. Blaise awoke and was immediately dazzled by the bright bedside lamp. Emily, lying beside him, had tilted the lamp so that it shone directly onto his face. He shut his eyes again. Then opened them and looked at his watch. It was three o'clock.

'I told you not to do that. It's absolute hell being wakened up like that.'

'And it's absolute hell lying awake and thinking the thoughts I'm thinking and listening to you snore.'

'Put out the light.'

'I want to tell you something.'

'You've decided to take Luca to Australia, well off you go then.'

'How can I bloody go to Australia when I've got no bloody money?'

'I see you've bought a fur coat. I asked you not to buy any clothes till the sales.'

'You notice everything, don't you. Well, clever-dick, it's not a fur coat, it's simulated, and I didn't buy it, Pinn gave it to me. I gave her a pound for it.'

'That's called buying it. Put out the light and let's sleep.

'Sleep, sleep, you just want to sleep all the time now. We

used to stay awake all night. Now you want to go beddy-byes at ten.'

'If we didn't stupefy ourselves with drink we wouldn't get so comatose.'

'I like that. You taught me to drink. I suppose we need the stuff now to get through an evening together. God!'

'Well, get on with what you want to tell me.'

'I was too frightened to tell your earlier. I'm getting feeble-minded.'

'What is it?'

'I usedn't to be frightened of you. Now I'm frightened of everything, even you.'

'*What is it?*'

'I've given up my job.'

'Christ! Why?'

'I've decided to retire. Other men support their wives. I'm tired. I'm getting old. You can start supporting me.'

'You know I can't afford to. You know we agreed —'

'Be quiet, you'll wake Luca.'

'He must be awake already. What's that noise? Christ, somebody's at the front door.'

'Relax, it isn't Mrs Placid with a blunt instrument, it's only Pinn letting herself in.'

'*Pinn?*'

'Yes, that's the other thing I was too timid to tell you. I've taken a lodger. Pinn lives here now.'

'You mean you've taken Pinn as a lodger?'

'I've just told you that.'

'How dare you do so without asking me.'

'Well, you aren't here all that often. I live here, I imagine. It's my home.'

'It's my home too. I pay the bloody rent.'

'That's about all you do do, to make it your home. And that reminds me, there's a third thing. You won't like this either. They're putting up the rent in October, it'll be nearly double.'

'You seem pleased. Em, how can you have been so stupid about Pinn? Do you think she's listening at the door?'

'No, she's gone into her room. She's my friend, isn't she? And she's made herself jolly useful.'

'Well you can tell her to get out tomorrow. I'm not coming here if Pinn's here. You can bloody well choose. How can I be with you when that woman's in the house snooping and listening?'

'What does it matter *now*?'

'You've done this on purpose to upset me. And you've given up your job on purpose.'

'Maybe I have. Maybe I feel it's time for a change.'

'Tell blasted Pinn to get out tomorrow or I will.'

'She pays rent you know. However it's up to you. You'll have to double my allowance, what am I saying, triple it.'

'I can't, you know I can't.'

'I don't know anything of the sort, I don't see your bank account.'

'Please, Em, have some consideration for me.'

'Why should I? You even grudge me the money to get my teeth fixed.'

'I can't afford it! Especially now. Harriet has to make economies too—'

'I told you never to mention that name. Economies! You mean do without the gold dinner service and the third car?'

'We only have one car—'

'I don't want to know. "We" and "us" and roughing it with one motor car!'

'If some of this dental work is really necessary—'

'God, you are crawlingly mean. Don't you want me to look nice?'

'I don't care how you look. We're too close to each other for that to matter.'

'Do you imagine you're the only person who ever looks at me? Well, you obviously do. Or are you afraid I'll attract another man?'

'Don't be a fool, Em.'

'Anyway, it's not just aesthetic. To eat, teeth must meet.'

'You know that if something is absolutely necessary—'

'And what about my holiday, if it comes to that, or don't I get one again this year? When am I going to see Paris?'

'Oh do shut up.'

'And I need new chair covers.'

'I suggest you persuade the bloody cats not to tear the place up.'

'Destruction is their only pleasure. Soon it will be mine.'

'We'll make a list—'

'I know your bloody lists. You make a list and then you feel faint and clear off. I give you notice, the years of heroism are over. I used to tighten my belt, Christ, I almost enjoyed it, I did enjoy it, suffering for you and all that. But not any more. The pain doesn't amuse me any more.'

'Well, what do you want? You know we're simply stuck.'

'We can unstick, even if it unsticks the world. You ask what I want. I want a bit of security at last. You pay the rent here, you say. Fine, but what happens if you go under a bus? You've always kept me on a shoe-string on purpose to keep me tame and humble—'

'That's not true. You know I'd be very glad—'

'If I went to Australia and was never heard of again. Thanks very much! No such luck.'

'That wasn't what—'

'I'm afraid of the future. I want to be set up properly. I'm sick and tired of living on hand-outs.'

'You're not living on hand-outs. I give you a regular allowance—'

'You've taken my life. Christ, I'm thirty-one, and I'm terrified of poverty and old age. That's what you've done to me!'

'You know exactly where you are financially—'

'Up Shit's Creek without a paddle! I want a house. I want you to buy me a house.'

'I can't! You know what houses cost now!'

'Well, sell something. Sell your other bloody house. Let her live in a flat for a change.'

'Oh Em dear, don't be silly. Don't let's start up this sort of mechanical argument again. We had it last week, we'll have it next week—'

'We haven't had *this* argument before. Remember. I've given up my job and I'm bloody well—'

'Please. When you use that awful tone we both stop being human beings and become machines.'

'We used to be two happy machines stimulating each other.'

'Oh go to sleep.'

'You wish I was dead, don't you, *don't you?*'

'Stop speaking in that tone.'

'Go to sleep, he says. Do you imagine either of us can sleep now?'

'Look, kid, please. I've got to work tomorrow.'

'Work! Don't make me laugh! You call it work chatting with women about their sex lives? Nice work if you can get it!'

'Just stop talking, will you.'

'Do you imagine I'm going to let you go to sleep and leave me with the thoughts I've got?'

'I've got thoughts too—'

'What's the use of sleep anyway, when it's nothing but a nightmare.'

'We're in this hell together. Let's at least be kind to each other.'

'I've been being kind to you for years and getting kicked in the teeth for it.'

'I've done what I can.'

'What sort of ruddy nonsense is that, I'd like to know! "Done what you can"! You wait and see what you'll be able to do when you have to! People never get justice until they start being violent about it, then the others cough up pretty quick. I'm going to make you cough up. It's just about my turn, isn't it?'

'I'll show you my bank account—'

'I don't mean money, I mean real stuff, action, blood. God, I've been fading away, I hardly know myself. I've got all tame and timid. No wonder you've stopped loving me. Maybe a little violence will make me real again.'

'Stop it, kid. You've said all this before.'

'That's right, look at your watch! Soon you'll be saying that you've got to go. You haven't got to go. You can stay here all day if you want to. You don't want to.'

'I'm not free any more than you are. Do you think I enjoy this situation—?'

'Change it, then.'

'You know there's nothing we can do.'

'I'm not talking about we. I'm talking about me. God, you've made me into a bloody wet. I'm a fighter and you've made me into a weak person. I'm not a weak person. I'll never forgive you. I'm a fighter by nature but because I loved you I put up with it all without a whimper. God, what I've put up with! I've been as quiet as a little mouse for years. No wonder you think you can make me accept anything. Well, you're fucking wrong.'

'You haven't been quiet for years, you've been screaming. And now that vile Pinn is here to listen.'

'Perhaps I want a witness for when you kill me.'

'Don't be silly, Em.'

'I know you want to kill me. I know I'm just a nightmare to you. You'd like to strangle me. Well, go ahead.'

'You're drunk.

'So are you. You ought to see your face now. You look like a bloated gangster. All right, now tell me what I look like.'

'Em, *stop*. Use a bit of self-control.'

'You used to say your relation with Mrs Placid was so dull because there was no violence in it.'

76

'I'm tired of violence.'

'You mean you're tired of me. I was just for kicks, I suppose.'

'Please, dearest Em—'

'Oh don't get smarmy, that won't let you out. Handsome is as handsome does. At least Pinn's always stood by me and helped me.'

'She's in love with you, can't you see that? She's always been a mischief-maker. I won't have her in the house, I've told you, I mean it.'

'If you don't like my friends you can stay away.'

'I won't keep bloody Pinn in drink.'

'You come less and less often anyway. Why don't you stay away altogether. That's what you'd like to do.'

'You know I'll never abandon you, you know I'll be faithful—'

'That's machine talk. I wish I had a quid for every time you've said that. Anyway, do you call this faithfulness? You do the bloody minimum and you know it. All your faithfulness does for me is prevent me from finding someone else who'd really love me and look after me. God, to think I've given my whole life to you and it's bloody dust and ashes.'

'Em, be a little kind to me, please. Just for a change.'

'Not that I'd care if you did come less often. Sometimes when you aren't around I feel almost happy, well not happy, that's impossible, but sort of contented, for a minute, now and then. Your visits just upset everything, they're so bloody meaningless, they upset me, they upset Luca—'

'Em, just try—'

'I pray every day that I'll stop loving you.'

'Please, let's break out of this circle.'

'All right, let's! Suppose you go tomorrow and tell Mrs Placid all about me and Luca and how you're going to set us up in a house and live with us and visit her in her flat once a week!'

'You know I can't do that—'

'I don't know anything of the sort, that's the point! Can't you see this thing from my position for bloody once? Why shouldn't she suffer for a change? Why shouldn't she share the suffering, why should I do it all?'

'It wouldn't be sharing. You wouldn't suffer less if she suffered more.'

'Wouldn't I just! I'd never stop laughing!'

'You don't just want revenge—'

'Why shouldn't I want revenge? Your bloody bourgeois genteel set-up over there, I'd like to smash it to pieces.'

77

'All right, let off steam, you don't mean any of this.'

'Don't I? You wait. I'll carry the war into the enemy's camp. War on the bloody rich. I know how the poor live. I only took up with you because I was afraid of poverty and what it does to people. Night after night I saw my step-father bashing my mother until at last he killed her.'

'I'm not responsible for your step-father.'

'Yes, you are. You're the principle of evil in my life. You're just my stepfather by other means. There's psychology for you.'

'Let's stop this slanging match, shall we? You always boast of coming out of the gutter, but at least you can behave like an educated person—'

'You mean like a lady. Like dear Mrs Placid. I know it's a class thing. She's top drawer and rich—'

'She isn't, actually—'

'Of course I want revenge. I want her to know what a heel she's married to.'

'It's not her fault—'

'What do I care? It's not my fault either.'

'Yes it is. It's mostly my fault, but it's partly yours too.'

'Do you want me to scream?'

'Anyway, she does suffer. She doesn't suspect *this*, but she knows she's lost my love.'

'That valuable commodity! That was true once. I think you've gone back to her. Do you make love to her?'

'Of course not!'

'I don't believe you. You lie to her. You probably lie to me. In a year or two you'll ditch us both and go off with a young girl. You're just a typical male chauvinist.'

'That's Pinn's mindless terminology. At least do your own thinking.'

'If I hadn't torn up all your love letters in a rage I could have sent them to Mrs Placid in a parcel. I'm going to ring her up tomorrow morning.'

'You know you won't do anything of the sort. Do you imagine our relation would survive if you did?'

'I'm getting a bit tired of that old bogyman. Why not let's try and see what it'll survive and what it won't survive. I'm tired of waiting for my rights so that Mrs Placid's boy won't be damaged. Am I to wait till he's thirty? Let him take his chance. My boy's damaged, why shouldn't hers be? You saw what Luca was like this evening.'

'Is he talking more?'

'No. He hasn't spoken to me for a week. He talks to Pinn though.'

'What about?'

'I don't know. I overheard a long spiel the other day about wriggly tadpoles. But if I come near him he plays dumb. He'll be a fair mess when he grows up. And you won't even go and see his schoolmaster.'

'There's no point—'

'I hope you'll be prepared to support him in some genteel mental home. That'll be another little item of expense.'

'Well, I suggested adoption, it was you who wanted to keep him.'

'I wanted to keep you.'

'So it was just blackmail.'

'Have you really got the face to taunt me now because I wanted to keep my own child? You're a bloody phenomenon.'

'You deliberately turn him against me.'

'Don't be a clot. It's automatic. "Where's Daddy?" Not that he ever asks that now, he never mentions you, God knows what goes on in his little head. Remember how we used to think of pretending you were a sailor? God, we were pathetic.'

'Yes, I remember that. We've gone a long way together, kid. Let's still look after each other. Please please be patient a little longer.'

'O.K., but what are we waiting for? For her to die, or what?'

'Emily, need we have this endless fruitless personal talk?'

'What do you want us to talk about, Racine? I thought personal talk was your thing.'

'It isn't. I don't talk personal talk all the time with Harriet.'

'Don't mention that name! I don't want to hear what happens in your other set-up. Of course you don't, you don't need to. She's secure, she's got you, she doesn't have to bother about personal things, because they're all hunky-dory. She can think about the ruddy dinner service and whether she'll go to evensong. Oh I'm the flesh and she's the spirit, don't tell me, I know! I'll write it all up for the Sunday papers one day. "I was an every other Tuesday wife." God, sometimes I feel like people who go to an airport with a machine gun and just shoot everyone within sight. You simply have no idea how much I suffer.'

'You feel jealousy and spite and resentment. I feel guilt. That's worse.'

'Is it? Get rid of it then, do what I'm always asking you to do!'

'It's no good, that wouldn't do it. We're simply trapped, caught—'

'Who's "we"? You say that just in order to stop thinking. You're such a bloody coward. You stay with her out of cowardice, you daren't step out of line. You daren't think, so you live in a dream. At least I used to bring a little reality into your life. Over there you live in a bourgeois dream world.'

'Do stop using the word "bourgeois". You don't even know what it means.'

'It means dream. At least here it's real. It may be bloody ghastly but it's real.'

'You said a little while ago it wasn't real. Or did I misunderstand you?'

'I could kill you sometimes. You know what I mean. Her place is real, it's part of society, people come there, she's somebody. This place is nowhere at all. I'm just loose, lost, rattling about, a bit of bloody scrap. No wonder I can't make friends or look anybody in the face. The women down at the school just stare at me and pass by. They know I'm an unmarried mum. I see bloody no one except you and bloody Pinn and the Welfare busybody. Welfare! Christ! And then you have the face to complain about my conversation! If we had some friends together like ordinary married people do, we might have something else to talk about except ourselves. We could have ordinary talk and gossip and that and look at other things together, and not be always staring at each other. Why do we have to be shut up all the time in this cage? Why can't we have friends together? I'd like to meet your friend Montague Small, I've been watching his Milo Fane series on telly, it's smashing. He's an interesting person. I'd like to meet him. He wouldn't tell Mrs Placid, would he?'

'It's impossible.'

'Why? Do I just have to live by your bloody decrees? Oh God, if you knew how much I wish we could live together in a proper house like real people and give dinner parties, instead of living in this hole like blasted criminals.'

'I'm sorry, my darling—'

'I daren't even cry in front of you now, you get so ratty. It seems mad to say it, but I've simply lived on love all these years, I'm like a bloody saint living on the bloody sacrament. I've got all thin and fine by living on pure love! Christ, I'm tough. If I wasn't I'd be dead!'

'Yes, you're tough, kid. You're my tough girl, my Berlin prostitute, my little blackamoor princess.'

'You've gone smarmy again. You're trying to make me stop. I know your tricks.'

'My glinting jewel, my jack of diamonds —'

'My Queen of the Night. Remember how you used to call me that? I'm fed up with being Queen of the Night. I want to be Queen of the Day for a change.'

'Darling, just pity me a little. I'm miserable and desperate too.'

'If it was just you and me I'd comfort you, I'd stop you being miserable. I'd make you happy like women do. But you can't expect me to feel sorry for you when you're mostly somewhere else. You do see. You asked for my love and got it and now you're deliberately destroying it. I said I prayed to stop loving you, but I don't really want to. It's what my whole life is for and I can't change that now. Oh my sweetikin, how can such a love as ours stop, it can't stop ever, can it? It is a great love, isn't it, isn't it?'

'Yes.'

'You must come to me properly, you must find a way through, you must, you must, you must.'

'Yes.'

'I know we quarrel, but I love you so much, you are my whole life, you are everything. I haven't got anything else. You will make it all well, won't you? You can, I know you can.'

'Yes.'

'And soon?'

'Yes, yes.'

'When?'

'Emily —'

'All right, all right. God, I'm so tired and now it's nearly time to get up. There's the sun shining outside. You know what. You've killed me and sent me to hell, and you must descend to the underworld to find me and make me live again. If you don't come for me, I'll become a demon and drag you down into the dark.'

Blaise tended to leave Putney earlier and earlier. These early morning departures were terrible, and were indeed largely symbolic since he could rarely hope to get back to Hood House before Harriet was awake. He wanted to represent each occasion to her as exceptional ('I simply couldn't get away') and also to be able to tell himself that he had not really 'spent the night.' He condemned himself for inconsistency and meanness and cowardice, but could not now resist the sheer longing to get away as soon as he decently could from Emily's accusing voice and vicinity. He could, when once away, put himself together again with remarkable speed. He longed for the return to Harriet and calm. And mad as this might seem, he actually did feel calm a good deal of the time at Hood House, and Putney then seemed hardly to exist.

Emily was either asleep or pretending to be as he pulled his trousers on. Her head was well down under the sheet, only a tuft of black hair showing. Last time he had lifted the sheet and found her crying. Today he felt unable to care whether she was crying or sleeping. Richardson and Little Bilham, who always jumped onto the bed as he left it and occupied his warm place, regarded him, like stray malevolent intelligences escaped from Emily's consciousness, with cynical unwinking eyes of an almost Egyptian antiquity. He did not even stay this time to shave, but tiptoed quickly out, dreading any recall whether angry or tearful. Out in the little hall he gathered up his things and pulled on his new grey herring-bone overcoat of very light tweed. He felt utterly exhausted, lacerated, wearied to pieces. The sun was well up, but the morning was still cold in its brightness. As he moved quickly to the front door he saw that the door of Luca's room was open. Luca, in pyjamas, was standing motionless just inside the door and now became visible to Blaise. Blaise stopped. His son looked at him with his round dark eyes, but without any change of expression or attitude. Blaise, to say something, said in a whisper, 'Mummy's still asleep.' Luca said nothing. A sort of anguish leapt at Blaise's throat like a wild animal, but he remained as expressionless as his son. He raised his hand in a vague salute and hurried on and out of the door.

With immense relief he closed the door softly behind him and walked quickly past the silent curtained windows of the other flats along the tiled path to the road. He breathed deeply, already beginning to feel better. The cold clarifying sun shone upon innumerable garish roses in the little gardens of the trim rows of semi-detached villas by which he had to pass on the way to where he had prudently left the Volkswagen, just short of the Upper Richmond Road. For security reasons he never parked outside the flats, and never twice in the same place.

He had nearly reached the car when he realized that someone with an accelerating pace was walking along the pavement behind him. He half turned and saw Constance Pinn.

Pinn was, as she sometimes described herself, a founder member of the situation. She had become Emily's char and then Luca's baby-sitter (Blaise used to take Emily out to dinner in those days) soon after the inception of the *ménage* at Putney. Emily had early on told her everything over a drink. Blaise had scolded Emily for this indiscretion, but as Emily pointed out Pinn was both necessary and hard to deceive. Pinn had indeed been useful and, apparently, reliable.

Blaise's view of Pinn had changed a lot during the time in question. Pinn herself had changed a lot. It was difficult now to remember her as a char: although Pinn had always made a joke of her charing, thus indicating that it was a temporary expedient, taken on simply because she was, to use one of her own favourite words, 'skint', and was not to be regarded as in any way placing her socially. In fact, socially speaking, Pinn was in fairly rapid motion. She had managed, during the time Blaise and Emily had known her, considerably to 'better' herself, not only financially but in profounder and more important ways. Emily unconsciously and Blaise consciously had helped her a good deal in what she herself called 'Operation Excelsior'. She had acquired a new voice and had learnt how to dress herself. Blaise suggested books for her to read, told her the answer to large and carefully posed questions ('Which are the most important plays of Shakespeare?' 'Which are the ten great novels?') and provided a controllable testing place for her new and more ambitious personality. Pinn's ambitions were laudible, her conduct modest and discreet. Of course (Blaise early saw) Emily had to have a woman to talk to, and this one seemed remarkably harmless. All the same, when he heard those sharp accelerating footsteps behind him and turned to see those slinky spectacles glinting in the sun, Blaise's heart sank.

It was of course largely his own fault. He now saw that he should never for a moment have encouraged any sort of complicity between himself and Pinn. To do so was not only disloyal to Emily, it was dangerous to himself. He ought to have remained, with Pinn, bland benevolent and aloof. He ought

83

thereby to have boxed Pinn firmly into her roll as Emily's necessary confidante. He should have behaved with Pinn as if there was nothing odd in the situation at all, he ought never to have betrayed any weakening of his confidence of his own complete mastery of it. It was easy to see all this now. *Then* he had had another urgent use for Pinn. In the earlier years leaving Putney had been a very different matter. Then he had left as late as he dared, and felt in every parting the anguish of a possible loss. How could it be that such a young and devastatingly attractive girl should not be surrounded by admirers, and that those admirers should not besiege her with passion, with cunning, with costly gifts, with temptations of every sort? Blaise did not doubt Emily's love (it would have been impossible to do so) but the fact was that he was married and had not yet managed to set himself free. Emily was often solitary. Supposing some eligible suitor were to appear when she was feeling depressed? It could happen. Did young men come to the flat? Were there people who simply waited for him to go? Of course Emily denied this passionately, but of course Emily would. How could he find out the truth? Pinn practically proposed herself for the role of spy. It seemed hard to believe it now, but Blaise could recall on many occasions pressing pound notes into Pinn's hand.

Pinn clearly enjoyed her work and relished the 'reporting sessions'. She never had anything adverse to report in the matter of rivals, but she gave Blaise long and often alarmingly penetrating analyses of Emily's states of mind. Blaise only gradually began to realize how intelligent, how *conscious*, this comparatively uneducated woman was; and he began to feel uneasy. It was not exactly that he feared that Pinn was capable of blackmailing him, though this idea did flash on him occasionally. He had begun to feel vaguely 'involved' with her, though not in any obvious way. (Of course they never touched each other.) He felt a desire to get rid of Pinn, but could not see how this was to be done. He simply did not want to have the implications of what he was doing rehearsed to him all the time by this appallingly clear-eyed observer.

Whose side was Pinn on anyway? At first Pinn had seemed to be almost sycophantically upon his. She had seemed to him too critical of Emily, to the point of disloyalty. 'That girl just doesn't know how lucky she is' and so on. Later on he felt that now keener edge of criticism being turned against himself. He began to dread the interviews, which invariably depressed him. The pound notes stopped passing. Blaise tried to elude his

84

relentless agent, he tried to indicate that *that* relationship was at an end. But Pinn refused to understand. She still kept discreetly accosting him, conspiratorial and smiling. More lately Blaise had begun to fear something else, nebulous but horrible. What was Pinn, anyway? He now thought that he discerned in her, something which she tried to hide from him, a definite possessiveness about Emily. Pinn claimed to have numerous men friends (though Emily said she had never met any of them) and professed to lead what she called a 'helter-skelter life' (though she kept it well away from the Upper Richmond Road). But supposing Pinn was just quietly getting her claws into Emily? Suppose in some awful way she and Emily were ganging up against him? Emily seemed to need Pinn more and more and was always quoting her. And now Pinn had actually got herself inside the house.

'Wait a sec.' Pinn never used his name.

'Let's sit in the car,' said Blaise. They walked on and Blaise let Pinn into the passenger seat of the Volkswagen. They sat side by side and Blaise simply waited.

'You're off early,' said Pinn.

'You're up early.'

'I wanted to see you.'

'You mustn't trouble, you know.'

'No trouble at all, it's a pleasure.'

'Anything special?' He could not get away from the conspiratorial tone.

'You know she's let me a room?' Emily was always 'she'.

'Yes. Good idea.'

'You don't object? Naturally if you objected I'd find other accommodation.'

'Of course I don't object, I'm delighted.'

'How obliging of you.'

Pinn's new voice, clear and a little loud, though low in pitch, still somewhat precise and deliberate like that of a stammerer, was perfectly adapted to the concealment of feeling. Pinn now spoke more purely than Emily (who exaggerated her provincialism for Blaise's benefit), but with remarkably little expression. The effect of power was not lessened.

'Where did she get that fur coat?' said Blaise. Machine, machine, he thought. Oh God, that conversation last night or this morning or whenever that devil-ridden scrap of nightmare had been. How could two rational beings go on and on simply saying the same awful things to each other week after week, month after month?'

'I sold it to her.'

'How much for?'

'Twenty pounds.'

Someone's lying, thought Blaise, presumably Emily.

'I don't see why she shouldn't have a new coat,' said Pinn. 'I see you've got one. Very nice too, if I may say so, it suits you. And hers isn't even a *new* coat. It's genuine squirrel though. I bought it off one of the rich kids at school.'

'I don't mind her having the coat!'

'Good. I thought you did.'

'What on earth possessed her to give up her job?'

'She didn't jump, she was pushed. Did she tell you she'd given it up? She's a bit sensitive and touchy about it all. She got the sack.'

'Why?'

'It was this Kiki St Loy.'

'Who?'

'Kiki St Loy. She's the one I bought the coat off. She's a French girl, well partly French, she just began to break up Emily's classes, made a dead set at her, made her life hell. Em simply couldn't cope and the Head asked her to leave.'

'I see.' Poor Emily, thought Blaise, feeling hatred for Pinn.

'This Kiki St Loy is very beautiful and just eighteen, and I think that got Em's goat too. Em's got to an age when—'

'I see. Nothing else special?' This question, also mechanical, meant: any men?

'No, no, nothing of that sort. She lives like a nun. Since school's packed up she hardly sees anybody. She just sits at home all day and watches the television. No fun and games. You needn't worry about *that*.'

Since when had Pinn managed to turn all her remarks into veiled accusations? 'Well, I must go now. Thanks.' Blaise never used Pinn's name either.

'Wait another sec or two. There's something I want to tell you.'

Blaise turned to Pinn. Pinn was not bad looking, with short slightly fluffy auburn hair, very round cheeks and pouting lips. Her new spectacles were narrow, oriental, with long shining spurs rising up on either side. The intelligent eyes behind the glass were mottled light brown and green. Pinn smirked. It was an accomplice moment.

'Yes?'

'It's about Luca.'

Luca. Blaise had gone on and on refusing to see Luca's

86

schoolmaster, though he knew that he *ought*, if that word still had any sense, to go and see him. It was not that Blaise feared a breach of security, though that anxiety was always with him. He was afraid of what he might learn, afraid of an involvement, a development, the necessity of another visit, discussions, decisions, problems. He simply had not the time or the energy, or rather he passionately did not want to give his attention to this matter, to have these difficulties as well as all the rest, however much his conscience might torment him about this extra and especially unforgivable failure. Of course Emily did not understand, any more than she understood about holidays, because Blaise could not explain, could not tell her his reasons, which were even shabbier than those she attributed to him. He had refused to give her money to go to Paris not out of meanness (as she thought) but out of jealousy, out of primitive dog-in-the-manger possessiveness. She might meet men in Paris; and he dared not tell her this in case it should put the very idea into her head.

He still felt jealousy; he still felt, in spite of everything, panic and frenzy at the thought of her taking another lover. That was another complication for which, beset as he was, he simply had not got time. It was mad. He kept Harriet (who never complained) short of holidays so as not to seem to Emily to be grossly unjust, and he could not help feeling that this was something else for which Emily ought to be grateful, only he did not dare to tell Emily this either, because he must not be seen deliberately to condone and continue a situation which of course they both knew he deliberately condoned and continued. He offered her enough provocation to violence as it was. It was crazy. And now Pinn, in her role as his needling mentor, was going to talk to him about Luca and to tell him that he ought to go to the school. Luca had said nothing to Blaise for over two months, although Blaise had tried to talk to him and had bought him a woolly pig and a mechanical mouse, and a chemistry set. Emily said Luca chattered to Pinn. She had heard him telling Pinn about some 'wriggly tadpoles'. Why would his son not talk to him about the wriggly tadpoles? Everything now was an accusation. Blaise stared at Pinn with fear and resentment.

'Did you know that Luca has been over to your place?'

'Been over — where?'

'To your place. To Harriet's place.'

'*What?*'

'Yes. He's been over several times. Twice anyway.'

The sun was blotted out. Blaise saw in a rent and jagged darkness Pinn's pert round-cheeked face ablaze with interested malice. 'It's impossible.'

'Not at all. He certainly went.'

'But—no, no—it can't be—how could he know where to go? How could he get there?'

'He stowed away in the back of your car. The first time anyway. He hid under a rug.'

Blaise turned round, half expecting to see his son's grave intent little face gazing at him from the back seat.

'How do you know this?'

'He told me.'

'How did he know it was my car?'

'He's known about the car for ages. I didn't tell you as I thought it might bother you. He must have seen you arriving some time when he was coming back from school. Or he might have followed you out one morning. He's very sly.'

'It can't be true, it simply can't be true. Children invent the most fantastic things. It's all an invention. What did he say exactly?'

'He says he hid in the white car and went over to Daddy's other house. He said it was a big house with long windows down below and little square windows up above, and he hid in the garden behind a big tall tree. I asked him about what else he did, and he said he saw a beautiful lady and a boy, a grown-up boy he called him. I said "I wonder who they are", and he said, "I know." Then he said, "I went again on the evening of school sports day. I saved my dinner and took it to the dogs." He said there were a lot of dogs.'

'Oh, my God. What else did he say?'

'Nothing else. He started talking baby talk. And I thought I'd better just smile and keep quiet in case he started shouting about it.'

'How can a child of that age have done that journey by himself?'

'He's very independent. All those children are. He's travelled all round London on the underground. He plays truant from school and he often just disappears in the evenings and comes in late. Emily says he's out at play, but really she has no idea where he is.'

'She never told me this.'

'There are plenty of things she doesn't tell you because she's afraid you'll get angry. She likes to save them up and then spill them all at once when she's in a rage herself.'

'Yes, yes. Christ, does Emily know this, about Luca going over —?'

'No. I said nothing of course, and he hasn't told her. I'd know if he had, she'd be screaming the place down.'

Blaise looked ahead along the road. People were beginning to leave their houses to go to work, opening their front doors, closing them again, walking down their garden paths, unlatching their gates. The clear sun shone upon the well-mown lawns and the bright orange roses. The sheer quiet ordinariness of it all made Blaise want to gesticulate and shout. How could such quietness exist all about when in one soul there was such a tumult?

'Don't tell Emily,' he said.

'Of course not.'

But he felt, this is the end, it must be. This is it. At the thought of Luca standing underneath the acacia tree he felt an emotion too confused and intense to be identified as either misery or fear. The inconceivable, the unimaginable, had happened, already it had entered his life, defeating logic, impossible, destructive. There. How *could* those two worlds meet? Their utter separateness was the guarantee itself of any intelligibility and order. Their separateness was the prerequisite of any thought, the presupposition of the world, it was what thought was about, what the world was about. Blaise had never feared mental breakdown. But at the idea of what Luca had so simply done, passing through a steel barrier as if it were paper, passing through the looking-glass, he glimpsed for a second the terrible underlying chaos of his own mind. Luca had gazed at Hood House, had seen Harriet and David, had fed the dogs.

Blaise's face expressed nothing. He said to Pinn, 'Well, thanks. I must go now.'

'What are you going to do?' said Pinn, as she got out of the car.

'I don't know.' He drove away in the direction of Putney Bridge.

Pinn looked after the white car. The interest, the dramatic unpredictability of it all, had enlivened her plump face, making it almost beautiful. Out of a sheer momentary excitement she began to laugh.

Monty was looking out of his bedroom window into the garden which the grey light of the dawn was just revealing. He had never noticed before that it was possible from here to see into the orchard. How huge the orchard looked in this light, almost like a forest, a multitude of tree trunks under its umbrella of gathered dark. As Monty stared at it he saw with a thrill of alarm that there seemed to be some people moving about under the trees. He peered, trying to discern the shadowy intruders. Three figures were now visible upon the lawn, clear of the trees, three figures in long black flowing robes. They are nuns, he thought with amazement. What are three nuns doing in my garden in the dawn, shall I go down and speak to them, what shall I do? As he hesitated he saw that the nuns were hurrying down the long lawn towards the house, their dark habits flying. They were running. He realized: they are frightened, *terrified*. What are they running away from? Terrified himself he watched the fleeing figures approach the house: and then saw with sudden clarity the face of the leading nun. It was Sophie, her face contracted with fear and anguish. Why, she is an old woman now, he thought. And what is she so frightened of, what is she running away from? Yes, she is an old woman, quite old, her face is wrinkled and her hair is white. I thought she had died, but she has simply grown old. Perhaps death just *is* growing old, and nobody told me?

Monty awoke. He experienced the split-second interval, then the searing memory. He remembered Sophie's face in the later stages of her illness, all wrinkled up, like a child's, with fear and pain, tears constantly in her eyes. Death had so cruelly separated her, still living, from him.

It was five o'clock and the birds were singing with crazy joy. He rose and pulled back the curtains and looked out into the garden, smaller and brighter than in his dream, but still alienated and menacing and strange. A black shape moved round the corner from the orchard and then proceeded with deliberation across the lawn. It was Ajax. Near to the house the dog looked up, saw him and paused. Ill-omened animal, thought Monty, as he and the dog stared at each other in the early light.

'How was poor Magnus?' asked Harriet, brushing the crumbs off the red check tablecloth and conveying them in her hand to the kitchen sink.

'As usual.'

'What?'

'*As usual.*'

'Poor you, you are so tired,' said Harriet. 'Can't you put off this morning's patients? You can't stay up talking nearly all night and then work properly the next day.'

'I've got Dr Ainsley and Mrs Batwood coming. I have to see them.'

'Well, tell them you're exhausted and get rid of them quick. You look utterly worn out. I wonder if you're getting the 'flu?'

'I am perfectly all right!' said Blaise, returning his coffee cup to his saucer with a crack which made Harriet wince.

She was silent for a moment, swilling some water around in an unwashed saucepan and watching her husband. He was very tired and edgy this morning.

'Well, I wish Magnus would hurry up and get better. I see him as such a kind sweet man, but he's so inconsiderate to you.'

'He pays through the nose. That's all that matters, isn't it.'

'What were you discussing with him?'

'It is not a discussion.'

'Talking about then. Had he had any good dreams? I think Magnus has quite the most original dreams of any of your patients.'

'He dreamt he was an egg.'

'An egg?'

'He was a huge white egg floating in a sea of turquoise blue, and he was everything that there was.'

'It sounds a nice dream.'

'No dream is nice for Magnus. All dream experiences fill him with terror. He now feels that all his limbs are withdrawing inside his body and his face is flattening out and his features are disappearing. He keeps looking in the mirror to make sure his nose hasn't vanished.'

'But he doesn't really think he's turning into an egg?'

'It's not clear what "really" is with someone like Magnus. The fears are real.'

'Did he cry a lot?'

'He always does.'

'Poor thing. What does the dream mean?'

'Fear of castration.'

'What a pity. It sounds so beautiful,' said Harriet. 'It's a painter's dream.' She pictured the great white egg, tinged a little with ivory, floating in the deeply saturated turquoise ocean. She saw it clearly in her mind, and the image soothed her.

'It's connected with his compulsive eating. Men who are failures often disguise their castration fears as a desire to engulf everything. When you've swallowed the world there's nothing left to be frightened of. It's the pattern of the failed artist.'

'Did he say anything about the bishop with the wooden leg?'

'He said he was catching up.'

'Did he say anything about me?'

'He said, "give my respects to the lady".'

'I love the way he calls me the lady, it's like something in a legend. I feel I very much exist for Magnus. I'm sure I could help him just by talking to him a bit.'

'Magnus doesn't need vague emotional female chit-chat. He probably needs electric shocks.'

'You've always been against shock therapy.'

'Someone like Magnus is better off dead anyway.'

'You *are* cross today. He's not suicidal, is he?'

'Of course I'm against shock therapy. Anything serious and scientific would put me out of business.'

'Darling, do have a rest before the doctor arrives.'

'Is that fat friend of Monty's coming in again? What's his name?'

'Edgar Demarnay. Yes. He wants to talk about Monty. He thinks he can help Monty. I want him to meet David, only they keep missing each other. You know he's head of a—'

'God, I'm so fed up with helping people. And all this sympathetic bloody hand-holding you go in for. You seem to be collecting men now like you collect bloody dogs.'

'Darling B, if you'd rather—'

92

'Oh go ahead, hold his hand. He'll probably fall in love with you too.'

'You know Monty isn't in love with me.'

'He soon will be if you go on playing the ministering angel. Monty needs electric shocks, he should just bloody pull himself together. Well, let them all come. I'll turn my patients over to you and you can hold their hands.'

'Darling—please—you're just tired—'

'Oh hell—Sorry, dear girl—Sorry, sorry—' Blaise left the kitchen and pulled the door violently to behind him.

Harriet felt as if she might cry. She never quarrelled with her husband, because she simply never answered him back when he became angry. But these scenes, which happened rarely, though recently rather more often perhaps, hurt her deeply, although she knew that they were simply signs of tiredness and strain. He always uses such bad language when he's been with Magnus, she thought. He gives himself so much to Magnus, he comes back drained. He is so absurdly generous to people who need him. She did not ever doubt her absolute connectedness with Blaise, but these momentary breaks of contact were simply very painful, and she suffered them like headaches without regarding them as deep signs. At such times she felt how stupid she was, she overheard her own remarks as those of a stupid woman, uneducated, insensitive, unable to say the right thing. No wonder Blaise got crosser and crosser. He must wish sometimes that he had a witty intellectual wife.

'What did you do with Kiki last night?' said Emily. 'You were bloody late.'

'We drank.'

'Where?'

'At the pub. Then in her car. We drove out into the country.'

'So she climbed in again?'

'Yes.'

'That school's a laugh.'

'Well, she is eighteen. Or pretends to be.'

'God, I wish I was eighteen again, I'd do a few things differently!'

'How was Blaise?'

'Bloody. He's so spineless. I think he's simply frightened of wifie. Well, he's frightened of everything, frightened of scandal, frightened of having to make a decision. I put on the heat but it's no good. He just wants to be let off and I let him off. Jesus wept!'

'Men are terribly conventional about marriage,' said Pinn. 'They chase younger women, but they want their lovely virtuous home life as well. Blaise is conventional and timid. Naturally wifie wins in the end.'

'When is the end?' said Emily. They were sitting over their coffee after breakfast. Luca had gone to school. Gone anyway. The kitchen was hot and smelt of frying and an overflowing bin. Grease, which seemed to drift in through the window on the warm urban air, lightly covered everything. Any object touched showed fingerprints. Even the tablecloth did. The distant traffic snarled and screamed. 'I wish I had the guts to kill myself.'

Pinn was picking her teeth with the orange stick which she had been using to press back the cuticle on her fingernails. She said, 'You ought to get really tough with him.'

'I'm always tough! It gets me bloody nowhere!'

'You complain endlessly, but that's just a form of weakness. You just feebly annoy him, and that gives him energy to resist you. You must use real force. Tell him he's got to tell his wife or else you will.'

Emily was silent for a while. She was still wearing her pink quilted dressing-gown. It seemed hardly worth while getting dressed. Last night she had dreamt of a cat with a terrible deformed head. The cat had fallen down a drain and Emily had tried to pull it out. But there was nothing in the drain except black blobs of mud. The cat had disintegrated. 'I'm timid too,' she said. 'I'm afraid of losing him. There's Luca. And I just feel I can't cope with life any more. At least as things are Blaise is loyal, and he's as kind to me as I let him be. I'm the one who draws blood. I know he won't abandon me. I just can't face a bust-up, I can't face it. If I wrecked things for him, he might go mad with anger. Anything might happen. God, I'm a coward.'

'I agree,' said Pinn. 'You are a coward. I wouldn't stand for it in your place. At least I'd have a jolly good try at smashing

94

up his lousy marriage. Of course wifie has the edge when it's all hunky-dory and conventional and peaceful and great Mr Man is having the best of both worlds. But if wifie knew that Mr Man was a rotten liar and if she knew that he loved you like crazy and had been duping her for years, she'd have to change her tune. Home life wouldn't look so nice and cosy then. After he'd heard her scream and sob for a change he might decide to leg it to you. As things are his lovely legitimate home is a bolt-hole. He can go back there and lick his wounds. Spoil it, smash it, and he'll have to run somewhere. That's your chance to catch him properly. Have you thought of that?'

'Christ. I've thought of everything,' said Emily. 'I just feel I can't be sure — what would happen — he would hate me — it's all so absolutely — unpredictable.'

'Maybe,' said Pinn. 'Still if I were in your place I should want to see her tears.'

My darling boy,

I am thinking of you with so much love, I see your dear face so vividly before me, I feel I could reach out and touch you. Do understand? Perhaps no man can conceive what a mother's love is. Surely God should be thought of as a mother. But need I tell you my feelings, dear? We two have always vibrated in unison. We two, then and now and always. Such love is so great that it cannot but help in affliction. Nay, I know it does. I think about you all the time, though I am busy with my little village cares as usual. Today for instance you have been with me to the alms houses, to the rectory, to the antique shop, to the play group, to the Women's Institute Committee. I *carry* you, dear child, as I did once when you were a babe. I will come to you soon. Meanwhile make no decisions about real estate . . .

Monty had torn up the letter after one quick perusal. His mother had written him love letters when he was younger, but never since his marriage. The change of style had been designed to hurt. Now there could be love letters again. How much his dear mother must enjoy these fluxes of feeling. God is mother, mother is God. Leonie had never deeply or absolutely loved her curate husband, there had been reservations. Marriage had been a social and emotional disappointment to her. She had played earnestly at religion as now she played earnestly at Social Work. Monty had been for her the erotic, the mystical. His literary success and fame had crowned her life.

Monty had not given up his mother. He had never disloyally assented to Sophie's frequent criticisms of her mother-in-law, though he had laughed at Sophie's spiteful jokes, of which the sheer *joie de vivre* seemed to lessen the bite. He did not feel appalled by the great machine of maternal love which, silenced, purred strongly away. Sensitive to those vibrations, he simply averted his attention, rose to no challenge, understood no hint. With precocious prescience as quite a small boy he had decided that he would not let his mother kill him, as it seemed that she might easily do, by the sheer intensity of her love, like a huge sow rolling over on its young. The small boy stiffened, receded. There was a scarcely perceptible coldness. Leonie felt it and was mortally afraid and concealed her fear. Monty felt the hidden fear and learnt an enduring lesson. They eyed each other like circling adversaries. Somewhere inside that silent contest there came into being the embryo of Milo Fane.

Monty was lying in the orchard grass. It was the afternoon. The sun, which had filled the whole sky as if attempting to blot out its blue with sheer gold, sizzled through the green leaves in sudden stars and needles of dazzling light. A very very distant cuckoo drew attention to the silence. Under the canopy of the leaves the air was hot and sultry and smelt of hay. The little haystack in the corner of the orchard exuded a damp delicious almost burning smell as if it might burst into flames at any moment. There could be thunder later but there was as yet no menace in the thick sweet air. The grass was still green and lush in its second growth. Though sun-warmed, it had a jaunty seeming of coolness. Monty, in shirt sleeves and sweating, was lying on his stomach, propping his chin. David, in flowery beach shirt over swimming trunks, was extended close by, lying on his back. They had been talking intermittently.

'I dreamt that a large blue flying-fish was wandering about my room,' David was saying, 'it was wandering about in the air just above my head and I was terribly worried because I felt I ought to catch it and put it in water otherwise it would

96

die, and I kept running after it with a butterfly net, and then suddenly I was in the school chapel, and the fish came down quietly like a bird and lay on the altar . . .'

How beautiful the boy is, thought Monty. That glow of youth, the perfect object of desire. How bitter, the fading of the body, the absolute condemnation to the loss of the first lustre. How stupidly he had wasted his own youth, joyless, pretending, building up that cold 'frightful' *persona* which had so much impressed fools like Edgar Demarnay. His brief love affairs had been self-conscious egocentric dramas. He had not even studied with passion. Perhaps surviving Leonie had impaired his strength. Perhaps that little whiff of her terror had inspired him too early with an unholy sense of power. No wonder Milo Fane, the remorseless killer who never smiled, had been his nemesis and the grave of his talent. Until Sophie he had been only half alive. Sophie's little neat splendours, her bright-faced energy, her crazy joy had glorified him, and given him the sheer strength required to support the pain which, with the other hand, she dealt him. Sometimes he felt like a victim constantly revived in order to suffer more. If only, he felt, he had not had to be so jealous, he could have got rid of Milo, he could have let Sophie, artless, thoughtless, brilliant, transform him into a human being, into an artist. If only jealousy had not had to mar that perfect love before death ended it. If only he had somehow known how to conduct himself differently. Well, he had tried, in hours of meditation. And what a wreck he was now. Was he destined to begin his manhood as Milo Fane and to complete it as Magnus Bowles?

'Dreams are rather marvellous, aren't they,' David was saying. 'They can be beautiful in a special way like nothing else. Even awful things in dreams have style, not like real things which disgust one, like watching the dogs eat.'

'There is a fresh pure innocence about some dream images,' said Monty, 'only one mustn't interrogate them too much.'

'You mean like my father?'

'Just let them come, visit, like birds.'

'You don't believe in "the deep dream life from which all life emerges" as my father puts it in his latest article?'

'No,' said Monty. 'A dream is a story you feel inclined to tell at breakfast time.'

'You can't mean that! Don't you think there are deep causes, machinery sort of, that it all means something?'

'It depends what you mean by "deep".'

'Is this like what you were saying earlier on about religious imagery?'

'Religious imagery is partly aesthetic,' said Monty. 'It's worked on. But it's *complice* in the same sort of way.'

'You mean — ?'

'It's all to do with the hygiene of the ego. A successful religion is a recipe for an innocent-feeling fantasy life and happy sex.'

'Even if one's a hermit or an ascetic on a pillar?'

'Especially if one's a hermit or an ascetic on a pillar.'

'My father says religion is based on the need for self-punishment.'

'Your father has his own favourite viewpoint. Some aspects of religion are self-punishment. Religion is a big business.'

'You don't believe in religion, do you, Monty?'

'I don't believe in that sort of religion.'

'But you believe in some sort, in the sort that would really be "deep"?'

Monty was silent for a while. He did not want to talk about these things to David, only David's youth made the conversation possible, but this also made it fruitless. Monty did not want to find himself seeking gratification in uttering impressive half-truths. In fact none of this could really be explained at all. 'Varro said that some gods died out of sheer neglect.'

'So — ?'

'When all the gods have died of neglect real religion can begin.'

'I don't understand. What about me and Jesus Christ?'

'Oh never mind about Jesus Christ,' said Monty. 'He'll go away. Like a rainbow goes away.'

'Well, I wish he'd be quick about it,' said David. 'Come to think of it, he was in that dream too. Yet how can he have been? He was the one who was trying to catch the blue flying-fish in his net, and we were in the school chapel — or was he the fish?'

Monty was looking at David's outstretched arm which was lying close to him in the grass. He studied the haze of short curving light-golden hairs, and the blue veins inside the elbow where the skin was delicate and almost white, and he felt a sudden impulse to lean forward and place his mouth there in the moist pit of the elbow and feel upon his lips the warm beating of the blood. Sophie is dead, thought Monty, and I am wanting to kiss a boy's arm. Is this some first horrible signal of a mindless return to life? If so, I reject it. But no, he replied to himself, it means nothing, or rather, like David's Jesus Christ, it doesn't matter. I must get beyond, I must get through, or else my fate is Magnus and the white egg.

'Why don't you try putting water into it?' said Harriet. 'Just put more and more water in and that will gradually reduce the dose.'

'I'd just drink more water to get the same amount of alcohol,' said Edgar. 'You see, my system knows, you can't dupe it.'

'Have you tried prayer?'

'What a wonderful woman you are! Not a woman in a thousand would ask me if I'd tried prayer. Yes, as a matter of fact I have. But the effects are temporary. I'd have to make myself a better man for the prayer to be effective and part of becoming a better man would be giving up drink.'

'Can't you just *decide* to give it up?'

'I've tried that too. The pain of it, it's like physical agony.'

'Like drug addicts have?'

'Ordinary consciousness simply becomes pain. I've just thought of something that might work though, something that I've never tried before.'

'What?'

'If you were to *order* me to cut it down—'

'Me?'

'Yes. You see what puny faith I have, I only say cut it down, not cut it out, but if you were to *order* me—'

'Why me?'

'Because—you know why—Harriet—darling—'

'Oh you are silly! All right. Edgar, I order you to cut down the drinking.'

'Thank you. I think I'll just have a little more now, all the same.'

'No, you must forgo this drink.'

'Must I? Well, good, yes, if you say so.'

Harriet laughed. They were sitting in the kitchen at the

round table. Harriet had been tailing strawberries and the thick dappled smell of the fruit hung in the room like a gaudy cloud.

'What a lovely dress you're wearing, Harriet, it's all strawberries and cream, or more like strawberry trifle. Girls are so clever.'

'I'm so glad you met Blaise and had an interesting chat about that Greek man who cured people by talking.'

'Antiphon. Yes. Your husband was very kind to me.'

'He's a kind man.'

'If I was your husband I should view me with suspicion.'

'Why ever should he? We're very married. I have various men friends.'

'Have you? Oh dear. I hoped I was the only one.'

'Well, you know there's Monty. Fancy you're having known him such a long time.'

'People always go off onto Monty as soon as they know I know him.'

'I'd love you to tell me what Monty was like when he was young.'

'That's exactly what Sophie said to me the day she met Monty.'

'Fancy your having introduced them. It's so historic. How did you meet Sophie?'

'She was acting in a verse translation of the *Agamemnon* made by me. She was Clytemnestra. I got the chop all right.'

'But—before Monty came—did Sophie love you?'

'No,' said Edgar thoughtfully, 'she loved Mockingham.'

'Who's that?'

'My house. Will you come and see it?'

'So you brought Sophie and Monty together.'

'It was fated. *This* was fated. There are some people who, all through their lives, seem to regulate your destiny, even if they despise you.'

'Monty doesn't despise you.'

'I don't know,' said Edgar. 'I am despicable. Why shouldn't he despise me?'

'What nonsense you talk. Monty needs you.'

'I wish that was true. I think I just remind him of too many things. People can be detested for that.'

'Besides you're so clever and learned. Monty said you were a famous scholar. You still haven't told me what you're a scholar of.'

'Oh early Greek stuff, nothing important.'

'But what? Tell me a little about what you know about.'

'Very little is known about what I know about. That's why it's so easy.'

'Tell me some of the people you study.'

'Anaxagoras. Anaximander. Anaximnenes. Antiphon. Alcman.'

'I haven't heard of any of them.'

'Aristotle.'

'I've heard of him. Why do they all begin with A?'

'Because they were servants of Athena and lived at the beginning of the world. But then there was Thales.'

'What did he do?'

'He thought.'

'What did he write?'

'He wrote nothing.'

'How can he be important then?'

'Socrates wrote nothing. Christ wrote nothing.'

'What sort of thing were they all discovering, your people?'

'That the universe is ruled by laws.'

'But isn't that obvious?'

'It wasn't then. The human mind is a funny slow old thing.'

'Would everything they thought seem obvious to us?'

'No. Parmenides thought that nothing really existed except one changeless object. And Empedocles thought that Love could fuse everything in the universe into a spherical god which did nothing but think.'

'That sounds to me like Magnus Bowles's white egg.'

'Who is Magnus Bowles? Is he one of your numerous men friends?'

'No, he's a patient of Blaise's. I've never met him. A poor chap.'

'You say that with such sweet pity. Won't you pity me too? Let me be one of your poor chaps.'

'I certainly don't pity you! All right, you may have a little more, but I'm going to put a lot of water into it.'

'Heraclitus said dry souls were better than wet souls. A dry soul goes up, a wet soul goes down.'

'Surely your men were poets, not philosophers.'

'It's ages since I talked to a woman properly. I don't mean I talked improperly. I mean I talked at dinner parties.'

'What made you decide to be a Greek scholar?'

'A man called John Beazley.'

'Who was he?'

'A Greek scholar. A god. When I think about Beazley I curl up with unworthiness.'

'Were you his favourite pupil?'

'No! I was a worm. Unrequited love has always been my lot. Look at this situation.'

'There is no situation, Edgar.'

'Not for you. You are the unmoved mover. Yet in a way unrequited love is a contradiction. If it's true love, it somehow contains its object. There's proof of God's existence like that.'

'That sounds like your chap who thought love could roll everything up into a ball.'

'Never mind. I may not know much about Empedocles, but I know quite a lot about love. Don't you worry. Just let me love you. May I hold your hand? Would Blaise mind? I'm terribly harmless you know.'

Harriet laughed. She did not know what to make of this big boyish clever middle-aged man who had suddenly appeared in her life. It was true that she had a few men friends, mainly people she had met through Adrian and had known for years and years. But Harriet was not a flirt and had no gift for *badinage*. There was nothing playful and certainly nothing unpredictable in these relationships. Edgar seemed to have come close to her in some hitherto unknown way, by some route which she did not know existed. Laughing, she let him take her hand for a moment, squeezed his, and rose. 'Let's go out into the garden. I want you to meet the dogs.'

'I wish you'd come to Mockingham. Blaise too of course. Would you? My mother was a great gardener.'

Harriet pushed open the garden door. Leaving the strawberry canopy behind them, they went out onto the lawn. The dogs who had been sitting and lying in a group, holding a meeting, rose respectfully and advanced. Edgar stroked Ajax, then sat down on the grass and let the dogs, who suddenly became excited, climb on top of him. Chuckling explosively he lay back on the grass. Pushing each other, they began ecstatically to lick his face.

Monty, who had just presented David with a pair of Bohemian glass finger bowls and sent him away unkissed, observed this scene from the shadow of the orchard trees. It filled him with anger. He walked slowly back towards Locketts, meditating upon this anger, its nature and its cause.

Emily McHugh was sitting on the floor in her sitting-room. The floor was covered with newspaper. She had set out Luca's big drawing board, pinned paper to it, laid out his coloured pencils, his poster paints, brushes, water. Sometimes he could thus be persuaded to paint. He never sought out the paints for himself. When he did paint it was often very good. Emily had a huge multi-coloured picture of a cat pinned up in the kitchen. It was as good as Matisse. It gave her much consolation.

This morning in Luca's bedroom, she had found the woolly piglet which Blaise had given Luca, hanging by its neck on a string from the end of the bed. Emily released the animal.

It was Sunday. The weather was still hot but murky, the sun shining through a haze. Pinn was out drinking with a chap, a bank manager, with whom she always went out drinking on Sunday mornings. Emily could not find the Italian cameo brooch which Blaise had given her in the first days of their love. Had vile Pinn borrowed it? Or had Emily lost it? She often lost things and forgot things now.

She sat down on the floor with her legs stretched out, wearing her old pink quilted dressing-gown, sipping a glass of sherry, her back against the tattered chair which Richardson used as a claw sharpener. Peach and grey Richardson was lying like a long warm sausage against one of her bare legs. Little Bilham sitting on top of the bookshelves opposite, his tail curled neatly round his front paws, stared at Emily with golden unwinking eyes. How wicked cats' faces are, thought Emily, even the faces of dear cats, one's very own, are somehow alien and cruel. Or do I just see cruelty everywhere now? Below Little Bilham Emily's French texts, battered and dirty, reeled on the shelves. Emily never looked at them now. She hardly read anything except the newspaper. Blaise used to bring her books once.

Luca was kneeling on the floor and energetically making a pencil scrawl on the corner of his drawing board, not on the paper but on the board. Emily had been sitting in silence with him for some time. She often did this at weekends, or tried to. Sometimes he went away, leaving any room she entered. Sometimes there was, she thought, a kind of silent communion.

At least he tolerated her presence. Emily had learnt on these occasions not to watch him too closely. As long as she looked at the cats and not at him, and above all refrained from tears, he might stay. At any sign of emotion he quietly went, leaving the room noiselessly like an animal, vanishing like a fox. So Emily sat quietly, breathlessly, rapt as if in prayer, letting her heart simply fill and brim over with pure thoughtless love for her son.

Now without moving her head she surreptitiously moved her eyes and looked at him. He had stopped scribbling and was kneeling with his head on one side, his lips slightly parted. He seemed to be listening. Emily wondered if she dared ask him what he was listening to. The pain of an unanswered question would spoil the morning, perhaps the entire day. Was it worth risking? She said, 'What are you listening to?'

'Beetles.'

'Beetles?' Emily listened hard. At first she heard nothing. Then she became aware of the tiniest tiniest crepitation somewhere in the room. 'Where are they?'

'Inside the table.'

Dislodging Richardson Emily leaned across, then listened again. He was right. It was wood beetles inside the oak table leg. One could actually hear the sound of their tiny jaws eating the wood. 'I can hear them too. Isn't that nice?'

Luca smiled at her and began to draw on his paper.

Emily sat listening with rapture to the beetles and daring now to look at her son. She felt a flood of wild dazed joy as if golden rain had descended upon the room. She seized Richardson and hugged him hard. The cat lazily adjusted himself to her embrace and began to purr.

After a while Emily decided to dare a little more. She moved slightly and peered at what Luca was drawing. 'What's your picture of?'

Luca said nothing. Emily peered at the paper. In coloured crayons Luca had drawn a house with big windows, and a tree beside it. In front of the house there was a woman in a long dress and a thin long-trousered boy and several dogs. Near the front of the picture, and looking at the other figures, was a man in an overcoat. Luca was filling in the coat with brown crayon and Emily recognized the herring-bone design of Blaise's new overcoat. She was about to say, 'That's just like Daddy's coat,' when something seemed to leap at her face. Emily gasped. She got up quickly and left the room. Luca continued quietly to fill in the picture.

His failure to achieve the lotus position had always seemed to Monty symbolic. Sophie, who was as flexible as a boy, could sit easily thus, turning the soles of her little feet upward for Monty to kiss. She thought meditation was nonsense. By some dispensation which seemed to Monty entirely felicitous, religion had been left out of her make-up. Monty had 'tried various positions, and had at last settled for kneeling, sitting back on his heels. This he could maintain for long periods, becoming rapidly unconscious of his body. At first he had resisted the idea of kneeling because of its unsavoury associations. His aim had nothing to do with self-abasement or worship or rubbishy personal prayer. Later he saw that these details did not matter.

Last night Monty had had a dream which struck him as interesting. He had been a pupil at some sort of grand school, somewhere near the sea, huge and built out of marble. The school was set upon pink rocks, pitted with azure pools, and across those rocks Monty had to scramble in order to reach some class or seminar which it was very important that he should attend. The rocks were slippery, but at last he reached a flight of marble steps which came down among them, and mounted the steps into a large hall surrounded by pillars and partly open to the sky. A man in white robes was standing in the hall obviously waiting for him, and Monty realized that before he could go on to the classroom he had to pass some sort of preliminary test. The white-robed figure said to him, 'You must simply mime what I tell you now. Pretend that you are scooping up water in your hands.' Monty leaned down to the ground and began to scoop up imaginary water in his hands. As he did so he glimpsed his mentor's face. It wore a sad disappointed expression and Monty knew that he had failed the test. Then he realized that a saintly man would have imagined himself to be immersed in water up the chest, up to the neck.

Monty smiled, thinking what Blaise would have made of this dream. What a load of lies he had told Blaise about himself at various times, not so much deliberately as because he found he simply could not tell Blaise the truth. In Blaise, truth would not be truth. Besides, Blaise believed in the dreary old historical self, lived indeed by that belief, made his money out of that fiction. Of course dreams were rubble. All the same they could be images of faith, little momentary trinkets offered for consolation by mind to mind.

Philosophy, the anxious connecting of one thing with another, the satanic proliferation of programmes of conceptual dominion, the doubling of an already doubled world, had long seemed to him like the pointless journeying of insects. None of his negative certainties however made him able to judge the worth of his failed spiritual vocation. That it had failed, that his life was for these purposes over, was a condition for his continued efforts, as if he could thus harmlessly dupe himself. This inbuilt assumption of failure had, especially since the evidence of the later days with Sophie, related him more quietly to time. Since there was no hope and therefore no urgency, he could live without ambition from moment to moment, thinking no historical thoughts about what he still persistently attempted to do.

But what was he attempting? Was it that he had lived too long in his mind and was tired of the scenery? or was it simply a sophisticated rescue operation for an ageing insufficiently talented man who was beginning to be aware of death? By sheer diligence it was possible to set up a huge machine onto which one could gear oneself in a second. Some such machine existed, Monty had, in a number of years created it. He had only to kneel, to droop his eyelids and take some deep breaths and the sensible world ceased to be. He knew at least enough to know that this, in his case, was merely an experience. However much his technique might improve the enlightening spirit was absent. Except in dreams he had no teacher. It would have been, he felt, artificial, another occasion for lying. No, Monty did not imagine that he had, by his pains, won anything of value. He had not even glimpsed his freedom. The obsessions which made Magnus Bowles's life a misery simply travelled with him like dormant viruses. The gods, who had nothing to do with enlightenment, unplacated, undefeated, were still there.

His latest idea of becoming a schoolmaster rather than, say, buying a luxurious villa in France and trying again to write a straight novel, was no symptom of a changed direction, the acquisition, say, of new 'social views'. The politics of his days of 'frightfulness' had long ago withered within him. He had lacked the sort of passion required to make him, what he would now have despised himself for being, a 'reactionary'. The miserable issue of all that had been Milo Fane, ascetic hedonist, discreet sadist, cynic. The schoolmaster idea was superficial, an interim measure, a new makeshift device aimed towards an old end. Towards a sort of simplicity and openness of living. An ostentatious hatred of pretention and the bogus (except of course in so far as these informed his own style) had impressed his Oxford contemporaries and probably made them overrate his intellect. He had carried onward within him an ideal of unbogus lucidity, of a contextless clarity of truthful utterance, which he had somehow never been able to crystallize into any ordinary mode of living. What he pursued on his knees was connected with this, but in a way that was full of crucial puzzles. Spirit, after all, can provide a much more durable holiday from morality than sin ever can. What was he seeking, truth or salvation or goodness? Sometimes it seemed to him that these roads diverged absolutely and only conceivably came together at some end point which he would never reach. Sometimes he felt as if he was simply seeking knowledge, or, more simply still, power. More drearily still, he had once imagined that to discipline his mind would be to help his work. But the discipline seemed merely to have stifled what was left to him of spontaneity and *joie de vivre*.

This business of trying to get rid of the ego often seemed idiocy. Years could pass in the attempt to centre the consciousness below the navel. The whole thing was laughable rot, oriental unBritish rubbish. How Sophie had mocked. It might be perfectly true that there was no deep sense in things, that nothing and no one had real dignity and real deserving, that 'the world' was just a jumble and a rubble and a dream, but was it not supreme cheating to make this senselessness seem to be the very essence of one's being? He might be a very shoddy artist, but he had the artist's capacity to cheat. Better surely to live as ordinary clever people live, by wit and pain and sex, finding these at last in the pinnacle of one's spirit. Better to resort to the holiness of suffering and to consent to give some name ('love' for instance) to the ground of one's being, rather than to attempt this radical undoing of a natural essence.

Yet Monty went on, and in the awful clarity of affliction after Sophie's death found *this* curiously unchanged, as if it had in spite of everything wedged its unconscious spearhead into a region beyond. Since the part of him which this hypothetical region concerned was infinitesimally tiny he experienced no sort of alleviation or insight. But misery did not make him alter his routine, even guilt did not. This much at least, in its automatic way, 'the machine' had done for him.

'Monty, Monty, are you all right?'

Monty regained his perception of his little Moorish drawing-room with one lamp alight, the window open upon darkness and the rain beating down. A certain sense of being *battered*, it now seemed to him, had been with him. The rain had come in and stained the carpet. Blaise was there, staring down at him. Monty tilted himself sideways and then slowly got up. He looked at his watch. It was nearly midnight. Blaise's unheralded visit was unusual. He must have come round into the garden.

'Why, you are soaking wet,' said Monty.

Blaise looked distraught, his darkened hair plastered in long streaks upon his brow. 'Were you in some sort of trance?'

'No, no, gone to sleep more likely.' Monty had only ever jested to his friend about these matters. 'I'll turn on the electric fire. I'll get you a towel.' He fetched a towel and closed the window, pulling the curtains carefully across. The battering rain was more remote. Blaise buried his face in the towel, then began to dry his hair.

'What's the matter?' said Monty.

'I am afraid,' said Blaise, 'that the game is up.'

Monty stared at him for a moment in silence. 'Have some whisky.'

'Thanks.'

'What has happened?'

'Luca has found this place. He's been over here. He's been in the garden.'

'I saw him,' said Monty. 'Odd. *That* never occurred to me.'

'You saw him?'

'Yes. Standing in the garden a couple of nights ago, looking at the house.'

'Oh, Christ. It means the end. Well, I suppose it does, doesn't it? I can't think.'

'Sit down, sit down. How did Luca come, how did he know?'

'He stowed away in the car.'

'What does Emily think?'

'She doesn't know.'

'How do you know then?'

'The char told me. Luca told her. It can't have been an invention. He said there were a lot of dogs. Anyway you saw him. It's the end.'

'Well he's been pretty discreet so far. He hasn't knocked on the door and asked for daddy. Though I suppose he might at any moment.'

'Exactly. But it isn't just that—it's the separation being— broken through—'

'Have you been drinking?'

'Yes. It's the two worlds, suddenly one sees—they're really —one world after all.'

'I suppose you had some inkling of this before. What are you going to do?'

'I'll have to tell Harriet. And yet I can't, I can't, I *can't*. And David. It's the end of my relation with both of them.'

'You underrate them.'

'But it is clear, isn't it—I'll *have* to tell them now—before Luca starts asking for daddy. It is clear. Just tell me, would you?'

'It's very interesting,' said Monty. 'Yes, I imagine so, but let's think. Suppose Luca could be persuaded to keep quiet—'

'He's not a rational being. He's a force. One couldn't treat him as predictable.'

'I should have thought forces were more predictable than rational beings. But come, he's just a little child.'

'He's a demon. He's come here to ruin me. Oh it's not his fault—'

'All right, one thing at a time. We assume Luca is fatal. Now let's consider your state of mind. Don't you find that you, a bit, want to tell?'

'No!'

'Won't it be a relief in a way to pull everything down on top of you?'

'No, it won't! That's just abstract. I've got to decide whether tomorrow morning to say to Harriet—'

'Don't think of the decision,' said Monty, 'Think beyond it. After all, we've talked about this before, it's not a new idea.'

'It is a new idea, as *real* it's new. I've never really imagined what it would be like. David's face, Harriet's tears—Oh God—'

'Don't be so tragic. Try to be intelligent. I admit I am fascinated by your dilemma. Are you not now simply being forced to do what you ought to do, and ought you not to be grateful? You always said it would have to come out sometime, and why not now when there's a motive?'

'Mephistopheles as usual. We've had this conversation before. I don't think it is what I ought to do, ruin Harriet's happiness.'

'You've already ruined it.'

'Ruin David's exams. Of course it'll have to come out sometime, but why now? There's still not enough reason—'

'Yes there is, because of Luca. You're lucky to have your hand forced.'

'But it's not being forced, as you said yourself. Luca may—there may be nothing more—I'll ask him not to—Oh God, I hate myself.'

'You speak as if you were losing your virtue now, but it was lost long ago. Anyway, your virtue doesn't matter here. What matters is the general happiness. You're not really thinking about Harriet—'

'Since I knew about Luca coming here, I've thought of nothing but Harriet and David—'

'No, no, you're thinking about yourself. Now try to picture it—'

'I can't, I can't—'

'You've told Harriet. Well, what will she do, what can she do? She'll have to accept the situation. She won't divorce you, you know that.'

'It's simply the fact of her knowing—'

'Exactly. So you haven't thought. You've been telling me for years what hell it all was, leading a double life. The new scene may be hell too but at least it will be different and it may conceivably be better. You're so obsessed with the loss of your virtue—not even that, that's serious, but that's done—with the loss of your reputation, you aren't thinking how the others may save you.'

'Save me?'

'Yes. Harriet can save you.'

'You mean forgive me? That's impossible. Simply her knowing would divide us absolutely. Anyway I don't want to be forgiven, such feelings would just be obscene. And even if Harriet could forgive me, David never could, ever, ever, ever. There isn't—there isn't—the machinery—for me to be forgiven—by David—it doesn't exist.'

'Let's think about Harriet. Harriet is a wonderful woman, intelligent and strong and good—an angel as you've often said —and she loves you. Why not cast yourself onto Harriet's love like people used to cast themselves on God? Stop thinking about your sins and your reputation and think about Harriet's love.'

'It's such an outrage against her love. I can't rely on her just where I've hurt her and damaged her most.'

'I don't see why not. You're thinking about yourself again, you can't seem to stop. Anyway, if you tell, you won't be making yourself morally worse, you may even be making yourself morally better.'

'What I need is for all this not to have happened at all.'

'You need what all sinners need, a salvation which blots out the fault. You just happen to be luckier than most sinners since something like that is just conceivably possible in your case.'

'I don't know what you mean—You've never said this to me before. You encouraged me to go on.'

'I didn't encourage you to. You were determined to. I just listened.'

'You encouraged me. It amused you. Anyway, what the hell, I wish I was dead.'

'You can't go through the looking-glass without cutting yourself.'

'Sorry. I'm drunk. I drank a hell of a lot of whisky over there. I kissed Harriet and sent her to bed, and she told me not to work too long—Oh God, perhaps it's the last time—and I was reading them their book—it's all so precious—and I've destroyed it forever.'

'And you must think about Emily too.'

'I'd like to kill Emily.'

'Imagine you've told. What will Emily do?'

'Celebrate. I don't know what she'll do.'

'Of course, you must resign yourself to losing the initiative.'

'You're loving every moment of this, aren't you. I wish I'd never said anything to you. Sorry. I know I'm behaving like a child, wanting to be told what to do. I suppose I want to be convinced that it's inevitable.'

'You need a salvation which will redeem your fault. Your two victims can provide it. No one else can.'

'You mean Harriet and David.'

'I mean Harriet and Emily.'

'You don't understand. I've never really—conceived they both exist—one or the other—but not both.'

'I know, I know. This is your ordeal. Simply Harriet knowing.'

'I feel if Harriet ever knew about Emily the world would simply end in a huge explosion.'

'Your ordeal is that it won't. You'll all go on existing, sleeping and eating and going to the lavatory.'

'It's unthinkable. Literally. Like modern physics. I can't think it.'

'Blot yourself out. Give yourself to them, really give yourself. You may find that, surprisingly enough and little as you deserve it, they may look after you.'

'It isn't a matter of Harriet saying "I forgive you", even if she did. It's cosmic.'

'Only for your consciousness.'

'I live in my consciousness.'

'Why be resigned to that? You imagine even now that you will sort out your life as an emperor sorts out his kingdom and that it all really depends on you. Don't play it so tragically. Life is absurd and mostly comic. Where comedy fails what we have is misery, not tragedy. You don't exist all that much, anyway. Your breaths are numbered. Of course you can't solve it all now by a rational act of will. And of course there are deep automatic retributions for any wrong-doing. Because of what you have done things will happen later which can't possibly be foreseen. But don't look on yourself as a tragic hero. Think about right acts, right moves. You ought to tell Harriet. That has always been so. Now you have a chance to take the idea seriously. Let the value of truth help you, let it shed light. Would it not be a relief and a simple good thing to tell the truth?'

'I can't feel the value of truth here,' said Blaise. 'Perhaps that's what corruption is. Anyway I've always felt that I must digest my own scandal.'

'You've always known that it would come out sometime. You will act when the pain and the fear become too much. Perhaps that is now. Better move before you get used to the new pain and the new fear.'

'You are right. I will tell Harriet tomorrow morning. Oh God help me—'

'Better tell her in a letter,' said Monty.

'Why in a letter?'

'Because in a letter you can use your intelligence. You speak as if there was just one huge fact to be revealed. But there are many lights in which you can present the situation to her and many lights in which it can be seen. Of course you will lie a bit to both women, that can hardly be avoided—'

'Perhaps you'd like to compose the letter for me!'

'I will if you like. Seriously. I mean, for instance you can tell her that you no longer love Emily, that she's a burden to you, that you only stuck to her out of a sense of duty—if that's true—and even if it isn't.'

'Mephistopheles, Mephistopheles—'

'Well, intelligence does help in hell. It helped Milton's characters. Once you can start thinking about the situation instead of being crushed by it you'll immediately suffer less.'

'What else should I say in the letter?'

'Talk about the children and their rights and the importance of their happiness. Two children, two separate unavoidable problems.'

'That makes sense, I suppose.'

'Good. You're thinking.'

'No, I'm not. I couldn't write this letter. You'll have to write it.'

'All right, I'll make a draft. Make Harriet see it as a set of soluble problems, not just as one huge enormity. And tell her you rely on her love. Come, do cheer up. You may be the wickedest man in England, but even wicked men perk up occasionally.'

'I do feel a little better.'

'You may even find yourself closer to Harriet in the end.'

'If I thought that I could bear anything. But—you know, I'd better see Emily first—it may not be necessary at all—you said yourself—I'll see Emily tomorrow and decide after that.'

'Let me go with you to Emily.'

'Why? To satisfy your curiosity at last?'

'That, yes. But I feel you need a witness, a second. You know what will happen if you see Emily and then decide. You'll just fall back into the old double state of mind.'

'If I tell Emily I am going to tell Harriet—then I suppose I shall have to tell Harriet. At any rate it—'

'You know, I've never advised you at all and I'm not really advising you now.'

'Oh, yes you are. Will you write that letter for me?'

'Yes, yes—'

'Why am I feeling better?'

'Because you've set yourself some little tasks which still don't commit you to anything. Because you've decided somewhere in your mind that it's not necessary to tell Harriet after all.'

'But it is necessary?'

'It is necessary, I think.'

'Maybe you had better come with me to Emily's.'

'By the way, please don't ever tell Harriet that you told me about Emily. Let her think I only found out after.'

'Why? You seem to be worrying about your reputation now.'

'It would hurt her to think I'd known all along, and deceived her.'

'Oh, Christ. Magnus Bowles. What about him?'

'Let him be. For the present anyway.'

'You mean don't tell Harriet he doesn't exist?'

'She'll have enough nightmares without that crazy little jape.'

'I can never make out whether you are bottomlessly cynical or not. Actually Magnus is the only bit of style in the whole thing. The rest is low, vulgar and low. You've always seen me as a rather vulgar man, haven't you, Monty?'

'I would not use that terminology.'

'Well, whatever bloody terminology. I am vulgar. Even my sins are in rotten taste.'

'In the case of sin, it is ultimately the stuff and not the style that stupefies. I doubt if Harriet—'

'I wonder if you see yourself as consoling Harriet?'

'You know how I see myself at present. You are lucky that I know *you* exist and am able to talk to you.'

'Sorry. Sorry. You've been damn good to me, Monty, throughout this ghastly business. You've been my therapist, my tutor. I am grateful, you know. Have we decided anything or not?'

'Yes. Go to bed. I'll draft the letter. I'll go with you to Emily.'

'The blasted dogs are barking. Perhaps I'll find Luca in my bed. That child always was a sort of practical joke. I wonder if I can really face it all? What will it do to my mind? How mysterious the psyche is, there's no science of it really. Morality baffles science, chucks everything about. Christ, I'm drunk. I wonder if I shall ever be a doctor?'

'Why not? Hold onto anything you know is good. That, Harriet's love. Especially Harriet's love.'

'You know what Harriet said about Milo Fane? She said he was going soft and getting all sentimental and high-minded.'

'She said that? Ah well. Milo is gone, there's no more Milo any more. Go now, go. Don't tell Harriet about me and

Magnus. And don't hate me for all this later, will you? Go, go, good night. No, wait. I will lend you an umbrella.'

Pinn, whom Blaise had failed, as he now realized, to explain to Monty, opened the door. It was also at once evident that Monty thought Pinn was Emily, and found her rather attractive. Pinn flushed up and smiled. 'This is Constance Pinn, Emily's friend,' said Blaise quickly.

Ever since Pinn's revelation Blaise had been living in a fantastic world. He could hardly recognize himself, his self-awareness had so much changed in quality. The easiest thing to think was that he was going to die. This was not exactly an intent to commit suicide, though he did consider suicide, it was rather a sense of the impossibility of surviving much longer, whatever he did, whatever he chose. He felt rent apart by an unremitting mental, felt as physical, strain. When he was alone he groaned aloud. He did not, except in a very shadowy way, speculate about what Harriet would do when she knew; though when he did wonder about this he felt how little he really knew about his wife. He had never seen Harriet in any really awful situation. Theirs had been such a sunny marriage. Her character, which made this so, had also its enigmatic side. What *would* she do? This question however he soon sheered off whenever it occurred to him. What was unimaginably awful was not what Harriet would do when she knew, but simply her knowing. To know that Harriet *knew* would change the entire universe. What would Harriet's face look like with that knowle 'ge inside her head?

Pinn was smartly dressed in a green linen coat and skirt with a white silk shirt. Emily, who now appeared in the doorway of the sitting-room, had abandoned her usual slacks and jumper and was wearing a blue and black zigzag pattern dress with a low square neck which Blaise particularly disliked. She had fixed the Italian cameo brooch (which Pinn had borrowed and returned) onto one side of the neck, a little too far out towards the shoulder, where it had come undone and was hanging down. Pinn's greater discretion, as Blaise suddenly saw the two women with Monty's eyes, made her look much the handsomer of the two. They were both of course dressed, not for Blaise, but for an exciting meeting with a famous writer. He had telephoned to say that he was coming over with Montague Small, but had not said why. It was eleven o'clock the next morning. How little Emily looked, he thought, how tiny and insignificant, almost dwarfish. Thin lines of grey already soiled the blackness of her hair. 'This is Emily McHugh,' he said. It did not sound like an introduction.

Emily smiled, revealing a smear of pink lipstick upon her teeth. The Italian cameo brooch fell off onto the floor and she stooped quickly to pick it up, and laid it on the table. 'Do please sit down. Get the sandwiches, please, Pinn.'

The best white cloth with the lace edges had been put onto the little bamboo table. Monty, smiling, sat down on an upright chair. He scooped up Little Bilham off the floor and began stoking him hard, as one might stroke a dog. Little Bilham turned to regard Monty with his wicked eyes. Blaise sat down on another upright chair and Emily upon the arm of the armchair. Pinn brought in sandwiches and a jug of coffee and stood there like a servant, also smiling.

'Or would you rather have a drink?' said Emily to Monty. 'I mean, there's coffee, but would you rather have sherry?'

'Coffee is fine.'

'You don't mind my puss? Are you a catty person?'

'I'm very fond of cats.'

'I've read all your books,' said Pinn.

'We've been watching the television series,' said Emily, pouring out the coffee. 'It's so exciting. Did you write the script?'

'Partly.'

'I do think Richard Nailsworth absolutely *is* Milo Fane, don't you?' said Emily. 'Did you choose him?'

'No, I didn't actually,' Monty seemed unable to stop smiling. He was wearing a white shirt and one of his narrowest silkiest indigo ties and suit of speckless close-grained black. He looked like a rich discreetly foppish eighteenth-century curate.

'Is Dickie Nailsworth queer?' said Pinn, who had gone to stand opposite Monty, her hands on the back of Emily's chair.

'I don't know.'

'He can't be,' said Emily. 'He's so virile. One can tell by the movements. Are you working on another Milo book?'

'Not at present.'

'How do you *begin* a book?' said Pinn.

'I've come to tell you something,' said Blaise to Emily.

'Shall I go away?' said Pinn. Blaise's tone had changed the atmosphere abruptly.

'No,' he said. 'I want a witness. Two witnesses.'

Monty stopped smiling and stopped stroking the cat.

Emily was rigid. Unconsciously she reached out and picked up the Italian cameo brooch and put it up against her cheek. Her vividly blue eyes shone like gems. She looked at her lover with a stern grim expression which made her suddenly beautiful.

'Monty,' said Blaise. He did not know why now he was suddenly addressing Monty. 'I mean—' He turned back to Emily. 'I have decided to tell my wife everything.' He had meant to say 'Harriet' but said 'my wife' instead at the last moment.

Emily was magnificent. Her face did not change at all. She contrived to stare at Blaise with an almost intellectual sort of intentness, as if he were a chess problem. Then after a pause she said 'Why?'

The question, though it might have been anticipated, took Blaise by surprise. He said 'Because it's right—I mean, it's time—I can't go on any longer—' He had not thought out whether he would say anything about Luca. He now decided not to. With things as terrible as this Luca was a side issue.

'Then you will live with me?' said Emily. They stared at each other.

'I don't know.'

Emily put the brooch down and began unsteadily to pour coffee into her cup, not looking at him. 'What's the point then?'

'I want to tell the truth.'

'Go on then.'

'I want to make—'

'I think you're lying,' said Emily. 'This has nothing to do with the truth. You've thought of something, you're up to something. I don't care whether she knows or not. I want you to live with me properly. That's what I've always wanted.'

Pinn said, 'When he's told her, if he tells her, he'll have to live with you.' Pinn, half-smiling in a self-consciously subtle way, was watching, not Blaise or Emily but Monty. Monty too could not help looking at Pinn.

'I don't see why,' said Emily. 'It could work the other way, couldn't it? His telling her could be a way of getting rid of me. Suppose she orders him to stop seeing me? That would be reasonable after all. She's his wife, as he pointed out just now. Then he'd have to choose either her or me, and he might choose her. As things are at the moment at least he doesn't have to choose.'

'If he tells her you win,' said Pinn, still looking at Monty with a pensive smile as if her words were addressed to him.

'Why?'

'Because it unties your hands. When you can fight her in the open you're bound to win. You can break all that up, once you're free.'

'I wish I shared your optimism,' said Emily. 'What am I supposed to fight with, bottles? Mr Small, won't you have a sandwich? I can't think why Blaise has brought you here to listen to this rather squalid conversation.'

'Have a cucumber sandwich,' said Pinn. 'They slip down like oysters.'

'You don't seem very interested in what I've just told you,' said Blaise. 'Perhaps I won't tell her after all.'

'Please yourself. Pinn, could you bring a wet rag, dear? I've just spilt some coffee.'

Pinn brought a rag and together they manoeuvred it under the cloth where the spot of coffee was. Emily then began to pin the Italian brooch back onto her dress, in the middle this time.

'Why have you never written a Milo Fane play?' said Pinn to Monty.

'I tried once, but it didn't work.'

'I've written a play,' said Pinn. 'About a girls' school. It's a bit saucy. I suppose one has to have an agent?'

'For a play, yes.'

'Perhaps you could recommend one?'

'Emily,' said Blaise.

'Yes?'

'You've been asking me to tell Harriet for years.'

'No, I haven't,' said Emily. 'What I've been asking for for years is you. Her state of mind doesn't interest me. I ask you if you're going to live with me now, and you say you don't know, which means no, I presume.'

'I can only do one thing at a time. If you only knew how difficult this thing is—'

'Well, don't do it then. Do you want our sympathy or what? Could you get some more hot milk, Pinn?'

'In fact,' said Monty to Emily, putting Little Bilham down on the floor, 'he is right to point out that he can only do one thing at a time. He probably can't foresee what will happen later. But I think I agree with your friend that this change could augur well for you. And at least it will be a change.'

'Oh thank you very much!' said Emily.

'Mr Small is right,' said Pinn, returning with the milk.

'I wanted you to tell her,' said Emily, 'because I thought this meant honesty and truth and a square deal for me. Christ, I started out wanting everything and I've been content, well I haven't been *content* for a second, I've put up with having very little, the least mean little little that you dared to have the face to offer me in return for my whole life. I still want everything and I still hope for everything. I daresay I am very stupid indeed. I'm a stupid woman and a millstone round your neck and so on. But the fact remains that I love you (yes, I must be stupid) and I want you to be my husband, my real husband, and live with me in a real house and look after me and your son, and Christ we need looking after, look at us. Talk about deprived, we didn't drop out, we were pushed. The sheer cruelty of it all just beats description. It's like famine and pestilence and war. You're cruel, you're like Hitler, you deserve to be assassinated for what you've done to me and Luca. You come here today with your bloody ''witness'' to tell me grandly you've decided to tell your wife I exist. What am I supposed to do, cheer? I don't want to chat to you about her. You can't chat with people who are starving, people who are perishing. I don't care any more whether you tell her or not. I want justice. If I decide to tell her she'll know anyway. I could tell her now this minute by telephone if I wanted to. It doesn't just depend on you. Oh God, why did you have to spring it all on me like this, with your blasted witnesses! Oh get out, get out, get out.'

Emily, whose face had been first pale, then red, burst into sudden loud sobs. Tears covered her face as with a veil. She sobbed angrily, wailing an 'ow! ow! ow!' like an animal which is aggressive because terrified. She put one hand over her mouth, biting her palm.

'Oh, *stop it*!' said Blaise.

'Take it easy, Em,' said Pinn.

Emily rose, and still biting her hand left the room, closing the door quietly behind her.

Monty put the damp limp cucumber sandwich which he had been holding down onto the tablecloth. He said, 'I'd better go,' and rose.

Blaise got up too. 'I'll walk down the road with you,' he said to Monty.

They left the flat and walked down the tiled path to the

road in silence. They began to walk slowly along the road. It was a grey warm morning, threatening more rain.

'I'm sorry,' said Monty. 'My coming was a bad idea. I'm sorry.'

'I thought she'd be delighted,' said Blaise. They halted at the corner.

'You'd better go to her,' said Monty.

Pinn came up, her heels clicking a good deal on the pavement. 'Aren't you coming back to talk to her?' she said to Blaise.

'Of course I am!'

'She's hysterical now.'

'Sorry not to be able to run you back,' said Blaise to Monty. 'If you walk towards Putney Hill you'll get a taxi. See you later. Thanks for coming.' He turned away along the road, leaving Pinn and Monty together.

'I want to see you again,' said Pinn. Her eyes behind her jaunty glasses were sombre, and she uttered the words expressionlessly, the way some purists read poetry.

'Sorry—' said Monty vaguely. He was upset by the scene that had just ended. He felt that he had been made a fool of.

'I want to see you again,' she said. 'It is important to me. Things are not often important to me, but this is. I don't want you to say anything now. I mean, you needn't even answer this remark. You are Montague Small. I am nobody. A cat may look at a king. I will come and see you sometime. Just don't say that I can't. That is all I ask of you. Good-bye.' She turned sharply and walked away and her heels clicked off with a slightly echoing moist sucking noise along the still damp pavements.

Monty loosened his tie. His umbrella was locked inside the Volkswagen and it was beginning to rain. He felt irritably dissatisfied with himself. Then his old huge familiar misery gradually returned like an old friend.

My darling Harriet and my dear wife. I am too cowardly to tell you what follows face to face, so I am telling it to you in a letter. I shall try to explain *clearly* because clarity and truthfulness are of the utmost importance here. You will be surprised, shocked, horrified at what I have to tell you, but I *must* tell you, not least because I love you absolutely, and lying to you has become ultimately intolerable to me. Some years ago (over nine years ago to be precise) I took a mistress. Her name is Emily McHugh and she is now over thirty. I was physically attracted and I succumbed to temptation. This, I know, is indefensible. But I did not intend to continue this brief unworthy liaison, and I should certainly then have confessed it to you had Emily not become pregnant. A child now exists, a boy, aged eight, and my duty to this innocent being is a reason why I have to tell you the truth, and should have told it long ago only I was a hopeless coward and did not want to shatter your and David's peace and destroy your respect for me. I put this down simply and perhaps crudely but you may imagine the suffering and the shame which lie behind these words. I have to tell you now, to lay it all before you for judgment. I was never really 'in love' with Emily and have long ago ceased finding her attractive. I wish heartily that all this had never happened, not only because of the shameful and damaging consequences, but because it was so evidently from the start a complete mistake. There was and has been no real love, only a dreadful bondage, an involvement tormenting to me and exasperating to her. We would have separated years ago, in fact very soon after the start, had it not been for the child's existence. I have during these long years visited her at intervals and have of course financed her and the child. This was a responsibility which I could not shirk however much I yearned to be rid of the whole matter and to be what I seemed, and what in a deep way I feel I have indeed been, utterly yours. The rich reality of my life with you has inevitably filled me with joy, though with a corresponding separated pain, as the years have passed and I have been living a lie. I am profoundly ashamed, and in now confessing this can only cast myself onto your love as a religious person casts himself onto God. Harriet, if ever I needed your love I need it now. I need it to continue to breathe, I would die without it, and I ask you for it on my knees. As you *know*, I love and have loved only you. I deserve punishment, but I ask for grace. Please, my darling, my sweet dear girl, forgive me and help me to deal with this awful situation. Let me at last share this trouble too with you and let us look at it together. I dare to ask you this, having in mind not only my own fault and my own suffering, but also the sufferings of a wretched woman whom I have also wronged, and a little innocent child whose father I am. Emily has long known (ever since, as I say, almost the start) that I do not love her, and resent her as a burden and as the spoiler of my perfect happiness with you. She is a very deprived and unhappy person, full of vexation, and having lost the charm of her physical good looks. I do not belittle this crime which I have committed against you and against her. But I ask you, madly perhaps, for your love as the only instrument of salvation. Can you, dare you, wretched and miserable and unworthy as I am, love me *more*? I know that by making this confession I am thrusting us both out into the unknown. I do not know how you will feel, and you yourself perhaps do not know, even as you (oh God, I can hardly bear to think of it) read these words, how you will react. Time will be needed to show us this. But I do with utter humility and full consciousness of my fault beg and beseech you to pity me and not to stop loving me. If you love me all can somehow be, if not retrieved, at any rate compassionately ordered, and the value of truth itself may cast a little light on the desolation which I have so unwittingly wrought. I am very very sorry and I feel I could die of shame and misery of loss, only if you will love me I shall live. I feel, as I write this, that I have never loved you more or valued you more. You are all that matters here, you and your saving love. Oh do not abandon me in my pain. It is, even though I am so frightened at what you may feel or do, a blessed relief to tell you the truth at last. It has needed something little short of heroism to do so. I so long felt that this, which I am doing now, was impossible and beyond my powers. Pity me and succour me and do not, I beg you, let me wait long for your judgment. I deserve anger, but give me love, or if anger, anger with love. The extra power which will save the world can only come from your perfect love, my angel and my wife.

I will put out this letter for you after breakfast, and I will leave the house until about noon. Then I will return to throw myself upon your loving mercy. Needing you oh so desperately my darling, and hoping that you will not abandon me — your devoted husband

B.

Blaise wrote this letter late at night. Of course it had proved impossible to use Monty's clever draft, though it had given him one or two ideas. In fact when he began to write he found himself unexpectedly inspired. A kind of weird excitement rendered him eloquent. He moved himself.

He had spent most of the afternoon with Emily. (He told Harriet later he was with Maurice Guimarron.) Emily had wept and stormed and Blaise had held her in his arms feeling a strange calm blank open-eyed sort of emotion rather like a strange pride. For he had now really decided to tell and he fully measured the perils into the midst of which he was going to launch them all. He said little to Emily and his silence eventually impressed her. 'You've got a funny look, sweetikin,' she said at last. 'It suits you.' They drank a lot together and finished the rest of the sandwiches and Blaise felt, in a crazy way, a bit cheered up.

When he had got home, talked to Harriet, had supper, sent her to bed, the terror returned. He began the letter dripping with perspiration and gasping with fear. As he went on writing however a sort of calmness, almost of hope, returned to him. The eloquence came, and a sense of having gripped the situation in his own way, and this feeling of an initiative gave him energy. He did not exactly enjoy writing the letter, but there was a zest in it, as of a man fighting for his life. He was glad that he had made some sort of peace with Emily. And he felt, as he now told the truth to Harriet, his love for his wife miraculously strengthened and refreshed simply by the act of truth-telling. To feel Harriet's power and to cast himself down before it was somehow invigorating and exciting. What a fool he had been not to tell the truth long ago now that suddenly it seemed possible, almost easy. And, as he begged and begged for Harriet's love he felt sure that it could not be withheld.

The next morning he awoke sick with terror and with the unspeakable thought that *still* nothing irrevocable had occurred. He could still tear up the letter. Everything could still go on quietly as before. He left the letter conspicuously on the table in the hall and ran out of the house. He spent the morning walking at random in the nearby roads, staring at the houses and reading out their names.

Harriet held the letter crumpled in her hand. She had read it. When she saw the envelope she already felt a pang of fear. Now she sat in her little room, panting. Simply breathing was a task. Opening her mouth she filled her lungs with air which it then seemed impossible to expel. An age passed and she expelled it. Another age and upon the very brink of unconsciousness she inhaled again. What she had read seemed impossible and her whole mind rejected it. It must be a *mistake*, Blaise had made a *mistake*. This could not be true of her Blaise, the past could not be changed in this way, after all it was well known one could not change the past. The person who was saying these things was automatically a stranger and could not be saying anything which could alter her life. Yet at the same time she believed. The eloquent pleading which had moved Blaise was invisible to Harriet. All she saw was the huge inconceivable intolerable fact.

I have got to deal with this, she told herself, I have got to be strong, this is catastrophe such as I knew must sometime come. Now I must find out whether I am brave or not. Still holding the letter she went into the bedroom and lay down on the bed. The ignorant familiar furniture crowded affectionately about her, the familiar row of trinkets paraded upon the chimney piece, a tie of Blaise's lay upon the table and his blue enamel cuff-links which she had given him. She could not breathe lying down, so she sat up again and tried to cry. A few tears came and then the gasping once more. I must be strong, Harriet said to herself, this is the catastrophe, and I must be strong.

What hurt her most at first was a sheer almost savingly objective jealousy. Could a fact hurt so intricately? He had taken a mistress and she, his wife, had known nothing of it. He had deceived her. Other husbands were deceivers, but not hers, and yet he was. He had given his love to another woman, he had broken the completeness of the world, and darkness was staining all the intricate channels of what had once seemed so perfect. Blaise looked suddenly alien and mean, and her love for him shuddered with pain. Then, there was the boy. A boy, his son, not hers, another fact. Harriet then recalled the boy she had seen in the garden, but she did not think it was *that* boy. She thought vaguely of the twilight boy as a symbol or prefiguration of what had come to pass. Blaise had *another family*.

Harriet went to the dressing table and sat down and looked

into the mirror. The calm face she had known all these years was gone and a strange woman stared back, big eyed and distraught, her mouth ugly with grief. Harriet felt giddy and exposed as if very quietly, as in a silent film run in slow motion, the house had been hit by a bomb leaving her sitting amid wreckage. And she remembered an Annunciation by Tintoretto in which the Virgin sits in a wrecked skeleton stable into which the Holy Ghost has entered as a tempestuous destructive force. Only Harriet was not glorified by ruin. Her house was destroyed indeed.

Hold on, she said to herself, hold on. Think. Blaise will come and I must be able to say something to him. She looked at the crumpled letter again. Emily McHugh. How terrifyingly particular the name was. He had been tender and sweet with this woman, laughed with her, had little private rituals of domesticity. The gross details of infidelity did not touch Harriet so much as the theft of that intimate personal *tendresse*. The fact of the child made it all so mysterious and huge, made of it another rival place where Blaise was hidden and whence he looked at Harriet with strange alienated eyes. She moaned now and wept freely, her hands over her nose and open mouth, gazing at her crumpled face in the mirror.

Hold on, she said, hold on, soldier's daughter, soldier's sister, think. What can help me, what can help him, now? I must find a way of thinking about it. It all happened a long time ago. He no longer loves her. She is a hateful burden to him. He has a duty to her and to the child. Of course he ought to have told me. But how he must have suffered, with his kind truthful nature, tied to a woman whom he no longer loved and lying to one whom he loved. For amid all her sense of a world devastated and defiled Harriet did not for a second doubt Blaise's love for her. She clung to him in her heart and her thought, and as she did so she seemed to see Emily McHugh and her son drifting away as if they were upon a raft. They were drifting away and she was with Blaise upon the shore.

Harriet jumped up and ran down stairs through the wrecked house. A lurid light of unhappiness and fear shone onto everything. It was only ten o'clock and Blaise had said he would return at noon. Oh where was he, where was he, he who had always in every sorrow supported and consoled her? And would he not aid her now? She felt a desire to run, to run wildly along the street looking for Blaise, calling out his name. She sat down and clutched the red and white tablecloth convulsively in her hands. After all she had not lost him, he was not dead, he needed her now more than he had ever needed her. The warmth of Blaise's pleading began at last to stream through for her comfort. He needed her love, her *extra* love. Had she that extra power, that grace, to help him in his extremity? Harriet now knew that she had, she felt brimming over and faint with it. She moaned aloud with desire for the return of her husband, so that she could console and reassure him and herself. They had not lost each other, had they? They could not lose each other. There was just a new and awful pain to be suffered together.

Blaise came back about eleven. Harriet, who had by now schooled herself to wait until twelve, was sitting stiffly like a prisoner who has been pinioned in some tormenting way and who sits still, wondering just how bad the pain is. Then suddenly she heard a footstep and there he was before her. The sun had come out weakly and the kitchen was filled with clear pale light, and there was Blaise gazing at her with a look of frightened agonized entreaty. Harriet rose and, almost carefully, as if to encompass something huge, put her arms around him and laid her head to rest upon his shoulder and felt his hands gripping her, gripping her dress, almost tearing it. His cheek touching her brow was blazing hot. They stood thus in silence for some time.

At last she thrust him away. 'Sit down there. No, get me something, some whisky.'

'Harriet, girl, do you forgive me?'

'Yes, of course. Oh don't worry, that's all right, *that's* all right.'

'You still love me?'

'Of course, of course. Don't be silly. Get the whisky.'

Before Blaise's return Harriet had remained submerged in a confused agony in the midst of which she simply held onto *him*. There was perhaps a comfort in thus isolating him and collecting him to herself. *He* was what mattered, and in this mattering she could almost forget about Emily McHugh. It was as if Blaise had suffered some disaster, had been maimed or disfigured or subjected to some awful menace, and only Harriet's thoughts, only her unremitting attention, could save him. She thought of him blankly and with absolute love and suffered her prisoner's pain hardly knowing what it was. Then as soon as Blaise appeared, quite suddenly, in a great white flash, she was able to think again, even to think logically and clearly, to see what was important, almost to see what had to be done. Only the house was still desolate and the day had a livid ruined atmosphere, time had been damaged in some deep way, like on a day of bereavement or frightful national disaster.

Blaise got the whisky, then stood looking down at her with a fixed grimace of fear.

'Don't look so awful, so frightened,' she said. 'I love you.'

'You won't leave me?'

'I wouldn't leave you in this misery. What do you think I married you for?'

'You won't want a divorce?'

'No. I'm just so glad you've told me the truth at last. You should have told me years ago. Aren't I here to help you in trouble?'

'Oh thank God, thank God, thank God,' said Blaise. He jolted the whisky bottle down onto the table and began to cry, rubbing his wet trembling mouth to and fro upon his knuckles.

'Of course it is—terrible,' said Harriet, 'it's a terrible shock. Oh you shouldn't have deceived me, you shouldn't, you should have trusted me, oh it does hurt so. Don't, please don't cry like that, I must keep my head clear. No, I won't have any whisky, you have some. Sit down, sit down. What is—the little boy's name?'

'Luke. Only we—we call him Luca. Sort of—Italian—'

Luca. We call him Luca. The details, the details were what would kill, and they were only just beginning. 'And where do they live—Luca and Emily McHugh?'

'In a flat. South of the river. God, just to hear you utter those names is so catastrophic.'

'Well, these people exist. You have been visiting them for years. I've got to get used to their names, haven't I? Who else knows about them? Did you tell anybody—our friends—anyone?'

'I only told one person,' said Blaise.

'Who?'

He hesitated. 'Er—Magnus Bowles—I told Magnus a little —just because—well, I had to tell someone.'

'You told Magnus? When?'

'Oh, years ago—I didn't tell him much—I just—'

'You told Magnus. That hurts me somehow. What did he say?'

'He said I ought to tell you.'

'Did he? He's good, he's wise. Still I'm glad it was only Magnus. I couldn't bear it if everyone had known but me.'

'Girl dear, how could you imagine—'

'I don't know what to imagine here. I'm still in a state of shock. So it was all a secret. Will it stay a secret, now?'

Blaise stared at her blankly. He did not know. He had not looked beyond the absolute barrier of confession. Beyond that there had been simply an obscure vista of pulverized wreckage. Now with a sudden deep surge of joy he realized that the barrier was passed and he was still alive. He was having a conversation with Harriet. She had forgiven him, she had said she loved him. There were thoughts and possibilities and explanations, not simply blood and screams. 'I don't know,' he said vaguely, looking at her with wide suddenly joyful eyes still wet with tears. The thing he had dreaded for nine years had happened, easily, almost painlessly, in a moment, it was done, it was over, he was released, he was free, he was free at last to be sane, ordinary, happy, good—

Harriet immediately understood his look. 'I know. I didn't think when I read your letter—Oh that seems ages ago now—But the extraordinary thing is that I can—stand up to it. It's as if—one were to go over a waterfall—over Niagara Falls—and find one's still alive, one's bones aren't broken—one is at least alive.'

'Oh my queen and my saviour, my own dear girl—'

'Well, we don't really know yet, do we.'

'If you still love me *now* we can manage anything together.'

'I married a man who was honest and good, and this—scrape—,' the word seemed ridiculous once she had uttered it, 'doesn't really alter that.'

'God, why didn't I tell you years ago!'

'But will it be a secret? Oh my dear, we've got to live it now, and it will change things. You aren't in love with her any more, are you? I know you said in the letter—'

'No, no, no, I can't stand her, I regard her as—'

'I don't want you to talk like that. It's just that it is terribly important—it is absolutely important—to be clear about this —that you don't love her?'

'I don't, I hate her, she's a snake, she's a poison, spoiling

128

my marriage, it's only you that matter to me, only you, girl, believe me, if you don't I'll—'

'All right, all right. You mustn't say unkind things. I don't want you to sort of sacrifice her like that, it's enough that you —I know that there can be no question of your abandoning her and little—Luca.'

Blaise who had been sitting opposite to her, breathing hard, clutching his whisky glass in the passion of his declaration, met her intense but now strangely calm stare. He dropped his head.

'Of course you can't abandon them,' said Harriet. 'But life will be different—here.' She gave a little gasp. 'You know, you have been very cruel to her, haven't you?'

Blaise mumbled 'Yes.'

'Yes. Very cruel. You loved her—yes, you did—then you ceased to love her—you neglected her. You have neglected her, haven't you?'

'Dreadfully,' said Blaise, still hanging his head. He said. 'I didn't really love her—not with real love like I love you—it was just a—'

'You must be absolutely truthful now,' said Harriet, 'absolutely literally carefully truthful. That's part of what will help us, isn't it? You will be, won't you?'

'Yes, yes.'

'Have you told her about telling me?'

'I told her I was—probably going to.'

The idea of Blaise conversing with Emily McHugh about herself was something Harriet could not yet contemplate. She said hurriedly. 'What about telling David?'

'Oh Christ. Oh Christ. David's knowing this—is—just— utter—hell.'

'I will tell David,' said Harriet. 'I'll tell him at once, tonight. Will you tell Monty?'

'Monty? Er—must Monty know?'

'I want Monty to know. I want somebody *else* to know, somebody who is my friend, who is friend to us both, to know. That will help to make it more real—I've got to see it's real— I've got to feel it all really exists—it still seems like an awful dream—'

'All right. I'll tell Monty.'

'The secrecy hurts, you see. Everyone thinking it's all right, like it was, when it's all changed. I've got to accept—'

'Yes, yes, I understand. I'll tell him. But let's not be in a hurry—'

'And when shall I see her?'

'*See her?*'

'Yes. You don't imagine it's all going to go on as it did before, do you? We're agreed that you aren't going to abandon her, but did you imagine—?'

'I don't know what I imagined,' said Blaise. 'But there could be no possible point in your meeting her.'

'Why not?'

'Because—well, she's a rough tough London girl—'

'Are you afraid she might swear at me?'

'No, no, I mean she's just a poor fish, she's a waif, she'd resent it anyway. You simply couldn't talk to each other, it would just be a horrible shambles, it's not necessary, you'd regret it—sorry. I've never conceived of your meeting, it could serve no purpose—do try to understand—sorry, I can't concentrate—'

'I don't see that *her* resentment should decide anything!' said Harriet.

'Sorry, sorry—but it's pointless—and if there was some sort of row—'

'I don't want to reproach her, I'm not a complete fool. I don't want to help her either, even if I could. That would be impertinent. But now that I know she exists I've got to see her —and to see—Luca. Don't you understand? I've got to *see* them. You can't just announce their existence to me and go slinking off to visit them now and then as if nothing had changed except that I *knew* and had forgiven you—is that what you want?—and expect me to put up with it! Of course you can't desert them and I'm not trying to force or change anything in your relationship to them or your duty to them, though heaven knows I might want to—Only—you know— this is between you and me—not what other people might do, but what we two, in *our* place, in *our* marriage, are going to do. And if we are going to act together, really together, I've got to see it all, not just listen to you, but see for myself. I mean— perhaps you should be kinder to them—I'm sure you should, perhaps I can help you to be. All this is part of—saving us— and it may not be at all easy—only we have got to save each other, and we can, I know we can. I didn't know this morning, when I read the letter, but I know now. But I must see them, both of them, at least once, however much pain this causes to me—and to you—and to her. And now please you must tell me everything exactly and truthfully in detail from the very start. Where did you meet her?'

Blaise stared at his wife. She was glowing with an energy and a certainty, almost an exhilaration, of moral force. Here was the gentle creature whom he had cherished and protected, whom he had feared to try. What a fool he had been. He felt her will, her strength, her new strength, the strength he had made in her by this ordeal. He had hoped perhaps for an angel's kindness, but he had not anticipated an angel's power. With resigned helpless gratitude he began to talk.

Harriet had told David. He listened to her in silence, only, after the start, turning his face away.

It was evening, the shorn grass of the lawn golden as stubble in the parallels of the rich light. Harriet had eaten nothing. She and Blaise had talked till three. Then she had taken aspirins and gone to lie down. Blaise had gone out for a walk. After that, he said, he would go and tell Monty. Perhaps he was telling Monty now. Harriet felt that she had heard the whole truth, and Blaise's obvious sincerity and relief in telling it had brought a kind of comfort. The weird wrecked feeling of the world persisted, as if a tornado had knocked everything over onto its side, letting in a sort of white glare. Harriet had fed the dogs, her tears falling into their food. All precious domestic rituals were alienated now. Amidst all this wreckage she was upheld by an intense loving pity for her husband and by a stiffness of her own, the absolute need for courage. After all, as she had firmly told herself, she was a soldier's daughter and a soldier's sister. She recalled Adrian saying, when some incident was being bemoaned, 'but soldiers are supposed to be shot at, it's their job.' Harriet was determined to stay upright now in the gunfire. She summoned up a sort of fierce bravery which she had never had to use before. The pain was very great however and she could feel obscure things in the depths of her mind shifting about in order to endure it. The crisis seemed already to have lasted for days and days. Soon there would be a new phase, not of collapse she was sure, but of now quite unpredictable thoughts and feelings. This was one reason why she felt she had immediately to perform the task of telling

David. She had not foreseen how hard, how awful, how extremely *peculiar* it would be to tell her son these things.

'Well,' said Harriet, 'there we are.' She had adopted a cool tone which, also, was new. What a lot of new armour she had suddenly had to forge. She was sitting on David's bed. He was sitting at the table, occasionally moving his books about, looking at them, straightening them. She could see, beyond the haze of his fluffy golden hair (recently washed) the curve of his cheekbone, the flush of his cheek.

After a silence David said in a similar tone, 'I see.' He turned towards her, not meeting her look but deliberately presenting his face, stiff and red with fiercely contained emotion.

'Your father wanted to live in this free way,' said Harriet. What an idiotic meaningless remark, she thought. I can't discuss or comment, it isn't possible, I had much better go away, only I can't do that either. I must talk to David, I must get some comfort from him, we shall have to comfort each other, both now and in the future. Only the bright eloquence which she had been inspired to use with her husband was utterly lacking here. She had no words for David, no ardent grace with which to cover up the horror of the facts. She wanted to cry but she knew she must not. 'He is very sorry,' she said in the cool brisk tone. 'We must be kind to him, mustn't we, and help him. He needs us very much, you know.'

'Is he going to leave those people now?' said David, after a pause. He had returned to fingering his books.

'No, of course not, how can he? There's the little boy.'

After another pause David said expressionlessly. 'Thank you very much for telling me. Now I think I don't want to hear any more about those foul people.' 'Foul' was a word of Monty's which David had recently acquired.

'But, my dear heart, you must try—I know it's hard, it's a terrible shock—but it's a fact and we have got to live with it.'

'I am not going to live with it. I don't want to know any more about it.'

How hurt he was in his youthful fastidious chastity, how outraged and ashamed. Harriet yearned to touch him, to embrace him, but two cold dignities kept them stiffly apart. 'Well I'm going to meet them,' she said.

'No!'

'Yes. Blaise is my husband. He has told me all about it. It just can't be all hidden again. I don't want part of his life to be hidden from me.'

'You are going to meet that woman?'

'You sound like someone in the nineteenth century! That woman is a very unlucky and very unhappy person.'

'I regard her as a criminal and a thief.'

'But it's all over, all that's over—'

'It isn't over, as you just said yourself. It can't be, and how do you know you've heard everything, you can't possibly have.'

'Your father told me all about it, all the truth,' said Harriet, fighting the tears out of her eyes with a fierce exertion of will.

'I think it's lunatic of you to want to meet her. It'll produce a sort of awful connection. It'll just make the thing go on and on.'

'But there is a connection and it's got to go on and on!'

'Well, there you are.'

'You're deliberately misunderstanding. While Luca is still a child—'

'I don't want to hear any names, please.'

'Blaise can't just abandon them, he's responsible for them, he supports them, it's a matter of money. We can't just wipe them away. Luca is your brother. You've so often said you wanted a brother.'

'I don't want this sort of foul brother.'

'Please don't speak in that ugly tone. At least the little boy is innocent.'

'This talk about the "little boy" is making me feel sick.'

'Please try to help *me*. I've got to support this, I've got to find some way of thinking about it, without screaming. You don't think I like it, do you?'

'I am trying to help you. But I feel it's all so—vulgar—and everything's sort of—spoilt forever. Can't we just go away together, you and me?'

'Go away?'

'Yes. To Italy or somewhere. Just the two of us. Leave him to clear up this mess. Tell him to get rid of these people somehow. He can give them an annuity or something, can't he? I will not have these people in my life.'

Harriet felt: a little while ago I would have been so rapturously happy that he wanted to go to Italy with me! But now it is impossible. A prophetic sense of being *caught* in deeper and deeper awful muddle made her suddenly gasp with pain. Would that old happiness, which for a moment in David's presence seemed so close, ever come back again? 'I can't go away, I can't leave him in all this misery.'

'You've forgiven him. He needn't be miserable.'

'Oh don't be stupid!' said Harriet. Some tears rushed into her eyes and she tried to repress them with her fingers. Then she said, 'David, you must forgive him too. Can you? It's terribly important.'

'I just don't think I can talk about it, with him or anybody. I suppose anyway it's a secret. I don't want people at school to know all this muck.

'It is a secret,' said Harriet, 'for the present—' But *could* it now be a secret? What would things be like now? 'Anyhow you see why I can't go away.'

'Are you afraid of leaving him with them?'

'Of course not!'

'I'm sorry to be stupid,' said David, looking at her now, pushing back the golden torrent of hair, his mouth pursed up with self-control. 'I just can't tell you how awful I feel about this, *awful*. I think I'm just going to cut it right off, I've got to. As far as I'm concerned it does not exist. Please don't talk to me about it any more. And those people must never never never come near this house. I live here too and I won't have it. Do you understand?'

They stared at each other with a sudden harsh puzzlement, seeming scarcely to recognize each other. It was a new world and they were new people, not knowing how to behave. 'All right,' said Harriet, as if making a concession. She felt she was about to be dismissed and that it was her last chance to speak to him with feeling. 'Please, dearest one, be gentle with your father, be kind. You can't just pretend nothing's happened, that would be so cruel. He'll feel so ashamed when he sees you.'

'Don't use these words, please. Don't you see, you mustn't use these sort of words at all. Please try to understand.'

'I will try. But you mustn't be cold—'

'I can't tell you how uncold I feel. Please go away now, mother, please go away.'

'You mustn't—'

'Please go away.'

'She's sitting outside in the car,' said Blaise. 'Well, not just outside, round the corner.'

'Why not outside?' said Emily. 'Who are you kidding now?'

'I thought it better—in case you didn't—'

'You could have warned me.'

'I did warn you! Christ, I said it three times over the telephone!'

'I didn't believe you. I thought it was a joke.'

'A *joke*?'

'So you've really told her at last. Poor old Mrs Placid. How did she take it?'

'Marvellously.'

'Marvellous old Mrs Placid.'

'I mean, she wasn't angry, she understood, she doesn't expect me to leave you.'

'How awfully kind of her.'

'Emily,' said Blaise, 'stop talking in that tone. Help me. I need your help. *Help* me.'

'What am I supposed to do,' said Emily, 'cheer because she's being nice to you and not demanding a divorce? What's in this for me? Nothing.'

'She wants to meet you. She isn't bitter. She's terribly hurt and shocked, but she's doing her best to—'

'I don't want to meet her. I don't want to know what her stupid face looks like. I'm not *interested*. Don't you understand? I'm just not *interested*.'

'I've brought her here—'

'Well you can take her away again. I've been hating her very existence for nine years. I've wished her dead. The fact you've owned up and evidently been forgiven doesn't alter any of that. All it means is that you've stolen my trump card, my secret weapon. At least in the past I could always threaten to tell her. Not that I got anything by it except seeing you shitting with fear, but that was something. You've deprived me of a minor pleasure, that's all. Except that it's not all. You're looking twice yourself. Seen yourself in the mirror lately? You're like a fat cat, you're glowing all over with satisfaction at being forgiven. You've fallen in love with her again now that she's forgiven you. You're happy! Oh Christ, you're *happy*!' Emily, who had been holding a glass of sherry in a trembling hand, hurled the glass down violently into the fireplace. A quick storm of tears blurred her eyes and she turned abruptly away. When she turned back Harriet was standing in the doorway.

Years later Emily McHugh still remembered this moment with the greatest clarity. It was a moment of revelation, when deep feelings, which have seemed leaden and immovable, suddenly begin to skip like the mountains of the psalmist, and intellect, like a flash of lightning, reveals a completely new configuration. Briefly put, Emily realized that she could not hate Harriet. At any rate, she realized that 'the hated wife' was now over and done with and some quite different problem had come into being. She also felt, and was horrified at herself in the same second, both guilt and shame. She felt, before Harriet, the legitimate spouse, guilty and ashamed.

Harriet's face was scarlet and she was looking thoroughly frightened. She was wearing a long white linen coat with the collar roughly turned up, supporting her massive bun of dark yet shining hair. A light blue silk scarf, tied in a bow, was sitting awry. She looked plump and tall and desperately old-fashioned and awkward, she seemed to Emily like a being from another era, and it was hard to imagine how they could both inhabit the same moment of time. Perhaps Emily had never attempted to imagine this. She felt riveted, curiously impressed, by her own ridiculous guilt, but she stared at Harriet in an almost contemplative way.

'I am so sorry,' said Harriet, 'I am *so* sorry.' She gazed at Emily with a look of intense apologetic pleading.

'Get a dustpan for this mess,' said Emily to Blaise. He went into the kitchen.

'You see,' said Harriet, her head moving to and fro like a tennis-watcher, speaking to both of them. 'I just couldn't wait in the car. I followed Blaise a little way and saw where he went in — I meant to wait in the garden but I couldn't. I've only just this moment arrived,' she added, thereby making it clear that she had not just this moment arrived.

Blaise came back with a dustpan and brush and awkwardly, leaning down from his waist, pushed some of the broken glass into the dustpan . 'Oh leave it!' said Emily. She took the dustpan from him. 'Now fuck off,' she said to Blaise. 'Go and sit in the bloody car.'

'Wouldn't it be —' Blaise began.

'Fuck off. Leave her here. You go.'

Blaise hesitated. There was a moment of apparently insolable tension and mute staring. Then Harriet stepped smartly aside and Blaise, as if thereby set in motion, left the room and the flat without looking at either of the two women, leaving them together.

136

Emily said quickly, 'I think since you're here, we should have a very short talk and then you must go. I didn't want to see you, it wasn't my idea, and it's pretty pointless if you ask me.' She set her trousered legs apart, looking at the taller woman, aware of the shame but now cool, a hen on her own dunghill. Emily was glad of the coolness. Her fists were clenched and she felt as if she were made of pliant steel, she felt hard and flexible and young. She was glad to be able to talk so calmly and firmly, but she could not imagine what was going to happen next.

'I'm sorry,' said Harriet. 'I feel I'm intruding. I hope you don't think that I — I expect Blaise told you that he's only just told me. It was a terrible shock.'

'Poor old you,' said Emily. She stared, very deliberately, balancing forward onto her toes and putting her still clenched hands behind her back. She was glad she was wearing her oldest sweater. When Blaise had told her Harriet was outside she had had an impulse to change.

Harriet's gaze had been straying round the room, looking at the cheap sideboard with the missing door, noting the torn chair covers and the stain on the carpet and the broken glass and Richardson sitting in an old cardboard box. 'Have a good look,' said Emily.

'Don't be angry with me,' said Harriet, now studying Emily with the same look of sheer curiosity. Harriet too was calmer. 'Naturally you know it isn't my fault — but I can imagine how you feel. I'm sorry you've had such a bad time. Blaise has behaved badly to you, I know, he has told me everything.'

'I doubt if he had told you *everything*,' said Emily. At least I hope not! she thought. 'And I haven't had a bad time, though I'm sure you'd like to think so. I've had the fun. You're the one who's been swindled. Poor old you.'

'Don't,' said Harriet. Then she said. 'Do you think we could have some tea?'

Emily suddenly laughed, a barking aggressive laugh, not mirthful and difficult to stop. 'Oh God. Look, have some sherry.' She took glasses from the sideboard and poured two drinks. She put Harriet's on the table.

'It's not just curiosity,' said Harriet. 'Though of course I am curious, I suppose. But you can have no conception what it's like suddenly learning something like this — and the little boy and all —'

Do I want her to cry? thought Emily. No. If she cries I cry. No tears. Just get through the scene, don't let her win points.

Keep cool and polite, get her out, then you can scream the place down. Harriet's handsome well-bred face loomed large in the room, shimmering through a haze of controlled emotion. She is good looking, thought Emily, and not ancient. He lied. No tears. She stared in resolute silence.

'It was just essential to see you,' said Harriet. 'I had to make the thing absolutely real to myself by establishing some sort of relation with you.'

'I don't want any relation,' said Emily. 'As far as I'm concerned you don't exist.'

'Oh but I do exist,' said Harriet. She said it in a quiet explanatory tone, her face very grave, her eyes huge.

Was this the point at which some sort of screaming slanging match was going to start? I've got to win, thought Emily, but not by violence, that would be too easy. I could frighten this poor lady out of her wits, I could reduce her to cringing tears in a second, but it would be too easy and I'd hate it afterwards. Only let the scene end soon and without any horrors. 'You flatter yourself, dear,' said Emily quietly. Then, unexpectedly to herself, she added with fearful sincerity, 'I want Blaise. I want him to live with me properly in the future. I want the lot. Sorry and all that. This is what this is about.'

'Of course he must see more of you,' said Harriet quickly. She picked up the sherry and twisted the glass without drinking. 'This is part of what I wanted to say. I know he's been negligent. You may have thought that—when he told me I— well, I don't know what you thought—'

'I didn't imagine you'd want a divorce,' said Emily. 'No such bloody luck. But *that* isn't going to make any difference!'

'After all, we are women—'

'What is that supposed to mean?'

'Please listen to me seriously and with forebearance. Of course it's been a shock and I am very unhappy—'

'Poor—' began Emily.

Harriet raised her hand. She had set the glass down again. 'Something very perfect, which seemed very perfect, very precious to me, is gone. Well, damaged. But I have to think now of Blaise and of our marriage, this is a problem in our marriage and I want to face it honestly, and that involves thinking of you. You said there could be no relation between us—maybe not in the ordinary sense—but we simply have to recognize each other. I just wanted to say that—I would never want to prevent Blaise from—seeing you and—carrying out his—and financially too—I wouldn't want to—'

She is breaking down, thought Emily, and then felt she wanted to rescue her. 'Drink your sherry, dear.'

'Thank you, thank you. You see,' said Harriet, desperately starting again, 'we can't now pretend, especially after we've seen each other, and it wouldn't be right, and we've got both of us to help Blaise, and there's your little boy to be looked after, and there are just a lot of *duties* —'

'What are they?' said Emily.

'You see, I regard you as a victim and not as a criminal —'

'Thanks a million.'

'And as I see it, and please you must help *me*, the question is simply what can we all do for the best. I want to be reasonable, I want to help Blaise to help you, I must. I haven't even any alternative.'

'Oh this is *rubbish*,' said Emily. 'It's soppy empty guff. I've told you what I want. Now I suggest you go back to your husband and let him drive you away in his motor car.'

Enter Luca. The child came in quietly, carrying in his arms the woolly piglet, the strangulating ligature once more tied tightly about its neck. He came straight towards Harriet and stood looking at her. Harriet said 'Oh . . .'

'Go away,' said Emily, 'go *away*.'

'Please don't,' said Harriet, to Luca, not to Emily.

Luca continued to stare. Then he said to Harriet, 'I've seen you.'

Harriet's serious huge-eyed mask had changed. Tenderness, anguish, pain squeezed her features. Her eyebrows shot up in an effort of communication. 'I've seen you too,' she said, almost in a whisper. They gazed at each other.

'Oh, stop it!' cried Emily. 'Clear off, damn you!' she shouted at Luca.

Luca, still ignoring his mother, lifted one hand and waved rather formally, agitating his fingers beside his cheek. Then quietly he made for the door. Harriet gave a rudimentary wave after him. Tears began to stream down her face.

Emily looked for a moment at Harriet's tears. Then, in a storm, her own tears came. She sat down at the table and put her head in her hands. She said through her wet hands, 'Go, if you've any decency, go —'

'Sorry —' The door closed. Emily put her head down on the table, she took the tablecloth between her teeth, she began to utter muted screams.

Luca, sitting in the sun in the middle of the lawn, surrounded by dogs, caused a variety of emotions in the breasts of his hidden human spectators, to whom, with the natural exhibitionism of a small child, he was displaying himself, seeming perhaps a provocation or perhaps some sort of moral sign or portent. He was wearing a grubby T-shirt with Micky Mouse upon it, a school blazer, very short shorts and sandals. His thin smudged legs, which appeared now daily longer, were extended. All the dogs were there of course. Luca was holding Seagull, paws upwards, in his arms and rocking him a little. Seagull's bare pink and black spotted stomach heaved with heat and emotion, his eyes were closed with privilege and bliss, his lightly-fringed black lips parted to give a glimpse of fine white teeth. The other dogs, with the exception of Lawrence, watched with respect, humble envy and awe. Ajax, always dignified and responsible, was sitting neatly up in an Egyptian attitude, his black moist nose twitching, his dark rather dewy eyes with their fine lashes (which Harriet likened to the eyes of a handsome Jewess) fixed upon the privilege-bestowing boy. Babu and Panda, the inseparables, were consoling each other, lying just in front of Luca, Panda on his back in empathetic imitation of Seagull, his dirty brown scanty-haired tummy and sexual organs shamelessly exposed, while Babu, lying behind him and supporting him, shifted a shaggy black visage uncomfortably about on his friend's ribs. Babu and Panda were well known to be the dirtiest of the dogs. They were mysteriously dirty. Little Ganimede (always somehow designated as the little one, though Seagull was equally small) was lying in his slug position, his head near to Luca's richly fragrant sandalled foot, which he licked ecstatically from time to time, his eyes like glowing damsons swivelling upwards. Buffy, always conscious of inferiority, always the odd man out, with a dark tear in the corner of each amber eye, sat behind the enlaced inseparables, staring his soul out of his light brown rather stupid whiskery face (which had so instantly won Harriet's heart at the Dogs' Home) and whining occasionally for attention. Lawrence the collie, who thought he was a human being, leaned familiarly against Luca's shoulder and

140

looked with superior indulgence upon the canine congregation.

'Who's the boy?' said Edgar to Monty. 'Some little cousin, I suppose?'

A talk had led them several times round the circle of the clipped orchard path, between the tall flowering grasses. 'Just like we used to walk round and round the cloisters at college,' as Edgar said sentimentally. The sun shining powerfully once more, had dried and burnished the scene until it looked like a little paradise out of some mediaeval Book of Hours. Green and white were the predominant colours.

White foxgloves were growing in a row along the fence between the two gardens. Monty had picked one of the flowers and was examining the extraordinarily vivid scattering of purple spots on the lower side of the interior. Did Shakespeare mention these spots somewhere? Or was it some other flower? Should he ask Edgar? No. Edgar would certainly know. He put the white cap on to his little finger like a finger-stall. He had had to let Edgar in because of Harriet. Harriet had asked Monty to tell Edgar. Monty did not want to tell Edgar. These emotional revelations were binding. He did not want Edgar to be bound to himself or bound in any way to the weird and fascinating scene which was developing at Hood House. Something about the scene was home to Monty, such home as he now had. He did not want Edgar in it. But he had to obey Harriet. Edgar had been talking of departing to Oxford, and this revelation would doubtless delay him. Thinking these thoughts and waggling the foxglove flower upon his finger, he turned back towards the house, saying nothing.

'Who's the little boy?'

'Blaise's other son,' said Monty. He crushed the flower up and threw it away.

'What on earth do you mean?'

'Blaise has another establishment with a mistress and a son. Harriet has only just found out about it. That's the son of Blaise's mistress, Emily McHugh.'

Monty expected some sort of immediate exclamation, but Edgar remained silent so long that he turned to look at him. Edgar's face was red, screwed up in an almost comical expression of incredulity and distress and outrage.

'Really—is this really so?'

'Yes,' said Monty. 'Harriet told me.' He added. 'She wanted you to know too. She's being very good about it.' Idiotic words. They entered the dim hall where the slim creamy pilasters grew up into trees and joined the pitted ceiling in a quick swirl.

'You mean all this time — all these years — that boy must be — Blaise has been deceiving his wife — had this other place and never told Harriet?'

'That's it. Come and have a drink. Then you must go.'

They entered the Moorish drawing-room. Mr Lockett had had a fountain there, in a recess, between the saffron and grey lentils, but Monty had replaced it by a bookcase. The vivid de Morgan tiles still peered out over the tops of the books.

'I can't bear it,' said Edgar. He sat down heavily in one of the elaborate white basket chairs, making it scream a little.

'You don't have to.'

'It means I can't go there any more.'

'Really?'

Edgar in tweeds (it had not occurred to him to remove his jacket) was sweating freely. Monty was in white shirt and black trousers with the narrowest conceivable leather belt. The room was cool, as he had remembered to keep the shutters closed earlier in the day. He poured out drinks into tall glasses. Gin and freshly pressed lemon, and slices of a lime which Harriet had given him, and soda water and a little parsley floating about, like his mother used to make in the old days. Sophie never drank long drinks even in summer.

'How can I, with that grief in the house. I can't imagine anything more awful. Oh poor poor Harriet —'

'Poor Harriet,' echoed Monty. He felt extreme irritation against Edgar and his self-regarding reactions.

'And I'd want to punch that swine. He has that wonderful wife and —'

'It's more complicated than that,' said Monty. 'Probably. Anyway we'll never know.'

'That's just it,' said Edgar, draining his glass and holding it out for more,' we'll never know. We can never ask. Of course Harriet is blameless. You aren't insinuating anything are you?'

'I insinuate nothing.'

'How did she find out?'

'Blaise told her. His nerve broke.'

'The swine. Oh dear, oh dear. I can't talk to Harriet like I used to any more.'

'You have known her for less than a week.'

'I couldn't expect her to confide in me about that, could I? How can I even offer her my sympathy? Oh God, what awful suffering.'

'Yes, it is awful,' said Monty, 'but as you said, we can't enter in. Better to keep clear. You'd better shove off to Oxford. Just drink up and go, will you?'

Edgar had drained another glass and was in possession of a generous third. 'I suppose I could write her a letter. Could I write her a letter?'

'That's it, write her a letter. From Oxford. Now drink up and go.

Harriet was coming to see Monty on the following morning for what she announced as a long talk. Monty looked forward to her visit with a mixture of alarm and excitement. He wanted Edgar to clear out. He wanted to think about Harriet.

'What on earth are you doing?' said David to his mother, in the vivid kitchen where the red and white cloth glowed in the indirect light of the hot sun. She, in a pale mauve dress with white smocking, was setting out the best tea service, thin bread and butter and honey and sugary fruit cakes. The Gavender household never had tea. The sugary cakes were for Harriet's elevenses.

She turned her gaze towards the window.

David's pale face flushed, but his features did not flicker. 'I suppose that's him.'

'Yes.'

'Is she here?'

'No.'

'Are we going to have visits like this often?'

'I don't know.'

'Did you invite him?'

'No.'

David moved towards the door.

'Where are you going?'

'Out. Till he's gone.'

'Please,' said Harriet. 'To please me. Please go and talk to him. Say just a word to him. Go and talk to him and ask him to come in to have tea.'

David looked at his mother. Her neck above the high mauve collar was as red as that of some strange bird, her face was red and seemed swelled with emotion, though there was no sign of tears, rather a sort of tremulous uncertain excitement.

'I know it's difficult,' said Harriet. 'But it will be harder next time if you run away now. We've got to make this somehow ordinary or we won't be able to bear it. Please. Please. *Please.*'

Blaise came in. He had a transformed look. He looked

humbler and stupider, not unlike Buffy, his face patchily pink, his short gingery hair jagged, his big jaw unshaven and covered with gleaming points of red. 'Look who's outside,' he said, smiling humbly and idiotically at Harriet. David turned his face away, as he had used to do as a child when his parents ate messily. 'What shall we do?' said Blaise diffidently.

Harriet said. 'I've asked David to say hello to him and ask him in to tea.'

'Is that — all right — darling?'

'Of course it's all right. We can't just leave the child sitting on the lawn.'

Blaise turned to David and was about to say something.

David walked out of the garden door and went quickly across the grass. A primitive awful sense of sacrilege and sheer trespass swelled his chest and made him want to scream get out, get out! He strode up to Luca and stood in front of him. The recumbent dogs all jumped up. Seagull twisted round and plopped out of Luca's embrace. There was a faint general growling. The small brown-eyed boy looked up at the tall blue-eyed boy.

'My mother says will you come in to tea.'

For a moment Luca said nothing. He simply stared up at the stern unsmiling face. Then he said, 'Would you like to see a toad?'

David, who had until now been simply hot with that confused boiling of misery and outrage, and who had uttered his mechanical words as ungraciously as possible, felt suddenly that characteristic cleavage of the soul which is the cold call of duty and, even in his anger against it, recognized it. He breathed deeply and said, 'Yes.'

Luca, moving himself gingerly, knelt up and gently introduced both his hands into the pocket of his blazer. The hands emerged holding a small brown toad. The toad wriggled a little, and then settled into the supporting hands, looking upwards with its bright bulging eyes and an air of concentration which was oddly like a frown. Its dry dark spotted skin glimmered in the sunlight.

David looked at the toad. He knelt down on the grass.

'They're looking at something together,' said Harriet.

Her voice was a little quavering but she was well in control. What had become plain to Emily at the moment of meeting had been as plain to Harriet as if she could have looked into Emily's soul as into a box. Where Harriet had expected the terrifying challenge of hatred, suddenly there was none, there

144

was only an object of pity. For Harriet had seen the guilt and the shame which Emily had so greatly wanted to hide from her; and all these things had been for Harriet a sort of searing consolation.

She had not attempted to describe their talk to Blaise, in fact she felt that any mundane description of it would simply mislead him. So much had passed between them which words did not then express and could not now explain. She felt that her meeting with Emily had been an achievement. She had done, against Blaise's judgment, what she thought to be right, and she had behaved to Emily with all the self-assertive dignity and kindness which she had intended in her heart. She had, in Emily's territory, planted her own standard and with no censorious device upon it. The vulgar brawl which Blaise had mutely feared could not have been more impossible, and this impossibility had been imposed by Harriet's own firm gentle will. She had done the very best she could, she had been brave, and the little meeting with Luca, that had been a success too, something so mysteriously important and so curiously easy.

At the same time, Harriet knew that the shock wave had not yet really come. She was simply, before it arrived, carrying out as many quick sensible movements as she could, shoring up her place, her home, against the tornado. Awful grief and fear hovered somewhere near to her, hanging in the still atmosphere like a faintly restless black balloon which she would touch lightly with her hand and push gently further away. But she was in control of herself, and as she suddenly realized with an absolutely new feeling of energy, she was simply in control. All these people now depended upon *her*. She, and only she, could, if it were possible at all, help, heal, and avert disaster. And now in the livid light before the storm she could see Blaise very clearly too. She could see him now and understand him perfectly, as he looked with amazement out into the garden where his two sons were kneeling on the lawn together, looking down at something and talking.

'My God,' said Blaise, 'Oh my God.' He felt from within his idiotic humble smirk. It was the best that he could do to hide a sort of stupid relieved joy, improper and insane. Harriet had said that her meeting with Emily had 'gone well'. Clearly there had been no slanging match. Blaise had not returned to Emily. He had driven Harriet home to lunch. Lunch had been an empty ceremony since neither of them could eat at all. They had conversed awkwardly, gently, about Emily, then about their own past, the early days of their marriage. After lunch Blaise had slipped out and telephoned Emily from a call box. She said in that heavy way he knew so well. 'Oh, it's you.' 'Yes. Forgive me.' 'Fuck off.' 'You were kind to Mrs Placid.' 'There is no Mrs Placid.' 'You were kind to Harriet.' 'She was kind to me.' 'May I come and see you tomorrow morning?' 'Do what you bloody like.' Emily rang off. It had been a very merciful conversation.

Blaise had returned to the house and tiptoed to his study. Harriet was lying down. He lay down too, relaxing upon the sofa, gazing at the ceiling, and letting relief lift him up like a tide. So far, so good. So far, they were both being kind to him. Had he, oh Christ, got away with it? Would God, in the form of two wonderful women, forgive him, grant him salvation after all? It was too early to know. But today there had been such mercy. I am unworthy, he said to himself, blinking and grinning at the wonder of it all. Was it conceivable that the worst was over? Blaise too saw the black balloon of grief and possible catastrophe and he tapped it away from him with a light touch. He felt love for Harriet and love for Emily welling up in his heart, and realized that he was experiencing this double love for the first time in his life as innocent.

Now as he saw David and Luca so impossibly together he wanted to yell out to the universe in gratitude. He turned to Harriet and saw how tenderly, how perfectly, she understood all that he was feeling. 'Oh—you—' she said, in her way; and took him into her arms and pressed his beaming head down against her shoulder.

'Isn't it funny,' said Harriet. 'The only person he told was Magnus Bowles.'

'Really,' said Monty.

'I feel I'm living in a myth,' she said. 'I feel the pain itself is giving me the energy to bear it. Is that crazy?'

'No.'

'Of course there'll be shock later. Secondary shock, or whatever they call it. People die of that.'

'You won't.'

'I feel so talkative, as if I were drunk all the time. I feel as if I were seeing myself all the time, and admiring myself for standing it.'

'You are wonderful.'

'Did you tell Edgar?'

'Yes.'

'What did he say?'

'He wanted to punch Blaise.'

'How sweet of him. Oh Monty, it's all so extraordinary. I woke up in the morning and—oh it was such pain—just for a moment I thought it was all a bad dream.'

'Yes.'

'I feel I'm living on pain, riding on it, like a sea.'

'So you're on top of it.'

'Yes. Now. It's odd, but I feel so full of *power*, I've never felt this before, I've always depended on other people, on the strong people, my father, Adrian, then Blaise, even David. Now suddenly I feel—everybody depends on me. *She* depends on me. Oh Monty, the little boy is so enchanting.'

'You don't resent him?'

'No, how could one, how could any woman resent a child—'

'I suspect some women could,' said Monty. He was not sure. How much did he really know about women? Were they different from men? Somehow he had never quite classified Sophie as a woman. He was annoyed with himself because he found Harriet's state of mind so difficult to imagine and because he was disconcerted by her reactions.

'Luca likes me too—it's quite a thing—it's like a sudden new love in the middle of it all—like a—'

'Spring in the desert. Blossom in the wilderness.'

'You're laughing at me! Monty, you are doing me good!'

'I haven't said anything.'

'You don't need to. I feel—you see, you're the only person I can talk to, and I feel now for the first time that I can talk to you perfectly. There's perfect understanding between us, I can say anything and be understood.'

It was true. Harriet's amazing exhilaration, there was no other word for it, had swept away all the old barriers of her nervousness, his coldness. She was suddenly able, with a strong instinctive deftness, to run the conversation. She was, probably for the first time in her life, utterly obsessed with herself,

147

interested in herself, pleased with herself, with her ability to endure pain, with what she had called her 'power'. This great flowering of self-pleasure gave warmth, gave light.

'I took Blaise for better or worse. Suppose he had cancer or were disfigured or blind or lost his mind? I'd nurse him, I'd look after him. Of course I never conceived of *this* sort of trial, but how could I fail it? I mustn't, I can't. Really, Blaise and I have never felt closer to each other, never more perfectly in love, it's made us both so much more alive, like being shipwrecked together.'

'You are very good.'

'No, no. You see, he's so *relieved*, it's like being a priest and giving somebody absolution, seeing the burden drop off. His relief is so wonderful. I've never been able to *give* someone I loved something they wanted so much. It's pure hedonism.'

'Goodness is finding pleasure in right acts.'

'He's so humble, and oh he is so relieved, not to have to lie any more, to have all that awful fear and deceit swept right away. And he really is sorry, and so frank about it all, not sparing himself at all, he really is contrite, I've never seen him like that, I've never seen anybody like that. I just want to hug him and hug him and tell him that it's all right.'

'Well I'm glad it *is* all right,' said Monty.

Misfortune had crushed him like a worm, deprived him nearly of life. This woman seemed to thrive on it. Her eyes were all dazed and glowing, her dark goldeny-brown hair, tumbling in a thick involved braid down her neck, seemed to be done in a new way, or perhaps it was just a felicitous accident. She looked younger. As she talked, making vigorous gestures with her plump arms, her long blue and white striped dress swept the floor. He could smell the newly-washed cotton material, Harriet's face powder, warm flesh, roses.

They were sitting in a couple of the white basket chairs on the small tiled verandah, whose glass roof was supported by formalized teak caryatids, now the worse for wear and splitting a little like old ships' figureheads. The sun blazed on the glass, making a flower of light at one corner, and the hot thick perfumed air shifted slightly about in big perceptible polleny bundles. Monty, his shirt sleeves rolled up to reveal thin white black-furred arms, was sweating. It was eleven-thirty in the morning. He was drinking the gin and lemon and parsley mixture. Harriet, drunk with her own survival, was drinking nothing. Monty felt restless to screaming with a strange irritation. Had he hoped, like a vampire, to batten on his neighbours' trouble, and to be helped in his catastrophe by surveying theirs, and was he now disappointed to find a triumph of courage and decency where he had expected a shambles of resentment and grief, a holocaust of rage and hate? Had he really wanted to console a broken Harriet?

'All the same,' he said, 'your troubles are only beginning. Emily McHugh exists, and—'

'Yes, yes, I know she exists, I *know* it. Blaise is with her now, I sent him to her. Monty, you must meet her. I pitied her. I *liked* her, and she didn't hate me. I want her to come here, I want her to see it all, a real family, a real home. I want her to accept it and not to feel condemned or excluded. Monty, do you think I'm mad? I thought at first I'd die of grief and shock. But now—you see it's got to be all right, so it will be all right. And I feel so crammed full of will power, I think I could make the universe obey me.'

'You are wonderful,' Monty said again. In her own way she will make the other woman suffer, he thought, she will punish her; and he felt less annoyed.

'And I think I shall adopt Luca.'

'But Luca has a perfectly good mother of his own! He even has a perfectly good father of his own!'

'No, I don't mean literally. I'm not as mad as that. Of course he must live with Emily, but I want him to come here a lot, I want him to have his own room here. The poor child could do with a second mother. We've decided to move him to a better school.'

'We?'

'Blaise and I. I'm going to see Emily again tomorrow. Blaise is sure she won't refuse. Of course it will all take time.'

'But don't you feel any ordinary jealousy?' said Monty. Was it possible that those apparently automatic torments which had crippled his own marriage could be cured after all by simple magnanimity, if that was what it was?

'Yes, of course I do,' said Harriet, picking up the skirt of her striped dress and tucking it under her. 'Monty, I think I will have a little of that mixture after all. I'm talking big to make myself feel that I can manage, because if I can't manage we're all smashed up. You don't know how brave I'm having to be not to become a screaming mess.'

'I'm sorry,' he said. I am stupid, he thought. She is really brave and intelligent. I keep wanting to imagine it isn't genuine, but it is genuine.

'I feel such idiotic jealousy about the past, as if that mattered, it's gone, it doesn't exist any more. But he *was* in love with her, and he *did* sleep with her.'

'Doesn't he now?' said Monty. Blaise had always been a bit vague on this point.

'No, of course not! That's what it's all about. She's a remnant, a duty—'

Was Blaise lying, Monty wondered. And then he thought sadly, I shall never know. Blaise will not forgive me for being the calm spectator, he will not forgive me for sitting here with Harriet and hearing her describe his contrition.

'Oh I feel jealousy, yes,' said Harriet, gazing with her big vague eyes down the garden, where Panda and Babu and Seagull were lying panting in the sun. 'Only I'm determined not to go mad with it. I've got to be in control of myself and of them. They expect it of me, even Emily expects it, Blaise says. I've got to save them all. Of course it's a wreck, a crash. Many marriages would simply break. Only mine isn't going to. All claims will be met. It's like being bankrupt but determined to pay. We shall *make a place* for Emily in our lives, we shall have to. I won't enjoy it, I shall often hate it. But as you said, she's a fact, the boy is a fact. Of course if it hadn't been for the boy, Blaise would have left her long ago, she knows that. But given that the boy is here he may even help, he may make us all behave better. An innocent can help.'

'How about David?' said Monty. It was not that he wanted to needle her, he just wanted to be sure that she had seen everything, that they had looked at it together.

Harriet, still gazing, frowned with pain. 'He's very hurt and he won't say anything to Blaise. He may be—no, I won't say the most damaged, for I won't let him be damaged, I won't let him. And he's old enough and wise enough to carry it. I'll help him. He's not a child. But it will be a long task and we're only at the beginning, it will be a long daily task. It's like having been free all one's life, and then suddenly being conscripted. Oh Monty, you will help me, won't you?' Without turning, she stretched out her hand and Monty took it and held it. Ajax appeared from the orchard. He smiled briefly at his mistress and then lay down and panted with the others. 'Monty, tell me more about what Edgar said when you told him.'

Monty released her hand. 'He said he was sorry he wouldn't be able to talk to you any more.'

'Oh, but tell him he can talk to me! I don't want it to be

taboo. The more people I can talk to about it the better I'll feel. It's got to be public, like marriage itself, otherwise it will be a nightmare.'

'Have you discussed *this* with Blaise,' said Monty. 'I mean about it being public?'

'No, not exactly—we haven't decided—Anyway, do tell Edgar he can come and talk to me.'

'All right, all right,' said Monty. His irritation returned. Harriet's *exalté* mood had something ridiculous about it. No good would come of all these fine intentions.

'I'd like to talk to Magnus about it too,' said Harriet.

'I doubt if that will be possible,' said Monty.

'Isn't it strange how one gets extra strength to cope with something like this? I feel I'm out in the open, out in the truth, like an open field with the wind blowing. I thought at first I should never be able to stop crying and I felt so weak and crushed. Then somehow I saw that only loving Blaise much more would help us all out, and then I found I simply had that much more to give!'

'Suppose Emily McHugh won't play?' said Monty.

'She will play,' said Harriet. 'She'll have to. We're both in a new country where we've got to live. That sound's grim but —you see, I know she didn't hate me—I'll *get* Emily to play.'

'So you're the boss.'

'You're laughing at me again. And you're looking at your watch. I must go. Come, boys, good boys. Monty, help me to keep it up. You will, won't you? And don't forget to tell Edgar. Oh, Monty, you really mustn't give me another Lockett's thing! That cup must be quite valuable, look at all the gold leaf or whatever it is! Whatever will your mother say?'

When Harriet was gone Monty went into his study, which he kept dark on these bright days. Locketts had dark red wooden shutters, decorated with stiff pointed tulips with blue girls' heads for flowers. These he kept pulled to across the open window, and the room was full of garden smells but fairly cool, the marbled wallpaper dimly swirling, the coffered ceiling studded with shadows, the narrow stained-glass cupboards, designed for tall vases, and willowy madonnas, gleaming dully, their jewelled foliage extinguished. Monty fell on his knees in the accustomed attitude, but could not clear his mind of thoughts. He felt himself tensely seeking a healing blank which his anxious mind in the same movement rejected. Imagery of above and beyond was of no use now. He felt caught and full of unclassified resentment. After a while he sank down sideways, holding one ankle, and stared at the thin blurry line of gold between the shutters. What had he expected and wanted? To hear Harriet cry out, to feel needed by her, to see that marriage in ruins?

How readily, how naturally, one makes a home inside the misfortunes of others. If this was still an instinct for him he had achieved nothing. He felt an old hatred for himself which he knew to be the most fruitless thing of all. I must get away, he thought. But where to? Soon his mother would be arriving. Sitting there he grew gradually quiet. The image of Sophie reasserted itself, painful but with a sense of the accustomed. He saw her glinting spectacles, her little well-shod feet, her perky avid head, her small air of begging for attention, which betokened all that was, after all, so touching and defenceless about her. He recalled a dream he had had last night. He had been a big blinded animal, and Sophie, naked except for a huge floral hat, was leading him upon a chain. Such small breasts she had. He wished desperately now to weep, but there were still no tears.

'You should go now,' said Emily. 'You mustn't keep Harriet waiting, must you?'

'And you actually talked peacefully together?' said Blaise. Everything that was now happening seemed strictly impossible.

'No. I told you. She talked. I sneered silently.'

'But you didn't shout at her, you didn't tell her to go?'

'Why should I? What she had to say was interesting. And she seems quite a nice person. She's the one who's had the shock, after all.'

'So you—you accept the situation?'

'I didn't say I did. I don't know what the situation is. Do you?'

'But if you both—if you don't fight—there we are—.'

'Sometimes, I wonder how intelligent you are,' said Emily. She was arranging in a vase some yellow and white roses which Harriet had sent from the Hood House garden.

'No, no. I'm not crazy,' said Blaise, 'I know anything can

happen. One can't absorb a shock like this just—but you've been so wonderful, so kind, both of you—'

'So kind to all-important central paramount you. Yes.'

'All right, kid, I'm pure egoist—and—don't say it—most men are. Let me speak then out of my egoism. I want you both. This is what I've never been able in the past to say to you really frankly, I've been afraid to. This new truthfulness may help us all. It certainly helps me. I feel suddenly free. I feel better, I don't feel afraid, I can say what I think. You know, Em, our love was always somehow marred by my feeling so afraid. I can love you so much better now—'

'I wonder what it was you were afraid of which you're not afraid of now. The possibility of my fighting for my rights? Has that gone then?'

'No. I mean truth is sort of infectious, it spreads. I was always trying to placate you—'

'And now you won't? You were saying you wanted us both.'

'I wouldn't have dared to say that before. Of course I don't love Harriet in the special way that I love you. You know that. But I do care for her and it's not just duty, though there is duty, absolute duty to both of you. So I am caught and held. That has always been so really, only now thank God I can tell truth about the whole thing to both of you. Now for the first time somehow it can all be well—'

'I think you're a swindler. You're getting away with it, that's what you mean—you having both of us, you having everything, you loved and cherished. You, you, you.'

'Well—yes—'

'You're being very frank and imagining it suits you. However, I doubt if entire truthfulness has yet descended from heaven. You've been such an habitual liar. Remember, I concede nothing.'

Blaise was silent for a moment, watching Emily carefully planting the roses into a large purple cut-glass vase. Emily was wearing a summer dress, a cheap cotton thing of a pale green, with white daisies upon it, rather like an overall. She had paid today only the discreetest attention to her personal appearance, and she looked pretty, her dark hair boyishly neat, her face creamy pale, her amazing eyes very blue in the clear morning sunlight, flashing now a little with a kind of irony which Blaise could not understand but which he felt to be, in spite of her words, benevolent. He was trying hard not to display a disgraceful relieved happiness which Emily might feel as a provocation. The smallest gentlenesses to him of the two women were gifts which made him feel vastly rich and vastly humble. Never had these two, endowed now with such godlike power over him, seemed so thrillingly attractive. He waited on Emily's every word and gesture, his whole being vulnerable to her as never before.

'Well,' said Emily, tickling Little Bilham's nose with the final rose, then standing back to admire her vase, 'my point is that you won't be able to drop your old habits so easily. You're still trying to placate me with half truths and jostle me into the position that suits you. You say you love me in a special way and her you just sort of care for. Or did I misunderstand you?'

'No—no—,' said Blaise uneasily. The sun revealed with fearful clarity the little familiar shabby room which Emily had, in her new mysterious mood, meticulously cleaned and tidied. It occurred to Blaise that he had never seen flowers in this room before. Why had it never occurred to him to bring any?

Emily looked at him with the new indecipherable irony in her eyes. 'Oh never mind. I could tie you into such knots, but I won't bother. Today anyway. You won't tell me the truth even now, I know that. Only the situation will tell me the truth in the end. Never mind, never mind.'

'Em, kid, you won't ever, will you, tell Harriet about, you know, our special world? That's private, such things have to be. An outsider wouldn't understand. Harriet would just be upset. That's our secret, isn't it?'

'I daresay I won't tell her,' said Emily. 'All right, I won't, it would be pointless. I suppose I should be glad to have some secrets with you still. Is Harriet going to tell everybody about our jolly trio? Your celebrity friend already knows all about it.' Emily thus designated Monty, whom she seemed to have taken against, rather to Blaise's relief. 'Or do I remain boxed up, receiving thrilling clandestine visits from your wife?'

'We'll have to think, we mustn't be hasty. There's my practice. There's David.'

'When am I going to meet famous David? He looks awfully handsome in his photo, much handsomer than you.'

Blaise had shown Emily a picture of David. This action, hitherto unthinkable, had been part of the new sincerity.

'Soon,' he said. David was one of the more obscure parts of what he and the women now constantly called 'the situation'. 'I hope he and Luca will be friends.'

'A little modest hobnobbing with the bourgeoisie may do Luca no harm. The main thing is you've got yourself galvanized at last about changing his school. What does David think about all this? Does he see me as a horrible prostitute?'

'No, of course not. Don't worry. Everything will settle down. It will have to. We all have to live with the situation and we may as well do so as cheerfully as possible.'

'Cheerfully?' said Emily.

'Well, with resignation, with charity, without violence, without frenzy. I don't see that you should mind. You and Luca are going to be a good deal better off.'

'Are we? How pray? Apart from your sudden ability to cope with Luca's schooling?'

'You'll see more of me.'

'How super.'

'Well, you always wanted that, Em, didn't you?'

'I'm not sure,' said Emily. She was sitting now, staring at him with a peculiar intentness. 'I didn't mind about seeing you. I wanted you.'

'You've got me, with much greater security now.'

'Because Harriet has OK'd my status. Big deal.'

'Don't mock, Em.'

'She will require you to be kind to me, she will keep you up to the mark, is that it?'

'Because Harriet knows and accepts, you are that much safer. Surely that's obvious. There's a possible catastrophe which has been eliminated.'

'Harriet's knowing and forcing you to choose.'

'Yes.'

'Harriet may change her mind.'

'She won't. She's a moral being and a person of principle.'

'I may change my mind. I'm not a moral being, or a person of principle.'

'You won't.'

'You mean, I can't. Any more than I could before. Less than I could before. Yes.'

'I don't mean that—'

'Oh never mind.'

'If you're thinking—'

'I'm not thinking. That's rather the point. I am talking calmly and uttering sentences and we are having what looks like a rational conversation, but really I'm a hollow woman. I don't know what I think, I don't even know what I feel, I certainly don't know what I can bear.'

'What Harriet can bear is the question. And she can bear—anything. We rest on her. She is predictable.'

'I'm not,' said Emily. 'However, as you observed, what we've got to endure we will endure. It just makes me sick to think how lucky you are. You must feel like the Sultan of Turkey. You've got us both. You've got away with it, you've just absolutely got away with it.'

'Yes—forgive me—please—you will come and see Harriet won't you? I won't be there—'

'Yes, yes—'

'And, Em, be discreet with Harriet, won't you? I want you to be friends, but—'

'All right, all right. I don't have women friends anyway.'

'What about Pinn?'

'Pinn's not a friend. She's probably not a woman. She's a phenomenon. Buzz off now, will you, I want to be alone.'

'See you tomorrow and—we won't quarrel—will we?'

'Not any more?'

'Not any more.'

'All this predictability is getting me down. All right, Grand Turk, off you go, back to wife number one.'

'Em, thank you, I'm so grateful, and oh—Em—I do love you so much, you do know that—'

'Buzz off.'

After Blaise had gone Emily McHugh sat very still for a long time, sitting motionless in her chair and staring at Harriet's roses, while the sun moved in the room. She felt as she had told Blaise, hollow. She felt impersonal, characterless, echoing. Even the slight toothache which she had had all day wandered ownerless in the room like an irritating unobtrusive insect. She felt as if there had been a great natural catastrophe, an earthquake or a deluge, and she had been right in the centre of it, and yet appeared to have escaped unhurt. How could it be so? How could the house not be wrecked, her home not shattered? She was still alive—and yet also she was dead. Perhaps she had really been killed and was surviving as a ghost? She and Harriet had conversed without screams or tears. This evening she was actually going over to see Harriet at

Hood House. The unimaginable had not only occurred, but had occurred quietly, almost naturally. What could be the *matter* with her, with Harriet, with Blaise, that this could happen at all? Who was doing it, who was working it? Was Harriet? Emily had never felt herself less of an agent. She was, for the time, simply bereft of will, a dazed spectator of her situation and of herself.

For Blaise, for his relief, for his transparent cunning, she felt a kind of tender pity which was quite a new emotion. She loved Blaise, in all this, very much and felt close to him, though without this love and this closeness including any conception of the future. Would the strain be less? Would they stop quarrelling? Was there a new world? Were things better? Or were they in some deep way much much worse, appalling? She felt like someone who suddenly discovers that they cannot tell of something which they are seeing close to and in a good light whether it is red or green. Some fundamental power of discrimination seemed to have been withdrawn from her. Of course, she and Harriet could never be friends. Even Blaise did not really imagine that. After these first encounters they would probably hardly meet at all. It was important to go to Hood House. Harriet had been very anxious for that and Emily was equally so, though the prospect sickened her. If they were to start existing 'in the open' it was important to see where Blaise lived. After all, he had never lived with her; and painful as it would undoubtedly be she had now to recognize more fully than ever before that he lived elsewhere, that he had a real house with a genuine wife and son in it. The son she dreaded. The house she must and could face. After all she had faced the wife. Was this, seeing the house, meeting the son, recognizing it all, her inferior position, her 'status' as she had called it, fully at last and with her whole attention and her whole heart, was *this* the worst? Or was there some other worst which with her crippled mind she could not at present see, even though it was staring her in the face?

The humiliating guilt which she had felt when she first confronted Harriet appeared to have gone, charmed away, it seemed, by Harriet herself. Was Harriet 'good' then? Was Harriet doing them all good? Was it as simple as that? Had Harriet made the screams, the vile abuse, the whole degrading horror of such a rivalry impossible? Into what was she, Emily, being charmed or changed? What priceless advantage was she now losing? Or did it just mean that everything was going to be much the same, only slightly better—better, for instance, for Luca? Upon what she thought of as Blaise's cunning, his absurd disgraceful relief, his secret continued duplicity, she looked with indulgence and with love. The love between her and Blaise seemed strangely renewed and made innocent. Innocent: was *that* the important thing? Of course Blaise had lied to her about Harriet and was doubtless busy lying to Harriet about her. Emily did not even now imagine that Blaise had sexual relations with his wife because, though Harriet was neither ugly nor ancient, she was so absolutely 'not his style'. Her big genteel attractions must be for him inert. Whereas Emily believed, and had always believed with a simple faith worthy of a peasant, in the quite special and enduring nature of her own sexual link with her lover.

Emily had had to believe in that; sometimes there had seemed to be nothing else in her life. And she had contrived to believe in it, even when Blaise had cooled, when they had begun to quarrel, when they had left off doing their 'things'. She had once felt that she and Blaise had been made for each other at the beginning of the world. The way they 'fitted' was a perfect miracle. This was the absolute of what a love should be. And this feeling had never really gone away, and she knew of it now as it revived and warmed her in the very central crisis of 'the situation'. She and Blaise belonged together, like two animals in the Ark, the only two of their kind. In spite of Hood House, in spite of Harriet and David, in spite of Blaiseless days and nights past and to come, she owned Blaise in a way that no one else ever could.

'Would you like him?' said Harriet.

Luca was with her in her boudoir. Harriet was seated and he was standing in front of her, a little way away from her. He had picked up the red mirrorwork elephant and was holding it up in front of his face, the elephant's brow touching his brow, and looking at Harriet past it. He now nodded his head hard several times, keeping the elephant in place, and smiled at her his curiously conscious cunning smile. With that smile Harriet saw him at fifteen, at twenty, his charm. Then he folded his arms crosswise hugging the elephant against his (very dirty) Micky Mouse shirt.

'Then he's your elephant,' said Harriet, trying not to let tears of tenderness and sheer wild painful confusion race into her eyes. 'Will you give him a name?'

'Yes.'

'What's his name?'

'Reggie.'

'That's a good name.'

'Reggie was a boy at school, he was nice to me.'

'Aren't all the boys nice?'

'No. They hit me. I hit them.'

'You're going to a very much better school soon. Will you like that?'

'Have you ever seen an elephant going up some steps?' said Luca.

'No, I don't think so. Have you?'

'Yes. At the Zoo. He walked up some steps and his legs looked so funny, like planks inside a sack. Elephants are kind animals. An elephant wouldn't tread on a man. He'd try not to.'

'In India elephants help men to work. They carry trees.'

'They squirt water with their trunks. If a man annoyed them they'd squirt him. There are snakes in India, big ones.'

'I know. I was born there. My father was a soldier there. He taught Indians about guns.'

'Did you have a pet snake?'

'No. I left when I was a baby.'

'Men play music to snakes and they dance, I saw it in a film. The snake waved his head to and fro. He was in a basket. I'd like a snake. He could live in my pocket. I'd teach him to dance. We have two cats. But I'd like a snake too.'

'You must ask your mother,' said Harriet.

Luca was now stroking the elephant with a firm hard movement of his flat hand, and staring at Harriet with a bright-eyed intentness which seemed almost like amazement. His dark brown very round eyes glowed with a faintly bluish sheen. His dark straight now tousled hair was tumbled about on his head in a chaos of locks. Without moving, Harriet was willing him to come closer, to touch her; and the next moment he had dropped his gaze and with a cunning smile and a look

159

that was almost coy with deliberation he came and leaned against one of her knees. His gesture combined the shyness of a boy lover with the knowingness of a favourite child. Harriet restrained the impulse to hug him violently in her arms. She could play this game too. Lightly, cautiously, breathlessly she began to comb his hair with her fingers, caressing as she did so the dark soft dry cool tresses. He smelt of sweat, of boy, and of something cool and moist like wet earth or water.

'My snake could go to school with me and nobody would know.'

'Why aren't you at school today?'

'It's a holiday.'

I wonder if that is true, she thought. 'Really?'

'Will my new school teach me about God?'

'I expect so.'

'What is God?' Luca was looking up at her now, his chin on the elephant's back, one hand firmly on her knee.

'God is the spirit of goodness,' said Harriet. 'He is the spirit of love which we all have in our hearts.'

'Is he in my heart?'

'Yes. Whenever you love somebody or want to do something good—'

'But I don't,' said Luca firmly. 'Does God make us love animals?'

'He does that too.'

'I love the cats. And your dogs. And all animals, even the fierce bad ones. I found a bat in your garage. He was hanging upside down and I thought he was a bit of rag. Then I saw his face, such a funny little old face with teeth. A bat would bite you. You couldn't tame a bat.'

'After all, you love your father and your mother,' said Harriet.

'Can you talk to God?'

'Yes. Anyone can. It's called praying.'

'What do you say to him?'

'You ask him to help you to be good and to love people.'

'What people?'

'All people.'

'You mean all people, like all animals?'

'Yes.'

Luca reflected for a while on the enormity of this requirement. Then he said, 'I love you. I saw you that night in the garden, and I knew you were magic like in dreams.'

160

Harriet drew him up against her, hugging him tight at last, and felt his arms fumbling then clinging about her neck.

Blaise, having just left Emily, was walking along the road in a daze. Something that very closely resembled happiness was making his whole head glow. He could not keep a lunatic smile off his face. The sheer continued kindness to him of both the women made him radiant with humility and innocence and relief. He felt he ought to be going everywhere on his knees. Thank you, oh thank you! he kept saying in his heart, to them, to the universe. And every moment which passed, every minute of continued acceptance and calm, made the thing that much more certain. Of course there was much to fear, Blaise told himself, though he could not now see *exactly* what there was to fear. The situation must continue for some time to be dangerously volatile. One of the women might break down. Yet even if she did, what could come of it? They were as caught as ever, they were all caught, and would have to make the best of it and had so blessedly early discovered that they could. They were caught now, why not look at it this way, in a cage of charitable forebearance and enforced truth. Why should either of them prefer a fruitless war which could only do them damage?

The black black spot was David, and from that place Blaise averted his attention. There was nothing he could yet do to mend that damage, whatever it should turn out to be. Harriet would help, could perhaps heal. Blaise felt so humble, so, he picked up Emily's word, hollow, so as it were transparent: he could not help feeling that David would have to forgive him in the end. His restored innocence seemed almost to blot out his fault. He felt, at moments, like Christian at the foot of the cross. Naturally what would strike David would be his father's lie, his crime, not his emergence into the truth. What would strike David would be the existence, and the continued tolerated existence, of Emily and Luca. But would not David *have* to forgive? David had looked at Luca's toad. Surely David would forgive. Blaise knew, and shied

161

from the knowledge, that his relations with his son would be, already were, radically changed. But surely surely David would give him back his pardoned being.

That belonged to the future, other aspects of which remained obscure. This was no moment for making plans, although huge questions remained undecided. Would Harriet and Emily really attempt to 'make friends'? Could Harriet carry this off too? In his heart Blaise did not believe it. He did not really want the two women to be together and to contaminate each other, and he did not believe that, after this first little exploratory honeymoon, they would want it either. Two quite separate places, like in the past only innocently, that was surely better. Would Harriet soon stop wanting everybody to know? *Ought* everybody to know? Blaise noticed the return of the idea of simple obligation into his life. However he felt no urge to immolate himself upon this altar. Honest reflection still gave the preference to keeping it all discreet and vague. There would be no point in a scandal which, in its dimensions, would be simply misleading. Blaise felt that he had courageously sorted out his life and should have the reward of continued privacy. His guilt after all really did now belong to the past.

Walking along, anxious and glorified, he was aware of something very unpleasant a moment before he realized that he had seen Pinn walking on the other side of the road. She crossed now towards him, smiling.

'Congratulations!'

'Er—thanks,' said Blaise.

'All well on both fronts, I trust?'

'Yes.'

'Emily is being marvellous, isn't she?'

'Marvellous.'

'I'm so much looking forward to meeting Harriet.'

'Er—yes—'

'It's like discovering a lot of charming new relations.'

'Yes.'

'You must give a party.'

'Mmmm.'

'You are a lucky man, you know.'

'I know.'

'It's the perfect ending, everybody happy.'

'Yes.'

'I expect you'll be over here rather more now, won't you?'

'I expect so.'

'You won't want me in the house.'

'Please don't feel—'

'Oh but I do. I'm going to move out. In fact I'm thinking of buying a place of my own. I wondered if you could possibly lend me some money?'

Blaise looked into the bland smiling freckled face. What was he being threatened with? He said, 'I haven't got any spare money, as you know.'

'Quite a small loan would help. Anyway, think it over. I'll let you know when I have some more definite plans. Bye-bye for now.'

There is nothing she can do to me, is there? thought Blaise. No. *Now*, there is nothing. But he felt very uneasy all the same.

'Who was that fat man who went away just as I came?' said Emily.

She and Harriet were sitting on canvas chairs on the terrace drinking tea. Emily was wearing slacks and a jersey, but had put on a clean shirt under the jersey and tied a red and black scarf round her neck. Harriet was wearing one of her Liberty lawn dresses covered with tiny flowers. The sun was still quite high in the sky and the garden hummed with light and warmth. The electric pink rose was glowing upon the box hedge. Emily kept looking round, staring at the garden, staring back at the house, staring at Harriet. So far, Harriet thought, the visit had gone quite well. The first moments had been the worst.

'He's a professor, Edgar Demarnay, a friend of Monty Small, a friend of mine.'

'Did he know who I was? Did he want not to meet me?'

'He just had to go.' In fact the answer to both questions was yes. Edgar, who had appeared after lunch, had been almost tearful with indignation on Harriet's behalf. Harriet had been ostentatiously calm, but she had been glad of his sympathy. Was Blaise, for all his reiterated gratitude, not taking her acquiescence a little too much for granted?

'You have men friends?' said Emily.

'Well, yes, I have a lot of friends, some of them are men.'

'I have no friends,' said Emily. 'All my grown-up life I've only had Blaise. I grew up into Blaise.'

'So did I!'

'Yes, but if you're married, you're much more free. I couldn't go anywhere. Blaise was so jealous. If you aren't married there's no bond, everyone's a menace.'

'But Blaise knew you wouldn't abandon him.'

'How nicely you put it. He knew I was stuck, yes. Anyway there was so little money. He wouldn't even cough up to let me have my teeth done.'

'About your teeth—'

'No,' said Emily, 'there are limits. I did not come here to talk about my teeth.'

'You did have a job though, you've been a teacher, you must have made friends there.'

'No one wants to know an unmarried ma, one just has no identity. The staff pretended I didn't exist, and the girls made my life hell, one in particular, a perfect little bitch.'

'I am so sorry—'

'I couldn't even tell Blaise about it. If I started to complain he just got cross. I suppose he reckoned he'd got enough troubles.'

'You've had such a bad time—'

'Blaise never believed in my job. He didn't believe I could do a job. He was right.'

'He never believed in my painting either.'

'Men despise us. They think we're just personal. Blaise was so bloody unsympathetic. He has no sort of physical sympathy either. When one feels like hell at the end of the month he just doesn't want to know. You find that?'

'Well—'

'Blaise is so revoltingly pleased that we've forgiven him. I suppose we have forgiven him, have we? All the same I'd like to knock that self-satisfied grin off his silly face.'

'You have been very kind to him and to me,' said Harriet.

'Oh don't talk stupid.'

'I mean it. Of course you're—as you are—'

'A fallen woman!'

'No, no, I mean it's you who've had the bad time and the —irregular situation—but I do want you to feel now that you can—lift up your head and—'

'My head's all right, thanks. When am I going to meet your son? He looks like a film star.'

'You will, I hope—' Harriet recalled David's implacable unhappy face. It was no use suggesting that meeting now or explaining to David how much it would relieve her mind if he would be at least briefly polite to Emily. Harriet's attempt, which so much amazed her male spectators, to 'welcome' Emily was not entirely dictated by that spirit of goodness of which she had spoken to Luca. Harriet needed to do everything that she could to make Emily real. To only half believe in Emily would have been agony. That would have been to try to live partly in a happy past which no longer existed. Harriet's own realism, her sort of strong spiritual domestic economy, demanded a complete acceptance of the new scene and a detailed vision of it. Harriet needed to swallow Emily whole, know the worst and be certain that she could survive it. To have had David on the reception committee would certainly have helped here. Also, David was something which she wanted to *show* to Emily.

Emily, seeming to read her thought, said, 'You have a lovely home.'

'It is pretty, isn't it.'

'And such a lovely garden. I bet you and Blaise never have rows.'

'Well, no—'

'Why should you, living in a place like this. If I lived here and had a clever normal son who looked like an angel, I'd never stop laughing.'

'You have a wonderful little son.'

'I've never had a proper home. First my lousy step-father. Then lousy Blaise. Christ.'

'I'm so sorry—'

'What a lot of dogs you've got. What are they supposed to be for? One of them growled at me when I came in.'

The usual dog group was in panting attendance on the lawn. Several black tails wagged feebly as Harriet gave them her attention.

'They don't bite. Luca's very sweet with them. He's so fond of animals.'

'Fancy his saying it was a school holiday, the little monkey. Kids should be beaten for lying. Blaise never bothered.

'But Luca is so—'

'Not having a proper father has done him in.'

'You do agree about the new school?'

'Oh, yes, yes. But it's too late. Luca's done for. He'll never be normal, never learn, never be an ordinary person. He'll be a sort of moron by the time he's twelve. He's had to carry such a burden, knowing Blaise wasn't a proper husband, having Daddy always disappearing, hearing the endless screaming rows when dear Daddy did turn up. He's had to use all his energy understanding that rotten scene. Sometimes I feel he hates his father, hates me, hates everybody. He's had a bloody awful childhood. Like I had. Those things get passed on and on.'

'He seems to me an immensely perceptive intelligent child, I can't think why you—'

'He probably plays up to you. He's good at pretending. The damage is done by the time you're six. You ought to know, your husband's a psychiatrist. So Blaise wants to give up the trick-cyclery and be a doctor, does he?'

'Yes.' Harriet had decided and Blaise had agreed, that she should tell Emily this, which Blaise admitted he had never done. Blaise said he would be glad for Emily to know. Besides, now Emily would have to know everything. 'He never told you because—it raised those financial questions and—'

'It's a lovely idea, but how do Luca and I eat?'

'You mustn't have less money,' said Harriet, 'you must have more. And Luca must go to that school. We can manage it all if we're careful. You see, David will soon be at college, Blaise can get a grant, we could sell the house—'

'You'd sell this house to send Luca to a good school? You've got to be joking. You're just too good to be true, Mrs Placid. We used to call you Mrs Placid, and it isn't a bad name for you either. What's the snag? Where's the string, Mrs P?'

'I'd do it to help Blaise too. Anyway we may not have to. We can borrow money from Monty, from Edgar—'

'Who's this "we"?'

'I mean all of us—you, me, Blaise.'

'Count me out. I'm not sure what I think about this doctor biz.'

'I feel we should try to pull together—'

'I'm tired of pulling. And we aren't in the same boat.'

'Blaise needs an intellectual challenge, he needs something really hard to do. He's lost faith in his psychological theories. It's all become too vague and easy for him. He needs—'

'Oh I'm so fed up with bloody Blaise! *His* needs, *his* theories, *his* challenges. Hasn't he had enough out of us, wrecking our lives, do we have to send him through medical school as well? What about my needs for a change? I've got a mind too.'

166

'My life isn't wrecked,' said Harriet, 'and neither is yours. We'll all manage somehow and we'll make everything better—'

'How will we? By magic? Well, maybe you could. You're so soft and kind, you're a magic lady.'

'That's just what Luca told me!' said Harriet with a smile.

Emily's cold bright blue eyes surveyed her hostess. 'You know,' she said, 'Blaise told me you were old and ugly and fat. Don't take on. He only said it to cheer me up. I expect he told you I was a common little south London tart.'

'He only spoke of you with the greatest delicacy and respect.'

'Well so I should bloody hope! Now you're angry. Don't be angry with me, be angry with him.'

'I'm not angry.'

'Yes you are. You really should get to know old Blaise one day. He has some pretty weird tastes. So have I, if it comes to that. He must have put in a good deal of play-acting with you in the old days.'

'What do you mean?'

'Never mind, never mind. Luca said you were magic, did he. He never says a bloody word to me.' Suddenly the fierce blue eyes were blurred with tears .'Oh damn! *Damn*!'

Harriet had seen her guest off. The tears were soon dried. Harriet had not wept. It had just been suddenly clear that the encounter was over and both of them wanted to escape. Harriet felt exhausted. She urgently wanted Blaise, to see his big rocky reassuring face, with the sweet diffident air which it always wore now, to smell his jacket, to be held and safe. She felt a sort of constant physical anxiety now about Blaise, like the anxiety she had felt about David when he was a baby. She would like to have had Blaise always within sight, within touch. But consent to his absence seemed now more than ever to be a duty. Today he had gone to the library so as to let her face Emily alone. He had even put off Dr Ainsley and Mrs Lister to do so. He would be giving Emily more of his time in the future: Harriet had insisted on this. She had questioned Blaise carefully (and he had hated it) about the amount of time he had been used to spending at Putney. It appeared that Emily's ration had been the occasional lunch-time and sometimes the earlier part of Blaise's evening with Magnus Bowles, who also lived south of the river. Harriet had declared that this was not enough. He must surely go sometimes for the whole day at weekends so as to see more of Luca. Blaise had been as vague as possible, but he had agreed. So, just when she needed him so much, he would be absent more. This had to be.

Harriet had never been in the habit of scrutinizing her states of mind. She had never needed to. She had always lived in a world of instinct and certainty. Her silly early loves, before Blaise came, had never required decisions of her, had never even puzzled her really. She had endured them like attacks of the 'flu, with as little probing of their nature. A world of sturdy convention plus a firm sense of duty, together with her fantastic luck, had kept her moving along without any real consciousness of her 'mind' at all. She saw the world, not her mind. Now, however, her emotions and her ideas preoccupied her, startled her even. She was aware that her whole mental being had altered since her first meeting with Emily, and was, with frightening speed, altering still. And for the first time in her life she had the unnerving sense that she could not predict either her actions or her feelings. What did remain clear and steady, and this com-forted Harriet in these days perhaps more than anything, was her simple sense of duty to her husband. She had *got* to support Blaise and help him to live truthfully henceforth and to do what he ought to do. It was morally unthinkable that he should abandon a long-established mistress with a small son. Harriet's marriage vows had indeed prepared her to travail for her husband, and she had always been ready to. Was she to repine that the ordeal, when it came, was such an odd one? If Blaise had become blind would she not have read to him, condemned to a wheelchair, would she not have pushed it?

Of course she was consoled and supported too, simply by what she thought of as Blaise's relief. This was so plain and palable as to be almost a kind of thing between them. As she had told Monty, it was wonderful to be able to give what was so much desired, to someone who was so much loved. She could help Blaise, 'save' him almost. She could help Emily too, though this now seemed easy less than it had seemed at the start. Harriet had been impressed by the fact that she could meet her husband's mistress without any approach to jealous fury. The comparative calm, the muddled decency, of that first meeting, the well-intentioned dignity which she, Harriet, had both displayed and imposed had given her an exalted feeling which she at once mistook for something rather like love. It was as if she 'loved' Emily. That much grace had been given her. Already, however, this impression was changing. Emily was becoming less of a formal trial and an abstract challenge and more of a very particular young women with a characteristic vocabulary and a characteristic voice. When Emily had said 'a common little south London tart' the phrase (which Harriet would never have dreamt of formulating for herself) had rung some sort of automatic bell in her mind. Of course Harriet did not own or endorse the reaction, but the reaction was there. What would her father have thought, what would Adrian think?

Already too Harriet was beginning to change her mind about 'publicity'. At first it had seemed the ideal that they should all live in the open: only this, it seemed, would really confirm and make perfect Blaise's return to the truth; and *this* had seemed at first practically the paramount thing. Also a total lack of concealment would, Harriet felt, help her in that necessary process of 'swallowing' Emily McHugh. And did not secrecy still lend to Emily a certain mysterious power? There were many considerations here, not all of them very clear ones, which later seemed to Harriet to have less force. There was David to consider. There was Blaise's practice. There was poor Blaise himself, still too diffident to say so, but obviously detesting the idea of this exposure. What *would* it look like to an outsider? Could she ever sufficiently explain her conception here of a world redeemed? She pictured Adrian's tongue-tied embarrassment, the pain it would cause him. He had never quite liked Blaise. Then there was the whole obscurity of the future. Even the idea of Blaise becoming a doctor seemed again disputable, though Harriet had felt combatively eager to expound it to Emily. Blaise, wrapped in the euphoria of his new innocence, seemed to have less grasp than ever upon his own arrangements. Harriet felt, with tender anxiety, his dependence upon her. She had spoken bravely of selling the house, but she had never felt less like doing so. The house had, as Harriet intended, impressed Emily. The house was, after all, the fortress and the symbol of their united family, Harriet and Blaise and

169

David, as it had always been. Certainly it would be foolish now to do anything irrevocable in a hurry, and perhaps discretion was for the present the wisest course; and Emily was not the sort of woman Harriet would ever have wanted to be friends with, or even be acquainted with, of her own free wish.

As Emily, the tears jerked away, was leaving, Harriet on a sudden impulse had asked her to come over for a drink on Saturday about six. 'And do bring your friend Constance Pinn.' Blaise had several times mentioned this woman with whom Emily had so long shared her flat; and although she did not exactly conceive of her as a chaperone, Harriet had heard with some satisfaction of this sharer. She did not now want to assure herself of Miss Pinn's existence, she did not doubt it. She wanted simply to feel the controls firmly in her hands. She wanted to be the recognizer, the authorizer, the welcomer-in, the one who made things respectable and made them real by her cognizance of them. The more she could 'oversee' the situation, the safer she would somehow feel. She had added, 'I'll ask Monty Small too, I'm sure you'd like to meet him. And David will probably be there.' Harriet wanted Monty to see Emily because she wanted to be able to discuss her with him. And she intended to beg David to appear at least for a moment, to remove a little of that anxiety from her. For she now more and more saw that the really important and central person was Luca.

It was of course because of Luca that Blaise had a continuing obligation to Emily. If there were no Luca, Blaise would have a very different set of duties now, and in respect of Emily possibly none. But more than that. In a way that almost frightened her, Harriet was conscious of having given her heart. With the characteristic cunning of true love, she was already manipulating the future. David must 'accept' Emily because David *must* accept Luca. Harriet felt that unmistakable possessive yearning, a yearning whose great strength would now have to be a secret even from Blaise. She would have to be patient, to be enduring, to be ingenious. She wanted Luca.

It was Saturday morning. David had left the house early. Breakfast did not really take place any more now. The kitchen, centre of consciousness of Hood House, was now disordered. The cups hung differently or not at all. Homeless objects lay about in heaps. The dark woodwork of the dresser was unscrubbed and the red tablecloth was last week's. His mother ate nothing and did not even sit down. Bright-eyed with her private anguish, she waited on his father who ate his eggs and bacon smiling and constantly looking up. David could not eat, but pretended to so as not to have the distress of being coaxed by his mother. He drank some coffee and tinkled his plate, then padded quietly out of the house and ran away down the road.

The previous evening his mother had given him a long talk. He had at first, at very first, feared that she would break down and weep tears upon him. He had pictured himself holding her in his arms and gazing steady-eyed at his father over her heaving shoulder. That had seemed an awful vision then. Now it was an image of an impossible consolation. Most horrible, most obscene of all, was his mother's courage, her compassion, her grip: his father's pink humble relieved face. Better the dignity of cries and fierceness. Besides, this dreadful tolerance was giving a sort of guaranteed continuity to the situation. David had received a very horrifying shock, but with the immediate sense that although everything was broken and could not be mended, at least the pieces would be quickly cleared away. His father had been 'found out' and would have now to put an end to his foul double life. The nightmare news was that the double life was to go on.

Last night David had dreamed that a mermaid with the face of his mother was holding a live fish in her hand. First she caressed the fish, then began, looking intently at David, to squeeze it. David tried to speak, to say 'Don't hurt the fish,' but he could utter no sound. He reached out his arms to her, pleadingly. But now the fish was dead, squeezed into a horrible nauseating pulp. David tried to scream and woke himself with the utterance of a tiny sound. He felt for a moment relief, the security of his room, then remembrance. He turned the light on. Upon his bedside table lay his Swiss penknife, his compass, a killer whale's tooth which Uncle Adrian had brought him from Singapore, a speckled granite pebble from a Scottish stream, a Georgian penny, and a very small teddy bear called Wilson, whom he always kept carefully hidden during the day. He now suddenly swept them all off with a crash onto the floor; and in the silence after the crash knew that they would never again accompany him upon the journey of the night.

He lay awake remembering the talk he had had in the late evening with his mother. She had come to his room and sat upon his bed, her face tremulous and coaxing, strained into that awful bright brave expression. She was explaining to him the inevitability of it all. His father could not abandon this woman and her child. They had to be supported and visited, they could not be just ignored. And since they were *there*, in his father's life, in her life, in David's, was it not better to pity them and to help them, rather than to regard them as enemies or objects of horror? 'They are—you see—poor things—like prisoners—like refugees'—his mother had said, trying to find the right words, trying to unlock, for her extremity, his gentleness.

David, expressionless, rigid, understood perfectly. He understood, as if he could physically see it, his mother's desperate need to dominate the situation, to as it were encircle it. In so far as his father still cherished this other woman, he must do so authorized, motivated, powered by his wife. Harriet was reaching out urgent tentacles to grasp it all and hold it by her own force together. And David read in his father's humble obedient look the present success of this holding. David did not try to explain to his mother how impossible any such acceptance was for him. These aliens were for him destroyers, defilers, foes, and could never be anything else. They had murdered his joy and could threaten his sanity. He hated them, he hated the faces of his parents as they struggled and shifted to survive, to manage, to forgive. He felt crammed to the gills with the violence of his hate.

And as he sat staring at his mother, who now seemed like an actress, he saw yet more terrible things. She cared for the little boy, his foul nightmare brother. He was to have a bedroom at Hood House. He would keep his things in that room. He would be there at night, Luca the vile toad boy, inside David's very own sacred place. His mother would go to him at night and kiss him. She was filled with a private excited tenderness which she attempted to conceal from David, but his ruthless judging eye saw all. This, in her anguish, was her strange unexpected and chief consolation. She had always

172

wanted another child. David had felt himself burdened by her too exclusive love. But he had, even as he thrust her petulantly from him, rested too in the absolute infallible earth-guaranteeing certainty that she thought about him all the time and that he was the goal and centre of her life. Now looking at her coaxing quivering lying face he realized that what he had thought of as troubles in *that* world had been idle discontents of the dweller in paradise. Suddenly, as if by the fiat of a wicked fairy, he had been utterly dispossessed.

How much the world was changed he experienced and tested as he ran, or now loped, along a way which he had made his own, down the leafy road, past the massive brick houses behind their wide lawns, under their big trees, along beside the high wall of the park, then onto a footpath which led into real country, tame but real, farmers' lands where black and white cows grazed upon a humpy green hill. Beyond the hill, now just visible, raising a huge unnatural brown flank above the fields was the new motorway. Blaise and Harriet had greatly bemoaned and vigorously petitioned against the coming of the motorway along their quiet valley, but David had rather liked it, had at any rate adopted it, having seen it grow from a few wandering men with flags, lost among the trees, to the huge juggernaut it now was, raised high up above the irrational little lanes and the winding hawthorn hedges, crazily out of scale with the rounded hillside and the black and white cows, sweeping onward with its white concrete surface glittering in the sun, almost now finished but still huge and silent as any abandoned lonely monument in the midst of that quiet country.

David in his flight had reached the place where, so dramatically it had lately seemed to him, the chaotic brown tumbled earth of the embankment, the great curving side of the thing, rolled like volcanic lava, like a strange immobilized sea, out onto the ordinary grass of the ordinary meadow: a meadow which David had known before the coming of the motorway, where he had searched for mushrooms in previous autumns, in lost quiet golden hazes. But now already the arrested volcanic sea seemed that much less strange, seemed a little to belong to the country. The big brown flank was no longer quite brown, was misted over with patches of grass and little white daisies and red poppies and starry clumps of red and yellow pimpernel and sky-blue birdseye. A large pipe which passed under the roadway already carried a captive stream which debouched as a sandy rivulet looking as if nothing odd had happened to it and it had been running along that pipe all its life. David paused automatically at the pipe which he usually shouted into (there was a weird echo) but then realized that the happy time of shouting into pipes was over for him forever. He began to climb up the side of the embankment. I am only a child, he thought as he climbed, I am only a child. How can they do this to me?

On the thick concrete surface of the road he was alone. In the distance a few lorries and figures of men marked the further progress of the monster, soon now to link up with another monster and become a humming lifeline of the New Britain, banishing silence forever, day and night, from that peaceful valley. These were the last days of the silence. David walked into the middle of one of the carriageways and lay down on his back, the sun dazzling into his eyes, a huge blue quiet heaven above him traced over by white trails of high soundless aeroplanes. And as with the pipe into which he had wanted to shout, he felt again the physical automatic memories of a lost happiness in the familiar feel of the warm gridded concrete touching his back through the thin cotton of his shirt. He felt too, as he lay down in the sun, something else which was now automatic, sexual desire, gripping him like a teasing tormenting hand reaching down from the blue vault of the sky.

How irrevocably spoilt, down to its minutest detail, his world was now. Even the countryside was spoilt, the animals, the birds, the flowers. There was nowhere to run to. Poor innocent toads had been desecrated forever. The rest would follow, all his secret private things. He had heard his mother say how much Luca cared for animals and how greatly he would enjoy exploring all the fields and woods around Hood House. How can I bear it, he wondered, and how can I bear it *alone*? His status of only child, which he had sometimes idly complained of, had been really the foundation of his life. He, his father and his mother had made one indivisible being, a trinity of scarcely separable persons where love circulated in a ceaseless life-giving flow. This had never ceased to be for him, even when he had of late become so sulky and so restless. He had still felt himself the invulnerable absolute focus of loving thoughts. Now suddenly this composite being was no more. He saw with panic the faces of his parents changed into unrecognizable masks by guilt, by revolting humility, by false lying compassion, by vicious disloyal

174

tenderness, by preoccupied alienated secrecy. His father, whom he had, even during his recent sulks, so unquestioningly admired, who had been a secure colossus in his life, was suddenly pitiful, guilty, tiny, found out and pathetically asking favour, while at the same time complacently continuing his crime. They do not know how I feel, he said to himself, they just do not know how *complicated* I am, they think I am simple and can be talked to simply. Oh if only I could take my mother away and never know of these things again. But it was impossible, the machine would go on and on and nothing would stop it. And no one from now on forever would know how much he suffered and what it was really like to be him.

How can I bear it, he thought, how can I go on bearing it without becoming something savage and awful? There seemed a *requirement* of violence, something he had never known before. The mild image of Jesus, never far from his mind, rose quietly over the horizon of his grief. Help me, Lord, he prayed, oh help me. Let me not die of misery and hate. So was he not alone? Was he then thoroughly and into his bitter depths *known* by Someone? Had he a benign Companion who could judge and console, and turn what was evil somehow into good? Was there even here some positive good thing which he and he only could perform? Was there invincible Good in the world after all? He gazed upon the calm pastel-shaded image of the Redeemer which hovered like a ghost within the sun-reddened cave of his now closed eyelids. And he knew, with a return of even deeper agony, that this appealing vision was only an empty fantasm after all.

'Your resemblance to the Old Man of the Sea is becoming tedious to me.' Monty's voice.

'Who was that on the telephone? Your mother?' A strange voice.

'That was Harriet asking me to come over at once. Emily's there. As I told you, you're invited.'

'I'm not sure that I want to come,' said Edgar, for it was he.

'Do as you please. If you stay here you'd better not drink any more of that whisky. Good-bye.'

Edgar and Monty were sitting on the verandah. David who, unseen, was listening, was standing in the Moorish drawing-room, beside the purple sofa, near to the de Morgan-tiled bookcase which had been a fountain in Mr Lockett's time. He had spent the whole day wandering about on or near the motorway. A haze of hunger and faintness travelled with him, buzzing lightly. He felt disembodied and mad as if he had become some sort of demon. No, not disembodied: the great hand of physical desire, descending from those heavens where his friend Jesus had once lived, had been twisting him all day. Vague images of girls floated around him, battering him like malevolent butterflies.

After five o'clock he had begun intensely to need to talk to Monty. The idea of talking to Monty suddenly, in a world without solace, presented itself as a refuge. He ran, sometimes staggering a little under the hunger and giddiness haze, back across the fields, along the lane, beside the wall and through the leafy roads as far as Locketts. And now Monty was not alone and was just going to go out to meet that dreadful woman.

Standing in the half-shuttered room, David decided to wait to see if Monty would leave the house by himself, and then to pursue him.

A book lay open upon the table. Poetry. In Greek. David's mind, switched like a well-trained engine, read the words, which he knew well,

'Then swift-footed Achilles answered him. "Why, oh beloved head, are you come here to tell me what things I should do? Indeed, Patroclus, I will fulfil them all and be obedient to your bidding. But please come nearer to me, and even for a little while let us embrace each other and satisfy our hearts with grieving." So saying he reached out his hands, but could not clasp him. The spirit like a vapour fled away beneath the earth, gibbering faintly.'

The terrible image of bereavement and loss, winged by beauty, seized on him like an eagle and he cried aloud. He sat down upon the purple sofa and wept, putting his face in his hands.

'What's that?' said Edgar, jumping up in alarm.

Monty threw back the shutter and the weeping boy was revealed. 'It's David. Harriet's son.'

Monty was in a mood of irritation and self-dissatisfaction

almost amounting to anger. He had intended to spend the morning in meditation and to bring his mind into a state of absolute calm. He was becoming now almost frightened by his mental condition. Other men suffered bereavements and did not seem to drift away into this state of almost unliveable consciousness. The idea of killing himself was now more real to him than it had ever been, and he understood for the first time how it is that men can prefer extinction to the continuation of agonizing mental pain. He simply must somehow stop himself from suffering in this way. A guilt about Sophie roved sharply inside him and a cinematograph in his head re-enacted and re-enacted certain scenes. He must, he thought, now somehow switch himself off or else move on into some new and even more awful mode of being. But even as he composed himself into slit-eyed immobility and called upon the stillness beyond the stillness where the fretful struggle of self and other is eternally laid at rest, he knew that he could not thus achieve what was needful. Such wisdom as he owned had told him that he could only survive his grief by giving in to it entirely, and though that way might seem to lead into madness there still appeared to be no alternative.

With a sort of mindless stubbornness he held onto the idea of becoming a schoolmaster. Before Sophie's death, though he had been in great pain (a pain which seemed like bliss compared with present pain) he had at least been able to think, and he had thought that it would be good for him thus to do an ordinary plain job. A complete change of world might even help him should he ever want to write again. He needed simple compulsory things in his life, to clothe himself in some humble serviceable role. Moments of vision suggested that to be forced to help people might be healing, might mysteriously make his long struggles with 'it' bear fruit at last, might at least help him to bear his (then future) bereavement without becoming in some way evil. For Monty well knew how untouched within him were certain dark things with which he could not 'play', as Blaise for instance played with his. Even Milo Fane, though certainly a product of the 'dark' things, was not really a part of them. Perhaps they had more to do with Magnus Bowles than they had to do with Milo Fane. Milo was a frivolity compared with *them*. Now that Sophie was dead the schoolmastering idea remained, drained of 'interest', but at least presenting a possible goal in a world without live ends, a way of countering this truly fearful self-absorption. The lack of 'interest' could even prove an advantage. Might not 'it' reward him for a motiveless decent act, if that was indeed what the schoolmastering idea represented?

However it was one thing to dream of a new and useful mode of life, quite another to get oneself out of a comfortable book-lined house in Buckinghamshire and into a masters' common room. This was where, Monty had reluctantly to admit, Edgar Demarnay came in. Edgar had taken over the idea with enthusiasm and had begun to give it body. Monty could teach history and Latin, could he not? After all, he had taught history and Latin long ago, before Milo. And he could teach Greek when he had had time to brush it up a bit. How enjoyable. Edgar felt quite envious. Teaching a fine dead language to clever boys was surely one of the most delightful occupations in the world. As for a job for Monty nothing was easier. Old Binkie Fairhazel, Monty remembered Binkie from college, was now headmaster of a school called Bankhurst near Northampton, and had written to Edgar as soon as he had heard of Edgar's appointment to ask him to look out for a classics master. Well, Monty's Greek was rusty, but he could soon bring it up to scratch. Old Binkie would be delighted. No doubt, thought Monty, recalling the contemptuous way he had treated Binkie at college. He scoffed at Edgar's idea but let a sense of destiny carry him nevertheless towards it. Must he not wait for 'signs' and was not Edgar one? Could he without help find himself a job before September? No. Where was he, will-less as he was, to go? Edgar pointed out that the Northampton school was not far from Oxford and was even closer to Mockingham. Would he, Monty wondered, ever sit once more upon the terrace at Mockingham, drinking brandy and smoking cigars with Edgar, and looking down at the river and the famous vista through the woods? He would need a few weekends off if he were to castigate himself to the extent of Binkie Fairhazel.

He also reminded himself that he wanted to be out of Locketts before his mother arrived. He wanted to be able to decide to sell Locketts. Only something detained him, something interfered with all his plans, and that something was Harriet. He felt, he told himself, no dangerous degree of affection for Harriet, but he did feel affection and a sort of sense of responsibility for her. He also felt a considerably less pure-minded interest in her predicament and curiosity to see how it would develop. This mean little interest and curiosity were, in their way, a sort of mediocre consolation

178

to him since they were a genuine distraction from his bereavement. Harriet was the only person in the world who now moved him in any way. Harriet, and of course David. Would it not be better to stay near them, even running the gauntlet of his mother's visit, and let the schoolmaster idea drift for a while? Besides, if he let Edgar help him he would be that much more bound to that Old Man of the Sea.

Harriet was the sort of 'soft' or 'angelic' woman whom Monty had always felt to be *his* kind of woman in the old days, in the days of his 'frightfulness'. Harriet's truthfulness, her unshadowed openness, her absolute obviousness, her naive untested goodness, her evident innocence calmed and cheered him a little, could do so even now. She was a gentle utterly harmless person who could make no one her victim. How was it that when Monty fell really in love he fell for a devious disloyal two-faced sharp-edged little monster like Sophie? Sophie's nose was the reason, or there was no reason. Or her shoes. He had simply wanted that alien unjustifiable unassimilable being more than anything in the world. Harriet was a consoler though and the picture of her sweetness and harmlessness was a good one to be held up now in front of his face. Perhaps after all he would stay with Harriet. And now he thought, as he listened to Edgar telling him about alterations he was planning at Mockingham and what the National Trust man had said and how he had seen a sparrow-hawk in the valley, it was nearly time for him to go to Harriet's idiotic party for Emily McHugh. Monty had rather disliked Emily and suspected it was mutual. He saw clearly the sort of demoness that sat enthroned inside that vital blue-eyed ferocious calculating little being. But what so moved Blaise here repelled Monty. Now he must go to the party, be polite, pretend to be meeting Emily for the first time, and listen to Harriet talking, as she invariably did when she met him, about Magnus Bowles. At that moment David cried out.

Monty, whose grief had no tears, gazed with sudden fury upon the blubbing boy. 'Stop that at once, will you!'

'Don't be angry about it,' said Edgar. 'He's got a lot to cry for. I think maybe I shall cry myself.'

'You're foully drunk.'

'I'm not—yet. There, David, don't cry, dear boy.'

'I'm sorry,' said David, rubbing the sleeve of his now filthy shirt across his eyes.

'Introduce us, Monty,' said Edgar.

'Oh God. David Gavender, Professor Edgar Demarnay.'

'Not professor now ac—'

'David, are you coming to this Emily McHugh party of your mother's?'

'No.'

'Hadn't you better get meeting her over with? You need only stay for a few minutes.'

'No. I can't—'

'You go,' said Edgar. 'I'll stay here and—hic—talk to David.'

'Oh—hell—' said Monty. He left them and walked quickly out of the house. He suddenly stupidly passionately did not want to leave Edgar alone with the tearful David. If only he had been by himself, a tearful David would have interested him, though he would have been angry all the same. Now Edgar would crawl over everything, interfering, misunderstanding, messing about, getting more and more *in*. He had to attend Harriet's ghastly party, but he resolved to return home very soon and tell Edgar to go. As he turned into the front garden of Hood House Seagull snapped at his heels. Monty kicked him.

'Are you the Professor Demarnay who wrote *Babylonian Mathematics and Greek Logic*?'

'Yes.'

'And *Empedocles as Poetry*?'

'Yes.'

'And *Pythagoras and His Debt to Sycthia*?'

'Yes.'

'And did that edition of the *Cratylus*?'

'Yes, but don't let's go on all night, dear boy. Dry those charming tears and tell me *all* about it.'

Monty had had several short drinks. With Edgar he had drunk slowly. Now he was drinking fast. So indeed was everyone else. There were some exquisite little sandwiches, but no one had eaten any. There was even about the strange gathering the semblance of a real party. No one seemed at a loss for words. There had been no disasters so far. Introduced by Harriet to Emily McHugh, Monty had bowed silently and so had she. Constance Pinn, introduced, smiled conspiratorially and seized his hand, scratching his palm hard with her index finger. Pinn had since then been trying to engage him in conversation and Monty had been determinedly avoiding any *tête-à-tête*. Pinn was handsome, dressed with ostentatious simplicity in her black dress with the lace collar. (Brussels lace, cast off by a girl at school.) Her sleek slightly domed auburn hair glowed wirily with health and confidence. Emily was handsome too and had got her clothes right for once. She was wearing a white blouse and the Italian cameo brooch with a blue velvet waistcoat and black trousers. She kept fingering her dark hair, which was newly washed and pleasantly floppy, and thrusting it back with boyish gestures. Her blue eyes were bright and brave, darting rather self-consciously about, observing furniture rather than persons. Harriet by contrast was pale and untidy, hairpins much in evidence and looking tired. She rarely wore jewellery, but had put on the silver-gilt bracelet with engraved roses which her father had given her. She kept clicking and unclicking its catch. The belt of her grey voile dress had come undone and trailed. She had whispered to Monty early on, 'Stay till they've gone, won't you.' So in spite of the horrid possibility of a David-Edgar entente, it seemed that he had to stay. In any case, now that he saw Harriet with her tumbling hair and her nervous hands and her trailing belt he wanted to stay.

Harriet had told Emily 'I hope David will come soon,' but David had not come. She had asked Monty about Edgar and he had replied vaguely. No David, no Edgar, and Emily and Pinn, who had both drunk plenty, showed no signs of proposing to go. Blaise, red in the face, was all smiles, agreeing quickly with anyone who addressed him. Harriet kept touching his arm reassuringly, perhaps possessively. Pinn, who was now getting the giggles, kept staring at him and laughing. Emily resolutely ignored him. She also ignored Monty and Pinn and addressed her remarks exclusively to Harriet. Monty, evading Pinn, talked mainly to Blaise who though incapable of listening or of answering rationally could quite respectably babble. Monty was beginning to feel, with the effect of drink, a sort of exhilaration. It was not exactly that he wanted something scandalous to occur, he was just horribly interested.

The Hood House drawing-room, a long narrow three-windowed room occupying the side of the house, had a bare bony look as of hollowed ivory, with its white walls adorned only by a quartet of water-colours and an oval mirror with a white porcelain frame. The room, a project of Blaise's, had somehow never been completed and was not frequently used. The thick yellowish Indian carpet left by the previous occupier had not yet, owing to disagreements between Blaise and Harriet about its successor, been replaced, and the furniture had at the best of times a tendency to recede to the walls. Upon the unprotected central area the company were now standing in an awkward ring like people who, at the blowing of a whistle or the striking up of music, would initiate some game or strenuous dance. Blaise, breathing rapidly and audibly, kept smiling a tremulous fading and returning smile and looking from one to the other of the women, distributing his attention, Monty noticed, equally between all three.

Conversation, not difficult though a little distraught, had concerned the theatre.

'The theatre is so artificial,' said Harriet.

'Don't you like Shakespeare?' said Emily.

'To read yes, but on the stage it's just tricks.'

'I can't think why people go,' said Monty. 'It seems to me a waste of an evening which might be spent in conversation.'

'Quite so,' said Blaise, 'quite so.'

'You're not serious, Monty?' said Pinn.

'I adore the theatre,' said Emily. 'It takes you out of yourself. I love those great glittering images that you remember for ever. But when can I ever get to the theatre with dear little Luca around?'

'You could take him,' said Harriet.

'He'd hate it.'

'How do you know?'

'He'd hate it.'

'You found someone to stay with him this evening.'

'Pinn did. Some school kid. Who did you get, Pinn?'

'Kiki St Loy.'

'What a pretty name,' said Harriet.

'You said you'd get Jenny. You never said Kiki.'

'Jenny couldn't make it.'

'Blaise could take you to the theatre sometimes,' said Harriet. 'I'd look after Luca.'

'You're kidding! Do a show. Well why not? Years since we did a show. Blaise is crazy about the theatre, aren't you, Blaise!'

'Yes, absolutely,' said Blaise.

'What a wet blanket I've evidently been!' said Harriet laughing.

'But *are* you serious?' said Pinn to Monty.

'What about?'

'About thinking plays a waste of time.'

'The only great plays are in poetry, and I agree with Harriet I'd rather read them.'

'Surely there are some good plays in prose?'

'I don't know. I never go to the theatre.'

'Then aren't you talking nonsense since you can't judge?'

'I don't claim to be right. I only claim to be serious.'

'You are a cynic! Is it true your mother was an actress?'

'Unsuccessfully. She taught voice production in a school.'

'I wish someone would teach me to produce my voice,' said Emily.

'You have a very nice voice,' said Harriet.

'I mean my accent. Blaise professes to like my accent.'

'I like it very much.'

'So you admit I have one? Thanks a lot!'

'Would you turn the lights on, Blaise, it's suddenly got so dark,' said Harriet.

'I used to want to be an actress,' said Pinn to Monty. 'I've written this play. Would you read it?'

'Wouldn't you like to sit down, Harriet?' said Monty.

'No—I think—standing is—better.'

'Why are the dogs yapping so?' said Emily. 'It's like a bloody wolf pack.'

'You could criticize it as harshly as you like, I'd want to know what you really thought.'

'There's someone at the garden door,' said Monty. 'It must be—'

'It's David!' cried Harriet. But instead of following Monty into the kitchen she went to the side of the room and sat down. The dogs continued in a frenzy.

Monty went through into the kitchen followed by Blaise. A figure just entering from the garden turned out to be Edgar. The hysterical barking was shut out by the closing door. Monty saw with surprise that the garden was darker, though the clouded sun still attempting to shine had given the scene the bedimmed vividness of a picture by Vermeer.

Edgar's bulky figure seemed to tilt. Then he reached the table, leaning there with his hands flat upon the red cloth. It was apparent to Monty, and also evidently to Blaise, that Edgar was very drunk.

183

'You deal, will you,' said Blaise, and was gone back to the drawing-room.

'Why come this way?' said Monty. 'Oh, I see, you came over the fence. You are a damn fool. And you're drunk. You'd better sit down.'

'I wanted to see — Harriet,' said Edgar, very carefully and clearly, rather loudly. 'I have something — to tell her.'

'Sit down. You've torn your jacket. And you're filthy. You must have fallen.'

Edgar stared down intently at a long tear reaching from his jacket pocket to the hem. The pocket sagged, showing its lining. Edgar's trouser leg was thickly encrusted with earth. 'Yes, I think I fell. I must have. I've got to see Harriet. No, I will not sit down.'

'Is David coming?'

'No. Oh he cried so. And now — I'm just going to —'

With a surprising turn of speed Edgar lurched past Monty and on into the drawing-room where there was already an expectant silence. He stopped in front of Harriet, who was sitting against the wall. 'Oh — Edgar —' said Harriet rather faintly, trying to smile. Emily giggled. Pinn said 'Ha!' Blaise smiled malignantly and poured himself another drink.

'Your son,' said Edgar swaying and exclusively addressing Harriet, 'has been in Monty's house for some time crying his eyes out.'

'I'll go to him at once,' said Harriet, but without rising. Edgar's bloodshot eyes and slightly dribbling lower lip seemed to hold her fascinated.

'Better not,' said Monty. 'Edgar, you come with me, there's a good fellow.'

'That *however*,' Edgar went on. 'That *however* was *not* what I came here to *say*. I have come, Harriet, to offer you my protection.'

'Really!' said Blaise.

'I have a house, Monty knows it well, a beautiful house called Mockingham, which I offer to you, to be of service, myself being absent, my housekeeper would, I think you should withdraw, into a kind of retreat, some kind of austerity, so as not to condone, there are things one cannot, without involving a falsity, some new wrong done, I must testify, I must testify —'

'I don't think you should testify,' said Monty. 'I think you should come home with me.'

'Offer you, as I say, my protection, not meaning by this

anything, a household has been dishonoured, it is not so simple to decide, how to treat this awful thing—'

'No one has suggested that it is simple,' said Blaise, who was evidently fairly drunk himself.

'Who is this comical man, please?' said Pinn.

'Don't answer him,' said Monty to Blaise. 'He'll stop in a minute and I'll remove him.'

'Dear Edgar'—said Harriet.

'Don't Dear Edgar me, you would have been kinder to me if you had not been so kind, I too have emotions, I too have needs, I am flesh and blood am I not, you let me hold your hand, of course you laughed at me, I can be laughed at, beautiful women have laughed at me—'

'He's rather fun, isn't he,' said Emily.

'He promised to forsake all others—'

'Naturally,' said Blaise, 'I value your observations and your advice, and I'm sure it's very charming of you to come here and hold my wife's hand and offer her your protection, whatever that means—'

'Stop drivelling, Edgar,' said Monty, 'come with me.' He tried to take Edgar's arm, but was shaken off. Harriet made a holding gesture.

'Because you are good you think that you can save them, but it is they who will defile you. You must not assent to what is wrong, that is not what the Gospel requires. You are a believer in Christian marriage. One must be in the truth and you are not. You must come away so that he can see what he has done. As it is he sees nothing. This is a lie, this man's lie, and he must live it and undo it. But you have put him in a position where he cannot stop lying. No one here, not even you, is good enough to redeem this thing. They will not tolerate your forgiveness, in the end they will hate you for it, they will go on intriguing as they have always done, they will not even be able to help it, and you will find too late that you have not been a healer but an accomplice of evil. He must decide, he must choose, that is where he has put himself. He has not acknowledged his fault, he is continuing in it, and you will be eternally his victim, abandoning him to wicked ways and conniving at his sin. For his sake you must not allow this foul thing to continue.'

'Oh come, come, come!' said Pinn.

'Thanks for the message,' said Emily.

Harriet said, 'Edgar, I am listening to you. But there is a little boy in the case.'

'Could you remove your friend?' said Blaise to Monty.

'No, I will not go. I must testify. I haven't said it clearly yet and I must say it *clearly*. Harriet, *listen*. Don't you see that you are putting him in a situation where he simply can't help lying to you? You have not required the truth of him. You must require him to decide. Vague tolerant pity is not true kindness here. You are trying to spare yourself—'

'We've all had enough of you,' said Blaise, putting his glass down and coming forward. 'Just shut up now, will you. Monty, for God's sake do something, take his other arm, or does this amuse you?'

'Please!' cried Harriet.

Blaise seized hold of Edgar, but Edgar with some violence pulled up his arm to defend himself and hit Blaise smartly in the eye with his elbow. Blaise subsided onto the floor. Harriet screamed. Emily ran to Blaise. Monty rushed to Edgar who was still vaguely flailing about with his arms, looking for Blaise who had so suddenly disappeared from his field of vision. With a robust though inexpert version of a blow used by Milo, Monty struck Edgar on the neck with the side of his hand. Edgar too subsided onto the floor with a crash.

'Quick, get him out,' said Monty. In a second Pinn was with him and they had somehow got Edgar upright and were propelling him towards the front door. 'Harriet— Harriet— Mockingham—' Edgar was crying out, like someone uttering a battle cry.

Once outside the front door they were suddenly in a different world. The clouded sun was already announcing twilight. A blackbird, bright as a toy amid the motionless swirl of the leaves, was singing in a tall snaky birch tree. He sang against silence. Mrs Raines-Bloxham passing by slowly to her house looked with curiosity at the emergent trio. She had always expected irregularities from a psychiatrist's residence. Edgar had fallen silent and was allowing himself to be propelled along by the other two. At the gate, watched by Mrs Raines-Bloxham, riveted now on her front door step, he gripped the gate-post and stopped.

'Come on, Edgar, there's a dear fellow.'

'I'm sorry,' said Edgar. 'I'm drunk. There was no need to hit me though.'

'Sorry. Come along now.'

More slowly they resumed their procession. They turned the corner. Mrs Raines-Bloxham entered her house.

When they got to the door of Locketts Monty said to Pinn. 'Thank you very much. I can manage now.'

Edgar lurched on by himself through the doorway. Pinn stood her ground. She said, 'Let me come in. Please.'

'Sorry,' said Monty.

'Please.'

'Sorry.'

'Why not?'

Monty stared at her for another moment, then went inside and slammed the door.

Edgar had lurched on into the little drawing-room. He sat down abruptly in one of the wickerwork chairs, smashing one of its arms with a rending sound. He was murmuring something to himself, 'Down in deep dark ditch sat an old cow chewing a beanstalk.'

Monty went slowly into the rather murky room. One of the shutters which had been closed against the sun was still across darkening the scene. He went over mechanically and pushed it and closed the window. Almost at his feet was David, sitting on the floor, his head pillowed against the purple sofa, fast asleep. At the same moment a snore announced that Edgar was asleep too.

Monty squatted down beside David and examined him carefully. The swollen reddened eyelids betokened the weeping spoken of by Edgar. The lips were slightly parted to show a glitter of teeth, and the 'archaic smile' was shadowily present, though a little downward droop at the corners had changed it into a rather tearful smile. The light golden hair was tangled, drawn forward over the brow perhaps by the distraught hand, which now lay open, palm upward, upon the sofa, as if imploring. The other hand was clenched upon the knee, the shoulder exposed. Suiting his breathing quietly to that of the sleeping boy, Monty slowly knelt, and then leaned forward to rest his head lightly upon David's shoulder, letting his body relax slowly. The boy's jacket was still damp with tears. In the darkening room Monty lay there open-eyed and gained, amid terrible thoughts, some kind of consolation.

Meanwhile in the Hood House drawing-room. The silence after Edgar's removal was broken by Harriet's weeping. The shedding of tears is of course not simply the semi-automatic discharge of water from the eyes, it is usually an action with a purpose, a contribution even to a conversation. Harriet wept now with a physical relief at being decently able to weep instead of having to be polite, and as an indication to whom it might concern that for the present she had had enough. She had tried very hard to be good and act rightly, this little party which had ended so disastrously was itself one of her right acts. Now there must be, she vaguely supposed, some sort of new phase. She had certainly done her best. And with a vague prophetic shudder, she felt a little as governments or as princes feel who, to placate opinion or to clarify their position, act with ostentatious tolerance towards some opposition group who, if they then misbehave, can be more firmly dealt with with impunity. Yet this was also, for her state of mind, too powerful and too conscious an image. It was psychologically necessary to Harriet to feel that she had played a good, even an absurdly good, part. But she was aware enough to know that the sheer awfulness of the situation had an impetus of its own which was beyond her will and beyond the will of others too.

She had not expected Edgar's 'testimony', but when it came it came with the same message, and an almost welcome helplessness overwhelmed her. She took what she needed from Edgar's outburst, and let the rest go, had already forgotten it. She had thought that she was in control, that she was the one who was looked to. But now it seemed that she was not in control after all, nobody was in control, that she was a victim, that they were all victims. There was nothing venomous in this collapse and it was not even intended as an appeal to Blaise. Harriet did not expect him to rush to her side, she did not even want it. She wept quietly, for and with herself, sitting gracelessly upon the upright chair beside the wall, as some derelict refugee might weep in an airport or a station waiting-room, unobserved and bereft of future plans. Wiping her hot face, kicking off her shoes and closing her eyes, she murmured a soft rhythmical 'oh, oh oh' and wept into her already soaking handkerchief.

Blaise at the moment was concerned about his right eye, which had made violent contact with Edgar's elbow. Still sitting on the floor, he covered and then stroked the bruised eye, opened it, shut it, opened it again. His vision had returned to normal but the area was painful and the eye already narrowing. Emily McHugh kneeling close by, not touching him, surveyed Blaise with a look which was strangely cold and bright. So might someone look who had suddenly seen, far off, not yet fully worked, yet somehow *there*, the solution of some long and baffling mathematical problem.

Blaise began slowly to get up. He said to Emily in a matter-of-fact way, 'I'm just going to bathe my eye.' He went heavily out of the drawing-room and into the kitchen leaving the door open. He turned on the cold tap and began clumsily to ladle water in his hands onto the burning painful area. Emily went out into the hall and put on her light fawn mackintosh and arranged her scarf. Blaise began to say something to her through the doorway.

'Good-bye,' said Emily. She went to the front door and left the house, closing the door quietly. Blaise leaned for a few moments over the sink, regarding his wet hands. Then, not pausing to dry himself, he turned and hurried after her.

Twilight was already gathering in the luxuriantly leafy trees of the long road and the clouded sky had paled to a sort of lightless hazy white. Emily was already some distance away, running as hard as she could. In silence Blaise began to run after her, and as the cool air touched his hot damaged face he felt a great pure clarity entering his head, entering his brain, flowing through him in a cleansing stream.

Blaise had never in his life before experienced quite the sheer confusion about his own thoughts and feelings which he had experienced in recent days. He had been unhappy before, guilty before, but he had usually understood *what* he was feeling, however powerless he might have been to change it. Since his confession to Harriet the only sensation which was at all clearly declared was his humble relief at having been forgiven by the two women. It was all so wonderful, so simple, so unexpected. A moment of confidence in truth, a moment of attention to duty, and suddenly what had been evil was all turned into good, with no punishment, without the loss of anything, not of any one thing, which he wished to retain. Well, there was David, but that problem was not insoluble, David would not vanish, Blaise knew that his son loved him. And there were the two women *held* in the new framework, offering him undiminished love, indeed enhanced love and accepting each other with a calm realism. The relief, the gratitude, had been violent indeed.

But Blaise knew that he could not live by this gratitude. What had been so wrenched about must have other huge consequences. His deepest attachments were in movement obscurely and without his will. More than he had realized, he had needed and relied upon the appearance (and as he often experienced it the reality) of a normal ordinary happy even conventional even dull home life at Hood House: a life where he mended things and mowed the lawn and cleaned the car. To this amalgam even his sense of wronging Harriet contributed something. And as, in recent years, his feelings had moved back towards his wife, his love for her was compounded with this present everyday guilt and pity. Harriet's ordinariness, her goodness, her legality shone for him in this light. She was good and sweet and she was wronged. And, as he now realized, the strength of his pity was a function of the secret strength and liveliness of his relation with Emily. He could perhaps have stopped loving Emily if he could have treated her, as he sometimes pretended to himself that he did, merely as an object of duty; and he would then have made a more challenging problem out of the task of loving his wife. As it was the mysterious chemistry of the situation, the familiar strong egoism of his own mind, had sorted it out thus for his comfort. His secret life with Emily somehow helped and certainly increasingly informed his love for Harriet.

Now Harriet, in what might have seemed a moment of defeat, with the revelation to her of her status as a wronged and cheated wife, had suddenly grown in stature. Harriet had become heroic. Her dignity, her monumental kindness, her power to hold and dominate the situation had amazed him and had been in effect a test of his love for her, which had in recent years become in its resigned guiltiness so calm and sweet. The changed developed Harriet must, when the resting time of gratitude was over, demand of him a changed developed love. At the same time the jerk of revelation had seemed to sever him from Emily. Everything that he had loved in Emily seemed now in eclipse. Never in those nine years had Emily faltered, never looked guilty or weak, though her strength had more and more expressed itself in fruitless punishing complaint. Now suddenly Emily had been picked up, as by a hurricane, and given a small but official place in this new Harriet-owned world, the world brought into being by Harriet's goodness. And Emily had looked guilty before Harriet and had obeyed her and had allowed Harriet to plan Luca's schooling, as if Harriet were Emily's mother and Luca Harriet's grandson.

Blaise had imagined himself before as inside a cage, and when he had felt nothing but the great blessed relief he had seemed to be out of it. But cages made of long wrong-doing are not so easily disposed of. Had he conceivably exchanged one cage for another? The deep falsity, the lie of which Edgar had spoken, still existed. But what was it exactly, *where* was it, and what did he now want? Truth, freedom? Where were they, in which direction? As Blaise ran along the darkening road in pursuit of Emily he began confusedly to feel that he knew.

Emily ran desperately, exultantly. She had stuffed her handbag into her pocket and swung along the road long-legged, like a schoolgirl. She too, since the revelation, had been utterly confused about her own feelings. She had felt of course a sort of disappointment, though she had also felt a sort of relief. She had always pictured the end of the long miserable deception as being brought about by herself, as involving the final loss of Blaise, and as signifying somehow or other, her own death. Extreme continuing unhappiness often consoles itself with images of death which may in a sense be idle, but which can play a vital part in consolation and also in the continuance of illusion. If *that* happens I am dead, consoles, and also dulls the edge of speculation and even of conscience. It is another way of saying, to me *that* cannot happen. 'The final bust-up' would mean either, almost impossibly, Emily's total possession of Blaise or else, almost necessarily, the withdrawal of Blaise from her life. Dreams of acquiring Blaise by means of revelation had certainly come to seem more and more empty, about equivalent to the visions of Harriet being run over or dying of cancer which had solaced the early days of Emily's unhappy liaison.

But now *it* had happened, quickly and with a weird ease, and there had been no explosion, no cataclysmic universal collapse. Blaise had been as it were politely handed back to her by Harriet, an authorized object inevitably and however reluctantly at any rate with kindness and composure to be shared: shared much as before except that the long deception was over. Of course there would still be life-giving lies. Blaise would never never tell Harriet everything. Blaise would go on lying to Harriet about how he did not care for Emily and never made love to her, just as no doubt he was lying to Emily about how he did not care for Harriet. Blaise's duplicity would remain, a little familiar haze upon the scene, comforting though also of course depressing. And there they would be, all three of them, as the years went by, the two guilty and the one guiltless. And Harriet would somehow run things and be unfailingly kind and play the older woman and help Emily, and help Luca, and Emily would be submissive and grateful and would gradually stop feeling guilty and. . . . But what had occurred to Emily after the liberating bang of Edgar's outcry, as she sat on the floor and unsympathetically watched Blaise stroking the damaged eye, was that none of these things had really got to happen at all, since she could prevent them. The power of pure destruction was still hers. She could still make it death or glory.

As she ran along wide-eyed and wild-eyed she expected and soon heard Blaise in pursuit. He did not call her name but she knew his running footsteps. Emily ran faster. She did not want to be caught. What she wanted now was to elude Blaise, to lose him, to know that he was frenziedly searching for her and not finding her. She had no notion how death or glory would work out or even happen and she did not want it to happen yet. She wanted a little time to gloat over her power, short of the agony which the exertion of it might bring on. Emily was fleet of foot and could easily have outstripped her lover, only a projecting paving stone caught her flying toe and the next moment she was full-length on the ground, her handbag disgorging its contents in the gutter and one sandal left behind her. As she sat up, investigating a grazed knee and torn trousers, Blaise arrived panting. Emily scooped back the contents of the bag and retrieved her sandal. She rose a little stiffly. Blaise was saying something. Emily gazed at the tremulous mouth and the swollen bruising eye. Then taking careful aim with her still swinging handbag she hit him across the face as hard as she could. Then she walked quietly on, limping a little.

The road was dark now, though the sky was still pale, become hazily bluer though cloudy. The street lamps came on making bowers of vividly green or red leaves round about them. The lazy capacious brick houses had put their lights on and uncurtained windows cast squares of brightness upon neatly raked gravel or attentive cascades of rambler roses. Emily walked on and Blaise walked first a little behind her, then beside her, holding a handkerchief to his eye. He made no attempt to touch her and there was silence between them. But now as Emily walked a sensation of pure bliss rose in her, rising from the warm paving stones, passing through her thin sandals up through her trembling knees. . . . She was simply filled with bliss, her blood had turned into some heavenly golden liquor which lightly scorched all her flesh and bubbled out at the top of her head, catching fire there and becoming a little dancing flame of joy, like the headdress of a Pentecostal saint. Emily walked along, gazing ahead down the dark road, aflame and yet immensely cool, immensely strong, immensely light.

When they reached the little suburban station Blaise went ahead and bought two tickets for London. They sat on a seat together in silence, they boarded the train in silence. On the train they sat opposite to each other and stared at each other without speaking or smiling, and the silence between them was like the silence of eighteen-year-old lovers who having suddenly and mysteriously achieved a perfect communion are simply silenced by joy, finding that now they can converse fully without words. Only Blaise and Emily were not eighteen-year-old lovers, but grown-up people who had made each other suffer for many years. And this made the silence between them even more beautiful.

Blaise had stopped dabbing his eye, which having received the full force of a second blow was now entirely closed and surrounded by a purple stain. His single eye stared and his mouth was straight with a grimness more moving to Emily than any tender smile. At Paddington they walked from the platform and with a single accord went and sat down on one of the benches near the paper stall on the main concourse. It appeared to be midnight and there were few people about under Isambard Kingdom Brunel's high cast-iron arches. Some sleepless pigeons walked about and pecked without optimism at screwed-up chocolate papers. A tramp dozed in a corner, so sunk inside a ragged overcoat that only a few tufts of hair proclaimed his head. Emptiness and night possessed the big brilliantly lighted station. Emily stretched out her legs and through a rent in her trousers scratched at the coagulated blood on her knee. She felt giddy with happiness and certainty. She would have been content to sit thus beside Blaise, not looking at him, not speaking to him, not touching him, for the rest of the night, for days, for weeks.

At last Blaise spoke. 'Well, we are a pair of babes in the wood, aren't we.'

'Perhaps the pigeons will come and cover us up with chocolate papers,' said Emily. She wanted to laugh and laugh and laugh, but her voice merely trembled slightly. Love possessed and shook her as a terrier shakes a rat. And between herself and her lover the old fierce strong electric current had been renewed and flowed once more filling her brimful with knowledge and with truth.

'Here we are then,' said Blaise. 'Here we are—again.'

'I hope you realize *where* we are,' said Emily, still not looking at him.

'Yes.'

'You realize that you've got to choose.'

'Yes.'

'And you've chosen.'

'Yes.'

She turned towards him at last, still not touching.

'You see, Edgar was quite right,' said Blaise. He spoke in a very cool analytical tone which made Emily tremble with desire. 'Although it looked like acting properly it wasn't, it was riddled with falsehood, it couldn't have gone on. You didn't have to hit me, though I'm glad you did, to make me understand. I understood back there in the drawing-room. I think all that was needed was a bit of noise. Then I saw.'

'We probably saw at about the same time then,' said Emily. 'What I saw was that I had to make you choose. What did you see, if I may, to make things perfectly clear, trouble you for an account of that?'

'I saw,' said Blaise, 'what I've really known all along, that you are my truth. For me you are the way the truth and the life. Only here can I be totally myself. I should have been faithful to this right at the start, only I fumbled and delayed out of sheer cowardice, and then being faithful began to be too painful and I deceived myself into thinking that I'd changed. But I hadn't changed. I ought to have been professional enough with myself to see the impossibility of change. But before Harriet *knew* I was simply spellbound, simply paralysed.'

'And now you're free.'

'And now I'm free.'

'And you're mine. Really. Absolutely. Forever. That's your choice.'

'That's my choice.'

'If you ever go back on these words,' said Emily, 'I will kill you. Not pain. Death.'

'Oh my queen . . .' he murmured.

A few minutes later they were locked in each other's arms in a taxi bound for Putney.

Monty awoke into an immediate scene of fear. He could not for a moment think where he was and why. He found that he was lying on the floor in his drawing-room, his head upon a cushion and a blanket over him. There was a strange light in the room. It was the full moon, now well risen above the orchard, sailing in a clear sky which it had turned to a glossy dark blue and shining straight into the room. This it must have been which prised his eyelids apart. But why was he there at all? Monty got up stiffly and went to turn on the light. Then he remembered the scene at Hood House, Edgar, David. But the room was empty. Who was it who had given him that cushion and that blanket? What had David thought after he woke up with Monty's head on his shoulder and Monty's arm round his neck? He looked at his watch. It was three o'clock.

He went out into his kitchen wondering if he was hungry. He was not. Did he want a drink? He did not. He realized that he had a headache and ate two aspirins and drank a lot of water. Then he heard the dogs barking in the Hood House garden. He went out through the kitchen door and stood for a while on the lawn which was glistening with dew which the moonlight was making to resemble hoarfrost. They would all be in bed over there. The dogs often barked pointlessly at night. Monty walked across the lawn, leaving a trail of frosty footprints, and turned the corner into the orchard. Now as he made his way down the clipped orchard path between the quiet pale presence of ladies lace in the long grass, he saw lights ahead of him. Lights were still on downstairs in Hood House, in the kitchen and evidently, in the drawing-room. Monty reached the line of white foxgloves and began to climb the fence.

The fence, scarcely five feet high with the transverse slats on Monty's side, did not present any serious obstacle to an agile and sober man. However, as soon as he put his foot on the lowest slat the dogs, who had fallen silent, started up again, rushing down the garden in a black torrent and barking and snarling in a very unpleasant way. Monty, now sitting on top of the fence, hesitated. Ajax was jumping up alarmingly near his ankles. To preserve these he jumped quickly, saying as ferociously as he could, 'Get out of my way, damn you! Get away!' The dogs retired, but returned again to give him a snarling and uncomfortably close escort up the garden. Monty, hurrying and holding his hands high, kept up a now more conciliatory barrage of talk along the lines of 'Come on now, stop it, you know me, I'm not a burglar, that's it now, who's a good boy then' and so on. The talk paid off, Monty was not bitten, and as he approached the house the animals drew back a little, except for Seagull who showed, in a mixture of animosity and respect, signs of not having forgotten being kicked on the day before.

As there appeared to be nobody in the kitchen, Monty walked along the side of the house where the uncurtained drawing-room windows were casting their light upon a feathery laburnum and an absurdly green *rhus cotinus*. He approached the windows and peered in. A strange sight met his eyes. Edgar and Harriet, Harriet leaning on Edgar's arm, were pacing the room, deep in talk. They reached the end, turned and proceeded back, then turned again. It looked, from the mechanical nature of their movements, as if they had been doing this for some time, and Monty thought he could discern a track made by their pacing feet in the thick Indian carpet. Harriet was gesturing towards the garden, doubtless in comment upon the dogs. She was, to Monty's eyes now, a weird figure. She had put on a long cashmere shawl over her dress which, deprived of its belt, billowed below with the effect of a shapeless robe. Her long darkish glowing hair was, as Monty had never seen it before, undone and streaming down her back, making her look, in spite of her pale tired face, ridiculously young. She looked too, so robed, with tangled streaming hair, like a priestess, like a sibyl. Edgar, shambling beside her, bent and dishevelled, much the worse for wear through sleeplessness and drink, his jacket torn, without a tie, seemed to be receiving from her advice, possibly admonishment. Socrates being instructed by Diotima perhaps.

Monty approached the window and tapped. The two inside turned in exclamation and shock. The next moment

Edgar had lifted the sash and Monty was climbing in. He scarcely had his two feet up on the carpet when Harriet enveloped him. The cashmere shawl wrapped his shoulders, then slipped to the ground, he seemed to be veiled by her flying hair, her arms were round his neck, his arms round her shoulders. He held her so for a moment, closing his eyes, feeling the plump warmth of her shoulders, the cold light touch of her hair. Then he stepped back, turning her round, moving away. Edgar and Harriet now both stared at him, haggard.

Wondering what sort of curious picture he made himself, Monty said in as flippant a manner as he could immediately put on, 'Well, well, where's everybody?'

'That's what we would like to know!' said Edgar portentously.

'Where's David?' said Monty. Had David given him that cushion and that blanket? He hoped so.

'He's upstairs asleep,' said Harriet.

'What are you two up to?' said Monty.

'We're waiting for Blaise,' said Edgar.

'What's happened to Blaise then?'

'Emily McHugh ran out,' said Harriet, 'just after you went away with Edgar' (Edgar groaned) 'and Blaise ran after her. We've heard nothing since.'

'I shouldn't think there's any mystery,' said Monty, feeling annoyed with both of them, but relieved to find that he could still function as a rational being, 'Emily was upset by stupid Edgar' (Edgar groaned again), 'Blaise saw her home and since it was so late decided to stay the night.'

'Of course that may have happened,' said Harriet. 'I wouldn't mind his—staying—since it was so late—but why hasn't he telephoned? He must know that I—that I—' she bit her lips drawing them in in a hard line, and tears mounted to her eyes, certainly not for the first time that evening.

'Oh my dear—' said Edgar.

'Have you telephoned Emily's flat?' said Monty.

'Harriet doesn't know the number, and it's not in the book,' said Edgar.

'I think you should go to bed, Harriet,' said Monty. 'It's stupid to upset yourself by staying up like this and all for nothing. Obviously by the time Blaise got to Emily's place he thought it was too late to ring you, he thought you'd be asleep. Have some sense and don't act the tragic queen so! You go to bed. If Edgar wants to do penance by staying up on duty all night he can. I might even stay with him. Now off you go.'

'No—no—I can't go to bed—I couldn't sleep—supposing something's happened to Blaise, he may have had an accident—I feel so—everything's suddenly become a nightmare—I must see Blaise, I must—I couldn't possibly go to sleep in this state—I'm so distraught, I feel I'm going mad.'

'My dear, my dear,' said Edgar, also clearly not for the first time that evening, 'I am so sorry, I am so dreadfully sorry, I was awful—'

'You're very kind,' said Harriet, 'you're both very kind. Oh, Monty, thank God you've come.' She clasped his arm.

'Well I'm hungry,' said Monty. 'Do you mind if I eat some of these sandwiches, since we're going to keep the vigil together? And I wouldn't mind some beer, if there was any.'

'There's some in the fridge,' said Harriet. They went all three to the kitchen, and sat round the kitchen table with the sandwiches and some cold lager. Monty and Edgar ate and drank, while Harriet sat between them, pleating up the red cloth and staring out into the garden where the dawn had already subdued the moon and made the lawn and trees colourlessly present in ghastly grey immobility.

'David wouldn't speak to me,' said Harriet. 'When he came in he just passed me and wouldn't speak. And I saw he had been crying so.'

'He'll recover,' said Edgar. 'Boys do.'

'He's not—just a boy—he's such a—deep person.'

'Don't grieve, Harriet,' said Monty. 'This is a bad moment, but things will sort themselves out.' God knows how though, he thought. I'm talking nonsense. A gust of sheer desire for Sophie's presence came over him, as if some distant door had been opened. If only she were somewhere and he could go towards her. At worst times, her simple presence had been complete defence, total comfort. At worst times, when she was angry, when she was lying, when she was dying.

'Oh God—if only Blaise would come—if only he'd ring—'

'He's probably on his way back,' said Edgar. 'He's been held up, and without the car it'll take ages. He'll turn up any moment now.'

'I suddenly feel,' said Harriet, 'as if he might never come. There are "nevers" in people's lives. People go away, people die, it does happen—'

'I think I'll just go to the lavatory, if you'll excuse me,' said

198

Monty. He left the kitchen, closing the door behind him, and went up the wide curving stairs which the big arched window showed quite clearly now in the horrible increasing light of day. On the upper landing, he paused. All was still. Then in the silence he could hear David breathing. Monty tiptoed to the door of David's room and very carefully depressed the handle. He stole in.

David, still wearing his shirt, lay half covered by the bed-clothes, his neck twisted as if in agony, his hair, as if in horror, streaming straight up across the pillow, one arm trailing towards the ground, in an attitude resembling Wallis's picture of the death of Chatterton. His face, once again made remote by sleep, blanched and smoothed by the vague light, looked like a beautiful death mask. Monty stayed and gazed at the sleeper for nearly two minutes and then soundlessly left the room. How mad, to hope to be consoled by a young boy, and one who was cram full of his own miseries anyway. To reveal his own emotional needs to David would be a folly, possibly a crime.

As Monty was gliding back down the stairs the telephone began to ring in the hall. Harriet came racing out of the kitchen with Edgar after her. Edgar turned on all the lights. Harriet had already lifted the receiver.

'Oh—darling—thank God—yes—yes—of course—oh, yes, why didn't I think—of course you did—I was so worried, but —it's all right now—yes, I'll go to bed now, I'll sleep, don't you worry—yes, see you then—oh I am so relieved—thank you, my darling, thank you for ringing—thank you, thank you—'

Harriet put the telephone down and moved to the stairs. In the suddenly brilliant light Monty saw her weary face all relaxed now, all smoothed and sweetened, radiant with relief.

'So you see, it was all right?' said Monty, questioning.

'Yes—yes—perfectly all right—I simply forgot—he's with Magnus Bowles—this is the day when he sees Magnus—he saw Emily to her train in London and then he went on to Magnus—he tried to ring me earlier but there was a break-down and he couldn't get through. He's having his usual all-night session with poor Magnus. Blaise is so kind to Magnus, so scrupulous, he never puts him off. So that's all right, you see. Thank you and thank you. Now I think I'll go to bed.'

'Good night then,' said Monty. 'I'm going to bed too.' He let himself out of the front door, nearly falling over Buffy who was lying on the step, and ran to the gate, followed by listless barking. Somewhere the sun was up. The road was brightening, entirely empty and full of detail, like a picture awaiting its central figure. But I am the central figure, thought Monty, seeing himself, black clad, haggard and wild as the others, his shirt collar up on end, his dark hair disordered, running along the road to his house as if horribly pursued. He hastened up the path and was fumbling for his front door key when he realized that he was in fact pursued. Fat Edgar, his colourless pale hair goldened by the vivid light, looking crazy and suddenly resembling his younger, his undergraduate self, a beseeching look upon his pink face, had swung in the gate.

'Monty—may I—'

'What was the name of that school?' said Monty.

'You mean where Binkie—? Bankhurst.'

'Well, tell them I'd like the job, if they think I could do it.'

'Oh good—shall I make an appointment for you to?—Monty, may I come in and—?'

'No.'

'But where am I to go at this hour? You see, my club—'

'Go to hell,' said Monty. 'Go back to Harriet. She'll give you a bed. She might give you her bed. That's what you're after I suppose.' He went in and closed the door behind him. Why in God's name did I say that, he said to himself. I don't even think it. How can I have been so foully vulgar and unkind? I must be going mad after all.

He went into the drawing-room. The *Iliad* was still lying upon the table. He had fetched the book in order to amuse Edgar by a test of his Greek. Only it was no test, since he knew that particular passage by heart. He shut the book with a slam. He picked up the blanket and began to go slowly upstairs. He felt Sophie's ghostly inaccessible being speechlessly about him. It fled away beneath the earth, gibbering faintly. But no, it was an illusion. She was nothing and nowhere, not a presence, not in any place.

'This one's very sweet,' said Harriet to Luca. But of course they had already made up their minds.

Luca looked up at her with the cunning almost seductively conscious look which made it sometimes seem impossible that he was just a little boy of eight.

'He has the longest tail,' he said.

It was true he *had* the longest tail, and Harriet's allegiance wavered slightly. Oh dear, would they have to take *two* dogs?

The smiling anxious friendly faces behind the wire moved with them in an ordered group, backed by the flailing tails. Oh how terribly touching they all were!

'I wonder if it tires a dog to wag its tail so?' said Harriet. 'I feel quite exhausted just looking at them!'

'Do they kill the ones that aren't taken?' said Luca.

'I don't know. No, of course not.' Harriet preferred not to think about that. She felt the immediate hot presence of tears, never far from her now.

The dalmatian with the very long tail was certainly a charming animal. Harriet had never seen one with quite so many spots either, and she was about to say this to Luca but resolved not to, because really they *had* decided, hadn't they? The dalmatian had a rather silly face, but Harriet could not make out whether this counted for or against him. They moved on to the next cage. There was a rather charming airedale, prettier than Buffy, with a brilliant autumnal coat and bright amber eyes, only of course Harriet never had two dogs of the same kind so he was not in play. There was a sweet long-haired dachshund. 'He's a dear, isn't he!' said Harriet, crouching and touching the long nose which protruded through the wire. How moving a dog's nostrils were, moist and dark, like the dark moist places of nature, hillside pools, rock crannies by the sea.

'He's too small,' said Luca, who had already made it evident that he had a set of standards, mysterious but firm, by which to make the anguishing dog-decision.

In silent accord they moved back to the first cage. The Cardiganshire corgi, somewhat resembling a huge caterpillar, with his glossy dark brown flowing coat (tweed colour, Harriet thought of it as) concealing his short legs and almost sweeping the ground, had been shouldered back by the taller dogs but was wagging his plumey tail with equal enthusiasm and in order to get a better view of his human visitors intermittently and clumsily rising on to his hind legs in a most engaging way. His face with its big muzzle, so absurdly large in relation even to his quite burly frame, glowed with intelligence and goodwill and his beautiful eyes, of a limpid colour of peaty brown, gazed upon Harriet with a curiously intimate and personal kind of beseeching. It was as if, already, he *knew*.

Harriet and Luca looked at each other. Words were unnecessary. Their communion was already perfect.

'He's *your* dog,' said Harriet. 'You know that, don't you?'

Harriet was more profoundly moved than she dared (fearing tears, a kind of soppiness which might embarrass her dignified friend) acknowledge even to herself by the excursion to the Dogs' Home. The combination of Luca and the dogs was almost too much. 'Dignified' was indeed strangely the word for the little boy. He was a child of great inwardness and entirely lacking in the anxiety which had characterized her own son at that age. Luca, barbarously under-educated, had something of a savage's self-possessed beauty. More than that. One was in the presence of a mind. What exactly went on in this mind Harriet could not conjecture. But she experienced the moment to moment perfection of their converse with the pleasure which might be associated with a successful love affair; and the partner who created the confidence and set the tempo was Luca. She felt, even, looked after. With what an extraordinary tact and deliberation he now took hold of her hand. She barred back the wild tears.

Harriet had more than this motive for weeping. Blaise had come back of course, everything was going along, not exactly 'as usual', but, under the dreadful new dispensation, with what should have been a fairly steadying degree of usualness, except that Harriet now knew that something awful would happen, was perhaps already happening. This conviction was totally irrational and she resisted it, but it kept returning. The old eternal communication between herself and Blaise had ceased. Of course, looking back, she knew objectively that in the early days of his association with Emily he *must* have been, with so much to conceal, alienated. But she had not felt the alienation, and it was as if by never recognizing it she had annihilated it. Something wonderful to do with the marriage bond, to do with perfect marriage vows, had made her able retrospectively to assimilate that disloyalty and make it as if it had never been. Blaise had repented and had returned, even long before she ever knew of Emily McHugh's existence, and Harriet need ask for nothing

202

more. She could, here, do the rest. But this present alienation was new and was another matter.

I am imagining it all, she thought. But there was so much evidence. The house itself bore witness to the dislocation. The objects in the kitchen, in the bedroom, in her boudoir, in Blaise's study, which usually, untidily and randomly placed as they were, coalesced into an organic interior, like to the world of a rich and well-regulated mind, were suddenly disconnected from each other. Some current which had joined them up into an aesthetic whole had ceased to flow. They lay about derelict, resembling the things in the house of someone who has died, surveyed by some stranger, his heir, to whom their histories and nature were unknown and uncared for. The house just looked a meaningless mess and Harriet had no will any more to cherish it. Customary activities such as 'doing the flowers' had simply lapsed. There were no fresh flowers in the house now, not even roses, which were so easy to pick and arrange. A vase of withered Dutch irises had stood in the hall for several days and the task of throwing away the flowers and emptying out the water had been monumentally too difficult for Harriet.

Of course everything to do with David was full of pains and problems. Harriet had, as it were, reconnoitred David with the greatest care, trying to find some way of reaching him. He remained polite, laconic, cold. However her bond with her son was profound and old and even across the estrangement they could still look at each other, there were momentary looks when she pleaded and he frowned, when she knew that their souls touched. She could not lose David and she would win him again somehow. She planned, and had said this to Blaise who distractedly agreed, to do just what David had asked: to take him abroad with her for a few days, just the two of them, to Paris perhaps. Once they were really alone together the barriers would surely fall. She had not yet put any date to this plan or spoken of it to her estranged son, but the idea of it consoled her.

Blaise was certainly in an odd mood, distraught, preoccupied, excited, but uncommunicative. He was *busy*. He had cancelled appointments with his patients in an unprecedented manner, and was absent for a lot of each day at, he said, the British Museum Reading Room. He was, he said, anxious now to finish his book, he was just on the last lap. Dr Ainsley, who rang up when Blaise was out, anxious to see him, sounded upset and also, unnervingly, as if he knew things which Harriet did not know, and was trying to find out how much Harriet knew. Surely Blaise could not have confided in the patients something which he had not told her? 'When are you going to see Emily?' she asked him. He replied with obvious exasperation, 'Oh next week some time. She's away.' 'Away? Where?' 'On holiday. With that girl Kiki St Loy. They've gone off in the car.' 'Who's looking after Luca?' said Harriet. 'Pinn is.' 'Where have they gone to?' 'How do I know? Just don't keep on about Emily, will you?' Have they *quarrelled*, Harriet wondered with a moment of wicked hope. But somehow it didn't feel like that. Of course questioning Luca, when he arrived on his mysterious visits, was out of the question. The 'dignity' of her relation with the boy forbade any such vulgar proceeding.

When at home now Blaise spent his time in his study, where as she could see from the state of the waste paper baskets, he was doing a lot of sorting and tearing up of papers. Perhaps it was something to do with finishing the book. He also made excursions to the loft, where old trunks of his held various treasures. He was even sorting out his *clothes*. He was putting his affairs in order. What for? Harriet's mind touched the possibility but instantly shied from it: was it conceivable that her husband was *preparing to bolt*? However she so knew that this was impossible that she could not so interpret the evidence, could not, in this light, even see it. Blaise was 'going through a phase'. She could not lose him any more than she could lose David. It was simply a matter of holding on, letting them both feel the absoluteness of her love and trust, and waiting for them to become open to her again. So Harriet waited and hoped. But, for whatever reason, the misery she now silently endured was more intense than any she had known.

'We'll have *that* one,' she said to the attendant.

The Cardiganshire corgi, separated from his less fortunate friends, emerged from the cage a free dog. Luca, kneeling with bare knees on the dirty ground of the yard, put his arms round the corgi's neck and had his face thoroughly licked. Luca's eyes closed in a rare moment of utterly rapt childish bliss as he embraced the dog. Harriet hastily wiped away the now inevitable tears.

'What shall we call him?'

'Lucky Luciano.'

'What name is that?'

'It's a gangster. Like what I want to be when I grow up.'

204

The weather had re-established itself. David, walking along the Upper Richmond Road, was sweating, although he had taken off his jacket. He felt the perspiration running down his ribs and glueing his white shirt to his skin down the whole length of his back.

Last night he had dreamt he was in China. In a wild mountain landscape he had seen, up a steep path, a wooden cistern fed by a warm spring. In the thick creamy water a naked girl was bathing. Then suddenly with horror he had seen the mountain shudder and begin to move. With increasing speed a great roaring avalanche was beginning to descend. The sea of tumbling rocks engulfed the cistern and blotted out the path. And now there was nothing but torn earth and piled up stones and a deep dark chasm out of which the steam arose in swirling clouds.

No one had told him Emily McHugh's address. He had found it for himself in an old address book of his father's cryptically entered under 'McH', together with the telephone number. David felt, as he walked along, almost faint with an emotion which he could not name, compounded of fear and excitement and grief. He simply had to see Emily McHugh. What he would say or do when face to face with her he did not know. He felt hatred for her, but no intent to reproach or revile her, that would be merely absurd. He simply had to *see* her, and then decide what happened next. He turned down the side street, and a few minutes later, with a violently pounding heart, was in the grubby corridor filled with rubbish boxes and children's tricycles, and was at the shabby door and ringing the bell.

An impressive auburn-haired woman in a green linen dress opened the door.

David looked upon her with bulging eyes. He said, just audibly, 'I am David Gavender.' The possibility then occurred to him for the first time that his father might be within.

'Well, I am not Emily McHugh,' said Pinn.

David felt intense relief. 'Is she — ?'

'She's not here. No one's here but me. I'm Constance Pinn. Have you heard of me?'

'No.'

'I've heard of you. You're much better-looking than your picture.'

After a moment's silence, David began to turn away.

'Wait a mo, handsome. What did you want with Emily?'

'Nothing.'

'Don't go away. Or, wait a bit. I'll come with you. I won't ask you in, the place is a shambles. Wait.'

David waited.

Pinn emerged wearing a matching green jacket over her dress. She seemed to be full of private glee and actually laughed, staring at him, as they set off down the corridor.

'Where are you going to, my pretty one?'

David gestured vaguely.

'Come along with me then. I'm going to the school where I work. It's a girls' school. Have you ever had a girl?'

'No.'

'Wouldn't you like to?'

David gestured even more vaguely. He walked mechanically beside Pinn, letting her touch his arm, tug him gently by his flapping shirt sleeve to guide him.

'What do you think of your daddy's carry-on?'

David was silent.

'You mustn't be too hard on him,' said Pinn. 'People get in awful messes. You'll be in a mess yourself pretty soon. Life is a series of messes. It's easier than you young people think to tell a lie and then have to tell another. And falling in love can't be avoided and has to be forgiven. You weren't going to be nasty to poor little Em, were you?'

'No.'

'There's a good pet. Emily's had a rotten life. Almost as rotten as mine.'

They were walking along beside a high brick wall, and Pinn stopped suddenly at a door in the wall and produced a key. They both went through the door and found themselves in a large vegetable garden, surrounded by three other high brick walls, along one of which ran a row of greenhouses.

'Where's this?' said David.

'Sssh!' said Pinn. 'This is the school. Keep your voice down. There are no men on the staff, only a few outside servants. A man's voice sounds very conspicuous in here. Just follow me and don't talk. I want to show you something.'

206

The tall walls seemed to exclude the sound of main road traffic or reduce it to a bumble-bee buzz, as the two figures crossed the garden by a diagonal path between beds of radiantly healthy lettuces. They reached another gate and passed through it. And as they did so a new sound came to David's ears, a sweet high-pitched jargoning as of a nearby aviary of little chattering birds.

They were now in what appeared to be a miniature park or meadow, with the uncut grass just coming into flower and covered with a reddish sheeny light. A little way off, almost black with their own density, stood two immobile very large Lebanon cedars. Beyond was an elm, green as the lettuces, and half hidden by some slightly farther trees, the slanted pale façade of an eighteenth-century house. To the right, leading along the brick wall, was a path fringed by golden elder bushes covered in flat saucers of creamy flowers, and along this path, finger on lips, Pinn led the way. The aviary jargoning was louder.

The wall ended, they turned its corner and the scene changed again. Across an obviously disused gravel drive, fuzzed over with little skinny wild flowers, was a high dark yew hedge with a neatly clipped archway in its midst. Pinn crossed the gravel on tiptoe and led her captive through the arch. A square of well trimmed lawn was here surrounded by four high walls of equally well-trimmed yew where, opposite to their point of entry, another archway was flanked by two yew-niches containing a greyly-naked hatted and booted Hermes and a mini-skirted Artemis selecting an arrow. As David followed Pinn across the grass he realized, had perhaps known from the start, that the aviary jargoning was the excited voices of girls. He could now hear their high-pitched laughter, the occasional little scream. He passed from sunshine to shadow to sunshine, moving on Pinn's heels under the second yew arch.

'Sssh—' Her hand gripped his as they emerged very cautiously onto a further stretch of lawn. Straight ahead of them was an immense tangled hedge of pink roses and it was from beyond this that the sweet hubbub arose. Pinn scanned the lawn in both directions before she drew him out after her, murmuring, 'Now *quick*, follow me.'

She released him and moved with long Artemis-like strides across the intervening space and almost with the motion of a diver projected herself into the rose hedge and disappeared into its interior. Panting after her and lowering his head David saw a rounded burrow-like space, like the pathway of a fox or badger, which led into the innermost part of the wide tall hedge, and with a similar dive, half stumbling over his jacket which he was still carrying over his arm, he fell on all fours and scuffled in after his companion.

He fell against something warm and yielding, Pinn's leg. They were kneeling close together on earth which was suddenly crumbly and moist, inside a sort of low domed hall, greenly twilit and surrounded by the robust reddish thorny stems of the roses, glowing and faintly translucent. The rose smell was overwhelming. David became aware of a long pain in his arm where a thorn had scored him in his precipitate entry. He covered his mouth to still his panting. The voices of the girls were very close.

Pinn, jostling to face him, her two knees now touching his knees, was suddenly glaring into his face and holding him by each forearm, sliding her hands in beneath the tumbled shirt sleeves. In a vivid momentary flash David saw Pinn's small hand with two silver rings upon it, dabbled with blood, presumably his. Pinn's face glared, round-eyed, puff-cheeked, like a comic mask, close to his, vividly smiling, and for a moment he thought that she was going to kiss him. But she had simply leaned forward to whisper. 'Not a sound. I'll show you where to look.'

She twisted about and lay down full-length, wriggling herself gingerly into a space between the glassy red stems where a similar but smaller burrow gave onto the other side of the hedge. David began to follow her, but was stayed by her sandalled foot pressing urgently upon his shoulder. There was evidently only room for one in the burrow. In a moment Pinn was wriggling back and kneeling to push him forward by the shoulders into the place she had vacated. David almost prone, edged himself towards a circle of leafy sun-shot brightness on the other side of the hedge. An aperture now at last showed him the scene beyond.

A whitish marble basin, half sunk in the grass, filled with water and with the area of a fair-sized swimming pool, lay in the foreground with, rising up behind it, an immense and very battered baroque fountain representing Poseidon surrounded by sea nymphs. In the marble basin, as lithe and pink as fishes, six or seven girls were disporting themselves. They were all entirely naked.

Only much later, as he endlessly rehearsed in his mind the brief vision of the bathing damsels, did David realize how much, in what turned out to be a very short glimpse of them, he had actually seen. At the moment of seeing there seemed to be nothing in his mind except the somehow terrifying distressing impression of those wet pinkish-brown limbs, those long agile legs, the dripping defenceless often graceless buttocks blanched by bikinis, the equally pale small scarcely-grown breasts, the long wet darkened strands of hair plastered to cheeks and necks and backs. Later on however he found he could fill out in memory the whole scene as he had evidently, in spite of his sheer startled terror, managed to perceive it.

Beyond the fountain was a big largely ruined portico, with a cracked and grass-grown pavement, between whose pillars a latticed fence well covered with white flowering clematis formed a screen. To the right of the basin was a high beech hedge, and to the left a fence at whose foot young beeches had been planted. The towering fountain, made of a pale coarse licheny limestone (the basin was also of limestone: only in David's first feverish vision of it had it seemed to be made of marble) presented a long-bearded and grimly magisterial Poseidon wearing a high, now brokenly, jagged crown and gazing abstractedly into the distance, while a messy tide of nymphs, dolphins, fishes and other merfolk climbed towards his knees, attempting in vain to attract his attention. A dolphin, held aloft by a two-tailed nymph, had evidently once, when the fountain was able to 'play', gushed water right up onto the god's curly beard, which cascading in involuted rings as low as his navel, had been stained in some now distant era of the nineteenth, or even of the eighteenth, century a vivid blackish green.

The basin, probably, on the evidence of the newly-planted beech hedge, only quite lately devoted to the sport of other than purely limestone nymphs, was not very deep and would not have admitted of diving. It was, however, both long and broad and contained the (David's memory now told him exactly) seven naked girls without overcrowding. The girls, all showy swimmers, were able at any rate to exhibit to each other their splashy crawls, with a great deal of spray and shouting, and some less than dignified clambering in and out, long legs scraping limestones, without too many actual collisions. A slimy sluice down which water had once flowed from the more elevated level of the fountain, well lubricated by the swimmers' splashes, even served the girl who seemed smallest and youngest among them as a slide, down which with shrieks she constantly descended, scattering her more pretentiously crawling companions.

David became aware that something hot and slug-like was lying on top of him. Pinn, to see the show, had insinuated herself into the burrow beside him, lying half above him, her arm across his shoulder. She began to speak to him in a whisper, though indeed the laughing and shrieking of the bathers would effectively have drowned a much more resonant tone. 'Aren't they lovely? Do you see that one over there, just climbing out, that's my special crony, Kiki St Loy, isn't she a peach? She wants me to find her a boy friend, would you like to be it? She's only seventeen, though she pretended to be eighteen to get a car licence. Isn't she just the prettiest thing? And believe it or not she's still a virgin. Most of them aren't, but she was never sure till now that she wanted a man at all. Just look at her, the way she's standing, admiring herself—'

Kiki had climbed up onto the rim of the basin and was standing rather awkwardly, with salient stomach, one leg firmly planted, the other dabbing a prehensile foot onto the wet curving intermittently broken edging. One arm was a little histrionically outstretched for balance, while with a quick busy hand she was gathering the long strings of her wet hair, squeezing them out and stowing them all neatly together, cast back over one shoulder. As she did this she contemplated her breasts with interested appreciation. Her body was slightly darker than could be explained even by a rich girl's sunburn, her breasts were brown. ('Touch of the tarbrush there,' murmured Pinn.) Her brooding face, quiet and clear in the bright sunlight, was a lucid milky brown, uniform in hue, long-nosed, large-eyed, with the striking appearance which Homer, meaning thereby to compliment Hera, qualifies as 'ox-eyed'. Her hair, drying a little in the sun, had now declared itself to be a radiant brown, somewhat fairer than might have been expected, when the expressive eyes, so singularly dark and large, turned suddenly in the direction of the rose hedge and seemed to dart their fire right in through the leafy aperture.

David at the same moment raising his gaze as far as her face felt himself, doubtless erroneously, to be observed. He felt the intolerable hot confining weight of Pinn, lying beside, half on, him and constricting his movements. Regardless now of disturbance or possible detection he began to struggle, half sitting up, pushing the obstruction away, and jerking himself out of the thorny tunnel into the middle of the hedge. A moment later he had rolled over and taking the other side of the hedge in a quick rush had burst forth at a run onto the sunlit grass. He ran fleetingly, desperately, the tips of his toes scarcely touching the ground, through the yew archway, across the yew-encircled quadrangle, over the gravel driveway, along the elder path, past the cedar trees, through the door in the wall, between the lettuces, and out through the second and blessedly unlocked door, onto the friendly safe expanse of the public street, where he slowed down to a fast walk. He realized from the strange looks given him by the passers-by, that not only his arm but also his face was liberally smeared with blood. He also realized that he had left his jacket behind, underneath the rose hedge. His flesh was blazing hot. He felt confused violent emotion. Shame. Terror. Wild joy.

'Didn't I tell you you'd have to descend to the underworld to find me and make me alive again?' said Emily.

Everything between them was as it had once been, only with the passage of the years, with the suffering which they had caused each other, with the shock of exposure and the fear of loss, deeper and steadier, more complex, more profoundly felt.

'Yes,' said Blaise, kneeling at her feet.

'Didn't I tell you that your real self lived with me?'

'Yes.' He stretched himself out slowly, luxuriously, like an animal, laying his cheek upon her bare foot.

'God, how you've made me suffer. How you've made us both suffer.'

'Yes.'

'You do look battered. It's not just the eye. You look a proper wreck. Well, you know it now, what you were saying yourself. You can't go through the looking-glass without getting cut. You know that now, don't you?'

'Yes.'

In the three days that had passed a certain violence had run its course. The fury had passed into them and become part of their knowledge and their strength and they had at last become quieter together. Blaise had listened to Emily speaking to him over hours and hours. 'It's her turn to suffer now. I suddenly felt sure what to do. I was prepared to be kind to her, but not to be bloody taken over. She assumed she was top wife, didn't she. She was bloody forgiving me, and I was taking it as if I were really some sort of blasted criminal. I was like a bloody culprit before her. She was running us both. She was running you, that was what I couldn't bear. You should just have seen yourself in a mirror, you should just have seen the expression on your silly face, like a little boy who's been let off his caning. I couldn't bear to see you so bloody meek and submissive before her, it drove me hopping mad. And her saying she regarded me as a wronged woman and an object of pity, and saying how badly you'd treated me and how she's make you treat me better, as if this was going to stop me feeling bad in front of her, and at first she just had me mesmerized, but then my God I could see it wouldn't do, I wasn't going to put up with a Christ-awful arrangement like that. I'm not vindictive, I don't want to watch her weeping, but it's just bloody time for me to have my rights and let her put up with the rotten end for a change.'

This outcry, hours and hours of it, which Blaise endured with dazed blissful pain, began to subside at last. Between them now Harriet's name was scarcely mentioned any more, except in so far as it entered into certain practical arrangements upon which Emily now dilated with a childish pleasure which stung Blaise's heart with humility and tenderness.

'We won't put off long your starting to be a doctor, will we? I want you to be a doctor. I don't want you to lose anything, anything because of me.'

'We'll have to put it off a bit,' said Blaise now fully dressed, holding the hem of her petticoat which he kissed at intervals, 'until we see where we are financially.'

'Here, let me sit down and you put your head here. I do think we should move out of this dump. I think it's important. It's not a silly extravagance is it, getting that other flat?'

'No,' said Blaise. 'We must have a new beginning in a new place.'

'It is psychologically important, like you said. You know, when I saw you signing the lease for the flat I felt as if we were getting married at last—like in my dreams—I've so often dreamt I was young again, getting married to you. Oh my dear sweetikin, you don't know how much I've suffered all these years from simply not being what I ought to have been, from simply not being your proper wedded wife.'

212

'I do know, kid,' said Blaise. 'I can't take that suffering from you. But for any future suffering, I'll be around, we'll do it together.'

'Together. Now and always?'

'Now and always.'

'We won't need new curtains. These ones will fit. Well, we'll need one lot of long curtains for the big room. Oh my sweet one, do you think I'm silly, when so many great big things are happening, to be so pleased about curtains and about having a balcony and a bathroom with a carpet in it?'

'No. That's a sign of love too.'

'Everything's a sign of love. Dear heart, I don't mind any suffering, you know, so long as you truly love me and so long as it's me you live with. And we'll have friends, won't we, friends of us both who come to the house, like married people have?'

'Yes, yes.'

'But not Monty Small or that fat man.'

'Not them, no.'

'You know, I think Luca went over to her again yesterday. That'll have to stop.'

'Of course.'

'I think after all a boarding school would be a good idea. I'll take a job. I feel I could work till I dropped now for *us*, for you and Luca. I just got so empty and idle and lazy because there seemed nothing to work for. I felt I'd lost you.'

'You never lost me,' said Blaise. 'Surely you knew that.'

'I'm not sure. I feel now so much more connected to our beginnings, to our very first deep true love. I feel that never ceased at all, it just waited, and if there were bad patches I've simply forgotten them.'

'Me too.'

'And you'll see her now and then and David of course. They'll get used to it. They'll see you haven't vanished into thin air. I don't want them to suffer much. I mean I don't *want* them to suffer at all, but somebody's got to, thanks to clever you!'

'I know, kid—'

'You'll keep faith now?'

'Yes, Em darling—'

'I'd better keep my foot on your neck all the same.'

'Your foot is always on my neck. I love it there.'

'And you'll really write to her tonight and show me the letter?'

'And we'll walk together to the post and post it.'

'That's my sweet prince.'

Blaise drew her over sideways and down towards him and studied that bright pert small very blue-eyed face, which happiness had illumined with even more than its former youthful loveliness. The old seductive vitality had returned, everything was back in place which had made her once so utterly irresistible to him. He kissed her, tasting the kiss with closed eyes.

How amazingly practical he had been in these three days. He had sorted out all his papers and business documents at Hood House. He had signed the lease of a flat in Fulham. He had put off his patients and told them he was moving his consulting rooms into town. He had done everything—except tell Harriet that he was going. Of course I'm not *really* going, he told himself at intervals, when the whole thing began to seem too dizzily dreadful. It's simply a matter of justice, it's like I used to envisage it when I was more clear-headed, nearer the start. There are two women, neither of whom I can leave. They must take their turns. I have to put this burden onto Harriet. She is strong enough to bear it, I can pay her that compliment. And her peace was shattered anyway. She'll live at Hood House with David and I'll visit her there like I used to visit Emily here, only oftener of course, as it'll be open and above board and so that much better. The *whole* situation will be better, and isn't that what's most important? One will simply have redistributed the pain. And that *is* just, after all. I tried for so wickedly long to overlook Emily's misery, simply not to see it. It's right that now I should have to gauge it and to try to make her some amends. Of course it's a terrible business but after all I've always known it was a terrible business. Anything I do is going to be somehow wrong. This solution is objectively the least wrong, and hang my motives. Anyhow, without *those* motives how could I make Emily so happy? And to make someone *so* happy is surely a good thing.

What am I supposed to do? What *can* I do for the best? Blaise inquired of some enigmatic power which still seemed, after all this, to be discontented with him and still to accuse him of something. Of what? Of a sort of awful *vulgarity*? Was that his sin, that too its punishment, that he was irredeemably *vulgar*?

Milo Fane, tall, cold, expressionless, stared into the muzzle of the gun which his captor now pointed at him with a hand which trembled alarmingly.

'Keep still, *keep still*,' said de Sanctis.

Contemptuously Milo turned his back and sauntered away down the room. He moved without haste, feeling the trembling lethal steel behind him. He counted the paces: two more to reach the table. As he suddenly side-stepped de Sanctis fired. The bullet passed Milo and struck the pier glass at the end of the room, shattering it into a glittering spray of tiny fragments. At almost the same moment Milo's hand closed on the heavy bronze: Neptune taming a sea-horse? his incurably literary mind suggested as, almost without turning, he hurled the object and then was after it with the speed of a panther. The bronze caught de Sanctis squarely on the side of the head and a moment later Milo had repossessed himself of his Mauser.

He looked down upon his fallen senseless foe. It was a moment for speed. A knife flashed in Milo's hand. With fastidious distaste he drew down the sock above one of de Sanctis's flashy Italian suede shoes and bared the ankle. With measured deliberation he severed the Achilles tendon. De Sanctis was screaming. Milo was wiping the blood off his hand with a clean handkerchief. He was walking down the stairs. He drew a bar of chocolate out of his pocket and began to undo the paper.

Monty stared fascinated at the television, which he had turned on intending to see the news. The long forgotten words of the book came shadowily back to him as he stared at Richard Nailsworth's stiffly handsome face upon whose unmoved ruthlessness the cameras were now gloatingly concentrated. He switched off the set. His watch must have stopped before he wound it, he had evidently missed the news. No consolations tonight in the form of floods, earthquakes, massacres, hijackings, public executions, murders or wars. Nothing to laugh at at all in fact.

He wandered out of the little downstairs dressing-room where, together with a painted wall cupboard large enough to conceal several pre-Raphaelite princesses, he kept the television set. He passed along the hall where the tea chests full of unanswered letters were now overflowing onto the floor. He kicked one of them as he passed dislodging a little stream of missives: messages of sympathy, appeals for money, political manifestos, bills, letters from lunatics, letters from women. He went into his study and crossed to the open window. It was already almost dark outside and a number of bats were dancing a tango over the lawn, taking sudden swoops towards the house as if they had dared each other to dart right up to Monty and touch his face with a passing wing. He watched them for a while, then turned on a lamp and closed the shutters. The stained-glass cupboards glowed dully like metal. Mr Lockett had had lights fitted inside them, but the effect had seemed to Monty garish. Sophie had sometimes turned the lights on to annoy him. It had been a fairly warm afternoon but now it felt cool in the house, almost cold, as if some diffused spiritual condition were declaring itself clammily. As he often did on such summer evenings, Monty had lit a small wood fire in the mosaic fireplace. How much this little room had comforted him once. He shuddered and felt the fear which lived with him now, the fear of his own mind.

He saw a letter from his mother, which had arrived by the morning post, lying upon the table, and he reached for it and opened it. The usual love letter. Still announcements of a visit and no date fixed. His mother was poised like a kestrel, waiting, watching, wondering. She was obviously afraid of coming too soon. He felt her fear, he felt her will, not even in her written words, but deep in himself, in the part of him that was her. Underneath his mother's letter was now revealed a letter from Richard Nailsworth once again urging him to come to Richard's villa in Calabria. Monty pictured Richard's face, so much more vulnerable and touching when he was not playing Milo. That, not. He crumpled up Richard's letter, then tore his mother's up carefully into small pieces and dropped both letters into the fire.

Monty had been alone now for four days. No one had come near him during this time except for Harriet, who had called in briefly, evidently upset and unwilling to talk. The telephone bell was still silenced. He had expected Edgar to turn up again to do his Old Man of the Sea act, but Edgar had not come and Monty was surprised to find himself disappointed. He looked in vain for Edgar's Bentley, in this road and the next. Doubtless Edgar had been offended by

Monty's horrible remark. Monty felt a vague urge to apologize but decided it was pointless. Where was Edgar anyway? Back at his London Club, or at Mockingham supervising the destruction of his mother's unsightly greenhouse? Monty had got as far as discovering the telephone number of Bankhurst School, but had not yet used it. He felt it as a sort of life-line however. He knew that he could force himself to pursue this job and that once he had put himself in a context where he had to behave normally he would probably find himself behaving normally. Writing was utterly and absolutely now out of the question. Getting through time was rather the problem. The cry of 'Help me!'—but there was no one there.

Devotion to truth might save him somehow: austerity, honesty, discipline; yet he had in his desert place to *invent* these things. He made his regular attempts to meditate, but their very formality gave admission to horrors. The depths where he had seemed to find silence and emptiness and peace now writhed with forms. He resorted to elementary techniques such as counting his breaths, but the numbers themselves became huge in his mind and enigmatically significant as if they were printed upon immense cards. He wanted to lie on the floor and weep but tears seemed eternally denied. No wonder he missed Edgar. Any human company was a relief. Yet there was no one whom he had the will positively to seek for.

Monty, who had wrapped himself in the white fur rug from the big armchair, had just decided to give himself a sleeping pill and go to bed when someone started ringing the bell and banging violently upon the front door knocker in a way suggestive of terror and desperation. Monty leapt up and raced through the hall turning the lights on. He opened the door and Harriet entered, passing him quickly by and going on into the lighted room. She was wearing the cashmere shawl which she had drawn up over her head. He caught a glimpse of her face and guessed instantly what had happened. Had he, during these four awful days, been waiting for it?

He followed her into the study. Without a word she handed him the letter and then sat down quietly. Standing beside the lamp Monty read Blaise's words.

Harriet my darling,
I have to tell you this and I beg you to accept it with all the wonderful courage and compassion which you have so far shown in this dreadful business. I am going to live with

Emily. I have to. I have simply got to choose. (Edgar was right.) I cannot live with you both and since it has all come out I have simply realized that I cannot now any longer ask Emily to take second place. She has suffered enough. I must now give her and Luca the comfort of a real home, a place where I am nearly all the time. Oh my God, if only I could divide myself in two, but I can't! Hood House already exists and will go on existing. And of course I shall come to see you there. And I shall trust you marvellously to keep it in existence, for David's sake and because you are some kind of saint. My dearest girl, I *pray* you to accept this new scene and to make it work. After the first shock, you will see that it is not impossible. The alternative to 'making it work' is just violence and chaos which you *cannot* choose. My mind is made up and I am certain of my course. I must now give myself to Emily, who has suffered so patiently and so long, during a time when you were happy. Oh do not despair of happiness again, my dear, I shall always be there. We shall just have somehow, shall we not, to learn each other anew and love each other anew in this different life. I *know* that you will attempt this and I bless you for it from the bottom of my heart. I shall be living with Emily in Fulham, in fact we are moving at once. (So there is no point in coming to Putney.) I think anyway it is better that we should not meet for a short while. Let there be an interval during which we both take stock. I feel so terrible and so desolate as I write these awful and irrevocable words to you. Do you remember when you first knew of Emily, you said, 'I love you. I just want to help you. What else would you expect me to do?' Can you, oh can you please, still say this under this further awful burden which I put upon you? You and only you can still save us all. You must do it and you will do it. I am acting with my eyes open. I *see* how awful all this is, what an outrage, what a crime. But I am placed between crime and crime and I have to move. Try to see it as an act of justice and forgive me. We must both learn, you and I, and we can learn to bear it. For this is anguish to me too, my dear. I cannot write more. Oh forgive me. And hold everything still in its place, my love and my saint.

B.

P.S. I hope you will understand when I say this: naturally in the new set-up Emily wants to have Luca all to herself, especially now that he has a resident father at last! We are planning a new school for him. (Not the one we decided before.) He must be made to fit in and to settle down. So *please* don't disturb him by trying to see him any more. You must appreciate that this is simply a matter of the child's welfare. Letters will be forwarded from the Putney address.

Oh my dear — I am so sorry —

Monty read this effusion slowly and with care and then looked at Harriet. He had seen the effects of strain, even of frenzy, in her face, and saw now the traces of tears. But her look was not that of a totally distraught woman.

'What do you think of that?' said Harriet.

Her steady tone made suddenly a kind of intimacy between them; and Monty realized at once how much better he was feeling. Harriet's troubles were a far more effective cure than catastrophes on television. He answered cautiously, 'Is he serious?'

'Of course!'

'I mean, won't he come rushing back in a couple of days saying he was in a muddle and please will you have him back? I mean, how *can* he exist without you?'

'He's in love with her again. He won't come rushing back. He'll be hanging the curtains at the flat in Fulham.'

Monty stared at Harriet in amazement. Was there no end to the surprises which this remarkable woman could spring upon him? Her stern controlled face seemed scarcely recognizable. She looked like a distant relation of herself. The features were similar but the expression was utterly new.

'He is mad with relief,' said Harriet. 'He has pulled it off. He is free, he is gone. He has done it at last.'

'But he said he didn't care for her any more.'

'He lied. Or else he has simply discovered he does. Perhaps she forced him to choose. Anyway, however it's happened, he's chosen.'

Facing this new haggardly beautiful Harriet, Monty, adopting a fresh tone and eschewing further efforts at comfort, said, 'Well, what are you going to do?'

'I'm not sure,' said Harriet.

'Are you going over to Putney? They may still be there.'

'I thought of doing so,' said Harriet. 'I only found this letter about an hour ago and I thought of going there at once and sort of—running mad. Then I decided it would be quite pointless. And then I began to feel—so cold.'

I can see the coldness, thought Monty. How much it becomes you! 'You won't stay cold though. The shock hasn't come yet.'

'Yes. I know. But I can already make decisions. I have made decisions.'

'What have you decided?'

'That letter,' said Harriet, 'is terrible. Awful. It is the letter of a wicked man.'

'Possibly,' said Monty. 'But the wickedness is not new and he *is* caught by it. What he says about justice is not totally insane, there's something in it.'

'Maybe. But the wickedness is there and it does change people. It has changed me. Monty, do you think you could give me some whisky please?'

Monty fetched a bottle and two glasses and poured some out. Harriet gulped and began to shudder a little, but quieted herself. 'How do you mean, changed?' said Monty.

'I'm not going to keep Hood House going for that man,' said Harriet. 'Does he imagine that he can walk out and have everything here all the same, cosily waiting for him when he decides to honour us with a visit? I will not keep Hood House going for him, not even for half an hour. I have already turned off the water heaters. Hood House is finished.'

Oh you wonderful woman! thought Monty. He said, 'Don't be hasty, Harriet. Blaise may be crawling back as soon as tomorrow morning.'

'Well, he'll find the place empty. Even if he comes tonight he'll find it empty.'

'Empty? Where are you going to go tonight?'

'Here.'

'Here? You mean Locketts?'

'Yes. Do you mind, Monty? I've simply got to get out of Hood House at once. I've got to be absolutely somewhere else. It isn't far to run to, but it's the only place I can run to immediately.'

'What about Mockingham?' said Monty. The idea of this transformed Harriet under his roof filled him with strangely mixed feelings.

'Oh, dear Edgar—he's been such a support—he's over there now helping David pack.'

'Helping David pack?'

'Yes. David's coming too of course. You really don't

mind? I feel I couldn't go to Mockingham. You're an old friend, you've known us for ages—if I went to Mockingham Edgar would expect too much—I don't mean—'

'You're not afraid I might expect too much?'

'Of course not. Monty, you've got to help me, only you can help me and David now. I feel—I can't tell you how clear-headed and determined—I'm frightened and wounded and desperately unhappy— but so determined. I feel I can, I must, simply commandeer your house if necessary.'

'It's yours,' said Monty.

'Thank you. I knew you'd say that. Edgar and David are following me over. Oh Monty, that awful awful letter—And about Luca—Monty, I'm not going to do without Luca.'

'Harriet, be sane! How can you—'

'I don't know. But I'll get Luca somehow. I can do that child good—his parents can't even talk to him—I can talk to him. The child loves me. How can they just decree that—'

'Because they *are* his parents!'

' "They"—"they"—that dreadful "they"—'

'Steady, Harriet.'

'Blaise simply doesn't know what I'm like or he wouldn't have written as he did.'

'Perhaps you didn't know what you were like.'

'No, I've never really had a crisis—'

'But, Harriet, wait a moment. Blaise says you're such a saint and so on. Mightn't it be better for everybody, what-ever you feel like now—running mad or whatever—whatever you *are* like now, if you just decided to *be* a saint, to bear it all, to carry their sins, to keep the Hood House heaters burning and all that? You did manage to behave so awfully well at the beginning of this thing—?'

'Yes, but it wasn't saintliness. It was sort of power—I can understand how she hated it—I had to be the one who decided things—and I so much wanted to console Blaise— and I thought he wanted it—and oh Monty, what can have happened, what can have happened—'

Harriet caught at Monty's hands. The front door bell rang again.

David and Edgar were standing outside under the lamp, with several suitcases on the step beside them. Monty had a crazy impulse to laugh. 'Come in, come in. Harriet is here and has explained everything.' He must not, he thought, sound jovial. How awful it all was, in fact.

David pale, stony-faced, moved the cases in. Edgar looked

sternly at Monty. Monty said, 'I'm very sorry I was so rude to you. I didn't mean it. I was just raving. Please forgive me.' Edgar broke into the sweet smile which had been hiding expectantly behind the sternness, a change of expression reminding Monty vividly of a big pink fair-haired appallingly diffident, appallingly clever, undergraduate.

Harriet had emerged from the study. About to start crying again, she stared at David and Edgar with a helpless tragic expression. Monty said quickly, 'Harriet, this is your house now. Could you organize everything please? David and Edgar will help you, and I'm sure you can find sheets and things. Decide which rooms you want. And the kitchen's all yours. I'm just off.'

'But where to?' cried Harriet. 'Monty, please, you aren't leaving me?'

'No, no. I'm just going for a walk.'

Monty bolted out of the door and down the path. It was darker now though the sky was still a slightly glowing blue admitting of few and huge stars. Monty had started quickly down the road when he heard a sound of running feet behind him. He stopped abruptly and David cannoned into him and they stumbled, clutching each other. David held on.

'You won't leave us, Monty, will you, you really won't?'

'I won't leave you. What do you suppose I'd do?'

'I could suppose you'd do anything. You could go to China. Anything.'

'I won't go to China,' said Monty.

Monty cursed, trying to get the stumpy tail of the hammer in underneath the twisted nail. A feeling of exasperated frightened impotence came over him. He felt clumsy and feeble and defeated. He had removed one slat of the fence and was trying to remove a second. The dogs, in whose interests this gateway was being made, watched malignantly and derisively from the other side. Ganimede's black nose and puffy moustaches had already been thrust through the hole. Monty kicked the slat violently, causing the dogs to

222

retreat. A chorus of angry outraged barks accompanied his reiterated kicks. The lower part of the slat splintered and came away and the smaller dogs began to squeeze through into the orchard.

Monty had made an appointment to visit Bankhurst School on the following Friday. (He had talked to the secretary, not to Binkie in person.) The actual taking of this step, the removal of his plan of salvation from the ideal to the real, had caused him no relief. He could not revive emotions which had once been attached to the idea of having what he had thought of as a real job. Even the idea of an ordeal or trial was devoid of interest. All that was clear was that it had once seemed to him a good thing to get out of his mind and into some ordinary compulsory setting. This was to be part of the purging of Milo, the deflating of Magnus. What was also clear was that if he continued as he was he would not go mad but would become something possibly worse. He was irritated and annoyed by the invasion of his house and he avoided his guests when he could. His sympathies, his feelings, all now seemed to him unutterably frivolous. If he could not set these aside for what had he striven all these years?

Though almost insomniac he had continued last night to dream of Sophie. He was lying in his bed, only it had become a box with wooden sides, and Sophie, lit as if by footlights, was passing silently by dressed in her wedding gown. (Sophie, who had married him with almost cynical casualness in a registry office, had never had a wedding gown, but Monty's mother kept hers religiously wrapped up in black tissue paper.) Monty thought, Sophie isn't dead, she has just become dumb. What a trial for such a chatterbox! At that moment Sophie looked at him, and he saw the glitter of her glasses—only it was not her glasses, but awful huge tears which sparkled all round her eyes like scales. Then as she passed him by Monty saw with horror that she was being followed, as if in procession, by the Bishop, his leg restored and wearing purple knee breeches. The Bishop moving slowly past, turned and smiled complicitly at Monty.

While Monty was kicking the fence and remembering his dream Edgar was sitting in the Locketts' drawing-room with Harriet. Harriet was watching with fascination while Edgar with his large clean white handkerchief was wiping off her hand one of his own tears which he had just dropped upon it. Harriet felt surprise, dismay, pity. Edgar had just made her a quite formal and detailed marriage proposal, which she had of course refused, explaining that she was married already. However, she was both consoled and touched.

'I know,' said Edgar, still holding her hand trapped inside his handkerchief. 'But I just needed to say all this so as to make it clear, I mean so that you could know, if ever you should need me in the future, that I am absolutely committed to you.'

'But Edgar, I don't want you to be! You are absurd! I don't want you to be unhappy!'

'Oh I'm not *unhappy*. You see, I need a woman to love. As I told you, I loved Sophie. I love you. It makes me so glad that you exist. There needn't be anything more, though of course I can't help hoping for more. I wish at least you'd come to Mockingham. You needn't see me there.'

'My dear Edgar—'

'You see, like I told you, unrequited love—and I haven't really known any other kind—if it's quite sort of hopeless—isn't it like unrequited love after all—I mean, like loving God even if He doesn't exist.'

'But I do exist.'

'The love goes and returns. It passes through the object and returns.'

'So it's really self-love?'

'No, no. I *will* you so much. I *will* you. Can't you feel it?'

'Not really.'

'And you can help me so easily, like Athena helping Herakles to hold the world up.'

'That sounds hard.'

'Not for a goddess. I'm rewarded for loving you. Even if I have nothing, nothing at all.'

'You have my hand.'

'Oh God,' Edgar groaned. Then carefully removing the handkerchief he kissed Harriet's knuckles and released her. She felt the moist streak of more tears. All this is mad, she thought, mad.

The state of prostrated reaction and shock which Monty had predicted had come. The sacred rage which had prompted her to turn off the immersion heaters and made her able to say 'Hood House is finished' had been totally withdrawn. Her mind seemed again to have altered radically since that strength. She now felt simply mutilated, and missing Blaise was an endless occupation. In bed she felt agonizingly incomplete, and by day a searcher. She reached for him. She had no further will for decisions. She did not want to return to

Hood House. She wanted desperately to do something about Blaise but could not think what to do. He had made no communication, no sign. No doubt he was waiting for her to *realise fully* that he had left her. A sense of the cruelty and injustice of it all was strong in her but vague. What *ought* she to do? She ought of course to help David. She had suggested taking him to Paris, but could not make out if he wanted to come, and had not the power to decide the matter. What she now desperately needed was Monty, his sympathy and his force. But though Monty was polite and helpful he had become horribly withdrawn and aloof. She also yearned for Luca, but Luca too had sent her no signal. He had been removed from her, imprisoned inside that awful new regime which she could not and did not attempt to imagine.

Monty was dreaming again. It was night and he was in his bed, and a tall woman in a pale robe who was certainly not Sophie was standing beside him looking down at him with glowing vindictive eyes. He was a sacrificial victim being scrutinized by the priestess. He was to be killed slowly, his flesh plucked from him slowly. He tried to move, feeling the horrible familiar impotence which he had experienced when trying to pull the nail out of the fence. He turned in his bed and then found that he was not dreaming at all. The moon was shining into the room and there *was* a woman there, standing close beside his bed and looking down at him intently. Monty lunged for his lamp and the light came on.

'Hello,' said Pinn.

Monty got quickly out of bed, pulled the curtains carefully together, then put on his dressing-gown. He put his hands in his pockets and stared at Pinn who was now sitting on his bed. She was wearing a rather long yellow mackintosh, and her face, restraining a nervous smile, was ablaze with interest and excitement. She said, 'Do you mind if I smoke? You don't, I believe? May I use this pretty bowl for an ash tray?'

Monty said nothing. He watched her light a cigarette.

'I thought this must be the master bedroom,' Pinn went on. 'I didn't intend to arrive so late. Not that it's all that late, I would have expected you to be still up. Then when I found the French windows unfastened it was irresistible. I felt like a burglar, it was thrilling. You looked rather beautiful asleep.'

Monty sat on an upright chair and continued to stare at her.

'They seem to be all in beddy-byes at the other house too.'

'The other house is empty,' said Monty. 'They're here.'

'Ah. What does that mean I wonder? You're very quiet aren't you. Won't you ask me why I'm here?'

'I suppose you were sent by Blaise to find out what has happened.'

'Yes, of course. Blaise and I understand each other, we're almost telepathic. I'm his hired murderer. I could have murdered you, by the way, quite easily. You oughtn't to leave your doors unlocked. Blaise wants to know what his crime looks like from here. He doesn't say this of course, but I understand him without speech. He's going to lend me some money to buy a flat.'

'What are things like over there?' said Monty.

'I'm glad you're curious. Do you mind if I take my coat off? It's just wonderful over there. They're dazed with love. She's so happy. I've never seen a woman so happy. The bones of her face are dissolving with it. She sings all day. She's crazy about the new place. She was nearly crying with happiness because she'd bought a tablecloth.'

'And he?'

'He's happy too of course, but he's much more conscious. He wants to know where he stands.'

'Does he intend to stick to Emily McHugh now, to live with her?'

'Oh yes, barring accidents.'

'What would an accident be?'

'I'm not sure. That's connected with the second reason why I'm here.'

'And what is that?'

'To find out which side you're on.'

'I'm not involved,' said Monty.

'You must be, you simply must be.'

'You, I presume,' said Monty, 'want them to fail.'

'Oh we are being frank, aren't we!'

'Don't you?'

Pinn was silent for a moment. Then she said, 'I ought to have been a man. I would have had eight sons and ruled them with a rod of iron. I once read of a sheikh who had eight hundred sons who could ride horses. I'd like to have been him.'

'Tell Blaise if he wants to know where he stands he'd better come and see Harriet.'

'I suppose she's still doing her saint act?'

'I do not know what she thinks.'

'Do you want her?'

'Do I what?'

'Do you want Harriet?'

'No.'

'I wish I could see inside your head,' said Pinn.

'There's nothing interesting to see,' said Monty. 'Now could you go, please? I want to go back to sleep. Please be quiet going down the stairs.'

'Don't be so cold with me,' said Pinn. 'Haven't you any ordinary pity?'

'Why should I pity you? Please go.'

'Ah, if only you knew how much I deserved your pity—'

Suddenly she began to undo her blouse, revealing a much freckled throat and a black brassiere. Staring at him, she let the blouse fall off behind her.

'Stop,' said Monty. 'Do you want simply to disgust me? Stop degrading yourself and go.'

'At least there's a little feeling in your voice at last. I thought maybe you were some sort of zombie.' She sat gazing, and a strong blush had spread over her face and down her neck.

'What *do* you want?' said Monty. 'And please dress yourself.'

'I want to startle you. I *have* startled you, don't deny it, even great you. I want you to look at me. It's a pleasure to me, I don't have many. I wish Harriet could see us. Shall I call her?'

Monty got up and walked away from her down the room. And as he turned his back on Pinn he seemed suddenly to forget her. He saw in a tall mirror Sophie in her wedding gown, weeping as ghosts weep.

'Don't be angry,' said Pinn's voice.

Monty paced back again and Sophie vanished. 'Cover yourself.'

Pinn pulled her blouse on again. She said, 'Surely you know that I love you. Surely you know that I am yours if you want me.'

'I thought you loved Emily McHugh.'

'I suppose I love her, if that frightful emotion can be called love. I'm not sure. But I *love* you. And you are worthy of me. You are the only man I've ever met who is. We are akin, you know, we are akin, I *recognize* you.'

'Please don't talk so loud,' said Monty.

'You *are* afraid Harriet might come. You *can't* be in love with that sopping wet.'

'I am sorry,' said Monty. 'I cannot respond to you in any way. I am just not sufficiently interested in anything you have to say.'

'God, you are a cold fish. What colour is your blood, for Christ's sake? Why not surprise yourself for a change? No wonder you can't write anything but sick detective yarns. Your bed is warm even if you aren't. Let me undress and get into your bed. you must want me, I can see you do. I'm yours, I tell you. God, you're lucky. Shall I tell you the story of my life?'

'No, thank you. Just go away.'

'You know nothing about real life at all. You don't know what it's like to be an outcast, a real outcast. You don't know what real horrors are. I'm going to tell you anyway, whether you like it or not. I'd like to lodge something in your cold fish mind. It will console me afterwards to think you saw my breasts and heard about my brother.'

'Your brother?'

'Yes. I've got a younger brother, two years younger. He's a moron. My father battered him. I saw it happening all through my childhood. My father hated him, he used to hit his head deliberately to destroy his mind, deliberately, and he did it. My mother cleared out ages before of course. My brother was as bright as a button when he first went to nursery school. By the time he was twelve he was done for, his brain was damaged. My father hit him again and again and again. He destroyed his brain. He's so beautiful, the most beautiful man I've ever seen. They let him wear his hair long. He's tall, like a picture. He's stone deaf and he's got the mind of a little child. They have to take him to the lavatory. I go to see him every month. He doesn't know me. He doesn't know anybody. He's a beautiful moron. My father married again. He's happy with his second wife. He's got a little girl to dote on. So that's how it is. I wonder if you can imagine what it is to live with that. No, you obviously can't. But I'm glad I told you. At least I've put it into your mind and you won't ever forget it. I've made my mark on your mind. You might even write about it. If you're capable of writing about anything which is really awful and not just fake.'

'I don't think it would make a very satisfactory story,' said Monty.

'Ah—' Pinn starred for another moment, then began to pull on her mackintosh. She said, 'I never told about him to anybody else, not even to Emily. You know, I would kill him if I

228

could. I sometimes dream I am stabbing him to death with a very long sharp knife. I dream that I've killed him and cut out his heart.'

'Please go,' said Monty.

'All right. You are a sort of thug. Not that I don't like it, of course. And after this you can't expect me to keep away from you. We might just as well have been in bed. You do appreciate me, you know.'

'I'll turn the landing light on,' said Monty. 'Please be very quiet.'

He went out noiselessly and switched on the lights. Pinn passed him and without looking back went away down the stairs. Monty returned into his room and lay down on the bed. He noticed that, for the second time since Sophie's death, he felt some vestiges of physical excitement. He forgot Pinn. Images of Sophie crowded his mind, causing him bitter pain.

'Pinn seems very happy all of a sudden,' said Emily.

Blaise said nothing. With Emily on the balcony, he was watching Kiki St Loy getting into the open sports car. Kiki was wearing a long shapeless scarlet shirt over very brief black velvet shorts. Her long legs, in apple green tights, folded themselves inside the car and the door banged. Pinn was already ensconced in the passenger seat. Kiki's long bright hair was neatly tucked down the back of her shirt. She now donned a floppy green hat and tied it over her head with a sort of motoring veil. Without looking up, she raised a brown hand in farewell greeting. Pinn, smiling up at the two watchers, waved, raising both hands in an almost ecstatic gesture. The yellow sports car leapt away with a roar.

'I said Pinn seems very happy all of a sudden.'

'Oh yes.'

'Christ, you aren't desiring that St Loy bitch?'

'Men are mechanical I'm afraid. No, of course not, no! Em, look at me. I love you.'

'You'd better. I wish to God that bloody girl hadn't been

in the house baby-sitting that night when we came home. And Pinn keeps bringing her over here. She and Pinn are as thick as thieves, I wouldn't be surprised if they were lovers. Not that I care. And I wish you wouldn't encourage Pinn so. I've had Pinn. I want Pinn out of my life now and she can take the bloody St Loy girl with her. I want us to be just us at last. You do want that, don't you?'

'But you wanted us to have friends.'

'Yes, new ones. All the old ones are spoilt. You aren't moping about Mrs Placid, are you?'

'Certainly not!'

'Because if you are—'

'Emily, I'm not! Oh Em, kid, stop it. I'm here. We've bought a refrigerator.'

'Yes. And a mixmaster. And an electric toaster. And a set of superior non-stick saucepans.'

'You're beginning to believe it?'

'And I've buttered Richardson's paws and Little Bilham's. Where are they, by the way? We'd better come inside and close that door. You don't think the cats would be silly enough to jump off the balcony, do you?'

'No, no. Oh Em, your happiness makes me so happy.'

'I hope you're happy in your own happiness and not just in mine?'

'I am, I am.'

'It's still not quite real yet. I wish you would work here properly, sweetikin. I wish you hadn't put off all your patients. Dr Ainsley rang up again, he seemed quite bothered.'

'I will work here. I just need an interval, a holiday.'

Blaise, seeing two of his patients (Jeannie Batwood and Angelica Mendelssohn) had found himself explaining to them the change in his situation. He had been unable not to tell them all about it. The change of locale, the change of woman, could in any case hardly be allowed to pass without some comment. Blaise had spent the hour on each occasion talking about himself. His patients had eagerly played the analyst. Later he felt bad about this and had cancelled all appointments. Ordinary life must start again soon however.

Blaise, when he could enforce some repose upon himself in the midst of the vortex of feeling in which he now lived, was amazed at his coolness. Not that he felt in the least cool, but there was a metaphysical coolness about his proceedings which fairly took his breath away. He seemed to be fully aware of what he had done, he could measure its enormity, and yet

230

he felt practically no guilt. This was not because he vulgarly 'analysed' his guilt away. He simply did not 'take' the situation in this manner. He felt rather a kind of humility, a recognition of fate. What a *shred* I am, he thought. How embryonic, how partially formed any human being is. How can we not be dooms to each other? Perhaps in the years before Blaise had simply 'used up' all his guilt. He thought with awe of what he used to feel, and could not help conceiving that in a deep way things were better now, even though he had done something terrible (but what exactly?) to his wife and his elder son.

Blaise coexisted in these days with his mind with a certain frankness. There was a part of him that believed (and he let it believe) that all could still be well in the way in which (with such relief) he had believed it could be after the revelation. Only now it was the other way round. Could this little alteration matter so much? Now he would live with Emily and visit Harriet. Why not? Human beings can get used to anything. Blaise had in fact not at all abandoned the idea that Harriet's goodness would somehow save them all. Harriet would 'hang on' through any ordeal and would in the highest sense make the best of things. Of course any moral idea by means of which he could defend himself (such as that he was acting 'justly') was fully entertained in his mind. But in his conception of an ultimate state of peace Blaise was not deeply concerned with the 'justice' of which he had made so much in his letter. 'Justice' (and any other moral concept for that matter, such as 'honesty', with which he also occasionally conjured) was too abstract to fit the dense texture of the real events. It was not justice he was now offering to Emily. He was not now 'offering' her anything. Things which he and she had done and been in years past were having their deep inevitable consequences. The time for guilt was over since the crime had been committed so long ago.

Intense mutual erotic love, love which involves with the flesh all the most refined sexual being of the spirit, which reveals and perhaps even *ex nihilo* creates spirit as sex, is comparatively rare in this inconvenient world. This love presents itself as such a dizzily lofty value that even to speak of 'enjoying' it seems a sacrilege. It is something to be undergone upon one's knees. And where it exists it cannot but shed a blazing light of justification upon its own scene, a light which can leave the rest of the world dark indeed. Blaise felt that he was experiencing this miracle fully for the first time, since in what he described to Emily as their 'first innings' his joy had been crippled by the necessity of deceit and shocked by his sense of a desecrated innocence. Now there was no deceit and its very disappearance was the honest recognition of the desecration which had after all happened and could not be undone. How, really, can one *think* about such a tangled business? Blaise wondered. He could conceive that a better man would not be in his situation, but he could not conceive that a man in his situation could act better.

Truthfulness was its own reward and fed what must seem to him a pure fire; and freedom was its own reward too. He had a burning sense of his own identity which felt like a justification. *Now* he recalled how often, on nights when he had felt his lack of deep rapport with Harriet, he had wanted to *run* out of Hood House, to *run* to Emily and *be* with her that other self which was so much more him. Of course he and Emily had quarrelled as the years went by under that intolerable strain. Emily's sheer endurance under that strain was a further guarantee of the rightness of their union now. After all they had let the world try to part them, they had even helped it! And how utterly the atmosphere of those years had vanished, now that they gazed at each other at last, breathing deep of the tangy air of freedom.

Blaise knew that he must soon go to see Harriet. He must endure her tears and encounter again that part of his divided self which, however inanimate it might seem at the moment, he knew still lived at Hood House. Of course he still loved Harriet, and as soon as he saw her that other self would revive, though it might be weaker and smaller. I shall just have to live with a split personality, he told himself philosophically. He delayed going, not because he feared Harriet's reproaches and the sight of her woe, or even because he feared the unnerving transition to his other mode of being, but because he could not bear to blot Emily's joy. Naturally Emily was afraid, naturally she needed reassurance and it was a marvellous delight to him to give it to her. Her childish pleasure in the new flat moved Blaise to tears. He saw her again as the almost-child whom he had first loved, a creature utterly uncorrupt, utterly unspoilt, an image of truth, of *his* truth, his own special personal tailor-made incarnate truth.

All these were the ingredients of Blaise's 'coolness'. He felt many pains and many fears but he did not feel agonizingly undecided or distraught. There was a great obscure pain about David. And more superficially he worried about Monty, about what Monty thought about it all and whether he had discussed it with Harriet. But the image of Harriet herself was solid and solitary. Even if she was wretched, even if she was angry, ultimately Harriet would be faithful. Harriet would wait. And meanwhile Emily McHugh was singing as she put away the new sheets and pillow cases into the airing cupboard. And as she sang Luca was sitting on the stairs watching her and smiling. Luca was happy too. Out of guilt and wickedness and violence a new stronghold of innocence had been born.

Emily, stowing away the linen, was singing like a bird out of a warm sense of renewed life, physical well-being, sunshine, sex. Sheets and pillow cases. Towels. Tablecloths. Even damask serviettes! Wow! She had never had a linen cupboard before. She had never *bought* so many things one after the other in her life, and each new purchase further guaranteed the palace of her love. Emily felt like a martyr who, at one moment being chewed by lions, is at the next in the presence of God being congratulated on her performance. She had indeed endured and now had her reward. She felt so perfectly justified, it was like being endowed with a heavenly body. She was cleansed and soothed and all that tormented angry love for Blaise which had carried her through those horrible years was pacified, purified, beatified. She was intensely and happily in love for the first time in her life. No wonder she sang. Of course there were fears. She needed Blaise's presence, his eyes, his touch. She needed constant draughts of reassurance. But then these were constantly available. Blaise did not need to tell her that Harriet's power was broken. The revelation, the smash, the entry of truth upon the scene like an announcing angel had sufficiently made a new world out of which there was no way back. This violence was not the dangerous herald of more. It was not the beginning of the war, it was its end. No wonder Emily, waking every morning to the amazing reality of it all, gritted her teeth with rapture.

She turned now and saw Luca behind her, sitting on the stairs. How much, in these days, Luca had the air of an interested spectator. He was smiling at her now. Could so young a child actually be looking sardonic? That could not be the meaning of his smile. 'You little hobgoblin you!' she said and seized him and shook him roughly in her embrace. New springs of love for her son had risen in her expanded being, and the perfect physical connection between herself

and Blaise made her able to touch and hold the child in a
new way.

'I'm sorry,' said Monty. 'I'm very sorry.'

He and Harriet were sitting on a rather skeletal rain-worn
teak seat on the lawn by the study window. Fast small clouds
bowled along, occasionally blotting out the sun. Monty in a
flimsy black summer-weight jacket, felt cold and would like
to have gone inside to the wood fire in the study, only the
nature of the recent conversation made any immediate such
move seem frivolous, even heartless. Harriet, very tense, was
staring down the garden at the Douglas firs, stroking Lucky
(his surname had been early dropped), who was sitting
beside her on the seat with a responsible air, his huge wide
paws upon her lap, gazing up into her face with calm contemplative affection, while her mechanical hand lightly
lifted the ruff of rusty brown fur about his big long-nosed
face. On the lawn Babu and Panda lay watching with jealous
concentration, while Buffy, wrapped in his unhappy thoughts,
sat erect behind them.

Harriet had lived through universes of feeling since the
moment, years ago it seemed now, when she had received
Blaise's second letter. Her certainty and promptness about
leaving Hood House had seemed later to be a sort of pointless
pique. In such a tragedy why run anywhere? Then it had
seemed right again, an impulse of self-defence which had
landed her in just the proper place. The flight symbolized
her surprising determination not to forgive her husband.
When Harriet had wanted to reassure Blaise and to take away
his pain she had felt utterly at one with herself. She was a
woman, and perhaps there are many such, who lived, like
an embryo inside an egg, upon a supporting surrounding
matrix of confidence in her own virtue. No nineteenth-century
matron, or even one from ancient Rome, could have been
more confident than Harriet that she was a good person and
would always be able to act rightly. There was nothing
vainglorious or forced about this view, it even coexisted in

her with a good deal of simple humility. I just have that sort of temperament, she said to herself, the result of a cheerful orderly childhood and a good upbringing and a quiet way of life. Of course, I have never been severely tried, but I have resources and principles. I can rely upon myself and others will be right to rely upon me. This little confidence she placed, without feeling herself in any way remarkable, indeed conscious that she was the smallest of small fry, in the centre of her family life. She saw more of Blaise's faults than he ever dreamt of, and she supported him with the pure will of her own humble decency. That was how she felt it all and lived it all, and this was a great part of her happiness.

So it was that when the awful trial did come Harriet swung into response to it with an almost exultant and only momentarily surprised sense of her own strength. She suffered the shock and the pain, but there she was, where she had always been, in the centre, needed and able to respond. Distress had to be eased, tears dried, and she could do it, and the performance of these duties was patently more important than the indulgence of her jealousy or of her shocked disappointment in her husband. The performance of the duties was a real solace, and the power to perform them filled her up at need like divine grace. This had been before Blaise's second defection. The difference *then* she could never have conceived of beforehand. She could support and forgive a penitent husband who needed her love and her strength. But when all that power seemed no longer necessary, when Blaise cut the channel through which, for so many years, as he almost unconsciously made use of it, it had fed him, Harriet felt utterly deprived of her central certainties and no longer at all knew how to think about what she ought to do. Perhaps she had never known how to think about what she ought to do. What she had possessed were not principles but instincts, the warm wise possessive instincts of a happy wife and mother. For a situation where she was not needed she had no heroism.

Harriet had of course, from the start of the new time, wanted and required to believe Blaise's assertions about the deadness of his present relation with Emily. Feeling sorry for Emily had helped Harriet a lot. Also she could not imagine, after meeting Emily, how any man, let alone wise decent Blaise, could prefer such a woman to herself. That an erotic preference could so war with all the tried openness of married love she did not conceive, and in any case she knew nothing of Blaise's 'special interests'. *Now* she believed that he had loved Emily and that he still loved her. Blaise's second letter brought instant despair and sheer agonizing amazement to Harriet. And with these came afflictions which were quite new to her, debilitating crippling jealousy and resentment, anger, even hatred. Like a cloistered jungle native suddenly infected by the viruses of civilization, she keeled over. What a less secluded temper might have withstood laid her low. She simply did not know what to do with her mind. She needed support and someone whom she cared for to confide in. This after all she had always had. Adrian was in Germany. David had his own agony and repulsed all her attempts to speak to him. She turned with increasing urgency to Monty.

It now seemed to her that she had loved Monty for a long time. He alone of all her vague friends had held an important place in her heart. Her desperate need of him now made this temperate but deep affection turn into a frenzy. The sense of being laid aside out of the action, rejected, no longer needed, sent away, shook Harriet to the roots of her being and almost seemed to make her a different person. She felt as if she were back at the beginning again, though a much more empty beginning, as if she were young and in anguish, facing an open alien world and grasping wildly at what might save her. It was not just that she needed help and comfort, somebody literally to hold her hand. Her disowned rejected love needed another object. It was not that she now judiciously cast her husband off. She experienced him as gone, and she had to have the comfort of making someone else need her. Her powerful loving nature could not rest idle. She loved Monty, and could not remain silent or make little of it. Hence the extraordinary (to him) confession which she had just uttered.

Monty had felt enough affection for Harriet to be glad of her visits at a time when he wanted to see no one else, and enough to be thoroughly irritated by Edgar's attentions to her. This represented perhaps, for him, a good deal of affection. Now, however, he was alarmed. There are unhappy countries (Poland, Ireland) whose misery is aesthetically unpleasing and inhibits sympathy. Monty had been moved by the spectacle of Harriet the loving and successful wife and impressed by the confident forgiving wronged Harriet. He had even admired, at first glimpse anyway, the fierce decision-making 'Hood House is finished' Harriet. This latest Harriet (for indeed it was like meeting a new person) unnerved and puzzled him. It was as if (and how unjust this was) Harriet's innocence were gone, had been destroyed forever: that innocence upon which, he now realized, he himself had in his own way reposed. Now he saw in her the scars of jealousy and resentment and the relentless tentacles of need, and he pitied her heartily but he shuddered. He feared for himself. He feared the dreadful complexity of her urgent demand upon him. He did not want to have to change himself, to modify his being to meet her case. In fact all the time he knew that part of him was pleased by her strange declaration of love; and he was very much afraid of betraying any tenderness which should, in this dangerous state of things, sweep her towards him. I must be very hard and clear, he thought. That will ultimately help her most.

'I am very touched,' said Monty. 'But I just cannot help you in the way that you want.'

'I'm not suggesting a love affair,' said Harriet, in a new rather metallic tone, still staring down the garden. 'I might suggest marriage, I mean later. That's how much I feel. The point is I need you now. I need you to be with me and simply to let me love you. I must love you.'

'You mustn't,' said Monty. 'You don't know me. If I accepted your love it would do us both harm. One can't simply stand there and be loved. You want an involvement and I just absolutely don't. Sorry. Sorry.'

'You can't—I think—imagine,' said Harriet slowly, 'what it's—like—to be me—now. I realize a lot of things about myself. Obvious things perhaps. I married very young. Blaise has been my only man. I suppose that meant that in a way I never grew up. It seemed perfect. If Blaise had been what he appeared to be perhaps it would have been perfect, a kind of perfection anyway. I would never have needed to grow up and change and see the world as terrible, for it *is* terrible, it is terrible in its nature, in its essence, only sometimes one can't see. Some people never see. *You* have always known this, and I knew you knew, long ago, something I could not name in you attracted me, and it was this, that you *knew*. As Blaise never did. Blaise pretended to. He played at it with his patients, but he was too self-centred and too fond of pleasure really to see it. Blaise has always lived in a dream world.'

'We all live in dream worlds,' said Monty.

'And now that I'm *out*—now that I've had—all my possessions—ripped from me—it's as if I were back at the start, having to live by my wits, if you see what I mean, for the first time in my life. When I married Blaise I was just a piece of ectoplasm, and I might have stayed like that forever. Now I realize I've become a person—not necessarily a nice person at all—but a person, an individual, something with edges. When I was happy I was—you can scarcely imagine it because you've always been a person—maybe men always are more than women—when I was happy I was so *vague*. I lived in others and through others, I didn't live in myself. It sounds like a good way to live. Maybe it was a good way to live in some small sense, I mean that a part of the world was good, was contented and in order—and I was part of that part, not exactly causing it, but it lived through me and I through it. But I wasn't anything real or hard in the middle, I had no structure, or if I had I wasn't conscious of it and I didn't use it. I must have been changing though, and becoming, though I didn't know it, what I am now. I can't have *become* all this, and there's really a lot of it, in a few days, can I?'

'We discover ourselves in affliction,' said Monty.

'I suppose one way of putting it is that I'm free for the first time in my life. I have to make decisions and choices in an open field. I have to look after *myself* and make or mar my own destiny by reaching out for things or letting them go. I've been so protected, so shut up, so shut in. Now it's like a bright light, awful, too bright, one has nowhere to hide, one has to move. And it's in this light and in this way that I've come to you, Monty. You can't think how—significant this is to me—that I realize that I love you. It's as if it's my first free act—it's so—*valuable*—'

It is to you, he thought. But that does not necessarily give it value for me. This new intensely self-possessed Harriet was fascinating. Misery had certainly given her energy, a sense of identity, a powerful questing will. It was even impressive. His part however was to be lucid and disappointing and cold. The least tenderness or excitement, the least foothold in his heart, and he and she would both be in danger.

'And I feel so strong, Monty. I feel as if I can compel you almost. I've always thought of you as strong and myself as weak. But now I feel as if I had power over you, claims, rights. You've got to help me, I will make you love me, we have a future. This is a strange way for a woman to talk whose husband has just left her. But I won't sit at home and weep, I won't! I can make a new destiny, a new life, I've got to, whether I like it or not. And when I need you, you are here. You must see how *meant* it all is. You needn't work it out now—you think so much and that makes you cautious—I don't really want to capture you all at once—at least I do want to, but I know I can't—I want you simply to let something begin between us—well, it has begun, it began before, before I knew about Blaise. Just let it go on, let it live, let it be, let it become. I need you terribly, Monty, oh I do need you so. Won't you simply please *meet* these needs, I mean hour by hour, minute by minute, be with me, look after me, help me? Then you won't be able not to love me. You need love too, you know—not only to be loved, but to love.'

Oh if only you knew, thought Monty. He replied, 'Look Harriet, sober up. Loving confers no rights you know. You talk as if you had just emerged into the clear light of day. It seems to me that the opposite is the case. You've been knocked on the head, you're suffering from shock, you're in frightful pain. Jealousy is one of the most awful of all mental pains—and in order to help yourself bear it you've invented this great affection for me—'

'So you think I'm suffering agonies of jealousy?' said Harriet.

'Yes.'

She considered this, lifting Lucky's heavy and now recumbent front half off her knee, and setting him to lie curled up beside her, his big head against her thigh, as she gazed still down the garden towards the yellow privet hedge and speckled fence that divided Monty's property from that of Mrs Raines-Bloxham.

'The odd thing is,' said Harriet, 'I don't think I am. The shock has been somehow too great and that has actually helped, like when someone is shot and instantly paralysed so that the nerves are spared the agony which might kill. Of course I could feel jealousy and I may feel it. Only somehow that's already something small, and I do feel in this awful way so strong and solitary. I don't think that Blaise or my former life will ever come back to me in any form—that I could accept or be—pleased by—any more.' For the first time since her confession began her voice faltered a little towards tears.

That's better, thought Monty. He pursued, 'You say you are paralysed. But you won't stay paralysed. You say you may feel jealousy. You certainly will. You've got to see Blaise soon and when you see him you'll inhabit your love

239

for him all over again. Love for someone you've been married to for years can't suddenly end like this, it's an addiction. You've got a long road, Harriet, and don't imagine I can tread it with you. You've got to work this thing out with Blaise and you can't foresee how he'll act or how you'll act. Blaise is perfectly capable of changing his mind again.'

'I don't care if he does.'

'You will care if he does. He could undo everything, including this new you that you're so proud of, in a moment. Suppose he comes back and throws himself at your feet, you would be instantly metamorphosed back into what you were before. In fact it wouldn't be a metamorphosis because you haven't changed, you only have a comforting illusion of having changed. All this stuff about freedom and will is *false*, Harriet, *false*. Your real work, and your duty too incidentally, is to go on supporting your relationship to Blaise, living inside it over a long time while he decides what he wants and what he'll do. He is your husband after all.'

'What about what I want and what I'll do?'

'That has no importance. For these purposes you're still ectoplasm.'

'Why are you so unjust to me?' said Harriet, suddenly now turning to look at Monty, shifting herself and the dog a little way from him for a better view. Monty in black linen jacket and white shirt, his dark hair well combed and neat, his black shoes ludicrously well polished, was looking his most jesuitically untouchable. Oh I do love him so, thought Harriet, and this is new, new in the world. I must convince him, I must make him see. He can save me. *I can save him.*

'I'm not being unjust,' said Monty, still not looking at her, gazing at the dogs on the lawn. (Ajax had just arrived.) 'I'm being realistic, which I dare say you're incapable of being at present. Blaise just has absolute power over you. The whole situation holds you emotionally and morally trapped. You are not free. Come back to a few simple clear ideas, Harriet. The idea of your duty, for instance. If Blaise wants soon, or even not so soon, to extricate himself—and he may —to come back to you, to re-establish Hood House, it is your duty to help him. It mightn't be another woman's duty. It is yours. Please don't interrupt me. It is your duty for David's sake, even if there were no other reason, and there are other reasons. You are not capable of suddenly "living free". You are not prepared for it by nature or by training. You have got to act the humble powerless part. You cannot and ought not to claim the dignity of will and action. In other words you've got to behave like a saint however peevish you may feel, because you, being you, haven't any viable alternative. Years later, if Blaise has really abandoned you and you find that you can really abandon him, all right, you may have to make other arrangements, learn typing and shorthand, learn some new and uncongenial form of life, who knows. And *that* won't be freedom either. When that time comes all those things will be just as compulsory as the things I've been speaking of are now. At present you're simply foisting a false idea of liberty and power onto a mere bubbling up of emotion, a sentimental feeling you have about me, a feeble muddled desire to be helped. Wake up, come back to reality. You are a long way, perhaps years, away from any deep change in your life. Because of the circumstances and because of your nature you have got to be passive now and simply *wait* for Blaise and see what he does and what he needs. That is the only role of which, without dangerous self-deception, you are really capable, and I advise you to play it.'

'You are *awful*,' said Harriet. 'Of course I've always known that. But I think now, which I've never thought before, that you are being *stupid*.'

'Another relevant point,' said Monty, his eye moving over the group of dogs like one who 'reads' a picture, 'is that I haven't got what you need. I haven't the *interest*. I'm sorry to be brutal, but clarity is better. There must be no muddle here and no, as you put it, beginning. I am a bereaved man—'

'I know, I know, I haven't forgotten for a second.'

'Bereavement is my occupation and it absorbs me completely. You want me to touch you, to look at you with sympathy. I cannot.'

'I know—not yet—no woman can come near you in that way—but—'

'Bereavement is also the cause, or any way the occasion, of real changes in my life. I shall sell this house. I shall cease writing. I have already done so. My life as a fake artist is over and I am not capable of being any other sort of artist. I have to live alone inside myself without Sophie and without Milo. As Edgar may have told you, I intend to become a schoolmaster. I have an appointment at a school which I hope will employ me. I am going to strip my life in ways which have long been in preparation—'

'Monty, stop. You accuse me of living in a dream world, but it seems to me you're doing just that! You tell me I can't change, and then you show off about how you can! If you could only see how self-satisfied you looked just now! Are you really going to mortify yourself in this ridiculous manner? You are your own prisoner too, after all.'

'These are not impulsive emotional expedients, my dear Harriet. All this is the outcome of deep long things. I've never really talked to you about myself and I won't now, except to say this. I have seemed to some people to be successful—'

'And you've enjoyed it!'

'In a way of course. But I have a long deep unhappiness about my life, about my marriage, about my work, which now comes to a crisis. I have to resolve this crisis properly or else become a sort of bad person which in a sense I've always been but which I've never absolutely become. I haven't become it because of Sophie and the fact that I loved her and because of certain illusions about myself as a writer and certain other (doubtless) illusions about what some people would call religion and I would call I know not what. Things seemed provisional for me which seem now, in the light of her death, absolute. I have my own troubles and my own moment of trial and you have no place in the picture. I have to meet what I have to meet and do what I have to do and you are simply an irrelevance, a, forgive me, profitless distraction. I have absolutely nothing to give you.'

'No,' murmured Harriet, 'no. You accuse me of being in the dark. Perhaps I am more than I think I am. But you are in the dark too. You can't *know* all those things about your life. You too have to struggle on and see how it turns out. Just don't—in the dark—go too far away from me. I am certain I can help you. To help you would be my salvation, and I can *see* now that to help me would be yours. I am your immediate task. The schoolmaster idea is romanticism. *This* is where you should be. Oh dearest Monty, I hardly dare to say all this to you because I know it makes you mechanically avert your face. But don't avert it, please. Look at me, Monty, look at me.'

Monty got up abruptly and cast a frowning glance at Harriet. He said, 'I'm sorry. I have been as accurate as I can. I shall be leaving this house very soon. You can stay on if you wish to. I have said all I have to say and I don't want any more conversations of this sort. They are a form of self-indulgence to which I am not addicted even if you are.'

He moved quickly away and went into the house, closing the French windows sharply behind him.

Tears rose automatically and at once into Harriet's eyes, and she drew Lucky towards her again and began to caress his big long soft muzzle, stroking his black lips and touching the fangs beneath. It is unjust, it is so unjust, was her thought. I have never been recognized as myself. Blaise always thought of me as part of him, and I was part of him. This is the first time in my life that I have faced another human being as an independent person. How can he reject me! He must not, he will not. I need and must have his help. He will relent.

She rose, having dropped Lucky, and began to walk slowly down the garden, her copious tears comforting her a little. Lucky, Babu, Panda, Ajax and Buffy followed her slowly, at her pace. She turned into the orchard and along the winding clipped path, Hood House now visible between the trees. The light wind had stripped the whiteness off the ladies' lace and the seed heads were already forming. The smell of cut grass came to her vivid with memory, carrying ghostly pictures of the Welsh cottage and her sad defeated parents. She mopped her eyes, feeling the relief of a more general sadness. A turning in the path brought the fence and the row of foxgloves into view, and the dogs' gate into the next garden, now enlarged so as to allow the passage of Ajax, his organs no longer endangered. There was a small scrabbling on the other side of the fence and Lawrence and Seagull came through. Another animal followed, a dark head and then, on all fours, a complete boy. It was Luca.

Harriet exclaimed and immediately fell on her knees, holding out her arms. The boy, with a laugh and a gasp, ran to her, falling down before her and into her embrace. With eyes closed they held each other tight. The dogs frisked about them.

'I've come to call for Pinn,' said Kiki St Loy.

'I'll tell her you're here,' said Emily McHugh, and shut the door in her face.

243

She went back into the sitting-room where, as she noise-lessly appeared in the doorway, she saw Pinn passing Blaise a letter. 'Your little playmate's here,' she said to Pinn. 'You might have told us she was coming.'

'Sorry, I forgot. Won't you let her in?' said Pinn, stroking down her frizz of bright hair in front of a gilt mirror with cupids on top and candlesticks in front, one of Emily's more ambitious buys.

'Let her in of course,' said Blaise, a little flurried about the letter.

Emily returned in silence to the door and opened it. Kiki who, dressed in delicately faded jeans and a long blue silk shirt, was sitting on the stairs, put on a martyred air for a second and then smiled. Her smile expressed the sheer golden self-satisfied joy of healthy youth.

'They say you're to come in,' said Emily with undisguised sourness. Kiki followed her to the sitting-room.

'Hello, Kiki,' said Blaise, and his face, Emily thought, could not help reflecting Kiki's pleasure in herself.

'Hello, Blaise. Hello, P. Your chariot awaits.'

'We'll be off then,' said Pinn. 'Come on, little one. Ta ta, love-birds.' They departed with a wave, and Emily could hear them laughing wildly upon the stairs. Blaise had dis-appeared to the lavatory, obviously to read his letter.

Emily stood alone in her sitting-room. It was a pretty room, the prettiest she had ever created, in fact the only room she had, like that, created. She had chosen the russet carpet, the purple and blue blotchy curtains, the maroon armchairs of corded velvet (they could not afford a 'suite'), the long-haired tousled multi-coloured woollen Finnish rug, like a big animal, the long low glass coffee table, the gilt mirror. It had given her such joy. It had seemed so alive.

'What was in that letter?' said Emily to Blaise, staring at the curtains, as he returned to the room.

'What letter?'

'The letter Pinn gave you.'

'Oh that. She is ridiculously secretive.'

'What was in it?'

'Well don't look like that. Nothing much, nothing awful.'

'Well let me see it.'

'I put it down the lavatory.'

'I don't believe you. Turn out your pockets.'

Blaise turned out all his pockets onto the coffee table. No letter.

'Why did you put it down the lavatory? People don't usually do that with letters. It isn't even very easy.'

'I can't stand Pinn any more. I'm sorry, I know she's your friend. But she and her letters just seem—muck. I wanted to clean it off myself.'

'She isn't my friend, and you don't even think she is. I've felt like that about Pinn for some time. I don't trust her an inch. It's you who's always encouraged her. You had secrets with her over at Putney.'

'I never did!'

'Well, you have now. You must be encouraging her or she wouldn't pass you clandestine letters. What was in the letter?'

'Nothing except—well, only one thing really, and we thought that already. Luca is over with Harriet.'

'I don't need to be told that,' said Emily. 'When he disappeared I assumed that was where he had gone.'

'Well it's better to know. And it was kind of Pinn to tell us.'

'Why did she need to put it in a secret letter?'

'She thought you'd be upset and that I'd better sort of break the news to you.'

Emily thought for a moment, still staring at the curtains. Blaise had sat down in one of the maroon armchairs, his outstretched feet almost invisible in the shaggy tangles of the Finnish rug. He looked up at her watchfully. 'I don't *think* I believe you,' said Emily. 'I don't think I do. Maybe Pinn said that in the letter, but she said other things as well, things that are worrying you. I can see, I can feel, that you're worried.'

'Of course I'm worried, about Luca, about you—'

'No, you're worried about something else. You're flushed, you're excited. Why does Pinn keep bringing Kiki St Loy here and trailing her about in front of you? She's trying to arrange a meeting between you and Kiki. That's it. She once said Kiki wanted her to find her a man. And you're so bloody pleased to see the girl every time, what you want is written all over your face.'

Blaise got up and took Emily by the shoulders, forcing her to look up at him, holding her tight and shaking her slightly. 'Listen. *Listen*, you little fool. You deserve a hundred lashes. Are you going to ruin things now by mindless stupid jealousy? I'm here, I love you, you are my wife.'

'I'm not, actually.'

'You will be. We've talked the whole thing through to completion. Surely you know where you stand.'

'In a quicksand, on a volcano.'

'No! We're safe, we're home, Emily, the danger's over. We live here now.'

'You swear you aren't in love with Kiki St Loy?'

'You lunatic! Yes, of course I swear it! I'm in love with you, kid. Don't you see that you're being crazy? Look into my eyes. I love you.'

'Yes,' said Emily, looking up at him. 'All right. All right, darling. Yes, yes. You're hurting me.'

'Good.'

'All right, forgive me, sweet, let me off, but naturally I'm frightened, how can I not be, I'm frightened of everything and everybody, even of Kiki, even of Pinn. I wish things could get settled down and clear at last, and you were having your patients again and all. I didn't want you to go and see *her*, but now I want you to. I want to be certain that when you see her all this won't suddenly crumble into dust and seem like a dream.'

'You know it won't.'

'O.K. But go and see her, will you, Blaise darling? Don't just send Pinn to spy, oh I know you do. See her—and tell her about this—about the fridge and the curtains—make her believe it—make her know it's real, that she's really lost you, that you've absolutely *gone*. Will you do that?'

'Yes. You're quite right. I must go. I just wanted this place to exist first.'

'Because you needed support, I wasn't enough, you had to have the flat as well?'

'No, no, I just wanted you to feel how safe we were before I went away from you anywhere, especially before I went away from you there.'

'You won't stay long away, will you? If you did I'd come and fetch you. And I'd scream.'

'No, I mean just an hour or so. You could be nearby. You could wait in the car.'

'I don't think I'd like that. I'll wait here, in our place, with our things. Oh darling, you won't suddenly go back to Mrs Placid, will you? You won't feel sorry for her, you won't be moved by her tears? I'm not being vindictive about her, I don't want her to be miserable, though I see she's got to be. I simply want her to understand and lay off. It's better for her if she understands soon, isn't it? And of course I don't mind your seeing her occasionally. You needn't feel that it's such a tragedy anyway. She'll settle down, she'll have to,

246

she's got this wonderful cabbagey calm. She'll put up with it, and don't let her tell you she can't. I don't want you to feel when you see her that it's a great crisis and you're killing her or anything, you're not. You must simply be absolutely truthful with her and not leave her with any false hopes. Do you promise to be absolutely truthful?'

'Yes. I'll tell her the lot.'

'Well, no need to tell her the *lot*, but tell her enough. There. All right. I'm sorry I was awful. I'm so full of terrors. But yes, yes, all right. Now I must go quickly and shop, it's early closing. After that we'll go to bed, yes?'

When Emily had left the flat and he had heard her sandals clack away down the stairs Blaise returned to the lavatory and pulled Pinn's letter out from its hiding place under the linoleum. He had only had time to glance at it quickly. Now he perused it with care. It ran as follows:

Dearest Blaise,

herewith your humble spy's report from over yonder. Your wife is showing more character than might have been expected. She has abandoned Hood House and moved in, complete with David, on Monty Small. Not only that. She has fallen in love with Monty! Yours truly, entering the house with soft footfall, overheard a conversation between the two parties who were sitting just outside the window. Your spouse was in fact offering herself to the gratified Mr Small! So she's not Mrs Mope any longer. I expect you are relieved though. It must be nice to know that you are not missed and that she has found Another. So you needn't dread seeing her and being beseeched. I wouldn't be surprised if the devious Mr Small hadn't seen all this coming a long way off and encouraged you to drop Harriet so that he could catch her! He's a deep one! It is all working out rather neatly, isn't it. Luca is there too, by the way, and shows every sign of staying. Harriet, who behaves as if she already owns Locketts, has set up a nice bedroom for him. She had also bought him a dog. (All this I know from legit. conversation with Monty, he and I are quite cronies now.) So it looks as if you and Emily may have to say good-bye to that boy. As for young David, he too has distractions from his woe. He has fallen madly in love with Kiki St Loy! She however, as you will have noticed, has eyes only for you! A pity you are not 'free' just now, Kiki is longing to chuck her virginal status!

You might have been the lucky one. (Let me know if you want to be. Em. needn't worry. She's got you on a chain now, whatever you do.) That's all for now. I'll continue to report. *Thanks* for the cheque. Not a word to Emily about that of course, and you can be sure I won't say anything. You are sweet to me and I adore you.

Thine forever, your constant nymph,

P.

P.S. Of course if you decide you want Harriet after all you'd better act quickly!!!

Blaise read the letter and the flush which Emily had noticed came again to his face and he closed his eyes and laid his head against the lavatory door. I am rotten, he thought, rotten, rotten, rotten. Oh what will happen? What am I going to do?

'I want to see Harriet alone,' said Blaise.

'Monty, you are not to go,' said Harriet. 'If you go I shall go too. I mean it. I will talk to Blaise, but only with you here. Is that clear, Blaise?'

Blaise stared at her with amazement.

'Oh all right,' said Monty. 'I'll stay. I think you ought to talk to Blaise alone, but if you won't you won't. Whisky, gin, anyone?'

They were in the Moorish drawing-room. Monty and Harriet were sitting at the table as if in committee. Blaise sat in one of the wickerwork chairs, a rather low one which had been made even lower by being wrecked by Edgar. Feeling at a disadvantage he got up and moved first to the purple sofa and then to a rather botanical-looking chair against the wall. Monty shifted the table slightly with his foot so that it was still between himself and Blaise.

'I'll have some whisky,' said Blaise.

'Good. Here. Harriet?'

'Thanks. The usual.'

It was evening, an overcast day inclining to rain. A lamp in the corner, sitting inside what looked like a wrought-iron holy water stoup, lit up one of the mosaic panels.

The usual, thought Blaise. He stared at Harriet, thinking how different she looked and how beautiful. He said to himself, hang on, hang on. Keep calm. He gently stroked his eye where the bruise had faded to the faintest of green shadows. Some sort of utter chaos was now not far away and must not be tripped into. He was well aware that he had arrived with no policy, very upset and confused and with nothing clear to say. Pinn's letter had distressed him to an extent which was terrifying. Of course he had relied on seeing Harriet alone.

'Well?' said Monty to Blaise.

'I might say that to you,' said Blaise.

'As I seem to be chairman,' Monty went on, 'perhaps I may open the meeting. You asked to see us.'

'I didn't.'

'You asked to see Harriet and have presumably something to tell her.'

There was a silence. Harriet, breathing rapidly, but in control of herself, was staring at her husband. Blaise kept glancing at her, but without meeting her eyes. He looked at Monty.

'Oh come on, come on,' said Monty. 'Say something, anything, set the ball rolling. After all there's plenty to talk about.'

'I don't like your tone,' said Blaise.

'Sorry, I didn't mean to sound flippant. But you must talk. Or would you rather be cross-questioned?'

'No, I wouldn't. Not by you.'

'Harriet, have you any questions to put to Blaise?'

'No,' said Harriet.

Blaise regarded her again. She was thinner and her face looked harder, finer, older, as if she were her successful professional elder sister. A doctor, perhaps, or even a lawyer, or else a great actress playing Portia. She had done her hair with care, dividing and twisting it in a new way, and she was wearing a simple dark blue dress *which he had never seen before*.

'I didn't come to say anything new,' said Blaise, surprising himself by the humility and diffidence of his utterance. 'It's still all as I said in my letter. I mean, I have to stay with Emily, but I'll come here too. I tried to be in two places at once before and I'll still try. I know my position is an awful one and the result of wrong-doing, but it *is* my position, and I can't alter it radically without being guilty of a lot more wrong-doing. You must—both—see that. I've got to compromise. I can't make things right again however hard I try. This being so, the most sensible thing seems to be— to be honest with you—Harriet—as I have been—and to throw myself on your mercy. Things can't be as they were. But they needn't be terrible either. I'll be—you see—here some of the time, there some of the time. It's just that I can't any more ask Emily to accept a second best—it wasn't even a second best, it was a tenth best. Now that it's all come out and we've all told the truth, which is a good thing, it's just got to be a bit more equal. Of course I'll be here a good deal, it won't really be much different from what we thought before and you were so good about. It's just to begin with while Emily's settling into the new place I'll have to be away a bit more. Emily put up with a lot for years and now I'm asking you to put up with a lot too—and to— forgive me—for David's sake and—because—because—'

There was silence. Monty looked at Harriet with raised eyebrows. Then when she did not speak he said gently, 'Talk to him Harriet. And talk as kindly as you can. And remember what I said too. Nothing here can be settled quickly. Be as kind and forgiving as possible because, if I may finish Blaise's sentence for him, reconciliation is better than conflict, and mercy than justice.'

Damn him, thought Blaise, damn him.

Harriet looked at Monty and suddenly smiled.

It was a new smile too and the sight of it caused Blaise pain.

'I can't do it,' she said, her voice now trembling a little. 'I can't do it, Blaise, things have changed too much. I can't and won't put up with what Emily put up with. Perhaps it turns out that I'm prouder than she is after all, or less sort of—good-natured. Or perhaps it's just that having been your wife I can't bear to be less. Or that I simply don't trust you any more. My trust in you was absolute, was perfect—and now it's completely broken.'

Let her cry, thought Blaise, let her only cry and she will forgive me.

Harriet steadied herself. 'You sound to me so much like a liar—like the kind of liar I—oh God—now *recognize* you as, when you talk of dividing your time and so on as if this were the best possible solution of a bad problem. But you have made it clear, and you deliberately said that you had not

250

gone back on that, that you have *left* me for Emily McHugh — she is now your wife — and your coming here occasionally to see me and David could have no value. I wouldn't want that sort of you at all — and your timetable, your sort of programme, doesn't concern me any more.'

'Do you want a divorce?' said Monty to Blaise. 'Have you promised Emily you'll get one?'

Blaise was silent. He ignored Monty. Then he said, 'I know it's awful, awful, but I do just ask you to forgive me and not go away from me.'

'*You* have gone away,' said Harriet. 'You have abandoned me.'

'I haven't,' said Blaise. 'I know now, *now*, that I can't abandon you, it isn't physically, logically possible, it isn't a possible thing in the world at all. We are bound together. Oh help me, please, Harriet, help me —'

'It's no good,' said Harriet, in a shakier and gentler tone than she had yet employed, 'you are moved and upset to see me, of course you are. But if you don't see me you will soon learn to settle down with Emily McHugh. That is what you have chosen to do.'

'You are forcing me to choose?' said Blaise.

'Really!' murmured Monty.

'Emily forced you to choose,' said Harriet, 'and you chose her.'

'But you are — asking me to choose again —'

After a moment Harriet said, 'No, I'm not. I'm not. I am just telling you that I can't fit into your life in the way you suggest — or now that I don't trust you any more, in any other way. I cannot be — any more — in your life — at all.'

There was silence. Monty was staring down at the polished surface of the table and making rings in the dust.

'It can't be like that,' said Blaise, 'it can't be. I could die of this. So could you. I've got to see you and be connected with you, I *am* connected —'

'You could visit David, of course,' said Harriet.

'By the way,' said Blaise, 'I'm going to take Luca back with me. I believe he's here.'

'You are not going to,' said Harriet, throwing her head back. 'Luca stays here with me. I don't regard your mistress as a suitable person to look after him and I will maintain this if necessary in a court of law. Luca wants to stay here with me. He disowns you. Luca stays here. Unless you both want a public legal fight.'

'Oh Harriet, Harriet,' said Blaise softly, 'please see me alone. Send him away. I know you'll forgive me in the end, you will, you must, you'll have to. I know your gentle forgiving heart. This isn't you, talking to me in this hard way. We must sort this out for the best. Oh pardon me, dear girl, you *did*—do it again and redeem me from hell.'

'There is no "we" any more,' said Harriet. 'You destroyed us. Oh Blaise, if you only knew how utterly utterly miserable you have made me—' The tears came now in a flood, but with them Harriet leapt up and ran out of the room before Blaise could prevent her. Monty immediately moved and closed the door, keeping his hand upon it. Blaise stood facing him across the table. He said to Monty, 'You've bewitched her.'

'Oh, don't be *silly*,' said Monty. 'Here, drink your whisky, you haven't had any.'

'You've made her fall in love with you.'

'No, I haven't.'

'I know you have, I've got evidence. You did it all on purpose, the whole thing, on purpose. You encouraged me to go on with Emily, you invented Magnus Bowles to make it easier, you led me on, further and further in, always so interested and helpful and watching as I got deeper! Then when you got bored with it you persuaded me to confess, and all because you had your eye on Harriet. By that time you wanted her for yourself. So you decided to ruin me in cold blood. And now you've been making declarations of love to her to persuade her to cut me out.'

'I confess I'm easily bored,' said Monty. 'I am certainly bored by a silly vulgar rant. Use your intelligence, also try a little to remember why and how things happened. I persuaded you of nothing, I didn't want to be involved at all. I still don't. I'm not in love with Harriet, I have not, to use your horrible phrase, got my eye on her. You just don't seem to realize that your own rotten conduct has consequences.'

'You pretended to be my friend.'

'Maybe I did. More fool you for being taken in. I am no one's friend. I am incapable of friendship. Now please go away.'

'And leave you and Harriet alone together.'

'Not alone. David and Luca are here, and Edgar Demarnay who can't keep away, and I'm clearing off myself pretty soon. There's no bewitchment or any need of one. You offer Harriet a totally unacceptable deal, and she turns out to have more spirit than you gave her credit for, that's all. Anyway, as I said to her, this squalid business will drag on, no doubt. This scene hasn't settled anything. Only it will drag on without me, please at least believe that.'

'I don't,' said Blaise. 'You're a cold-blooded liar. You put all these words into Harriet's mouth, you coached her, it wasn't like her at all. You've been making advances to her, denigrating me —'

'Oh go away,' said Monty, 'go away. I'm sorry. I'm even sorry for you. But you must just sort the two women out for yourself. My guess is that you've lost Harriet, whatever you do about Emily, but I may well be wrong. Women are so volatile. If you go on begging her she may cave in. Anyway, I assure you her anti-you stand has nothing whatever to do with me. Now please get out, will you.' He opened the French windows.

'Oh damn you,' said Blaise.

'You can get round to the front by — but of course you've been here before, haven't you. I'm very sorry, Blaise. I've just got troubles of my own.'

'Damn you,' said Blaise. He stepped out of the French windows and half ran, slithering on the now rain-wet concrete of the path, round the side of the house and, without looking back, out into the road.

Here he began to walk along quickly. A little rain was falling and he was without coat or hat. He automatically registered how much he hated getting his hair wet. He felt so sorry for himself he could have wept, and now indeed, as he hurried along in the rain towards where, two roads away, he had left the Volkswagen, he actually did weep a little, the hot tears mingling with the cold rain upon his face. He pitied himself desperately. He knew he was not a bad man, not a wicked man really. He had got into this muddle in such a natural simple way. Lots and lots of men did what he had done and got away with it. He had just had dead rotten luck all the way along the line.

Where had he gone wrong, what was his absolute crime? Perhaps marrying Harriet? He had loved Harriet but had he not (it was hard to remember) felt just a little that she was not *the* one? Yet at that time he had been rejecting the very idea of that sort of the one existing. He had married Harriet to rescue himself from his peculiarities, and that had seemed to be the formula for happiness. Was Emily the crime

253

then? But how could he have resisted Emily? He could scarcely, at least, have resisted a love affair, and after all most husbands had love affairs for much less good reasons, under much less strong temptations. Then Luca had just been an unfortunate accident. And Emily *taking* it for all these years. Then when it had seemed right to tell the truth, Harriet had so wonderfully forgiven him. What had gone wrong? Of course he had to be just to Emily now and of course this meant tilting the balance a bit against Harriet and of course Harriet hated it. But she would come round, wouldn't she? She *couldn't* be in love with Monty, it was inconceivable, his Harriet in love with somebody else. Oh God, if only he could have held her in his arms for a moment and mingled his tears with hers! If she could only see how much he *suffered* she would forgive him surely. Should he go back, rush in, fall at her feet? He paused.

He had by now turned a corner and was within sight of his car, staring at it. He stared vaguely, wondering what to do. Then he noticed with a jerk that someone was sitting in the passenger seat of his car. Could it be Harriet, relenting after all? He went eagerly forward.

It was Kiki St Loy, in a sky-blue jersey and surrounded by a great deal of wet hair. She smiled at him; and that pure sweet seventeen-year-old smile had even then for him a power to console. He said as calmly as he could, 'Well, well, what new enchantment is this? Today is full of surprises.'

'Blaise, I'm so sorry,' said Kiki. 'Don't be furious with me, will you. It is a silly joke of Pinn's.' Kiki's voice was faintly undecipherably foreign.

'Pray explain!' said Blaise. He walked round the car and got in. The rain began to pelt down isolating them inside a dark silvery grille.

'You see, Blaise,' said Kiki, 'for a long time now I am at Pinn to get her to introduce me to Montague Small.'

Blaise started the engine and the Volkswagen moved slowly away.

'And she said today that she would take me to see him, then when we got here she saw your car and stopped and we both got out. She opened the door and said, yes it was your car, and then she opened the glove compartment, and we are looking in and laughing, when suddenly she ran back to my car and drove it away. I thought she will come back, and I do not know this Mr Small's address, so I wait, and then it begins to rain, so I sit in here. And now you have come to drive me back to London! But what is it, my dear?'

Kiki's soft lilting voice had wrought upon Blaise's torn nerves. He ground his teeth together in a sort of pant of agony—'Aaaah—'

'What is it? Tell Kiki.'

'You know what it is,' said Blaise, 'I daresay bloody Pinn has told you everything.'

Kiki, leaning towards the wheel, brushed the back of his hand lightly with the back of hers. 'I'm sorry.'

'You see, I love them both,' said Blaise. 'I'm crucified. I'm bloody crucified.'

'Then you must keep them both,' said Kiki, her voice deepening with sympathy.

'I can't. Oh Kiki, if you only knew what a mess I'm in, what a hole I'm in. I can't get out, I just can't get out. I hate myself for it all, I hate myself.'

'Do not do so. I am sure you are not much to blame. Won't you tell Kiki the whole story?'

Blaise stopped the car. They were outside the little railway station from which he and Emily had fled together on that momentous night. He turned to Kiki and looked at her gently, at her tangle of long damp hair and at her huge dark pure-brown eyes and at the limpid transparent unsullied young girl's skin of her eager face, brought by time and nature to perfect fruition and not yet by them marked in any way. And at how her breasts were *kept* inside her jersey. Kiki smiled again, so affectionately, so ruefully. She was an intelligent girl. 'I go home by train, isn't it. Good-bye then, Blaise. I do so hope it will all come right.'

'Don't go just yet,' he said, and retained her, holding the damp blue sleeve in a light grip. Then he put his arms round her and drew the beautiful dark head, so fragrant with youth and rain, up against him. He turned her head in his hands, crushing his shoulder against the wheel, and kissed her very carefully upon the lips. Then he pushed her away from him and she got out of the car. He did not see her enter the station.

Blaise drove on a little and then turned into a side road and stopped. He laid his head down upon the steering wheel and groaned out another long agonized 'Aaaah'. Was he doomed to go completely out of his mind?

Monty closed and bolted the door after Blaise. He sat down for a moment at the table. He felt disgusted with Blaise, disgusted with himself. He ought to have made Harriet see Blaise alone. Only because the scene had amused him he had consented so readily to be its chairman. What the hell was he up to? Had he ever been Blaise's friend? Had he ever been anybody's friend? Edgar's once? The idea was fantastic. And now his house, which had been so pure and desolate, was full of people. Harriet, Edgar constantly, the two children. There were two children in his house. How endlessly, after the miscarriage and before it too, Sophie had vacillated about whether she wanted children. How much Monty had hoped at first — and feared later. Later he would not have been sure who the father was.

Am I *responsible* for all these people? Monty wondered. David came and went like a ghost. Passing him in the hall, on the stairs, Monty usually took his hand as he passed, in a strange passers-by handshake. But he had shunned a long talk with the boy. He had felt annoyed one day hearing Edgar talking to him in the garden, but he had not attempted any contact himself. He did not want to see David's tears and he feared to be involved in David's affections. With Luca he had established no relationship at all. He felt a revulsion from the child on David's behalf, and also because of some unnerving changeling quality which Luca possessed. Luca (doubtless sensing hostility) had evidently determined to be 'difficult' with Monty, and stared at him without smiling whenever they met. Monty stared back. He knew that Harriet had been discussing Luca's education with Edgar. Nobody had consulted Monty.

The question is, what am I doing here, he thought. The strange ménage had existed now for days. Monty, sitting at the table in the darkening and lamplit room, realized that he was feeling a little faint with hunger. He had never yet, though of course begged to by Harriet, sat down to a meal with her and the boys. In fact 'the boys' rarely sat down together (or met, if they could help it) since David had lunch at school and usually took a late supper with his mother after

Luca's bedtime. Monty left them the kitchen, only entering himself at odd moments to cook an egg or open a tin. It was a pretty peculiar way of life, but then everything was so peculiar and provisional at present, it was perhaps less than noteworthy. And soon, after so many threats and delays, Monty's mother would arrive to join the throng! What a surprise for her to find the house thus occupied!

I suppose I had better eat something he thought. He looked at the three drinks on the table, all untouched. Life was so intoxicating these days, they hardly needed alcohol. He drank a little whisky and began to feel very strange, unsteady, visionary. I have not eaten all day, he thought, I'll craze myself. He drank some more whisky, then went out into the hall meaning to visit the kitchen, but as he emerged he heard a murmur of voices from his study. Edgar and Harriet. He changed direction and threw open the study door.

Edgar was sitting in the big armchair with the white fur rug and Harriet was sitting at his feet, one arm over his knee. The little wood fire was burning in the grate. Harriet was crying. She shifted slightly away, removing her arm, as the door opened. Monty felt blinding exasperation.

'Sorry to intrude,' he said.

'Oh Monty, what am I to do!' said Harriet.

'Go back to Hood House and wait for your husband to come home, I suggest,' said Monty.

'Don't be an idiot,' said Edgar.

Harriet knelt, wiping her eyes. 'Do you want us out of here, Monty?'

'No, of course not. I'm going myself soon.'

'Oh Monty, don't go. It was terrible seeing Blaise, I couldn't help feeling so sorry for him, and it seemed as if I could make everything all right, take him home again, and yet of course I couldn't. If you hadn't been there I'd have forgiven him.'

'Then it's just as well I was there,' said Monty, 'or is it?'

'Think what you are being offered,' said Edgar. 'The man is shameless, you mustn't pity him. He wants to make you into a passive victim.'

'You're quite right,' said Harriet, rising wearily to her feet. 'I mustn't give in. I couldn't *live* that situation—it would destroy me—yet he does need me—and now there's Monty—and it's all so—'

'There isn't Monty,' said Monty. 'There is no such person.'

257

'Monty, I do hope you don't mind—I've told Edgar—about us—'

'*Us*?!'

'You and me. I mean, how I feel about you.'

'Edgar must have enjoyed that.'

'It was no more than I expected,' said Edgar.

'It's no business of his anyway,' said Monty. 'I have put up with this fantastic invasion of my privacy. Must I have my private concerns discussed as well?'

'I'm sorry—'

'I hope you made it clear to Edgar that whatever sort of faked-up affection you feel for me is certainly not reciprocated.'

'Monty!' said Edgar.

'I told him, yes,' said Harriet, starting to cry again.

'Let me say it once more,' said Monty, 'with a witness. I do not believe in your so-called love, but whether or not it is serious does not concern me. I have no grain of love for you in my nature. I have helped you out of a sense of duty, or more precisely out of a sort of inertia, since you forced yourself upon me. I shall be obliged if you will leave me out of your daydreams. I will not tolerate any "interesting" relationship here, however shadowy. I say this for your good. Now please go away, go to bed. You too, Edgar. Clear off.'

Harriet, who had been staring at him with flowing tears, gave a cry, covering her face. Then she ran from the room. There was a moment's silence.

'Surely that was not necessary,' said Edgar, frowning.

'I think it was, precisely, necessary.'

'You could have been kind—'

'Kindness would be fatal. Now go away, will you. Drive yourself back to London or whatever you do at this time of night. Or do you want Harriet to allot you a bedroom?'

'No, I don't think I'll go just yet,' said Edgar, 'I want to talk to you.' He had remained solidly in the armchair. 'I say, Monty, is there any whisky around?'

'There's some in the drawing-room.' Monty sat down near the window and leaned forward, putting his head in his hands. The journey to the kitchen was, for the moment, beyond him.

'Here.' Edgar was thrusting a glass towards him. He took it.

'I wanted to talk to you about Bankhurst,' said Edgar.

'Yes. I'm grateful to you for fixing that business.'

'The point is, I haven't fixed it.'

'Oh. Then you haven't.'

'I've been thinking about you a lot,' said Edgar.

'Thanks.'

'I can't get to the bottom of you.'

'I am bottomless.'

'I mean, I feel I don't know you well enough. You see, Binkie asked me, naturally, for a testimonial. And I found I couldn't write one.'

'I'm not surprised,' said Monty. 'As I told Harriet, I don't really exist.' He raised his head and drank some of the whisky. The room was gently and rhythmically wavering and something was pulling at his scalp and elongating his face.

'I'm worried about you,' said Edgar's voice. Edgar was pouring some water into his whisky with a shaking hand. 'You see—you know what one writes in a testimonial—conscientious, trustworthy, good with his colleagues, good with the children, and so on. I found I couldn't write it.'

'You mean,' said Monty, 'that you felt I was not a proper person to be trusted with children. I daresay you're right. Am I conscientious and trustworthy? I daresay I'm not. All right. So forget it.'

'No, no,' said Edgar, 'don't misunderstand me—'

'I think I understand you very well, you have put the matter very clearly.'

'I don't exactly think ill of you. I just don't feel I can *see* you. I feel you may be having some sort of breakdown and—'

'No breakdown,' said Monty. 'I wish I could have a breakdown, but I'm incapable of it.'

'I do wish you'd talk to me frankly. Is it just—Sophie—or is there something else? Are you in love with Harriet?'

Monty laughed curtly. 'No. I used to feel fond of Harriet. But I'm—beyond all that—now.'

'I wonder if you really are. What do you mean by "beyond"?'

'There's only one thing the matter and that's everything.'

'Talk to me about it. Please, Monty.'

Monty said nothing for a while, and just kept swilling the whisky round and round in his glass and sipping a little. He could hear in the silence Edgar's heavy breathing, like the breathing of a sleeping dog. Drink, emotion, drowsiness? He would soon fall asleep himself. And he recalled how once, as undergraduates, drinking together, they had both fallen asleep simultaneously in the middle of an argument. He felt an impulse, but resisted it, to remind Edgar of the occasion.

He got up, intending to go off to bed. It was too late to eat anything now. He found that he had sat down again. He said to Edgar, 'Would you like to hear that tape of Sophie, the one I was playing when you came to burgle your letters?'

'Oh my God —'

'It's in that drawer. And the tape recorder is under the desk. Do you know how to work it?'

'No. But ought we to —'

'Bring it all here.'

Edgar tumbled the tape and the apparatus between Monty's feet, where the white bear rug was trailing on the floor, and Monty began to fix the tape on.

'Can you stand it?' said Edgar.

'Oh — what I can stand —'

'I'm not sure if I can.'

'She didn't know I was taping this,' said Monty. 'It was near the end. I wanted a little memento of my darling wife.' The tape turned slowly and a new voice was heard in the room, very clear, a little staccato, high-pitched, very slightly French, very slightly northern, a trenchant self-assertive actress's voice, the inimitable mixed and mingled voice of the one and only Sophie.

'Take it, take it, it's so heavy on my feet. The book, take it. Ach. Could I have the drops now. I have got the shakes today. Let me have the glass, will you — no not that — the glass, the looking-glass. *Mon dieu, Mon dieu.*'

'You were saying.'

'What was I saying? Why do you keep making me talk so. I want some peace now. Take it.'

'You were saying.'

'I thought you knew about Marcel, we hardly bothered, I was so sure you knew. I thought you heard us giggling that night when he went round and came in again and there was his coat in the hall, and we both got the giggles. You mean you didn't know?'

'No.'

'Oh well. Oh I do ache so. And my back itches. *C'est plutôt quelque chose de brulant.* No, no, don't touch me, that is no use now, you just hurt — Ach. You bored me so about Marcel, at last I hardly tried. You made me swear and of course I swore, what else could I do? Oh it was so boring. But you never believed me, did you, and the proof was when you said "He has told me everything" and I didn't know what to say.'

'You laughed.'

'Thank God I had still the power to laugh at you then. It was not true of course. *Toujours des ennuis.* If you could only have seen your face, that dreadful inquisitor's face, how I hated it. When you put that face on it was for a whole evening, a whole day. No, it's not the pain now, just aching so. *Mon dieu.* I hated you then. "Did you, did you, did you?" you could say for hours on end.'

'Well, did you?'

'You mean with Sandy? Yes, of course.'

'At the earlier time?'

'Oh what does it matter! No, at the later time. He would not leave me alone. What does it matter now what happened, nothing matters now. Are you to write my story? It would be something. You could not have invented it. And you have put on the face that I hate so. I hate you, I hate you, I hate you. You know that time that I went to Brussels to Madeleine, to her sculpture show. I was with Sandy then. We went to Ostend. It was boring.'

'You went twice to Madeleine, again the next year.'

'Why do you keep asking now, why do you even now torment me?'

'You torment me.'

'It is that I cannot be bothered now to lie. It was so wearisome to lie and I got into such muddles. Oh such muddles I got into.'

'You went twice to Madeleine.'

'Oh yes, who was it the second time. I think it was Edgar.'

'Edgar?'

'Surely you knew about me and Edgar.'

'Before I met you —'

'Oh but after we were married too. One could not get rid of Edgar. He was such an old faithful. If there was no one else there was always Edgar.'

'So you went to Ostend with Edgar.'

'No, no, to Amsterdam. We took the train. Madeleine sent off my postcards to you from Brussels. Only it was so funny I made a mistake. I said on a postcard I had been to Bruges and you said did I like Bruges and I said I had never been there, and you just looked at me as if you could kill me.'

'If you only hadn't lied so.'

'*Mais naturellement.* Such a husband deserves lies.'

'You ought never to have married me.'

'You made marriage a prison. You made my life so miserable with your stern face and always thinking and always these endless questions. *On se croirerait chez la juge d'instruction.* I have not had a moment's joy with you, and I felt so happy and free with the others always, and then the return to you with your face of a gaoler and a torturer. I have not had a moment's joy in this marriage.'

'I have not had a moment's joy either.'

'Switch it off!' said Edgar.

Monty switched off the tape and resumed his former attitude, leaning forward with his head in his hands.

'That's not true, of course,' said Edgar, 'about me.' He spoke quite softly and calmly, but his breathing was heavier, almost a panting sound.

'I didn't suppose it was,' said Monty. He picked up his glass again, circled it about awhile and then drained it.

'You believe me? I never went to Amsterdam with Sophie. I never went to bed with her ever, after your marriage, or before it either. I wrote to her when she was your wife, yes. But I hardly ever saw her alone. I came to tea that time. And I had lunch with her once when you were in New York with Richard—but I told you about that in a letter—it was at Pruniers and—'

'Yes, yes. You even told me what you ate. It doesn't matter.'

'You do believe me?'

'Yes, of course.'

'Why did you play me the tape?'

'I wanted to hear you say it wasn't true. If it wasn't true about you, it mightn't have been true about the others. I thought after she died I'd have to go after them all. There were dozens of them. Well, at least a dozen. I don't mean I thought I'd go and shoot them or anything. But I wanted to hear what they'd say, I wanted to confront them, to let them know I knew, to hurt them somehow. Then I decided it would be pointless.'

'I'm glad you decided that,' said Edgar softly.

'Of course she did have lovers. But I never knew quite which or how many. The ones she named may have been a sort of front for other ones I've never even heard of.'

'When did you make the tape—I mean in relation to—?'

'Her death. It was about three days before. It was typical of conversations we had been having over a period of weeks, months—and went on having till the end. I thought I should have a record of the death scene.'

'You oughtn't to have done it,' said Edgar.

'Made the tape? True.'

'And you oughtn't to have kept it.'

'True.' Monty took the tape off the machine and went over to the fireplace and stirred up the wood fire and placed the tape in the midst of the glowing embers where it began to sizzle and blacken. 'I'm off to bed,' he said. 'Good night. Forget about the Bankhurst business. You're quite right about me.'

'Wait,' said Edgar. 'Sit down. Please. Sit down.'

Monty moved his chair to the fire and sat gazing at the tape which was burning now.

'Has this done anything for you, Monty?'

'Has what? Oh you mean playing the tape and—No, I shouldn't think so.'

'Is *that* what's the matter, brooding about Sophie's lovers? You mustn't. My dear, she's dead.'

'You think I should forgive her? That's hardly the question.'

'Never mind the terminology. You must let her go.'

'There can be no speech between the bereaved and the unbereaved.'

'It doesn't matter now who her lovers were or how many. It doesn't matter at all. Death is more important than these things. I mean, it makes a different scene. You must calm your spirit. We are mortal too. You are tearing yourself to pieces, Monty. You mustn't. What's more you know you mustn't, you know all about it.'

'Do I?'

'Yes. You know what I mean.'

'Words, words.'

'Let it all go, Monty. The resentment and the jealousy and the reliving it all. Sophie is dead and you must *respect* her death, and that means not tearing away at a memory of her personality. Death changes our relation to people. Of course the relation itself lives on and goes on changing. But you must at least try to make it a good relation and not a rotten one. Sophie is dead and you are alive and your duty is the same as any man's, to make yourself better. You are making yourself worse.'

'You think so.'

'Yes. And somehow deliberately. You're making a drama out of it. Oh if only I could understand you and help you. I love you, Monty, I always have, since we were students, and I've always admired you so much.'

'You are mad,' said Monty. 'You admit I'm horrible and you must see by now that I'm not even talented.'

'Of course you're talented. Why don't you try and write a proper novel? Of course that's not the whole answer, but it's part of it. It's your job, if you've got enough courage. Anyway, stop being so secretive and ferocious. It isn't even that, it's being small-minded, petty, cowardly somehow. Oh I know my words are all astray. If only I could see what it *is*.'

'You think you haven't seen "it" yet?' said Monty.

Edgar looked at him in silence for a moment or two and the silence of the night all about them possessed the room. 'No, I don't understand. I think there's something else. And I think you'd better tell me what it is. Now.'

'All right,' said Monty. 'I killed her.'

'You—killed—Sophie?'

'Yes. Of course she would have died anyway fairly soon. But I killed her.'

There was a pause. The fire murmured, collapsing. The silence sighed.

'To save her from suffering?' said Edgar.

'No. I don't think so. Just out of anger or jealousy or spite or something. I dreaded her death, I dreaded her death agony, I kept thinking about it. But I didn't kill her for that reason. I killed her because she maddened me.'

'But you didn't—mean to?'

'Yes, I think I did. It wasn't premeditated of course. I'd often wanted to hit her and she often tried to provoke me to, but in all those years I never touched her. Then at the end it was like an obsession—to get her to tell me all those things before she died—which later I wouldn't be able ever to find out. Only then—all at once—I just couldn't stand it any longer—her talk—her *consciousness*—and I took her by the throat and squeezed—and—then I stopped and—she was dead.'

'Oh Christ.'

'So there you are,' said Monty. 'That was it! You have it, and can go away contented. More whisky before you depart?'

'No, no—you mustn't talk like that—what about the—doctor and—?'

'Dr Ainsley saw her. He saw the marks on her throat. He never said a word. He wrote "cancer" on the death certificate.'

'Oh Monty, Monty—'

'So you see your intuitions were quite sound. I would hardly make a good schoolmaster.'

'Stop. You don't understand—I'm not—But tell me, is it this guilt which makes you so—?'

'So—whatever I am. No, it isn't exactly guilt, old friend of my college days. It's more like—deep—shock. You see—I loved her—what I've been talking about sounds like—pure obsession—cruelty—but I loved her with—all my passion—and all my tenderness as well—I loved her—all her little ways of being herself—and it wasn't true what she said on the tape—and I said it too—about there being no joy in our married life—there was deep joy—she teased me and worse—but there was love between us and she relied on me so—it was just at the end—she was so *unhappy*, so *unhappy* and so *frightened*—she didn't want to die—she wasn't made —in her mind and her soul—to face a slow awful inevitable death—she became—with the misery and the fear—another person—and there was no one but me—to express it all to —all her misery—and she wanted to make me suffer and I ought to have—accepted that suffering on my knees—but I wouldn't, I couldn't, treat her like a dying person—I had to fight her—and I kept wanting to know and wanting to know—and so we tormented each other—all that time— until I killed her—it should have been so otherwise—but it's not guilt really, it's shock—I've felt almost mad with it— if she'd died naturally it would have been—but I did it—I stopped our conversation—which could have become different, better—I chose the moment of her death, I chose the moment when she should go—and that deprives it of all —inevitability—makes it seem—almost accidental—as if it needn't have happened at all—as if it can't quite have happened—but only half happened—and she's half here—and it's all—unfinished—and she's still dying—and she'll go on dying—and suffering—forever.'

Monty was shuddering as he spoke, his mouth trembling, his hands trembling. Now the fire, into which he had been gazing became hazy before his eyes, his eyes were wet, his mouth was wet, a flood of tears burst from him and he uttered a sob and his face was covered in tears and the tears were dropping down onto his jacket and onto the floor. Still sobbing he half rose, pushed the chair from him and knelt on the floor, resting his elbows on the chair and weeping without restraint like a desperate child.

Edgar, bright-eyed, collected, came and sat beside him on the floor. 'There. Cry then. But try and be calm. You will be calm soon. It is so good that you told me. So good.'

Monty gradually fell silent, subsiding to sit on the floor leaning against the chair, rubbing his face with the back of his hand.

'Come with me to Mockingham,' said Edgar. 'Come and stay for a long time and think what you're going to do next. Please, Monty. I may not be up to much. But I am an old friend. And I did know Sophie and I did love her. And now that you've told me this I feel we're somehow tied together, you and I, absolutely tied together.'

'The bond of a terrible secret,' said Monty in his usual voice. 'Ah well.'

'You are recovering. But don't behave as if nothing has happened and the world isn't different. Tonight I mean. A lot has happened and the world is different.'

'Is it?'

'Let me lead you. As if you were blind or lame. I can do it.'

'I am blind and lame,' said Monty.

'That's the most sensible thing you've said for a long time. Come with me to Mockingham. It's so beautiful there. And we could argue like we used to.'

'You don't then regard me with horror.'

'Don't be silly!'

'Of course this must be a great thrill for you, my breaking down like this. You must feel it as an achievement.'

' "The Prince whose oracle is at Delphi neither tells nor conceals, he gives a sign." '

'Oh him. I'm not sure—'

'You're not saying it's an accident, Monty?'

'Tonight? That it might have happened with anyone? No. It had to be you. As you modestly say you aren't up to much but—'

'I loved Sophie and—'

'No. No. Not just that or boyhood days either. You are you.'

'Oh—!' murmured Edgar.

'So you see. Yes.'

'Will you come to Mockingham?'

'Yes,' said Monty. 'And we'll smoke cigars, at least you will, on the terrace, and argue about the Line and the Cave and you will cure me—of my sickness.'

'Monty, are you serious? It matters so much.'

'Oh yes, I expect so. Yes. I'm so tired, Edgar. Please go. I've been asking you to go for an hour.'

'Well thank God I didn't.'

'You can go now. There's nothing more to learn. I am poured out and empty. Good night.'

'And you *will* come?'

'Yes. Yes. Yes.'

Harriet stood alone in her dusky lamp-lit bedroom, petrified with terror.

Monty's attack on her, his rejection of her, had been so vicious, so sudden. She had long wept with shock, and with sad disappointment of hopes and utter loneliness and lack of any resource. After their long conversation in the garden she had felt upset, but so connected with Monty that she had been unable not to imagine that all would be well between them. He *would* cherish her, he *would* love her! The rudeness and the bitterness were just his way, which after all she now knew so well. He was a bereaved man, she could not come near him yet. But gradually he would let her approach. She was sure that this would be. And then when he had so wonderfully protected her from Blaise, protected her from herself, from her own stupid slavish tenderness, staying with her as she had asked him to do in the presence of her husband, Harriet felt certain that he had done so out of some sort of love or caring for her. He had, after all, not wanted her to collapse, to return to Blaise on any terms. He had kept her, surely, for himself.

But now in a moment she saw it all as illusion. She could not interpret in any favourable sense, not even as a manifestation of jealousy of Edgar, those harsh words uttered so cruelly in Edgar's presence. Monty had rejected her. She had humbly and passionately offered him her love, virtually herself, and he had thrust her aside with repulsion. What contempt he must feel for the desperate humble need which had clung to him and become love.

After a long time her weeping ceased and she sat on her bed, twisting her wet handkerchief about and staring ahead of her blankly. What will become of me? Harriet wondered. Where shall I be this time next year, even this time next month? She got up, frightened at her thoughts, and went out into the passage. There was a murmur of talk from the study below. She looked at the closed bedroom doors. She stole along the carpeted floor to Luca's room and very quietly depressed the handle and sidled in. A little light from the hall, falling in a triangle on the carpet, showed the bed, the sleeping child. Yet was he sleeping? Something about the attitude suggested to Harriet that he was shamming sleep and would suddenly start up and call her to him. He lay so oddly. Supposing on the contrary he were lying dead. A dead child in a bed. To comfort herself she stretched out a hand to touch him, to feel his warmth and his breathing. She touched something strange and dark upon the bed, something that felt odd and moved slightly. Then she realized that it was Lucky, who was lying snuggled into the crook of Luca's knees and giving him that weird unfamiliar shape. As Harriet's hand touched the dog's thick coat Lucky growled very softly. Harriet withdrew her hand hastily and retreated from the room.

She stood still a moment on the landing and then went to David's room. She opened the door cautiously and slipped in, half closing it behind her. On this side of the house the moon was shining and there was a dim fine light in the room. David was lying very straight, as if tense and also, though differently, as if about to rise. This rising really would resemble the rising of a corpse. Harriet stood for some time looking at the long tense form of her son. The stiffness and straightness then made her think: soldier's grandson, soldier's nephew. Did she want David to go into the army? The idea had never entered her head. Then with a horrible shock she realized that the boy was awake, that his eyes were open, gazing towards the window. She could see the faint light reflected on his eyeballs, which glittered as if his open eyes were full of tears. He could not possibly be unaware of her presence. Yet he made no move, not imagining that she could see that his eyes were open. Appalled, Harriet murmured very softly, scarcely audibly, 'David'. The tense body did not move, but the eyes flickered and seemed to flash as if two tears had overflowed from them and caught up the faint light of the moon. Harriet withdrew.

Back in her bedroom her own tears flowed once more. Then she suddenly stopped weeping to listen. There was an odd new sound below her. It was the voice of a woman. How very strange, in Monty's study, a woman, talking to Monty. Harriet listened carefully and then with cold incredulous horror recognized that unique inimitable sound. It was Sophie's voice. Harriet ran to the door, ran back again. What had Monty done? Had he conjured up a ghost, had he that power? She was half willing to believe it. Or was Sophie really not dead but hidden somewhere in the house? Was that why Monty was so strange? Utter terror took hold of Harriet and she wailed with it. She ran out of her bedroom onto the landing and listened more intently. Now she heard Edgar's voice, Monty's voice, nothing more. Had she imagined that awful sound? Was she going mad at last?

She stood in the darkness holding her head. Then suddenly from below there was a strange wailing cry. And as Harriet stood there motionless with fear, it was as if a wind blew through the house, as if an airy shape passed through, passed by, and Harriet felt cold, cold. Something very cold and frightful seemed to have passed through the house and touched her in its passing.

Harriet hastened to turn on all the landing lights. She returned to her bedroom and turned on more light there. She thought, I must get out of the house, I must get away from Monty, I must get away from this awful haunted place. And in that moment she saw Monty, no longer as a refuge, but as a haunted, doomed person, filthy with his own ghosts. She took her handbag, put on her coat. Then she paused and tried to *think*, and with this effort came the certainty of what she must do. She sped quickly, silently, down the stairs, hearing again the voices of the two men in the study, and went to the front door and noiselessly out into the road. She breathed the soft warm night air with relief, looked at the reassuring street lamps making nests of green and red in the motionless trees. She walked along the road until she saw, not far away, Edgar's Bentley parked under a lamp, and she went to it. The solid familiar ordinary form of the car calmed her and she leaned against it and watched for a while the play of the bats as they swept round and round between the lights in their soft checked ellipses. The road was silent and empty.

At last the sound of a closing door and Edgar's footsteps. Hidden behind the car Harriet, peering, saw his face for a second before he saw her. Edgar was smiling, he looked pleased, dazed with happiness.

'Edgar.'

'Oh, Harriet! You startled me. What are you doing here? I thought you were in bed.'

'Can I talk to you a moment? May I get into the car?'

She climbed in and Edgar got in beside her. How big, how deeply comforting, he seemed, in that capacious dark leather gloom.

'Edgar—'

'Yes. You're all of a tremble. I hope we didn't—'

'I've decided. You have been so kind to me, so gentle— you have cared and been so kind. I think I will come to you, to Mockingham. You can look after me. Somebody's got to. I just feel that I've reached the end of things—the end of the light—and there's nothing but darkness ahead—and I'm so very grateful to you—I think I could love you—I think I do love you. So let us go—when you will—now if you like— only we must take Luca and David too—to Mockingham— where I'll be safe at last.'

There was silence in the car. Harriet could hear Edgar's heavy breathing and could now smell the plentiful whisky upon his breath as he turned towards her.

'Harriet—I'm so touched—'

'It's all right,' said Harriet. 'I really—do—care for you—' She reached out in the dark confined space and stroked Edgar's shoulder, stroked it as she might have stroked one of her dogs, feeling its warmth and the roughness of the cloth. And in that moment something which had been a little artificial and forced sprang suddenly to life and her heart was stirred within her and inclined to Edgar.

'I'm so—you're so kind—Oh I am so grateful—' said Edgar, 'but I'm afraid it isn't—possible just now any more—'

Harriet withdrew her hand. 'I see. You've changed your mind. I'm sorry.'

'No, not that, Harriet, *not* that. I haven't changed my mind at all. It's Monty. I can't explain. I'm taking Monty to Mockingham. It's very important. I think there must be —for a while anyway—just the two of us. He suddenly needs me, you see, and I've got to—so I can't have you there too —just absolutely now. Please forgive me and don't think I've changed in any way at all—I'm still, you know—it's just that now I *must* deal with Monty—but soon, well you know how terribly much I want you to come—soon, a little later—'

270

'I don't think I'd want to be there with Monty,' said Harriet, 'anyway.'

'No, of course it would be awkward—I mean—I quite understand—I am so sorry—and I'm *so* pleased and grateful that you thought you might—I'm so sorry—but we could meet here or in London—and you know how much I'd always want to help you—'

'Of course,' said Harriet. 'That's very kind of you. Well, I mustn't keep you now, must I, it's late.'

'I hope you do see that it's not—I'm so sorry—I do wish I could explain—'

'There's no need to explain,' said Harriet.

'And we will meet soon again, won't we? I do so want you to rely on me—'

'Oh certainly. We must meet for lunch—'

'In London, here, anywhere—you know I'd—only just now—'

'Yes, yes, I understand. Good night, Edgar. Drive carefully.'

'My dear, please—'

Harriet was out of the car before Edgar could offer his clumsy kiss. She walked quickly away and the Bentley slowly, reluctantly, moved off in the other direction.

Unable to take himself to bed Monty stood at his study window eating bread and butter and cheese and waiting for the dawn. He did not think, I have done well. He did not think, what imbecility ever possessed me to pour it all out to Edgar. He just felt, as he had said to his friend, emptied. He could not make out if the emptiness were good or bad. Perhaps it was good. It certainly produced a certain calmness. There was a hint of peace around, just as sometimes, early in the year, there is a hint of spring around. But possibly this was mere mood, illusion, even drink. I wonder if I shall really go to Mockingham, Monty wondered, and be shown up to one of those huge fantastically cold bedrooms with those four poster-beds that used to impress me so? And come down and have dinner with Edgar and drink port afterwards and talk about philosophy and college business. Was there such a world, could he see it, could he smell it? Was it the ancient unfamiliar smell of innocence? Perhaps all Sophie's love affairs had been imaginary, perhaps Sophie had been chaste after all.

After a while he let himself out into the garden and began to walk across the lawn. The sky was already pale with dawn, a very pale yet obscure blue, offering no light and yet somehow allowing things to body themselves forth as if they themselves were emitting a sort of spotty pallor. He could see the dense shapes of the fir trees, a prowling darkness which was a dog. A bird uttered a half phrase and fell silent again. He turned into the orchard and after a moment of strolling stopped suddenly and stared. He could see now through the trees the outline of Hood House and a light which had just come on in Blaise's study.

Monty's immediate feeling was fear, a kind of terror of the uncanny, born of the dawn light and of the deep abiding horrors in his own soul. Who could be there now in empty abandoned Hood House, turning the lights on and walking from room to room in frightful meditation? Blaise? Monty felt a fear of Blaise which was partly a fear for Blaise. It was not exactly that he imagined that Blaise might hate him, might wish to injure him, might wish to kill him. But the horror of Blaise's world touched him closely, and suddenly the more closely after what had just happened in his own. Blaise was a sort of pitiable walking danger, like something radioactive. Blaise had come there, searching, hoping, Blaise wishing it all undone, wishing himself dead? After a moment's hesitation Monty went forward and reached the hole in the fence and climbed through it and paused again. A downstairs light was on too, the hall light shining through the kitchen. The curtains were drawn in Blaise's study and the lighted square revealed the flowery pattern of the curtains, pasted onto the grey emergent shape of the house.

There was an aggressive scuffle and some barking. 'Who's a good boy, then?' He thought, I must see Blaise, I ought to. I must stop him from thinking of me as Mephistopheles, I must stop him imagining I somehow lured him on to disaster on purpose. Surely he cannot really think this. I should not have talked to him like that with Harriet, it was wrong. How strange that he should turn up now when I sort of require him. I must make my peace with him and not allow him to have the horrors alone in that house in the dawn. I must see him because I too need these things. Accompanied by desultory barks he moved across the lawn and along the side of the house. The front door stood ajar. Monty glided into the lighted hall and up the stairs. He knocked softly on Blaise's study door and entered.

'Oh!' said Harriet, dropping a number of cards on the floor.

'It's you!' said Monty. 'I thought it was Blaise. Oh, Harriet, what is it?'

Harriet said nothing for a moment. She was wearing her long white coat, and her face against the upturned collar looked grey, livid, as mottled as the dawn light. Her hands flew to her throat, pulling at the buttons of her dress as if she might faint. She looked at Monty grimacing with anxiety and shock, with fear, perhaps with aversion. She recalls my words, he thought, they are planted in her soul. That too should have been done quite otherwise.

'Nothing,' said Harriet in a dead voice. 'What do you want?'

'I thought it was Blaise.'

'Sorry. It isn't.'

She returned to her occupation. She was rifling Blaise's filing cabinet, of which several drawers were open and the contents lying scattered about the floor.

'What are you looking for, Harriet? Can I help you?'

The very bright direct light in the room made the scene seem unreal and horrible, the search a violation, a kind of violence, like a visit from the secret police. Harriet took up another handful of cards, glanced at them and tossed them onto the floor with a clatter.

'What are you looking for?'

'Magnus's address.'

'Magnus Bowles? His address?'

'Yes.'

'Why — ever — ?'

'I'm going to see him,' said Harriet. 'He knows all about it, he knows all about Blaise and me, he knew from the start, Blaise told him everything, he probably told him all sorts of things he never told me, and I feel so certain that Magnus is a wise person, a sort of kind good holy man. I've felt this thing about him for a long time. Blaise belittled him but then Blaise belittles everybody. Blaise can't *see* any kind of greatness. I've got to talk to Magnus, I've *got* to, I feel certain he could help me. Blaise said I was the only woman who really existed for Magnus. He must need me. And if he needs me I need him. And he's—the last one—' Her voice broke and she turned back to the cabinet and wrenched out another drawer.

'Oh dear!' said Monty.

'Of course Blaise took away a lot of stuff, but he didn't take the old files with the addresses. All the old papers are here, stuff from years ago, and there's a file for everybody, for *everybody*, except Magnus. I suppose you don't know Magnus's address, do you?'

'Harriet,' said Monty. 'You don't know then—about Magnus.'

'Don't know what?' she turned, glaring at him, fierce almost.

'Magnus is dead,' said Monty. 'He committed suicide—a little while ago. He took sleeping pills. He's dead.'

Harriet sat down slowly at Blaise's desk and with an automatic gesture cleared a space of papers in the middle of it. She gazed at the leather of the desk where the thick dust was crisscrossed with random trails. She said nothing, but sat stiffly, gazing down.

'I'm so sorry,' said Monty. He looked at her with pity, but also with a curious exhilaration. He tried to compose thoughts, words, in his head. He waited for her to speak, he waited for her to weep, but she did neither. She sat like a stunned condemned prisoner before him.

'Harriet,' said Monty, 'please forgive me for what I said to you before, with Edgar. It was stupid and—unnecessary. It was for your sake. I just wanted to warn you, I didn't want you to rely too much on someone like me. But I do care for you and I do want to help you. That was just a sort of act—it was cowardly of me—please believe that I do really want to be of service—'

Harriet turned to him her strange condemned face. 'Thank you, but your service will not be needed, your help would be of no help, any more than your—apology is. I was simply grateful that you made yourself so clear. I am going to make other arrangements in my life now. Tomorrow I shall move back into Hood House with the two boys. I am sorry to have inconvenienced you for so long. Good night.'

'It's morning,' said Monty. He pulled back the curtains. Outside the sun was shining and there was a little jumbled sound of birds singing in the orchard trees.

Harriet, who had turned back to the desk, did not reply

to him. She murmured something which sounded like 'end . . .
end . . .'

'I know you're angry,' said Monty, 'and you have good
reason. But please stay at Locketts and be a little kind to me.
Perhaps I need you—after all—'

'Oh I'm not *angry*,' said Harriet, in a voice almost inaudibly
without resonance. 'If you think I'm angry you have understood nothing. It doesn't matter that much.'

'All right. We can't talk to each other now. But just remember later that I do care—in spite of all those stupid things I
said. Now I'll go. Good—day—'

He paused, but as she did not move or reply he left her
and went downstairs, switching off the lights, and out again
into the garden. His own trail of footsteps in the thick dew
led away across the lawn. As he reached the hole in the
fence, Ajax, his coat wet with dew from the long orchard
grass, came through to meet him, sleek and dark as a seal.
Monty's hand touched his wet fur and felt the vibration of a
soft growl as he slipped through into his own garden. He
walked slowly along the path towards Locketts treading
upon a carpet of small white daisies. He must remember to
tell Blaise that Magnus Bowles was dead. How quickly and
rightly it had been done. The curious exhilaration he had
felt when he told Harriet the news came back to him now
as a feeling of freedom. Had talking to Edgar really made a
difference? Something had made a difference. Milo was dead,
Magnus was dead, and Monty felt himself increased by these
deaths. He felt better. He dared not yet return to any close
scrutiny of his deepest woe, not yet. He felt like a man who
has had plastic surgery for his burnt face, but dare not yet
look into the mirror. No, that's not the image, he thought
to himself. It's more like a leg operation, an eye operation.
And he recalled how he had said to Edgar, 'I am lame, I
am blind.' He must have been confoundedly carried away to
enact such humility. Drunk no doubt. No wonder Edgar was
pleased.

Monty entered the house and went into his study. He knelt
down for a while in his usual meditative pose, but without
attempting to meditate. He reflected in a relaxed way about
Harriet and about how he would try to make her trust him
again. He would write her a careful letter. She will come
round, he thought, she needs me and she really has nobody,
now even Magnus is dead.

The boys were stirring above. Monty emerged into the

275

hall and began to delve a little into the tea-chest of letters. Perhaps today he would look at some of them. It also occurred to him that he might now unmuzzle the telephone, and he went to it and began to pull out the piece of plastic wire with which he had jammed the bell. As he lifted the instrument he could feel it trembling and vibrating in his hand. It was actually at this moment trying to ring. He pulled the wire out and lifted the receiver, instantly stifling its outcry.

'We have a call for you from Italy,' said the operator's voice.

An English voice said tentatively, 'Hello.'

'My dear Dick,' said Monty, 'however many times must I tell you that I detest long distance calls, especially at breakfast time.'

'If you won't fetch Luca, I will,' said Emily.

'It's not so simple,' said Blaise. 'You know what that boy is like. We can't keep him here against his will, he'll just decamp.'

'I want Luca fetched.'

'Anyway with us like this he's better out of the house.'

'With us like what?'

'Like this!'

'I sometimes think you hate your own child.'

'Emily, do talk sense, things are bad enough—'

'All right, I know you regret what you've done, I know you don't want to be here—'

'Oh *stop* it!'

'The school rang up again.'

'Of course they did. If we aren't careful he'll be taken into care. Thank God it's nearly the end of term.'

'Dr Ainsley rang too. He sounded pretty crazed up.'

'Fuck him.'

'And Mrs Batwood rang.'

'Honestly, I'd rather Luca stayed with Harriet for the present. I've got enough trouble without that pixie. In the autumn we'll send him to that boarding school.'

276

'We?'

'You and I. In the autumn—'

'I don't know whether I shall still be alive in the autumn.'

'Is that a suicide threat?'

'No. I'm far beyond suicide threats. I just don't know whether I can stand the strain and what happens when I can't. And the autumn is far away. Anything may have happened to us all by then.'

'What are you complaining about? I'm here, aren't I?'

'Are you?'

'I've smashed up my life for you. I don't know what more you want!'

'You want to go back to her.'

'I do not!'

'Oh, well, never mind,' said Emily, staring at the table-cloth, not having raised her voice at all, 'never mind, never mind, never mind.'

'Oh *Christ*!' said Blaise. He did not want to quarrel with Emily, but he was near to screaming with exasperation and anxiety and indecision and sheer fear.

'I think it would be better if Luca and I just cleared off to Australia and let you return to your ordinary life with Harriet,' said Emily, 'if you'd pay our fare.'

'Stop saying that. You don't mean it.'

'I do. I think I may not have made clear to you just how much Luca matters here. He is my son. He is the only thing I've got in the world that's really mine. I'm not going to let bloody Harriet have him. All right, you needn't fetch him today, but I want him back here by the end of the week, otherwise I'm going over there to kick the place to bits. Got that?'

'All right, all right,' said Blaise. Emily's new quiet tone terrified him, and just when he had so much to think about. Oh if he could only *think*! And how very much he did not want Luca in the house just now. 'All right,' he said. 'I'll fetch him.'

'And when are you going to see the lawyer about the divorce?'

'Soon.'

'Which day?'

'Oh soon, *soon*!' said Blaise. 'I can't do everything at once!'

'No divorce, no go, you know that?'

'Yes, yes, yes!'

Blaise's hand in his pocket convulsively clutched the letters which he had received by the latest post and which he had concealed from Emily. One was from Monty, the other from Harriet. Monty's letter ran as follows:

Dear Blaise,
I thought I had better tell you that our old friend Magnus Bowles is no more. I assassinated him yesterday for Harriet's benefit. (She was proposing to go and see him.) He took an overdose of sleeping pills and is dead. As he had outlived his usefulness, I thought it would be less confusing for all concerned if he were liquidated. I am sorry I was not able to consult you first.

It remains for me to say to you most sincerely that there is absolutely nothing between Harriet and me. That at least is not one of your problems, as I hope by now you have realized. Moreover, if there is anything at all that I can do to help you, I beg you to let me know. (For instance, I could lend you money.) Please keep in mind this availability and forgive me for any clumsiness in the past. You cannot surely, on reflection, see me as, in relation to you, a sinister agency.

Finally an expression of opinion, which I hope you will not think is impertinent. If you want to keep Harriet in your life you can probably do so, but you should act quickly and decisively. I mean, come here, stay here, for a while at any rate, and *take over*. She has gone back to Hood House and whether she now expects you or not I don't know. But if you don't come she might do anything. I don't mean anything desperate, but she might clear off and vanish so as to make a real break. She is perhaps waiting, but will not do so indefinitely.

Excuse these observations. I wish you both very well.
                                        Yours
                                        Monty.

(Typical! thought Blaise of this letter.) Harriet's letter ran as follows:

Dear Blaise,
    the simple fact that you have not come back here, not written, not telephoned, not anything, tells me, I think, and it is meant to tell me, I suppose, all that I need to know. You have gone away. You have left me. You mean

me to understand it and I do. Would I now forgive you if you totally rejected Emily McHugh and came back to me? I don't know. Anyway you won't do that. I shall not dwell on my unhappiness. I suppose you want a divorce. I write to say this, that I will cooperate with you to get a divorce and will make everything easy for you on condition that I keep Luca. The child I must have and you can hardly grudge him to me. I have the impression that neither you nor his mother cares very much about him. He was thoroughly *neglected* at Putney. This could be proved if necessary in a law court. He passionately wants to stay with me and not to return to you and Emily. I am prepared to fight a legal battle for Luca, but I hope and believe that you own sense of his best interests will coincide with mine. He needs security, communication and love, and these I can give him. He will in every way be far better off here. I am prepared to devote my life to the upbringing of that child. You should be grateful to me. I am letting you have what you want without reproaches or difficulties. Oh Blaise, how can you have done this, how can it have happened, I can scarcely believe this nightmare! I love you as I have always done. That is what is so terrible. And if your other world should end—but what is the use of saying that. As things are now, I could never be an accepting slave. You have chosen her and must do without me. But oh it is so terrible—I did not intend to write like this. I mean what I say about Luca.

H.

As soon as he received this letter Blaise realized with anguish that the peace and joy which he experienced with Emily depended on his assumption that Harriet's situation was static. Harriet was to be 'frozen' in an attitude of waiting, of attention, while Blaise sorted out his emotions and settled down into at least as much of a new world as would satisfy Emily and make her reasonably happy. Was he still, *still*, so mad as to imagine that he could perfectly keep both women? Evidently. Harriet's letter put him into a frenzy, the sight of her handwriting made him feel sick, it was like being in love again. How *could* he have lost her after all these years? Now he longed for her, longed to hold her in his arms and *explain* it all. He had always had Harriet to tell his troubles to, and could he not turn to her now and tell her this trouble? If only he could explain to Harriet, explain his whole mind,

279

explain the difficulty he was in, lay the dilemma at her
feet. He imagined Harriet saying gently, as she had so often
said before when he told her his problems, 'Yes, yes, it is
difficult, isn't it—now let's see what can be done—'

'And you've fallen in love with Kiki St Loy.'

'Oh shut up,' said Blaise.

'You have. You said her name in your sleep last night.'

'You lie. We've got enough troubles without your inventing
this rubbish about Kiki.'

'You drove her back to London in your car.'

'How do you know?'

'I could smell her off you.'

'Pinn told you, I suppose. Pinn marooned her on purpose
so that I had to drive her. I only took her to the station.'

'Did you kiss her?'

'Of course not.'

'You lie. What fun our married life is turning out to be.
No wonder you want to go home to dear old Hood House and
Mrs Placid.'

'Stop it. Emily. Darling. I don't want to go raving mad.
If possible.'

'I don't want to go mad either,' said Emily. 'I just wish
I knew one way or the other what you were going to do.'

'I'm going to stay here with you and make you happy at
last.'

'Are you? Honest? If you fail now it's the end, you know
that.'

'Yes, yes.'

'You mustn't fail. I've bought three fuchsias for the balcony.
And collars for the cats.'

'I told you not to buy collars for the cats, they'll hang
themselves.'

'Maybe we ought to hang ourselves.'

'Oh Emily—'

'You look so unhappy. Oh my darling, why couldn't we
have just found each other properly, without all this hell,
why didn't you *wait* for me? Blaise, come here, kneel here
please, look at me.'

Blaise left his chair and knelt and looked up into the fierce
blue truthful eyes of Emily McHugh. He felt with a desperation which was almost relief, yes, I am hers. But oh what will
become of us, what will become of us?

'We must make our love work,' said Emily. 'It's everything
I've got. I think it's everything you've got now, unless you

intend to wreck yourself. Will you try, Blaise, will you be a hero for my sake?'

'Yes, yes.'

He means it *now*, she thought. He is utterly with me now, he is utterly mine. But can I hold him to it? I am becoming so cruel and frightened with him. I can't help tormenting him and making him wretched. There's such a flood of happiness waiting to be released, if only this thing were true at last. But he's so broken and rattling about, he's half demented with not knowing what to do, and I can't help him here, I can't even afford to pity him. He won't be loyal, he'll mess it about somehow, and will I be able to stand it if he does? Oh if only only only we could be happy and ordinary like other people. I'd work so hard for him, I'd give him my whole life and being with such joy. Oh if only he'd waited for me! How can perfect happiness be so near to two people and not draw them to it like a magnet?

Blaise was thinking, yes, I am hers. But what on earth am I to do about Harriet? If my whole life is stripped away and smashed how can I be of use to any woman? I've just got to fight for myself too, I've got to *look after* myself. And I'm in such a financial mess now and I can't borrow from Monty. (Or can I?) I must see Harriet. I can't possibly know where I stand until I've seen her again.

He said, 'I'll go over and fetch Luca. I'll go today.'

'You don't want to fetch Luca,' said Emily. 'You want to see *her*. I can read it in your eyes. No, don't go. Luca can stay there for the present. I think I agree with you after all, he's better away when we're both in this awful state. You won't go over there will you?'

'No. All right.' I will go though, he thought. I must invent some cover story. He got up slowly. 'Did I really say Kiki's name in my sleep?'

'So you think you might have done?!'

'Where's Kiki?' said David to Pinn. 'Have you brought her like you said?'

'What's the matter with you?' said Pinn. 'You look ready to faint. Are you that much in love?'

'My mother has just gone away,' said David.

'What, gone away without you? You poor pet. Look you'd better get inside and sit down.'

David had returned to find Pinn in the front garden of Hood House, peering in through one of the windows.

David let himself into the house and Pinn followed. Already the place seemed to echo. Automatically David went through into the kitchen. On the kitchen table there was a note from Harriet to Edgar about arrangements for feeding the dogs. David looked round the kitchen and the sad betrayed room was unbearable to him. He went out again and into the drawing-room and lay down on the sofa. Misery prostrated him with a kind of exhaustion which weakened every inch of his body, as in a bad case of influenza.

His mother was gone, flown. He was to have accompanied her. He had agreed to all the arrangements, the timetable of departure, the telephone calls to school. He had even packed his suitcase and placed it near the door. He had got up early and watched his mother and Luca at breakfast in the kitchen. His mother had run out after him with a cup of coffee. She had embraced him in the hall, hastily, passionately, in a corner like a lady kissing her young footman. He felt her hot face pressed upon his. She had whispered, 'Bear it — I need you so much.' She had never spoken to him like that before. The train left at eleven and the taxi had been ordered for ten-thirty.

At nine-thirty David quietly left the house. He set off on his usual route towards the motorway. He walked through the lanes which he knew so well and over the shoulder of the little hill where the black and white cows used to be. The hedges had been bulldozed and the ditches were full of blue plastic cement sacks. Soon there would be a housing estate. As David mounted the slope, trying not to count the minutes, he could already hear the hum of the motorway, which was now open. The concreted courtyard where he had once lain supine in the sun in a final act of solitude was now a racing track of glittering motor-cars. And upon the nearer carriage-way as he approached he could see, and shuddered at it, the squashed and flattened form of a hare, a monogram of fur and blood. The volcanic tumble of bulky red earth which had come to rest so strangely in the quiet field was alien no longer, it had been raked over and sown with grass. The young blades were already showing.

David had intended simply to stay away from the house until after the train had left and then to return. He tried not to reflect upon whether he would then find his mother still there. He felt like someone who has gone out to avoid a death scene or the removal of a body. When he came back it would be *done* and the house though terrible would be clean. Oh that awful uncleanness, as he had felt it in the last days, his own dear precious home haunted, infested! The spectacle of his mother and Luca, whispering, laughing, petting Lucky, petting each other. His own title of son usurped and caricatured. His mother could not know what she was doing or she would not do it. He had intended simply to stay away, but now he realized that his ramblings had brought him fairly near to the railway station and he could actually go and watch the train depart.

A piece of disused railway track curving through a cutting led towards the station where the ground evened out a little. David had often walked this way, striding upon the grass-embedded sleepers, crumbly as dark chocolate, and searching for old nuts and bolts, venerable relics, their sturdy cast-iron forms printed with vanished insignia. He hurried along now, springing upon the soft slightly rotting wood until the little station was almost in sight and he could see the glittering rails of the still open permanent way. A disused railwayman's hut, a wooden shack, solid and now quite hollow, stood just before the intersection. David glided in through the gaping door and looked along the line. The station was quite close and he could command a view of the platform. A few people were waiting for the London train. His mother was not among them. It was a quarter to eleven.

Perhaps she won't come, he thought. If only she could not fail this test, if only she could find it impossible to leave without him. He could go back and take her in his arms. If only he knew how to do this. But they had lost the language of their affections, they had lost the style. How repulsive to him had been that hasty embrace in the hallway, that awkward hot almost guilty kiss. He stood well back within the open square of the window, in the shadow, and watched the platform. He turned to consult his watch. It was dark in the hut and smelt of warm unpainted wood and elder flowers. When he looked up Harriet and Luca had come onto the platform. Harriet was talking to the taxi driver, gesturing, perhaps telling him to drive quickly back towards the house in case David should be coming from there. She looked about, her gaze even crossing the dark window of the hut, as if she expected him to come running up from somewhere at any moment. He saw that she had brought his suitcase with her. He could not see her face clearly but he could read the detailed symbolism of her movements with the lifelong sympathy of his own body. She was distraught. I will go to her, he thought. Then suddenly she knelt down and, pretending to be settling Luca's coat collar, embraced him with a frantic gesture.

A few minutes later the train was audible. It swept past, obscuring the view for a moment, and then stopped at the platform. Harriet had gone back to the barrier and was looking away down the road. The guard was calling to her. She returned and began pushing the suitcases into the train. She bundled Luca on. The door banged. David saw her still hanging out of the window as the train rattled away into the trees and curved out of sight. Its vibration hovered in the air for a while after it had gone and then there was silence. David emerged from the hut and walked up to the other side of the station, crossed the footbridge, and began to walk slowly along the road that led back to Hood House. It was a longer way than through the fields but he had no heart to walk in the fields now. The hot piney sandy smell of the railway was gradually left behind. He thought, I am entirely alone. I am entirely alone and abandoned for the first time in my life. I have neither father nor mother. She got into the train. She need not have done so. She got into the train and went away without me.

Simply the waiting, the vigil, the refusal had been his purpose. But what now? He was suddenly on his own, returning to an empty house. She will come back, he thought. But would she? When? He had, with his body's sympathy, felt her final frenzied need to flee, to run. Of course there was Monty, there was Edgar. But he felt alienated from Monty. Monty had refused to talk to him when talk would have helped so much. Monty had become aloof and mute. And David's mother too had rejected Monty. 'He is no use,' she said once, after she had virtually shut the door in Monty's face. Monty was 'no use' and Edgar would soon be going back to Oxford. David would be alone. He could not go back to his school after those telephone calls. All his life someone had fed him, provided his clothes, given him money, told him what to do—who would look after him now?

'David!' Pinn seemed to be calling to him from far away. 'Are you asleep or have you gone into a trance?'

284

'I'm all right.'

'Are you hungry, did you eat any breakfast, shall I bring you something, cook you something?'

'No, thanks.'

'Sit up for a minute. It makes my head swim to look at you.'

David sat up jerkily and leaned forward over his knees, panting and rubbing his face with one hand. He did feel a little faint, he felt very strange.

'She'll come back,' said Pinn. She took his free hand very gently yet firmly in hers.

'No.'

'Where's she gone?'

'To my uncle in Germany.'

'Well, she *will* come back. Meanwhile you're a big boy, aren't you.'

The telephone began to ring. David knew at once: It is my mother telephoning from Paddington. 'No, don't answer it. Shut the door please.'

Pinn shut the door.

'Will Kiki come?' said David against the muted clamour of the 'phone. 'You said she would come.'

Pinn said after a moment, 'No.'

'Why not?'

'She has fallen in love with somebody else.'

My father, thought David. He had seen them together in the car. Tears started into his eyes. 'Gone forever,' he said half to himself, 'gone forever', and he quickly checked his tears with one hand, letting Pinn continue to hold the other. The telephone went on ringing. Pinn removed her glasses.

'Well, what are you going to do now?' said Pinn.

'I don't know.'

Pinn was beginning to undo the buttons of his shirt. When she had undone them all the way down to his waist she put her hand inside and laid it very firmly upon his breast. The particular slightly cupping gentle and yet commanding pressure of that hand upon his flesh produced an instantaneous and very complex change in David's being. At one moment he was hanging in space, outstretched upon a huge grid of pain: jealousy, loneliness, fear, anger, resentment. He was disincarnate and scattered in terrible regions. At the next moment his body had assembled promptly and compactly round about him, obedient to the sudden authority of Pinn's caressing hand. He saw the details of Pinn's face become, through its own emotion, arresting and unfamiliar. He saw her frizzy red-gold crown of neat hair, her round and uniformly pink cheeks, her moist mouth and green eyes. 'I suggest you make love to me,' said Pinn.

'I can't,' said David, removing her hand, but holding it and retaining the other one.

'You could have with Kiki? You thought about her?'

'Yes.'

'And dreamt about her?'

David recalled the steaming abyss of his dream. 'Yes.'

'You don't want her. You want a woman. Love me. I am nobody, I am everybody. I am the figure in the temple that embodies the will of heaven. I am worthy of you because I am the messenger of your fate. You are looking at me for the first time but I have looked at you many times, you have walked about freely in my dreams. Your youth and your beauty are holy to me. I worship your innocence. Trust me and give it to me. It is the right time. And love me just a little in your heart without fear. I have no will to entangle you or to hold you. I will be kind to you and will set you free and even send you from me. How could I presume to speak about your mother if this were not so? I want you now and I need you now and this is something which your destiny and not mine has ordained. But I need your affection too. I have never begged for anyone's affection before, but I beg for yours now. If you can give it to me as you love me the world will be made anew in which your manhood begins. You will never understand me or know me, David, but at this moment we can do each other no harm, only good. Believe this and accept my wooing and don't be afraid. No other woman will ever speak to you like this and there will never be another moment in your life like this one. Come, will you, please?'

In the silence that followed David heard his breathing, heard his heart, or perhaps Pinn's, echoing the gathered momentum of her speech. The green-eyed face seemed to be transforming itself before him into a beautiful mask of pure gaze. He had never been so absolutely looked at before. The air around him had become exquisite and thin. They both rose.

'Wait,' said David, and his voice was gruff. 'I'll just go and –' He left her swiftly and went to the front door and bolted it, went to the kitchen door and bolted it. Then he returned to the hall where Pinn was waiting for him.

286

Her face was more muddled, more humble now, blurred with her own need. 'You can care for me a little, can't you, simply at this moment, it's not just—?'

'Yes, yes,' said David.

'You can't understand, but I've been a heroine and—you are my reward—and oh, because of so many things—just a moment of somebody's tenderness—'

'Yes, yes, yes—'

'Come then, my dear.'

They went up the stairs.

'Well, and how was it?' said Monty to Kiki St Loy.

'Super!' Kiki, now fully dressed, was putting on her sandals.

Monty had slipped on his shirt and was still lying reposefully against a pile of pillows in the disordered bed. .

He regarded the girl with tender amazement. How put together she was, with her sleek brown tights and her short lilac-coloured dress of feathery cotton, and the milk-white glassy necklace which she had just slipped about her neck, and her dark burnished gold-shot hair combed out and falling to its straight silken hem with not a strand out of line. So mint-conditioned, so complete and somehow beautifully public, she who had lately been to him a universe where thought and feeling, flesh and world, him and her had so tumultuously intermingled.

'What do you think?' said Kiki.

'What are you thinking.'

'What are you thinking?'

'You look so *presentable*,' said Monty. 'I mean so well-turned-out and uncreased and uncrumpled and neat. I can hardly believe you're the girl I've just been so marvellously in bed with.'

'I am that girl!' Kiki sprang at him, a foot dabbing the edge of the bed, landing beside him, on top of him, he felt her sandalled feet against his bare feet, her honey-nylon thighs against his thighs, her neat lilac dress bundling against his shirt, her lips against his jaw, her hair about his neck, about his head. He smelt the apple smell of her flesh, her sweat, the cottony dress, the tender cool smell of her hair.

'Mind your dress, you silly goose.'

'I want to be creased and crumpled, I want to be your creased and crumpled Kiki, I want to be undone by you.'

'You have been undone by me, and I hope you really *did* think it was super. At one point I wasn't too sure what you were thinking.'

'I was not thinking.'

'Feeling then. I didn't hurt you too much?'

'No, no, Monty, it was perfect — the hurt was there — but in the midst of all — Oh I am so happy!'

'Well, don't be too happy,' said Monty, pushing her away from him. 'Remember what I told you earlier. Get out of the way, I'm going to get dressed.' He got up and sought for his trousers.

'I love you, Monty,' said Kiki. 'Is that wrong?'

'If anything's wrong it's mine,' said Monty fixing his belt. 'Many people would call this a crime. If it has unhappy consequences for you that will be some evidence in favour of the view that it was one. This is something that you must look after for me. Part of it all was my trusting you with it.'

'I don't understand and yet I do understand,' said Kiki. 'But I can't help loving you forever and there is that too.'

'A girl of your age doesn't know about forever.'

'I think I do know though,' said Kiki. '*I* know about it. I am a remarkable girl.'

Monty came to where she stood beside the bed, her lilac dress indeed a little crumpled. He took her by the shoulders and looked into the big dark eyes where there were in the iris drifting depths of red, Mediterranean eyes, African eyes.

'Yes, you are a remarkable girl,' he said, 'and that is why I have done this to you and taken this risk. I have passed on some of my pain to you, which is what human beings ought not to do, though human beings constantly do it. And I have done this deliberately. I have victimized you, Kiki, because of your remarkableness and because at a certain moment you were suddenly there and able to make a change in my life.'

'You will be less unhappy?'

'Perhaps. Yes.'

'I think I will be more unhappy,' said Kiki, 'if you will

really not now—let me see you—though if I have made you less unhappy I will have extra happiness for that.'

'Less in quantity, my dear, but higher in quality! Let it be made up that way. Now you must go.'

'No, no. Monty, please. We can never be like this again.'

'I know,' he said. 'Don't you think this saddens me too? That is why you must go quickly.'

'But you *will* see me again—you didn't mean never—Oh, I feel so terrible, Monty.'

'I expect we shall meet, why not. But all this must pass.'

'It will never pass.'

'Come, come. Any pain I will have caused you is very pure, perhaps the purest pain you will ever feel. It may even help you one day, like a hard thing, to give you a foothold, somewhere quite else, to put your gallant little foot upon.'

'Let me see you tomorrow.'

'No. Go now, Kiki. I have nothing more to give you, except my blessing which looks like a curse, but is really a blessing. You are a brave child and I give this last remnant to your bravery. Go, remarkable girl. And my thanks.'

Monty went away down the stairs and opened the front door.

'No. Good-bye.'

Kiki passed him and the last he saw was the big dark eyes hazy with unshed tears. Then her long hair tossed and flying. But she left with a firm step and did not look back.

Monty closed the door and leaned against it. Then he sat down on the floor with his back against the door. His world seemed to be sailing, sailing in front of him, the pieces of it huge and coloured like storm clouds. Everything which had been so dark and tight as if he were crushed inside a nut, had loosened and become separated and airy and streaming and a little wild. Monty did not think now, is this good, is this bad? He simply responded to it, as he had responded to the extraordinary advent of Kiki St Loy.

Somewhere in the midst of all these jauntily sailing pieces there was what had happened that night. Sophie had not been in bed. She was lying on the purple sofa in the little drawing-room, in the canopied recess, dressed in a long robe of dark red and blue silk which in fact she had just bought by post from a West End shop. It was the first time she had worn it. She was propped up among the purple cushions and her face looked thin and pale, uncannily greyly pale like the wax effigy of a dead saint in a Spanish church.

How much her expression had changed with the vanishing of those plump confident cheeks. She had been saying again and again and again for nearly half an hour, 'I hate you, I hate you, I hate you, I wish I'd never married you.' It is simply the litany of her doomed pain, Monty told himself, as he had told himself many times in the last weeks, as Sophie reviled and tormented him, casting her anguish off onto him like an acid shower. He made his usual effort to be quiet, not to quarrel with her, to answer gently, to say to her again and again and again in a countervailing litany, 'Rest a little. I love you. Don't be angry with me. Forgive me, Sophie. I love you.' But once more he failed. 'All right, I wish I'd never married *you*! I wish I'd had a decent loyal wife and not a whore who went to bed with all my friends!' 'You have no friends, you don't know how they mock and despise you, all of them.' 'If they do it's because you teach them to,' 'I despise you, you are not a man at all, oh how I wish I had married a man.' 'Oh, shut up, Sophie, go to bed.' 'They all mock you, Richard mocks you.' 'Shut up!' 'You didn't know I made love with Richard.' 'It's not true.' 'It is true, here in our bed, we mocked you.' 'You'd invent anything to hurt me, wouldn't you.' 'I hate you, I hate you, I hate you.'

Monty caught his breath. The memory had risen like a noxious atomic cloud in the midst of his sailing thoughts. He checked himself, made himself rigid, while the hysterical voices went on and on in his mind. He had made them silent at last, seizing her throat. It had been like an embrace. He had to make her silent. He threw himself upon her and silenced her and held her, wanting to hurt her, wanting to dominate and hold that awful consciousness which filled him with so much pain and so much wild awful pity.

'Sophie,' he said aloud. 'Sophie. Sophie. My darling. Rest now. Forgive me.' She was part of him forever. Only here within him did she now exist. His love for her was still alive and would live always and would change as live things change. And perhaps as with the years it became softer and vaguer its imperfections would fade too. It could never be made perfect but it would carry fewer of its blemishes into the years to come. He and Sophie, bound together forever, married forever. His body relaxed slowly and then he began to remember Kiki and what had just been happening. How strange, he thought, how very strange. And he felt himself in change like a plant, altering in all his parts. What had made this newness? Telling Edgar? Something to do with Edgar himself, some place of innocent affection, some relic of youth even, providing a mysterious fulcrum? So Edgar had somehow made possible Kiki, and Kiki would make possible—what? What delusions were these? Had he not simply committed another crime, a little one? And it seemed then in his mind curiously like the big one, its counterpart. Sophie's death, Kiki's tears, to bring about for him, what?

The telephone began to ring. Monty slowly got up and went to it. A man's voice asked if that was Mr Small.

'Yes.'

'It's Fairhazel here—you know—er—Binkie.'

'Binkie!'

'I'm speaking from Bankhurst School.'

'Binkie! After all these years!'

'We were expecting you here this morning for interview.'

'Oh heavens!' said Monty. The whole matter had, since his conversation with Edgar, gone completely out of his head. It was not only the intervening emotion. When Edgar had said 'I cannot write you a testimonial' Monty had felt that the whole plan was automatically cancelled. But of course Edgar had not in fact cancelled Monty's appointment! 'I'm so terribly sorry,' said Monty. 'I am afraid a rather urgent thing detained me here—a—er—a matter of a forced entry.'

'Oh I'm sorry. I trust nothing was taken?'

'Well, one thing of value was taken, but I think it's going to be all right.'

'You're fully insured?'

'I hope so,' said Monty. 'Time will show!'

'Perhaps we can fix another day for you to come here?'

'It turns out that I have to go away after all. So I think— perhaps we'd better just leave it for the present. I'm so sorry to have been a nuisance—you've been very kind to be willing—'

'Not at all. No doubt you'll let me know later if—though of course—'

'Yes, yes, thank you, thank you.'

Monty put the telephone down and began to laugh. Then he stopped laughing and began to calculate how long it was since he had last done so. The huge multi-coloured storm cloud clouds continued to sail in the clear open spaces of his mind.

Blaise turned the key and pressed the door but it would not open. He pushed it in a frenzy, then stopped. It must be bolted on the inside. Why? Fear seized his mind. He rang the bell and waited. Silence. He rang again at length. Nothing. He ran round the side of the house to the kitchen door, but this too was bolted, or at any rate locked and he had no key to it. He peered into the familiar empty kitchen into which the sun was shining, showing the red cloth, some papers on the table, cups not washed up on the old-fashioned sink. He tried the kitchen window, then all the other lower windows, but they were all locked. His mind raced, picturing to him Harriet lying upstairs with an empty bottle of sleeping pills beside her.

That's nonsense thought Blaise. Harriet would never kill herself, that is not her nature. Of course she has simply bolted the door to keep me out. She is sitting upstairs listening silently waiting for me to go away. This image was nearly as frightening as the previous one. He seemed to see Harriet's eyes glittering at him venomously, glittering in his mind in a way which he had never seen in life. He felt as if she could see him now, must be observing him from above. He stood back and looked up but could see no one, no vanishing head or twitching curtain in the upper storey. He ran back to the front door and called 'Harriet! Harriet! Harriet!' through the letter-box. Silence. The dogs who had gathered to watch his proceedings, now followed him snappishly, barking round his heels. He kicked at them and they withdrew snarling. 'Harriet, Harriet!'

These desperate frightening cries seemed to him the awful climax of his day. The stupid quarrel with Emily about Kiki had gone on and on. They had continued it mechanically out of tiredness, neither having the creative energy to see how it could be ended. Then the telephone rang. It was a doctor whom he knew at a hospital in central London. 'I've got some bad news for you. One of your patients was brought here. We couldn't save him. He's committed suicide.' 'Magnus Bowles?' said Blaise stupidly. 'No, Ainsley. Dr Horace Ainsley.' Blaise laid down the 'phone. Betrayal of trust. He was to have

292

that pain too, that cue for wounding self-accusation and remorse, he was to be spared nothing. God, he had troubles enough without that too. 'What was it?' said Emily. 'Ainsley has killed himself.' 'I told you he rang, I told you to see him, I told you—' 'Oh leave me alone!' Blaise screamed. 'Can't you see I'm nearly round the bend as it is?' They went on fighting.

Blaise left her at last saying he had to go to the hospital to see about Dr Ainsley. He drove straight to Hood House. And as he drove along Western Avenue and came at last to the familiar turning and the familiar quiet roads with their confident capacious tree-surrounded houses, some consciousness in him which had not been told of recent events took form as a weary battered contentment, a relieved feeling of coming home. What he used to feel in the old days, when he returned from battling with Emily at Putney to the unconscious innocent untouched peace of Hood House.

I can't do it, he thought to himself, I can't *do* it, I must be let off this hook, and Harriet must let me off it. Yes, it all depends on Harriet, and if once she sees that she will help me. She helped me before, at the start, when she saw that only her help would avail. How did things go so wrong? I made a mistake, yes, it was just a *mistake*, and I now see it and can undo it. I was stupidly offensive to Harriet about loving Emily and going away. I should have been much vaguer and less direct. How do I know what I'm going to do even now? There was no need to offend Harriet in that way, I should have been much more careful. Of course she couldn't stand it, no woman could. She felt she'd been cut right out and that I didn't need her any more. A woman needs a man to need her. And by Christ I *do* need Harriet. She is the key. Why didn't I see it all along, it seems so clear now. Only Harriet can make the situation bearable at all. Of course I'm committed to Emily, whatever that means. Harriet must at least understand that, so perhaps it's just as well I was a bit brutal and got it across. But now I must try and calm her down, coax her, stop her from being offended and hurt, make her see how much I want her to help me. I can't live without Harriet's forgiveness and without Harriet there in my life somehow just like she used to be. Harriet can't change, she's not the sort of woman who changes, that's what's so wonderful about her. She was only pretending in that letter, angry and trying to hurt me, making me feel I might lose her so as to force me to come back. Yes, that was it. She was just provoking me to come back. It won't be easy, she'll need to be wooed a little, but my really needing her so is the essential thing. Once she understands again that she has real power and isn't just being put on the rubbish dump she'll come round and be kind and merciful again. I've *got* to have that quiet place to come to still where Harriet is sitting and sewing and David is doing his homework. I may not be able to be there all the time, but the place has got to exist. 'You have destroyed that place forever.' No, no, said Blaise to the voice in his mind. Harriet can make it exist for me and even now she will.

As he drove along, coming nearer and nearer to Hood House, he felt more and more that he had the solution. He could be saved after all, sanity, honour, peace of mind, the lot. Amidst all the muddle and horrors one thing, for his remaining sense of his integrity, had stayed clear. He *was* committed to Emily, to live with her mainly, properly, somehow. It was a new phase, yes, a new phase. These words too brought him comfort. It had all happened to him as automatically as the turning of the seasons. He had to stay with Emily and ride out the storm of circumstance without abandoning her. Of course they quarrelled and shouted as they had always done even in the days of perfection. But at nights as he lay exhausted by emotion and distress, quiet at last in Emily's arms, he had a deep sense of being in the right place. He said this to her more than once, and although she made a sarcastic reply, he felt her joy purring silently up against him and he thought to himself what a wonderful thing it was to make a woman happy.

I ran through it, with Harriet, he thought. There was a sort of cycle. That was good too, but utterly different. And now a new cycle begins. It's natural somehow. Only I *must* have Harriet too, absolutely there in the background. She must see that without her nothing can work for me. It's a lot to expect, it comes to asking her to sacrifice herself, but she's the sacrificing type and in the end she'll see it as her duty. She couldn't be happy really without that sacrifice. In fact it is probably the thing that will make her happiest to feel that she has saved me. That stuff about throwing herself at Monty was obviously false. Why on earth did I believe anything Pinn said? Harriet couldn't possibly love anybody but me.

I must see her, thought Blaise, standing once again outside the kitchen door with the intermittently yapping dogs in a group behind him. I must see her and explain it all while it's so clear in my mind. And he yearned now for his dear wife, to hold her again in his arms and see the light of forgiveness in her face. He rattled the door, trying to estimate whether it was only locked or also bolted. It seemed to be only locked, and the key would be there in the lock on the inside. If he broke the glass panel of the door he could reach in and turn the key. He looked about to find a stone or something with which to shatter the glass. There was a broken piece of paving stone lying on the terrace and Blaise picked it up, weighing it in his hand. As he did this Ajax, in whose mind (already disturbed by hunger: Harriet had forgotten to feed the dogs before leaving and they had been fasting for nearly two days) this action revived some awful puppyhood memory, set up a quick high-pitched hysterical scream, rather like the continuous loud crying of a human being in shock. 'Oh shut up!' said Blaise, menacing the dog with the stone. He moved to the door and struck the glass violently, shattering the lower part of the panel. The other dogs had begun to bark too, uttering an unnatural frenzied clamourous yell.

Blaise had put his hand through the jagged hole when suddenly the most agonizing physical pain he had ever felt shot upward through his whole body, and he stumbled, tearing his wrist upon the sharp glass. For a moment, in agony and amazement, he could not think what had happened, it was like a heart attack or being shot. Then he realized that Ajax had bitten him deeply behind the ankle, completely severing the tendon like a cut string. Blaise screamed and turned, grasping at the door for support and again bringing his hand down onto the broken glass. Ajax, snarling and baring his teeth, confronted him, and Blaise saw in a clear awful flash of vision blood, his blood, upon the animal's muzzle. The hysterically barking dogs were all about him now. He felt a tug and a grab at his trouser leg and Panda's strong jaws nipping his calf. Then Ajax sprang and Blaise's fist caught a glancing blow upon the blood-stained mouth, knuckles grating along teeth. I must run, thought Blaise, only I can't run, I can't. He tried to run, trying to overcome the agony in his foot, trying to be winged by fear to hop and leap his way out of the frenzied circle of yapping snapping dogs. Seagull had jumped up to bite his swinging hand. Blaise saw the blood flowing freely from his cut wrist and his gashed palm and complete panic overwhelmed him. He saw far off as if it were a refuge, a gap in the fence leading into Monty's garden and he tried to run, hopping on his sound leg and dragging the other. He must just manage to make himself run. For a few steps he simulated the familiar motion, while the maddened dogs tore at his clothing. Then he stumbled and fell and Ajax's strong white teeth came for his throat.

Harriet was not used to travelling alone. Of course she was not *alone* since Luca was with her, but she was responsible for him, he could not protect her from the brusque demands of officials, made now in a language she could not understand. Luca had done well however. He had brought his passport (of which he was very proud) along with him in a little bag of treasures from Fulham. He had even reminded Harriet that she would need *her* passport. He had held her hand all the time on the aeroplane. Though extremely excited, he was the more composed of the two. Harriet was distraught, tending to tremble and drop things. When she fumbled for passports, tickets, money everything seemed to come jumping out of her bag at once and falling on the ground. She felt clumsy and hot with embarrassment and anxiety. I suppose I ought to change some pounds into marks now, she said to herself, but she had no will to leave the seat in the Hanover airport lounge where she had taken refuge with Luca while they waited for their luggage to come through from the aeroplane. She snuggled the child against her side, drawing her arm around his shoulder, while he looked up at her with his shining calm dark eyes. He was hugging in his arms the mirrorwork elephant and also a small teddy bear in a tartan uniform which he and Harriet had selected at Heathrow.

Harriet was already regretting her flight, though she felt too that it was somehow an inevitable path which must now be trodden to the end. She had sent a wire to Adrian to say that she was coming, but had had no reply from him. Perhaps there had been no time for a reply. She had been incapable of counting up the hours. Perhaps he was away on an exercise or had been moved from Hohne since his last letter. Adrian, once a great letter-writer, did not write often now. Doubtless he had had nothing pleasant to tell of his life and prospects since he had failed the staff college exam. Hohne, though she had never visited it, was not a stranger to Harriet's imagination since her father had ended his career as Range Liaison Officer there. Adrian had pitied his father's fate. Now he was at Hohne himself, commanding the HQ battery, another unsuccessful Major Derwent. He had described to Harriet the bare sandy tank-ravaged ranges and the desert of Luneberg beyond. An end-of-the-world destination for an end-of-the-world journey.

Of course Harriet knew from her general experience of the Army that even if Adrian were away his brother-officers (she repeated this comforting term to herself) would assist her. But she did not know how, without a word of German, she was to get to Hohne. She must get money, she must ask somebody. But oh, she felt so hungry (unlike Luca she had been unable to eat on the aeroplane) and so tired and so bewildered and frightened. Blaise had always looked after her on journeys. The desire to reach the shelter of her brother's protection was at the moment her overwhelming urge. She needed to be where she would be quietly controlled and looked after. She pictured the near haven where she could put Luca to bed and then cry at last. And Adrian would say, 'Well, what are you going to do?' and she would say 'I don't know' and even that would be a comfort. Her brother was the mildest and gentlest of men. Perhaps he ought not to have been a soldier, only father pushed him into Sandhurst.

Exactly *why* Harriet had fled was now, in her weakness and her tiredness, obscure to her. It had seemed like a matter of principle. But what was the principle? She could remember saying to herself: I will not be Blaise's slave. I will not be *their* slave. Was that the principle? Was that what principles were like? Were not these just feelings? As feelings she could still re-enact and reinhabit them. She thought, it was somehow right to come away. If I had stayed it would have been impossible not to fall into a role of acquiescence. I know what Blaise is like. I have found out what he is like, he would make me pity him, he would make it a matter of rescue. I am not the good person I used to think that I was. If I were forced to be their victim I could not do it with clear eyes and a humble loving mind.

I would do it with secret resentment and hatred. Not even that, for resentment and hatred are forms of strength. I would become weak and spiteful and demoralized and crazed with humiliation. I would writhe like a half-killed worm and would have no way of thinking about myself. And Harriet recalled with anguish that wonderful calm self-possession which had seemed so invincible and would never now come again.

Yes, she could rehearse these feelings still, but her mind and her heart were already changing. She regretted bitterly having gone away without David. She had booked the flight for the afternoon leaving no interval in London, so great had been her haste to escape, her fear of some new appeal from Blaise. She had simply not had the will to change her plan. Here were the aeroplane tickets, like authentic messages from fate, and in default of other ideas about what to do she had simply obeyed them. She needed Adrian's support and counsel, not least because he seemed now to be the last person left. Blaise, Monty, Edgar, Magnus, all gone, and now David too had rejected her. The cruelty of his disappearance was an awful just judgment. That too was part of a machine from which she had not, for all her 'feelings' and her 'principles', the spirit or the courage really to escape.

Indeed, what made Harriet, as she sat paralysed, waiting for the luggage to arrive from the aeroplane, feel now most desperate of all was the slow automatic realization that running away had altered nothing. It was an empty gesture. It was not a life-giving leap into freedom. What after all could she do? In the end she had nobody but Blaise. Adrian would be very sympathetic, very rational, very kind, but he would soon want her to go away, to go *home*. There was no solution, it all came back to Blaise in the end. No one else needs me, she thought, except the children, and they can't save me. Blaise needs me terribly, he needs my forgiveness to perfect his happiness with Emily. He needs Hood House and a pretence that it can go on and on as before. Perhaps David needs that too. It is certainly what Blaise needs and wants. He cannot confront what he has done. He will beg to be let off and not to be punished. He will pester me for a token pardon and then he will treat me as he used to treat Emily, only it will be easier because I am so much less aggressive and Hood House is there. I can revive Hood House and turn on the heaters and pack up Blaise's clothes if he wants them and be there to be visited. And he will visit me and grovel and accuse himself and speak slightingly of Emily and indulge his emotions and his guilt and return to her feeling stronger and cleaner. And he will bless me sincerely and think I am good and tell Emily I am 'wonderful' and they will laugh together about me. And I shall be alone. This kindness to him, which is just weakness really, is my only and my last resource. I shall come to it, I am coming to it, I am thinking exactly what he wants me to think, and the only escape from this is a kind of violence of which I am not capable. There is no great calm space elsewhere, thought Harriet, where a tree stands between two saints and raises its pure significant head into a golden sky. What had seemed to be an intuition of freedom and virtue was for her simply a trivial enigma, an occasion for little meaningless emotions. She was caught in her own mind and condemned by her own being.

'Policemen!' said Luca.

Harriet looked up. There was a curious group of uniformed men standing in the doorway of the lounge. Harriet stared. The tense still attitudes of the men announced something unusual. Danger. Harriet's heart suddenly began to beat very fast. She turned and saw next to her a stout German whom she had noticed on the 'plane. His face struck her with terror. It had gone completely white, his mouth open, his eyes staring towards the centre of the room. Harriet looked there. In the midst of a deadly quietness and frozen immobility of everybody else, two young men were standing together, one of them holding a long glittering tube in his hands. More police appeared in another doorway. Someone called out peremptorily in German. A woman screamed. One of the policemen raised a revolver. There was a sudden crackling of deafening sound and the room became full of desperate agonized screaming. The stout man beside Harriet fell to the floor bleeding profusely. Screaming herself, Harriet covered Luca with her body.

'What did you think of Uncle Adrian?' said Blaise.

'Stuffed shirt,' said Emily.

'I think he's rather sweet,' said Blaise. 'We never got on of course. He always regarded me as a charlatan.'

'You are a charlatan, dear. But is he really a soldier? Why wasn't he in uniform?'

'They don't wear uniform off duty except in war.'

'He looked like a bank clerk to me.'

'I wish you'd stop buttering the cats' paws, it's a ludicrous idea anyway. Little Bilham has walked all over the Indian carpet.'

'I hope you liked my little touches in the drawing-room.'

'No, I did not. I told you not to change things without asking me.'

'And I told you I had to make it my house and you agreed. Wasn't it funny about Uncle Adrian wanting Lucky?'

'Rather touching. He said he wanted something that had specially belonged to Harriet.'

'I notice you didn't offer him anything valuable!'

'He didn't want anything valuable. I gave him all that stuff off her desk.'

'You are comically mingy. What are you making that face for?'

'Because I am in pain. Have you forgotten?'

'Oh, you mean your foot.'

'Yes. I mean my foot. I shall be lame for the rest of my life. You don't seem to mind.'

'Fortunately you have a sedentary occupation. I expect you're glad that dog's gone. I don't suppose you want to see another dog as long as you live.'

Blaise had had a narrow escape. He had had to have twenty-five stitches in his neck as well as an operation on his leg, but Ajax's teeth had not severed an important artery. Almost immediately after he fell David and Pinn ran out of the house and beat the dogs off. When Monty arrived it was all over.

In the long confused aftermath Ajax and Panda and Babu and Lawrence and Seagull had all been destroyed. So had poor Buffy, who had done nothing but stand on the lawn and bark, as usual not daring to join the other dogs in whatever strange thing they were up to together. Ganimede (certainly a guilty dog) was saved by the resourcefulness of Mrs Raines-Bloxham, who had had a clandestine relationship with him for some time, feeding him secretly in her kitchen, and who simply came round and removed him before the situation had been properly clarified. Lucky, exemplifying his name, survived too by accident. Possibly because he was not yet integrated into the pack and was not used to being fed regularly in the same place, he had shown more initiative when challenged by hunger and had wandered off to explore Monty's dustbins: in the course of which exploration he had been unwittingly provided with an alibi by Kiki, who had shut him unnoticed into Monty's garage when she moved thence her car, which she had thus secreted in case Blaise should see it in Monty's drive and be grieved. (She was a thoughtful girl.) So Lucky, discovered later, was deemed not to have been involved. Blaise had been about to return him to the Dogs' Home when Adrian appeared and, on hearing that Harriet had doted on the animal, adopted him.

Harriet had perished in the massacre at Hanover airport. She had saved Luca's life, shielding him with her bullet-riddled body. Blaise, telephoned by Adrian, had flown out to bring home his wife's remains and his shocked alienated child. Since that appalling moment Luca had not spoken, had not uttered a word or a sound, looking mutely out at the world with terrified eyes which seemed bright with pain as if bright with tears. He recognized Blaise and his mother, but put them aside gently with helpless animal gestures when they tried to tend him. Emily wept long and long over him, but consented to have him taken away to a special institute for mentally disturbed children. The psychiatrist there did not regard his case as hopeless.

Soon after the funeral Emily moved into Hood House and immediately after that Blaise and Emily were quietly married in a registry office. Pinn and Maurice Guimarron were the witnesses. Blaise had informed Monty by letter and Monty had sent good wishes but had not turned up. On Emily's arrival at Hood House David had moved back to Locketts where, so far as Blaise knew, he still was. Blaise had not yet set himself to woo and reconcile his elder son. Later there

301

would be a time for that, a time for all the things that had to be done and ought to be done so as to set the world in order again. Oddly enough the world *could* be set in order, that Blaise knew in the midst of the weary aching blank mood which had possessed him since the first shock had worn away. Secretly, cautiously, he felt that he had come through the fire and had probably emerged unscathed. He had *survived*. That Harriet should simply have been killed, meaninglessly slaughtered by people who knew nothing of *his* predicament, that his problem could have been so absolutely solved in this extraordinary way, struck Blaise first as being unendurably accidental, and later as being fated. It had all happened so quickly that for a time he could not believe that Harriet had gone, that she had been thoroughly and forever mopped up and tidied away. How terribly complete death was, how strangely clean. For a long time sheer shock kept him physically sick, but this sickness seemed unconnected with Harriet. Meanwhile he kept, in a kind of almost superstitious fright expecting her, looking for letters, listening for telephone calls. Was there no final message? And in the old ordinary accustomed parts of himself he missed her dreadfully.

'I miss her so, oh I do miss her so!' he kept moaning to Emily, as if this testimony were very important. He felt an obsessive need, in his conscience, to keep on as it were holding up her picture in front of Emily. And Emily recognized the need and respected it: which indeed was easy enough for her to do. The fates had done Emily an amazingly good turn, and she could afford to be generous. She was relaxed about it though. She did not pretend any sorrow, nor did she trouble her imagination about Blaise's sufferings which she regarded as strictly temporary. She concealed her satisfaction under a gentle cool tact, though every now and then she would murmur something like: 'How awfully considerate of Mrs Placid to go off and get herself massacred.' And Blaise respected *that*. Emily reckoned that these little brutalities, these attempts to trivialize the horror of it, would be good for him somehow, would make him feel that life simply had to stagger on without becoming a nightmare. And perhaps Emily was right.

Blaise never saw Harriet's body, which had been identified by Adrian. He was indeed determined not to see it, though Adrian said the face was unmarked and obviously thought that Blaise ought to see the body. Adrian organized all the formalities for bringing the coffin back to England. Adrian

302

in fact decided that it should be brought back. Blaise, in a frenzy of self-protective haste, would have preferred an immediate interment in Germany. Formality, which clearly comforted Adrian, did nothing for Blaise. Adrian also arranged the funeral and burial in a big London cemetery where their father and mother were already at rest. ('He will visit her grave regularly,' Blaise said to Emily with surprise.) Harriet, at death, passed back into the hands of the Derwent family with a naturalness for which Blaise felt weakly grateful. It seemed to diminish his loss a little if it turned out in the end that she was really theirs after all.

He dreamed continually about Harriet and felt in dreams a piercing compassion and also a fear which he dared not allow into his ordinary life. In one dream he saw her feeding the dogs and crying desperately over them with some dreadful anxiety. In another he saw her face badly bruised but not bleeding, looking at him accusingly. She is not dead, he thought, she is only hurt and I have hurt her. How could I have done that to my dear wife who is so kind and good? Waking, he soon put away these refinements of pity and terror. He aimed at simpler modes of survival and ways of passing the necessary time. He allowed himself, almost as if rationing them, periods when he grieved about her, mourning the maim in himself which her awful death had made. With swift mechanical efficiency his egoism took its countermeasures, and had begun to do so from the second when Adrian's voice on the long-distance telephone had informed him of Harriet's fate. I will not allow this horror to lodge itself deep in me, he thought. I will not let the abomination of death make a place in my life. I must immediately think about myself, about my future, about how Emily will console me, about how I shall one day be happy. I will not think that it is my fault. I will not think about Harriet's sufferings, they are over. I will not be destroyed by this, I will turn it to the best account I can and heal myself through my responsibilities to the living. I will try to lead a simpler, better, easier life without problems, and let the cleanness of death do at least this for me. After all I do need rest now. I will not live with a ghost. Go away, he said in his mind, go, go, go, as if he were cutting off the little hands or tentacles of dreadful pity which were reaching up at him from the grave.

Meanwhile he and Emily worked silently, surreptitiously, feverishly, like people trying to conceal a crime, to erase all traces of Harriet's existence from Hood House. A perpetual

303

bonfire burnt in the garden onto which the spouses, usually avoiding each other in this chore, quietly piled Harriet's more dispensable belongings, the poor rubble of Harriet's finished life : the contents of her desk, her childhood mementoes, the water-colours of Wales, her books of recipes, her newspaper cuttings about her father's regiment, picture postcards from her father and brother, drawerfuls of cosmetics and combs and ribbons and old belts, even underwear. The strange funeral pyre gradually consumed them all. Harriet's clothes and her few inexpensive jewels had gone to Oxfam. Only a silver-gilt bracelet engraved with roses had been coveted by Emily, who had prompted Blaise to urge her to keep it. She had never worn it however. The mirrorwork elephant and the uniformed teddy bear had returned from Germany with Luca, and the teddy bear had gone on with him to the institution. The elephant had somehow been left behind at Hood House. Blaise found its charred remains one day upon the bonfire and pondered the mood which had led Emily to decree its destruction.

Harriet's will made Blaise her heir of course, and he was interested as well as pleased to discover that she had possessed considerable assets, inherited from her father, of which he had known nothing. Did this concealment, he wondered, indicate some area of mistrust of him in Harriet's mind? Perhaps she had simply wanted to surprise him with her little nest-egg on a rainy day. She had spoken of 'securities' once when they had been discussing his plan to become a doctor. More probably she herself had not known their value. The money was certainly welcome now when there were so many expenses, such as redecorating the house and altering the kitchen to suit Emily. Fortunately too Blaise's practice was continuing to flourish, though with an almost complete change of clientele. A large number of the old patients had left, declaring themselves cured. As he now worked mainly with groups, he could take on many more people, and even then there was a waiting list. Blaise and Emily still occasionally talked of the possibility of his becoming a doctor, but neither felt that this was now an urgent matter.

(In fact, though Blaise never knew it, his patients had largely benefited from the triple shock of Horace Ainsley's death, of Harriet's, and of Blaise himself being nearly killed by dogs. Surviving these catastrophes, unhurt by them, increased by them, they all felt better. At a party given by Maurice Guimarron, Angelica Mendelssohn agreed with

Septimus Leech that they had never been taken in by Blaise for a single moment. 'And he imagined we adored him!' 'I can't think why I went on!' said Angelica. 'Neither can I,' said Stanley Tumbelholme, joining the group. 'I feel so much better since that ghastly creep passed out of my life. How I wish those dogs had eaten him up!' 'I've nearly finished my novel,' said Septimus 'and Penelope says she can sleep like a log nowadays.' Miriam Lister laughed archly. Septimus and Penelope were shortly to be married. Only poor Jeannie Batwood was silent. She was desperately in love with Blaise and could not now leave him, even though her husband was threatening divorce proceedings.)

Blaise felt, on the whole, relief at the removal of Luca from the scene, though he was distressed for Emily. It was a terrible thing to admit, but he had never really understood Luca or his own feelings about Luca and had never loved the boy as he ought. Luca, conceived as a burdensome problem, had remained one for Blaise. The strange child, as it grew, inspired guilt and fear. It was a relief to have it officially *classified* as subnormal and taken away to be looked after by experts. At this period a holiday from Luca's presence was in any case essential; later on decisions could be taken with a clearer mind. And although Emily cried a good deal about it, he felt that she too was relieved when that terrible incomprehensible silent suffering was taken away from before her face. This leaves more energy for other things, he thought, such as looking after David: though as yet he had scarcely attempted to do this, and Emily never mentioned the boy. Blaise had twice visited David at Locketts, but talk between them had proved impossible. David remained obstinately taciturn, then politely dismissed his father. Blaise, who had hoped for some little sign of mercy, felt he could not soon again so expose himself. He refrained from any reflection upon these meetings, quietly blurring them away. I will deal with David later, he thought. Just now he is better left with Monty and Edgar. What most immediately matters is Emily, settling her here, making our union real, making her believe in it at last. And once again he thought to himself how wonderful it was to be able to make a woman happy.

And now he was married to Emily McHugh. They faced each other as man and wife. The long fight had ended or had changed. There was to be a new era of wars and revolutions of an entirely different type. The badinage sounded the same but with the disappearance of real danger had lost

305

some of its cutting edge. Had fear really been an important ingredient in their old love? Had he perhaps at least enjoyed his sense of *her* fear? Now it was as if, behind each exchange, they were constantly saying, 'It's all right, darling, it's all right. One can't now be lost or ruined or destroyed any more. It's all a game, you know.' The ferocity in her which he had savoured so now seemed innocuously fake, or at any rate no longer sharpened by circumstance so as to pierce or thrill him. There was a gentler calmer understanding between them, almost a conspiracy, a conspiracy in favour of happiness. It was like an agreement of much older people. As he apprehended this Blaise found himself thinking hungrily of happiness and wondering if this less exciting prize were after all available to him and his second wife. He could not remember the quality of his very first pre-Emily happiness with Harriet, that time had become legendary and all but inaccessible to his mind. Nor could he clarify in memory that transformation of his early affections which had made him feel that Harriet was his sacred love and Emily his profane. As he now edged and nudged the past about, instinctively ordering it for a diminuation of pain, he could only remember clearly (or was he partly inventing it?) with a new emphasis and yet also as a form of pity for her, his unhappiness with Harriet, his loneliness with her, his sense of having made the wrong choice and being in the wrong place.

But in what place was he now? The fact of being *married* to Emily came to him with a kind of shock of innocence and blankness, like a very white light, and while it made him feel deeply tender towards her it seemed to diminish their old vertiginous feeling of a unique kinship. Perhaps this kinship had indeed been partly a product of adversity and of the excitements of fear. Now they were no longer living dangerously and must appreciate other qualities and see each other with differences. Yet the thought of their old love remained to them as a token, or as a sort of guarantee, a reassuring flag which at certain times they flew. They had been sure once that they were quite specially made for each other, they had walked through a fire for this and deserved a reward. And even if the reward was puzzlingly different from what they had expected, at any rate the fire had been real. Blaise felt the marks of mortality upon him. He would carry scars and limp for the rest of his life. And as he nursed himself carefully out of the horror of Harriet's death, he felt older and even more self-indulgent and noticed with pleasure the symptoms of a similar self-indulgence in Emily. They would have money, comfort, a pleasant house, a pleasant easy life. They had suffered together, and would now enjoy worldly consolations and rest at last. How ordinary we shall become, he thought without much regret; and he felt in himself a sort of achieved moral mediocrity, a resignation to being unambitious and selfish and failed which gave him a secret wry delight.

'I'm glad Adrian's over,' said Emily. 'It's another phase in the phasing out of you-know-who.'

'I thought he was never going.'

'Look, I think you should see Monty.'

'About David.'

'No. About the orchard. I want the orchard.'

'I'll write to him.'

'Why not ask him here for a drink?'

'I thought you didn't like him.'

'I did, only I wasn't going to let on. Anyway I like him now. He's the only celebrity we're ever likely to know.'

'Well I don't like him now.'

'I shall go and see him.'

'You won't.'

'You see, I can still madden you.'

'Lay off, kid, I'm tired.'

'I want the orchard, I want the orchard, I want the orchard.'

'All right. I'll try and get it for you.'

Of course it's not true that I don't like him now, thought Blaise. But what a sort of evil genius he has been to me. I don't want to see him, not yet anyway, because he makes me feel inferior. He always did, but I suppose I enjoyed it once. Now I don't and that's part of the 'failure' too, that Monty doesn't 'work' for me any more. Really in a way the whole thing was his doing, something he just did to amuse himself. He made my thing with Emily possible by inventing Magnus Bowles, and he made Harriet run away by killing him. Poor Magnus committing suicide was the last straw for Harriet. Monty really is the king of cynics. Or more like a dreaming god, making awful things happen in a sort of trance. That's what he's been like to me. And really I suppose, in a dreadful way, he hasn't done too badly as our local divinity. It has all ended fairly happily for those who are left alive. Out of so much guilt and muddle at least there is a new beginning for me and Em. And because of Monty

I don't have to think too badly of myself either. It was not my fault Harriet ran off to Hanover, it was Monty's fault. If he'd looked after her properly she wouldn't have gone. I didn't kill her, Monty did. He was the immediate cause. Let him have the guilt then and keep it for himself. He has eaten it up as he eats up everything. Let him burst with it like Magnus Bowles. Of course one can't be friends with a power maniac like that. The sin of pride isolates people more than any other sin. Monty likes to think he's Lucifer, but really in the end he isn't even Magnus. He's thin and small, as thin and mean and shrivelled up as Milo Fane. Yes, that's who Monty is after all, just Milo in the end with intellect instead of nerve. Well, I'll write to him about the orchard. I wonder how little I can decently offer?

He's jealous, the pet, the angel, thought Emily McHugh. He think's I'm going to start something with Monty, as if I would, or if I did it would be simply to stir Blaise up a bit. I mustn't let him get too sluggish or take me too much for granted just because we're married. Emily had never lived so richly and vividly inside herself in her whole life. She now experienced so much which she could not tell to Blaise (simply, like a mystic, for lack of a vocabulary in which to convey such transports) that she sometimes felt that simply by being conscious she must be constantly deceiving him. Also of course she had to draw a decent veil over her absolute satisfaction at the demise of Harriet. She did not feel wild triumph, rather the deep pleasant sense of a task well done, as if, in some quite guiltless and proper way, she herself had eliminated her rival.

Emily felt in these days that she had become something huge, as if her stunted and deprived nature had suddenly grown, expanding upwards and outwards so as to contain what had formerly contained it. She contained Blaise. She felt now, in the tenderest way, larger than he was, stronger, wiser, and she watched him and read him with meticulous loving closeness. She saw, as never before, his faults, his old faults and his new. She saw all in him that was bogus, all that made him the sublime humbug, the sheer dear old charlatan that he was. She observed the coiling protective mechanics of his anxious egoism, his determination not to suffer the horror, his quick busy instinctive destruction of Harriet inside himself. She even saw the imperfection of his love for her and saw it in the *light* of her own more perfect love for him. She too felt the diminution or change of their

308

so specialized 'kinship', but she did not grieve, understanding it rather as an opening out of their love to the wide world, which enriched them with a whole new territory of the emotions. All this she had somehow prophetically experienced at that wonderful moment in the little registry office when Blaise had at last slipped the longed-for wedding ring onto her finger, and Pinn and Maurice had kissed her and called her 'Mrs Gavender', and she had thought, Blaise and I are *married*. She was an ordinary married woman with a husband and a home. Everything now could be an exercise of her love, including the simple worldly satisfactions which were for her a part of the innocence bestowed by marriage. She loved Hood House, loved tending it and embellishing it and feeling proud of it, and she only wished she could somewhere find her stepfather, if the old swine was still alive, and let him see the stylish way she lived now in a real gentleman's residence.

Of course she was unhappy about Luca, but the unhappiness was circumscribed by a determination, similar to that of her husband, not to suffer to excess. Luca was at present, for her, in a state of suspension and she tried to feel about him as if he were asleep. The psychiatrist had advised no visits for a month or two. Later on they would see. Emily had burnt the elephant not because Harriet had given it to the child, nor even (which Blaise had not noticed) because there was a tiny smear of Harriet's blood upon it, but simply because the sight of it suggested the reality of Luca so dreadfully: the possibility of deciding to go and see him, the obscure idea of his ultimate return. How would Luca return? Would he return? All this threatened unbearable mental pain. But Emily was not going to destroy her heart with these questions. She dwelt rather upon the idea that Luca was being helped and healed; and she recalled the awful fear for him, and indeed of him, which she had constantly felt in the old days, when he was so strangely silent with her. Must she not now feel relief to know that, for the time, he had ceased to be a special vulnerable perishable little boy for whom she was so frighteningly responsible, and had become a case like others with which highly qualified experts knew just how to deal? She did feel the relief and took it intelligently for her comfort. The best possible was being done for him, and that must for the present suffice. About David, Emily had no worries at all. David was nearly grown-up. She could almost cross off upon the calendar the weeks and months which must elapse before David should be grown-up. And when that time came he would simply go away and not trouble them any more.

And Emily, as she sat in the bright transformed Hood House kitchen and gazed vague and wide-eyed with love and with cunning understanding pity at her husband, had another reason for feeling that she must spoil herself a little and keep all horrors far away. (The old wooden kitchen table had been banished to the garage and the red tablecloths had gone to Oxfam. Now there was a shiny round white Scandinavian table with a heat-resistant surface and six white chairs to match. All the crumbly shabby darkness was gone.) She had been to the doctor today and had confirmed her suspicion that she was pregnant. When she had heard this she had felt a sudden instant confidence that Luca would get well. He would be cured and come home and they would all live together happily ever after. She had not yet told the good news to Blaise, and now she was anticipating the pleasure of doing so. How he would fuss about it being a girl! For the first time in her life Emily McHugh looked at her future and saw it stretch out before her like a golden land.

'*Moules?*'
   'No.'
   'Not a seafood man?'
   'No.'
   'Well, *oeufs* somehow? *Mornay*? *Timbale de foie de volaille*? Avocado? Or how about smoked salmon? *Quenelles de brochet*? You can't foreswear all fish, we can't have a mockery made of serious eating. Smoked trout?'
   'You choose for me,' said David. A tear spilled from his eye to his cheek and he rubbed it away with a slow gesture.
   Edgar saw the tear and returned his attention to the menu. 'I suggest we both start with smoked salmon. Yes. The *poulet sous cloche* is good here, but—Perhaps a steak, we could have a *châteaubriand* between us. Unless you'd rather have the game pie? No, I think not too. Oh, wine waiter! Yes. Now

let me see, the *Graacher Himmelreich*—not *spätleser* that year, that would be really too sweet at the beginning. Then—then the Pommard '64. Excellent. Yes, we are ready to order now, thank you.'

'So you're driving Monty to Mockingham this afternoon?' said David.

'Yes. Don't be angry with Monty.'

'I'm not angry. I'm just sort of disappointed.'

'Because he hasn't had a big talk with you?'

'He doesn't seem to care. And he's so sort of spiritless.'

'Spirit-less. That he could never be.'

'He just doesn't seem to function any more.'

'For you, perhaps he doesn't. We all have our Montys, and they can be disappointing, but perhaps that's our fault for wanting the wrong thing. Monty is a good deal fonder of you than you seem to imagine.'

'I don't think Monty is fond of anybody. Sorry.'

'He just feels he can't help you at present. See it as humility. Some people help themselves by helping others, and this cheers them up because it's an exercise of power. But Monty mistrusts that sort of power. Maybe because he could have so much of it if he chose.'

'It doesn't seem right for Monty to be humble,' said David. 'I don't want him like that.'

'I know. We don't like our Montys humble. We want them to be proud. But that may not be good for *them*. You'll see him again anyway at Mockingham when you come. There's a lot of Monty ahead.'

Edgar had invited David to Mockingham. Edgar had invited David to come with him to the British School at Athens. David could go on a dig in the Peloponnese if he wanted to. The dig had already turned up a gorgeous torso by Phaidimos and a fine calyx by Douris. None of this helped at all. David could not live the terrible death of his mother, he felt hourly that he could not survive it. Compared with that *fact* even his father's obscene hasty marriage, even that woman living at Hood House and changing it all and spoiling it all, was just a foul irritation. His mind felt impossible, like an impossible visual object or like a huge tattered thing which someone was trying to drag through a narrow pipe by awful force. Nothing helped. Well, perhaps Edgar helped a little.

'Don't cry,' said Edgar. 'You can stop yourself. Try the hock and tell me what you think of it.'

311

'Don't be silly! All wine tastes the same to me!'

'No it doesn't, David. Now drink some and concentrate. I'll teach you all about wine at Mockingham. I've got a marvellous cellar there. You'll like it at Mockingham. I'm putting you in the turret room.'

'That's the nineteenth-century folly?'

'Yes. Thank God my mother never had the cash to pull it down. The turret is octagonal. My great grandfather admired Frederick the Second. There are windows all round and you can see the whole valley. It's jolly cold in winter though. In winter we'll put you in the west wing.'

' "We"?'

'Monty and I.'

'The west wing is Regency?'

'Queen Anne. It's less romantic than the Elizabethan part, but far more comfortable.'

'And you'll help me with Greek like you said?'

'Of course. When you're up at Oxford reading Greats you'll be quite near. You can come every vac, and at week-ends, and bring a reading party of your friends. You must regard it as a home.'

'That's just as well,' said David, 'as I haven't any other one.'

'Don't say that. They need you.'

'You keep saying so.'

'They do.'

'They don't. They are self-sufficient. They regard me as part of—her—'

'Steady.'

'They have cut her off, cut her out, it's as if they were killing her a second time, making her not to have been. And I've got to go too. They're just determined to forget the past and be happy. They are happy. If you'd only seen them at the door when some horrible new furniture was being delivered. They were like a couple of children, laughing, happy, petting each other in front of the van man. And they're burning all her stuff. They didn't even ask me. They're like Hitler, just destroying everything—'

'Steady, steady. They can't be happy. Your father can't be. Think, David, think. He must need you.'

'Why should he? He comes to see me now and then because I'm on his conscience, but he can't talk to me because we haven't anything to talk about except *her* and he's already driven her out of his mind.'

'Of course he hasn't. He's just too upset to talk. You must help him.'

'He's not upset. He's looking after himself.'

'And Emily. Remember she's had a bad time. You must forgive your father if he wants to look after her now.'

'Let him. But then he can keep away from me. I'm not going to license it all for him. I can't do it.'

'You can do something. You can be just a little gentle and kind.'

'It would be sheer hypocrisy.'

'Be a hypocrite then. To ape goodness is a bit of the battle. It may be even half of it.'

'You think he cares what I think. He doesn't. That's what's so — awful.'

'No, no, you have a lot of power, David. You are the final reconciler. In the end — without you — they will — starve.'

'Let them starve.'

'You have inherited your mother's part of reconciliation. It must be perfected in you.'

'I don't know what you mean. I hate them.'

'For your own sake too you mustn't. You have got to survive. I don't mean forget. You have got to become a whole human being and live as one. Hating will only hinder that. You must just — let them be — in your mind. They will need your mercy.'

'I feel I'm in my mother's place. I feel I am her. I'm all that's left of her. No one else cares. Well, Uncle Adrian does, I suppose, but he isn't anybody.'

'He is, as it happens, and you must be kind to him too. Did you write to him like I told you to?'

'No. They're totally wicked and they just want to be allowed to get away with it.'

'*Will* you write to Uncle Adrian?'

'Yes! They want me to *nod* and let them get on with it.'

'Then you must nod. One must not judge. One must nod. You must make your mind quiet. Have you tried? *Sauce bearnaise*?'

'Yes, I tried — of course I couldn't exactly pray — She taught me to pray when I was a child — Oh, God, I mustn't remember —'

'It doesn't matter what you call it. Keep trying. And stop being afraid of Christ. He's just the local name of God.'

'You don't think it's insincere?'

'No. I don't believe the dogmas, but still Christ is mine and I'm not going to be deprived of him by the church.'

313

'Did you ever discuss all this with Monty?'

'Yes, but—Monty is so ambitious. I daresay he's right to be for him.'

'You said he was humble.'

'Yes, yes, but he's an absolutist all the same.'

'And one shouldn't be?'

'I don't know. One mustn't worry too much. All human solutions are temporary. Pass your glass will you, dear boy? One has to live in one's own little local world of religion mostly. For nearly everyone religion is something primitive. We hardly ever get beyond the beginning any more than we do in philosophy. If it's natural to you to cry out "Christ help me!" cry it and then be quiet. You may be helped.'

'But how do I know what it means, how do I know what's true?'

'That sort of truth is local too. I don't mean any relativism nonsense. Of course there's science and history and so on. I mean just that one's ordinary tasks are usually immediate and simple and one's own truth lives in these tasks. Not to deceive oneself, not to protect one's pride with false ideas, never to be pretentious or bogus, always to try to be lucid and quiet. There's a kind of pure speech of the mind which one must try to attain. To attain it is to be in the truth, one's own truth, which needn't mean any big apparatus of belief. And when one is *there* one will be truthful and kind and able to see other people and what they need!'

'And you say you aren't an absolutist!'

'No. You see, it's awfully difficult really. I'm just talking. But you will be kind to your father?'

'I don't know.'

'Now what about some treacle pud, it's awfully good here and you haven't got a weight problem. Or all those gluey things from Asia Minor? Figs? *Crêpes suzette*? Just cheese? You don't mind if I have the *crêpes* and then join you on the cheese? Waiter! We need some more wine. I think a little Barsac with the pudding, oh of course you aren't having any— well, perhaps this Moselle—'

'I keep seeing my mother. I even see her in the street. It's like a constant presence, only it's so ghastly. And I keep wondering what it was like for her at that moment. I don't want her to become a nightmare to me.'

'Pray then. Ask for help. Take refuge. That can be done at any time. Whenever it seems like nightmare.'

'Yes, yes. I'll have the Camembert.'

'Wait. Let me inspect it. Nice and ripe. Yes, you should set up a lifelong habit.'

'Of eating Camembert?'

'Of quieting your mind. Or at least of watching it's strange antics from a serene viewpoint.'

'Talking of strange antics—in the middle of everything— I keep on having those fantasies—the ones I told you about— I can't stop them.'

'About Kiki St Loy and tearing her clothes off?'

'Yes. Isn't it awful? It seems so wicked now to be thinking about a girl in that way.'

'One's mind is such an old rubbish heap. All sorts of little bits of machinery start up. Don't bother about them. Watch them a while, then make a change.'

'They're so *detailed*—'

'I daresay they are. But if that's your sexual fantasy life I shouldn't think you have much to worry about. Everyone has sexual fantasies.'

'Do they? Do you still have any sexual fantasies, Edgar? What are they about?'

Edgar laughed considerably. 'Well—well—well—I say, shall we be devils and have Irish coffee?'

Edgar let the Bentley purr to a halt a little way away from Locketts. He had left David (who was now occupying Adrian's flat) in town bound for the British Museum. He stopped the car short of the house underneath a large cherry tree which leaned out over the roadway. He pushed his seat back a little and relaxed, reclining his head and looking up at the blue sky through the branches. He saw that the tree was in copious flower and thought to himself how odd, a cherry tree in flower at midsummer. And it's a wild cherry too, and they usually flower earlier. The woods at Mockingham are white with them in April, even in March in a warm spring. Then he saw that the flowers did not belong to the cherry but were the flowers of a huge white rose which had clambered up into the tree and climbed right up to the top and was spilling out over the

L

branches in pendant showers of small white blossoms. And as he looked up and saw the very blue sky between, beyond, its brightness lending a radiant transparency to the innumerable flowers, a few white petals fluttered slowly down and attached themselves with a deliberate gentle insistence to the Bentley's windscreen.

Edgar delayed so, for the luxury of a little period of reflection before going to fetch Monty. There was plenty of time. The drive to Mockingham would take less than three hours. They would take it easily. And arrive in time for evening drinks upon the terrace. How beautiful the valley would look in this perfect weather, the little mixed woodland all feathery and glowing with different greens, the river flashing its signal where here and there its windings became visible, the tithe barn, big as a fortress in the middle distance with white doves crowding on its stone-tiled roof.

As Edgar looked up at the rose-whiteness and at the sky and breathed slowly and deeply, he let the news come to him that in spite of everything he was happy. Was this disgraceful? Perhaps, but it was hopelessly natural. Two women had died and he had loved them both. How different they were and had differently touched his heart. What exquisite sweet pain he had felt when Monty married Sophie. He had carried that pain about for so long like a precious casket. Sophie had privileged him only by her endless teasing. The lie about Amsterdam was her final tease. She had never given him a moment's peace. But Harriet had reminded him of his mother and conveyed the promise of a refuge of total gentleness. Harriet could have given him, without even noticing it, a lot of joy. He had wanted so little from these women after all—or was it much?—some small secure affection, holding of hands. And now they were both gone. Yet Edgar knew that he was not desperate with bereavement, his case was not that of Monty or of David. Whereas for his mother he had really mourned and always would. At Mockingham earlier in the week he had tasted the old black misery, looking at the chair in the drawing-room where she used to sit with her feet tucked under her, showing yards of silk stocking and a hint of suspenders. How girlish she had remained right to the end.

The shock of Harriet's death had almost broken through into the terrible abode of his demons. He had for many years now been spared the demons, though he was constantly aware of their continued presence. He could hear them, as it were, moving behind the wall. They belonged to him and would doubtless go with him to the grave. His mind too, like David's, ran irresistibly to the horror. He watched his mind as one might watch a bad dog, tugged it a little, and waited for quietness to return. He had had other abominations in his life. He might resemble a huge pink baby and spend his time in libraries reading very obscure texts, but he had had his share of soldiering through nightmares, and things had happened to him of which he could not speak even to Monty. Guilt was always the worst of the problem. (The amazing business at Oregon, the catastrophe at Stanford about which thank God hardly anybody knew.) He prayed and some help arrived. The demons kept their distance. And he could now think steadily of Sophie and Harriet without the self-indulgence of any personal despair.

What he was reflecting upon now as he looked up at the sky through the half transparent papery screen of the climbing rose was how a miracle seemed to have come about lately in his life. Suddenly there were two people who needed him. He had two people of his own to love and cherish. Since his mother and his old nanny had died he had never had anybody. He had always been seeking and searching, sometimes tolerated, usually laughed at, never really wanted, always ultimately abandoned. Edgar had lived many years with his mind and needed no analyst to tell him of his peculiarities. It was no accident that he was unmarried and alone, that his love for women was unrequited, and his love for men undeclared. But now all of a sudden he had two people. How miraculous. Monty had never really known how much Edgar had loved him in the old days, he did not even know it now. And as Edgar thought of how things had turned out at last he was hard put to it to restrain his lips from uttering a triumphant little song of thanksgiving.

Monty's confession to him had made one of the most moving and exciting moments of Edgar's life. The matter of it had cost him a shudder, not exactly of horror as of reverent compassionate affection. But the all-importance of Monty made what he said of almost secondary interest. Edgar felt that he was *receiving* Monty, as one might receive a holy gift or talisman or the sacrament itself. And he held what he had been given with a breathless humble gratitude, hardly able to credit his good fortune. He had feared that afterwards, Monty would immediately draw back. But Monty had not drawn back. 'I am lame. I am blind.' These words of Monty's echoed in Edgar's mind and brought the thanksgiving often to his lips as he meditated upon them in secret. Monty would have understood perfectly of course and uttered his sarcastic laugh; only of such matters Edgar was careful never to vouchsafe any hint to his friend. He was so anxious not to seem to press any advantage that he might even have seemed stiff and cool, except that he knew too that Monty could read him like a book.

The humility and simplicity of Monty's behaviour to him since the confession filled Edgar with amazed gratitude, and also made him cautiously conjecture that he had been the instrument for doing Monty some sort of crucial 'good'. Edgar did not know, had never really known, what Monty's demons were like, but he saw his friend as now somehow emerging from a place of terror. Monty's curious docility was an aspect of it, the way, for instance, in which he had agreed to come to Mockingham. Of course Edgar wanted now to keep Monty at Mockingham forever, and of course he had not said this to Monty, and of course Monty knew and was coming to Mockingham all the same. They had discussed in a relaxed way various jobs which Monty might in due course do. 'And of course you could always stay on at Mockingham and write,' Edgar had said casually, changing the subject immediately afterwards.

The matter of Monty was of absolute importance. Perhaps it seemed to him now, it had always been the central thing in his life, even though he had long since become resigned to never achieving a real friendship with Monty. Doubtless he had only loved Sophie (or so frenziedly gone on loving her) because of Monty. Monty was ubiquitous in Edgar's being and represented a central need which, had it not in this form existed, Edgar would have had to invent. The matter of David was a marvellous unexpected bonus, from the gods. The thought of David as an Oxford undergraduate, even if he was not (but perhaps he would be?) at Edgar's college inspired a warm delight. The thought of David at Mockingham reading a Greek text under Edgar's supervision filled Edgar with sensations which would have been, had he had less confidence in his own self-knowledge and self-control, quite disgraceful. Edgar, who knew how attractive Monty too found the boy, had avoided any discussion of David, not out of possible jealousy (*that* his love for Monty, and what a test of it for one of a jealous nature, quite precluded) but out of simple propriety: though here again he realized how transparent he was to the gaze of those dark jesuitical eyes. At this point in his reflections he recalled David's question about his sexual fantasies and laughed aloud. Edgar's fantasies did not merely concern touching David's elbow over a text of the *Agamemnon*. In fact not only David but also Monty would have been astounded had they ever known what Edgar's sexual fantasies concerned.

Edgar leaned forward to start the car. The windscreen was now so covered with adherent rose petals as to hinder visibility, and as he did not want to crumple the petals with the windscreen-wiper, he got out and picked them all off carefully with his fingers. He was about to drop them on the pavement, but decided to put them into his pocket instead. He got back into the car and drove on the little way to Locketts. He let himself in with the key which Monty had given him.

It was ominously stuffy in the long hall which was usually cool and fresh with the moving airs of summer. Edgar called out 'Monty!' and went on into the Moorish drawing-room. The air here too was thick and breathless, smelling of must and dust as if the house had taken a journey in time. Edgar returned to the hall, looked into the study, and then went again to call at the foot of the stairs before going on into the garden. Then he saw, upon the table near the front door, a fat envelope addressed to him in Monty's writing. As soon as he saw the envelope Edgar's poor heart, never a stranger to fear of loss, gave a big sad frightened jolt. He picked the letter up and ran back with it into the drawing-room, tearing it quickly open. Monty's communication was as follows:

My dear Edgar,

You will probably not be too surprised to learn that when you receive this letter I shall be gone; and when I say gone I mean *gone*. (Not dead of course, no nonsense of that sort.) Did you really believe that I would come to Mockingham? (Did I? Yes, I think so for a time. But how does one know what one believes until one sees what one does?) It is possibly very ungrateful (or something) thus to give you the slip. I have indeed sincere feelings of gratitude. I am grateful for what you have done for me. (You know what I mean.) You were for me a felicitous instrument which perhaps only you could have been. I am also grateful, in a way I find more difficult to express, for your affection. For a short while this unwonted warmth made me feel almost

319

human. I had the illusion of conversing with a fellow being
without a barrier, without a steel door, without a black
hood over my head. (It was an illusion however; my state
was entirely subjective.) I have never, I think, impressed
upon you how almost impossible I find it to communicate
with anybody. These troubles are however not interesting;
and even if you are interested in them they are still not
interesting. There are dull areas of egoism and failure
which have no resonance and reflect no light. Such are my
lonelinesses, which I once thought that Sophie might cure.
But she was solitary too, though totally unconscious of it as
women often are. Figuratively speaking, we conversed in
brief shouts. That this was the sort of thing which *you*
would not put up with at any price I saw at once when we
first met at Oxford, and determined to scare you forever
into keeping your distance; a plan which would have
worked perfectly well had you not come upon me at a truly
desperate moment of weakness. Your nervous desire for
intimacy and communion of souls, your urge to sidle up
close and gaze into eyes and whisper into ears, has always
filled me (excuse me, dear Edgar) with a disgust which
prompted in turn the brutality which you have so suffered,
deplored and enjoyed. I regard your blundering kindness
and officious desire to 'understand' me simply as a rude
trespass upon the fastidious integrity of my being. Your
moral style sets my teeth on edge, just as your soggy so-called
religion makes me want to vomit. I pretended to myself for
a while that we could nevertheless be friends, partly out
of the aforesaid gratitude, and partly out of sheer desperation. But, soberly, no, my dear fellow, no, it simply won't
do. And pray do not pretend that you really think it would
or that you 'love' me so much that the loss of me will
prove of any serious importance. I do not say (though this
is true, my dear) that you are 'better off without me'. You
imagine that I have hitherto caused you pain. In reality
this was never more than mere self-indulgent discomfort.
At close quarters I would have caused you torment. The
merest *gifle* compared with the slow knife in the guts.
There is no need to dwell on this. I say simply that you
will not really miss me. You are about to enter a new
world full of people whom you will find (if you can now
terminate your schoolboy infatuation) far more interesting
than I am. I know that you will derive satisfaction from
helping David. (I would have done so too. Only you will

probably do him little harm and I might have done him much.) And (I do not say this cynically) Oxford will be full of Davids. So it would be hypocrisy to say that I am vastly concerned about you. In a way, you will have suffered from being *too* useful to me: like the Russian guardsmen who spent one night with Catherine the Great and whose bodies were found the next day floating in the Neva. (An image which may even, if you can staunch your grief at my departure, amuse you a little.) Yes, it's the Neva for you, dear Edgar, I am afraid. I don't want to see you again, so please don't try to make any overtures to me later on, should it occur to you to do so. I should regard them with the nausea I have already described. In addition (and what is more human?) I thoroughly resent your having not only witnessed my weakness but actually helped me to overcome it! So henceforth keep clear. You already know my capacity for kicking fawning dogs. Let us make a tolerably clean end to a tolerably decent encounter. You wished to serve me and you have done so. Be satisfied with that.

I am going to stay with a friend in Italy and will be away for some months. After that I shall sell Locketts and go and live in some more distant solitude (not near Oxford) with the person I shall by that time have become. I do not think that art or what I know of spirit will heal or better me. (As far as the latter goes I have always tended quite crudely to mistake my level.) Nor do I imagine that any deeper spring of inspiration or invention will ever flow for me as a writer. I may even produce another Milo story. So you see what a confession of failure and admission of defeat all this amounts to. Maybe there are times when one should welcome defeat, tell it to come right in and sit down. What I feel about this is not anything like despair (*that* has passed). I feel a resignation which I will not insult you by dubbing humility. It really does not matter tuppence to anyone, even to me, what I shall write or whether I shall ever write. Almost all one's thoughts about oneself are simply vanity. This letter is vanity, the attempt to attach interest and importance to what has none. (That stuff about how my friendship would have tormented you: pure vanity!) It is not even important whether or not I have been deliberately cruel in thus leading you on (if that is what I have been doing) until the very last moment. You may think what you like about it, and what you think does not matter either. There is a certain pleasure in writing to you.

I suppose this is a sign of affection. (I am not sure. I also enjoy picturing your dismay.) I am grateful to you and in an inert way I wish you well. You are one for whom every little thing matters. This sort of moral greed has always been a source of irritation to me. I am going now where things will matter less, and if this is to the devil then this does not matter either, since if there is a devil I am he. (Vanity again, my dear.) That's all, I think. Just close the front door when you go and leave the key on the table, would you. I have locked all the other doors and windows. Oh by the way, I found some of your letters to Sophie after all. They are on the bureau in my study. They are ridiculously touching and I read them with the greatest amusement.

Good-bye.

M.

Edgar finished reading the letter, sat down upon the purple sofa and dropped the sheets of paper onto the floor. Monty's final piece of frightfulness. He stared at the window and at the gently moving branches of the wistaria outside and listened to the profound airless silence of the house, and let these representations carry a sense of terrible solitude into his heart. Monty had given him the slip. Had he expected it? Had he really imagined that he and Monty would grow old together at Mockingham? Had it not trembled in his mind with the insecurity of a mirage? He had believed in his love for Monty, but in Monty himself had he ever for a second been able to rest? Monty had indeed defended himself ably, resolutely refusing himself as even an object of faith. How much it all mattered, yes, every little thing mattered, and how minutely, Edgar reflected, he would torment himself by going over and over and over every detail of it in time to come.

And the future for Edgar as he now poured himself out a glass of whisky, seemed suddenly shrivelled up and small. He searched in it for consolation and found none. Monty had wrapped up all Edgar's affections and taken them away with him. Nothing now in his heart reached out towards the world at all. Of course he would help David because it was his duty to do so, but the task had lost its charm. Any lustre which David had had for him was simply reflected from Monty. Any lustre which the world had had was simply reflected from Monty. The mad hope of Monty which had come to him on that evening when Monty had confessed, had robbed all other things of their light. Even poor Harriet had been so robbed. Edgar recalled now very clearly Harriet's face when she had said to him that she would come to Mockingham, and how her face had changed when he denied her; and he seemed to be seeing that sorrowful change as if for the first time. How simple and inevitable, how perfectly necessary, the denial had seemed at that moment. Yet if he had taken Harriet to Mockingham then she would still have been alive now. I preferred a ghost to reality, he thought; and yet I could not then have abandoned Monty, he held me in a grip of steel. O rapacious ruthless ghost!

Edgar picked up the letter and began to look at it again. Then he jumped up and hurried from the drawing-room to Monty's study. There was something live and moving in the room, the small wood fire still burning in the grate. There on the bureau tied up with string was a small packet of letters, the few remnants of so many which, over the years, he had written to Sophie. He undid the package. The envelopes were already faded. Mrs Montague Small. Mlle Sophie Artaud. Sophie's maiden name rang forlornly, like a bell in some abandoned palace moved by the wind. He recalled with a sudden gasp of memory the lyricism of days so different and so long ago when, always one of many, he had pursued Sophie through Europe. He recalled days rent with pain but overflowing all the same with the golden light of youth. She had made him dive into a lake after one of her shoes. Beside another lake (Como? Maggiore?) he had (it was the boldest thing he ever did) opened her dress and put his hand inside. And as he felt her heart beating he was suddenly *with* her, right through the barrier, and saw her face devoid of mockery, devoid suddenly of all defence, even that of the mask of personality. How sick he had been with love. What a child she had been, what a light airy mischievous spirit, Ariel, Puck. And what dust it all was now. He recalled the harsh angry voice which he had heard upon the tape. Yet it seemed to him as he held the letters in his hand that some part of her soul from which the grace of youth had never been withdrawn still fluttered unquietly within him. Because of Monty he had never really been able to make his peace with Sophie, never been able to let her, living or dead, come to rest in his heart. He was about to open one of the letters to Mlle Artaud, when he was startled by a sudden darkening of the study window. A girl was standing outside.

323

Edgar felt for a second that he was being visited by a ghost. Then he saw, feeling his own years, that it was only a young girl, a schoolgirl, a stranger. She was tall and dark-complexioned with long hair and very large dark eyes. She wore a loose blue cotton sweater which reached almost to the hem of her short skirt. Her hair, disordered by haste, had spread and looped itself about her like scales, like chain-mail. She had the urgent look of a runaway as she tapped upon the glass.

Stuffing the letters away into his pocket, Edgar went to open the window. Without waiting to be further invited, the girl still snuffling and panting in her haste, thrust a long brown bare leg through, then taking hold of Edgar's shoulder as a convenient support, steadied herself and drew the other long leg after. The room was suddenly filled with warm close animal presence, as if a beautiful agile beast, smelling of the woods and still glorious with its own speed, had leapt in. His shoulder still burning with her touch, Edgar backed away from her, murmuring 'I say—I say—'

'Excuse me. Where is Monty?'

'Gone,' said Edgar hollowly.

'But will be back when?'

'I don't know. He's gone to Italy. For a long time.'

'Oh.' Kiki St Loy sat down on a chair and consulted with her still heaving bosom about whether or not she should cry. She had felt suddenly quite unable not to come to Locketts, persuaded that both Monty was willing her to come and that he would be very angry with her for coming. When the combination of these two ideas had become irresistible she had felt winged with joy and under the orders of her deepest self, directed by cosmic rays expressive of the will of the stars. She had raced in her car, raced on her feet, panting with the declared necessity of love. And now she had run into an emptiness more final than any words of rejection. He was gone and would make himself a stranger to her forever. She struggled with her tears for a moment, won the struggle, and looked up at Edgar with eyes even wider and more glistening.

'I am Kiki St Loy, a friend of Monty.'

'I am Edgar Demarnay, also a friend of Monty.'

'Then we must be friends of each other.'

'Friendship is unfortunately not a transitive relation.'

'Ah, you are the professor!'

'Not any more actually.'

'But you are head of an Oxford College and are they not all professors?'

'No.'

'How can that be?'

'Very easily.'

'I want to come to Oxford to make my bachelor. When can I come and talk to you about it for a long time?'

'I'm not quite sure what you mean,' said Edgar, his hand on the door and his eyes upon the blue sweater where the wild hair had made a glowing veneer over each breast, 'but I am afraid I am just leaving—'

'I shall come to you in Oxford then. On Thursday, yes? I shall drive my car to your college and say I am the guest of the—what are you called—the Principal?'

'The Master,' said Edgar faintly.

'How beautiful. The Master!'

There was a loud banging upon the front door. Then a long steady peal upon the bell. Kiki, with one quick movement, gathered all her truant hair in a long hand and tossed it back over her shoulder. One stride took her to the open window and another precipitated her through it. As she turned to look at Edgar, waving farewell, her lips inaudibly uttering 'Oxford, Thursday' it seemed to him that there were tears in those huge dark eyes.

Dazed, Edgar went to the front door and opened it. Pinn, who was standing outside, one hand poised to ring the bell again, sidled quickly in. 'Where's Monty?'

'Gone,' said Edgar. 'To Italy.'

'Ah.' She looked anxiously round, as if trying to descry changes in the house, or as if she might after all spot Monty hiding under a chair. Then she went on into the drawing-room with Edgar after her. 'So he's escaped. I'm not surprised. He couldn't just stay and *be*, could he. Someone like Monty lives entirely in gestures. What am I saying? There is no one like Monty. And how are you, Edgar? Heart-broken?'

Edgar said nothing. He stared with respectful amazement at Pinn, at her glowing rounded cheeks and her neat healthy hair and her military handbag with the brass buckles and the very soft silky scarf at her neck and the Italian cameo brooch that held the scarf.

'Do you mind if I pour myself a drink? I can see a bottle and glasses over yonder. Thanks. Here's how. Cheer up, Edgar. Monty was some sort of monster. If he's gone back under the ice so much the better. Do you mind if I stay here and talk to you for a while? It's not exactly that I'm suffering from shock. I just feel it's the end of an era. Conspiracy and treachery and violence and sudden death. Did you know you gave Blaise a black eye that night simply by raising your elbow?'

'What night?'

'Never mind, my pet. I say, what do you think of the love birds over at Hood House? Do sit down and let's have a good natter.'

'I'm just leaving for Oxford.'

'Well, I must talk to you,' said Pinn. 'It strikes me that you and I are the only sane people in this story, so we must get together. I'll come and see you in Oxford. I've never been there, so you can show me the city. When can I come? Soon? Friday?'

There was a sound in the hall, the unmistakable sound of a key being inserted in a lock. Pinn and Edgar stiffened, then bolted out into the hall jostling each other in the doorway. A figure was entering the house. A tall dignified handsome woman set down her suitcase and confronted Edgar. She was hatless and wore her lustrous dark hair combed down onto her neck in a smooth metallic mane. Her linen dress, the colour of cornflowers, was long and full, caught to her slim waist by a belt of silver links. She appeared to be about thirty. Her radiantly cunning dark eyes regarded Edgar with a gaze that seemed suddenly familiar.

'Isn't it Edgar?'

'Yes.'

'Don't you remember me?'

'Yes.'

'You remember my visiting you at Mockingham?'

'Yes, Mrs Small.'

'Where's Monty?'

'Gone to Italy,' said Edgar. 'This is Miss—er—' Her name had disappeared.

'Pinn,' said Pinn. 'I won't keep you. See you in Oxford on Friday. Cheery-bye, Edgar. Don't forget our compact.'

'Who was that?'

Edgar felt unable to explain. Who after all was it? He waved vaguely, offering Mrs Small the house. 'I'm so sorry Monty—'

'Never mind. I expected it. Perhaps it's just as well. Now I can look after everything here. I hope he hasn't sold anything?'

326

'Not that I—'

'Now, dear boy, let us come in here and sit down and you shall tell me all about it. I know how devoted you always were to Monty. I want to hear the whole story.'

'I'm afraid I'm just leaving—'

'That's a pity. I might have wanted you to move some furniture. Now where will you be at the weekend?'

'At Mockingham.'

'Good. I'll come there. May I stay the—? How kind. Expect me Saturday lunch time. Now I won't keep you. I just want to look round the house and make sure there's nothing missing.'

The vision vanished. Edgar heard the soft determined footfalls mounting the stairs. He bolted quickly into Monty's study and shut the door. It all came swooping back to him, his unhappiness, his loss. Sophie was dead, Harriet was dead, Monty was gone, David was just a boy who would pass by as boys passed by. Oxford was full of Davids, bitter-sweet boys, each one a fruitless brief joy, perhaps a long sorrow. Come in, defeat, come in and make yourself at home.

Edgar thrust his hand into his pocket and pulled out the ruffled package of his letters to Sophie. As he did so a shower of white rose petals suddenly flew about him, adhering to his jacket falling upon the carpet and the warm dusty hearth stone. The petals of the big white rose which had clambered so high up into the cherry tree and whose flowers he had seen translucently alight against the brilliance of the sky. Edgar looked down at the strewn whiteness, like little messages, like confetti. He had always preferred white flowers. He then began to unfold one of the letters and to peruse upon the faded paper his own years-old writing. *Oh my darling darling girl.* How far away that love seemed now, and yet it was part of a whole, part of his own mysterious continuing self. I always wanted Monty's women, he reflected, perhaps it was a way of wanting Monty. And yet of course it was not just that. It was special, it was private, it was a part of history with its own unique sacredness. I won't read these letters, thought Edgar, these letters which so much 'amused' Monty. I couldn't reread them now with innocent enough eyes. Better not disturb the decent work of memory and of time. Better to leave them here. The wood fire, the fire which Monty had lit centuries ago in another era, was glowing red at Edgar's feet. He thrust the small bundle of letters into the hottest part of the fire and raked the embers over them and watched them flame. Good-bye to the past, with its mysteries which would never be fully unfolded. Come in, defeat.

No, thought Edgar, no, I may be in the Neva but I'm damned if I'll drown! If I ever believed in divine grace now is the time to make a grab for it. Every little thing matters, yes it does, and if Monty thinks it is greed and not love that says this, well Monty need not be right. Monty is simply a chap with his own troubles, a chap just like me after all. Monty will change his mind, thought Edgar. He is not the dear awful monster I have sometimes thought him to be. He is an ordinary human fellow with his muddles and his needs. He will change his mind. I shall see Monty again.

The letters were all burnt. Edgar moved away from the fire and quietly opened the door into the hall. Upstairs there was a sound of drawers being opened, objects being shifted. He tiptoed across to the front door and let himself out into the bright sunshine. And as he did so he thought to himself, and now there are no less than three women, three powerful handsome women, wanting my attention, needing my help, insisting on coming to see me. Fascinating women would stroll again upon the terraces at Mockingham, mingling with the reading parties of charming young men, all of them affectionately flirting with their genial host. The heart would be touched again, not dreadfully perhaps, not divinely, but touched. There would be innocent frivolous unimportant happiness once again in the world. Three good-looking women, he thought, and all of them after *me*! And he could not help being a little bit cheered up and consoled as he got into the Bentley and set off alone for Oxford.

Also available in Vintage

Iris Murdoch

A FAIRLY HONOURABLE DEFEAT

With an introduction by Philip Hensher

'A distinguished novelist of a very rare kind'
Kingsley Amis

'Iris Murdoch really knows how to write, can tell a story,
delineate a character, catch an atmosphere with deadly
accuracy'
John Betjeman

In this dark comedy of errors, Iris Murdoch portrays the
mischief wrought by Julius, a cynical intellectual who
decides to demonstrate through a Machiavellian experiment
how easily loving couples, caring friends, and devoted
siblings can betray their loyalties. As puppet master, Julius
artfully plays on the human tendency to embrace drama and
intrigue and to prefer the distraction of confrontations to
the difficult effort of communicating openly and honestly.

'The most important novelist writing in my time'
A. S. Byatt

VINTAGE

Also available in Vintage

Iris Murdoch

THE SEA, THE SEA

With an introduction by John Burnside

Winner of the Booker Prize

'There is no doubt in my mind that Iris Murdoch is one
of the most important novelists now writing in English...
The power of her imaginative vision, her intelligence and
her awareness and revelation of human truth are quite
remarkable'
The Times

The sea: turbulent and leaden; transparent and opaque;
magician and mother.

When Charles Arrowby, over sixty, a demi-god of the
theatre – director, playwright and actor – retires from his
glittering London world in order to, 'abjure magic and
become a hermit', it is to the sea that he turns. He hopes at
least to escape from 'the women' – but unexpectedly meets
one whom he loved long ago. His Buddhist cousin, James,
also arrives. He is menaced by a monster from the deep.
Charles finds his 'solitude' peopled by the drama of his own
fantasies and obsessions.

'A fantastic feat of imagination as well as a marvellous
sustained piece of writing'
Vogue

VINTAGE

BY IRIS MURDOCH
ALSO AVAILABLE IN VINTAGE

☐ Under the Net	0 09 942907 1	£6.99
☐ The Flight from the Enchanter	0 09 928369 7	£6.99
☐ The Sandcastle	0 09 943358 3	£6.99
☐ The Bell	0 09 928389 1	£6.99
☐ A Severed Head	0 09 928536 3	£6.99
☐ An Unofficial Rose	0 09 928538 X	£6.99
☐ The Unicorn	0 09 928534 7	£6.99
☐ The Italian Girl	0 09 928523 1	£6.99
☐ A Fairly Honourable Defeat	0 09 928533 9	£7.99
☐ The Black Prince	0 09 928399 9	£7.99
☐ A Word Child	0 09 942912 8	£7.99
☐ Henry and Cato	0 09 942908 X	£7.99
☐ The Sea, The Sea	0 09 928409 X	£7.99
☐ Nuns and Soldiers	0 09 928535 5	£7.99
☐ The Philosopher's Pupil	0 09 928359 X	£8.99
☐ The Message to the Planet	0 09 928379 4	£7.99

FREE POST AND PACKING
Overseas customers allow £2.00 per paperback

BY PHONE: 01624 677237

BY POST: Random House Books
C/o Bookpost, PO Box 29, Douglas
Isle of Man, IM99 1BQ

BY FAX: 01624 670923

BY EMAIL: bookshop@enterprise.net

Cheques (payable to Bookpost) and credit cards accepted

Prices and availability subject to change without notice.
Allow 28 days for delivery.
When placing your order, please mention if you do not wish to receive
any additional information.

www.randomhouse.co.uk/vintage